D0426277

DEVIL'S GAMBLE

BOOKS BY FRANK G. SLAUGHTER

Devil's Gamble
Plague Ship
Stonewall Brigade
Women in White
Convention, M.D.
Code Five
Countdown
Surgeon's Choice
The Sins of Herod
Doctors' Wives
God's Warrior
Surgeon, U.S.A.
Constantine
The Purple Quest
A Savage Place
Upon This Rock
Tomorrow's Miracle
David: Warrior and King
The Curse of Jezebel
Epidemic!
Pilgrims in Paradise
The Land and the Promise
Lorena
The Crown and the Cross
The Thorn of Arimathea
Daybreak

The Mapmaker
Sword and Scalpel
The Scarlet Cord
Flight from Natchez
The Healer
Apalachee Gold
The Song of Ruth
Storm Haven
The Galileans
East Side General
Fort Everglades
The Road to Bithynia
The Stubborn Heart
Immortal Magyar
Divine Mistress
Sangaree
Medicine for Moderns
The Golden Isle
The New Science of Surgery
In a Dark Garden
A Touch of Glory
Battle Surgeon
Air Surgeon
Spencer Brade, M.D.
That None Should Die
The Warrior

UNDER THE NAME C. V. TERRY

Buccaneer Surgeon
The Deadly Lady of Madagascar

Darien Venture
The Golden Ones

DEVIL'S GAMBLE

A Novel of Demonology

FRANK G.
SLAUGHTER

Doubleday & Company, Inc., Garden City, New York

Better to reign in hell,
than serve in Heav'n.
. . . So Satan spake.

JOHN MILTON: *Paradise Lost*

BOOK ONE

THE FIRST IMPOSSIBLE

Impossible things, as history constantly reminds us, have an uncanny way of becoming possible when given enough time.

CHARLES PANATI: *Supersenses: Our Potential for Parasensory Experience* (Anchor Press/Doubleday, 1976)

1

As he took the exit ramp off I-495, the Washington Beltway, and headed toward the westward extension of Dulles International Airport Road, Dr. Michael Kerns was listening to the eight o'clock news on his car radio. On an average Monday morning in June, when returning to Washington from his weekend river-front hideaway, a cottage on the east—and Maryland—bank of the Potomac River near Indian Head and the U.S. naval ordnance station, Mike would have crossed the river into the teeming Washington "bedroom" suburb of Alexandria on the Woodrow Wilson Bridge. From there he would have taken the George Washington Memorial Parkway and the Key Bridge into Georgetown and his office near the huge University Hospital adjoining the medical school. Today, however, he was taking an early flight to a meeting of the prestigious Congress of Plastic Surgeons, hence his presence so far west of his normal route. Also his preoccupation, now that traffic had thinned out markedly on the road to Washington's newest and least used airport, with thoughts of the paper he was to present that afternoon to his fellow specialists.

Twenty-eight years old and an Assistant Clinical Professor of Plastic and Reconstructive Surgery in the medical school, Mike was still on the bottom rung of his climb to pre-eminence in his profession. With a residency at University Hospital in his field behind him, and an additional two years as a Fellow in Cosmetic Surgery at Bellevue Hospital in New York, his surgical credentials were sound and his future assured.

Six feet tall, with wavy hair, a curly mustache, the blue eyes and mobile features handed down to him by Scotch-Irish ancestors who'd settled in the Shenandoah Valley apple country in the mid-1870s—plus the lean compact body of the tennis and swimming letterman he'd been at the University of Virginia, from which he'd also graduated in medicine—Mike Kerns had attracted the interest of many a young woman on the way but had so far managed to remain unattached.

"Speculation is still rife," the voice of the network newscaster broke into Mike's thoughts as he guided the small convertible toward the airport, "concerning just where the FBI has spirited Lynne Tallman, femme fatale of the Chicago devil worship cult believed responsible for at least ten bombings in that city during the past six months and for causing nearly fifty deaths.

"The trial of Lynne Tallman in a Chicago federal court ended abruptly yesterday with her dramatic offer, communicated to authorities by a newspaperwoman close to the prisoner, to reveal details of the cult, its operations, membership and connections with similar groups throughout the country. In return, the Justice Department is reported to have agreed to accept a lesser plea than first-degree murder and it is also believed that federal authorities will bring Miss Tallman to Washington soon to testify before a special federal grand jury investigating senseless violence and death to innocent people.

"With some attempt likely to be made by other cult members to kill Lynne Tallman before she can testify, extraordinary precautions for her protection are being taken by the FBI. In fact, she is thought at this moment to be on an airplane, somewhere between Chicago and the national capital, where the grand jury will shortly be starting another day of the secret hearings. . . ."

The roar of a passing airplane descending for its approach to the Dulles International Airport some thirteen miles away drowned out the news broadcast momentarily. Reaching across the instrument panel, Mike switched to VHF Frequency 119.1, used by the ground controllers at Dulles in communicating with planes in the air. Since the top of the small car was down, Mike was able to glance up in time to see that the plane—a Boeing 727—was almost directly overhead. He realized, too, with a sudden start of apprehension and horror, that the pilot had not yet lowered the landing wheels—an observation confirmed seconds later when, amidst a burst of static on the VHF radio, he heard the voice of the pilot of the sleek 727.

"Dulles Tower, this is Tri-Continental Six-twenty. Something's blocking my landing gear."

"Six-twenty, this is Dulles Tower. Climb to five thousand and hold over the airport." Mike wondered if the controller could possibly be as calm as his voice sounded, with an emergency belly landing in prospect for the crippled plane. "Any idea what's wrong?"

"I've sent the copilot down to see if he can lower the landing gear manually. Meanwhile, you'd better clear a runway and start laying down foam. . . ."

"Roger, Six-twenty." The tower controller was still calm. "We'll initiate preparations for an emergency landing."

A second burst of static brought another voice, sharp and authoritative, into the conversation between the pilot of the stricken plane and the airport tower.

"This is Washington Center." Mike could envision one of the FAA air traffic controllers at nearby Leesburg hunched before a radarscope, watching the green blip indicating the position of Tri-Continental Flight 620. "Anything wrong?"

"Six-twenty's landing gear seems to be stuck," said the Dulles Tower. "We're preparing for an emergency landing."

"Roger, Dulles," said the Center controller. "What about you, Six-twenty?"

"We're climbing to five thousand and holding," came the somewhat anxious voice of the Tri-Continental pilot. "My copilot should be working on the landing gear now."

Seeing the stricken plane rise above the tops of the pines once again in the direction of the airport, as the pilot sought to gain altitude, Mike pulled off the road. Taking a pair of powerful binoculars from the glove compartment, he focused them on the 727. The landing gear was still up, he saw at once, but, while he watched, the hatches covering the folded-up wheels started opening and the bottoms of the wheels appeared as they descended slowly.

They should give that copilot a medal, Mike thought. *He's probably saved a lot of people from being killed.*

"Dulles Tower, this is Six-twenty." The pilot's voice betrayed his relief. "The copilot is lowering the wheels manually."

"Roger," said the tower controller. "Let me know when they're down and locked."

"Roger. This is one cargo I'll be glad to get rid—"

The pilot's voice was drowned by a dull boom over the radio. Observing the big plane, now just above the pines and headed for one of the North–South runways, Mike Kerns didn't need to be told the cause. While he watched through the powerful binoculars, rigid with horror yet fascinated by the grim drama being played out there in the sky above the green Virginia countryside, the underpart of the forward fuselage started to expand, like a child's toy balloon being blown up. Even before the sound reached his ears through the air—after traveling some ten miles line-of-sight distance from the scene of the aerial disaster—he knew the manual lowering of the wheels by the copilot had somehow triggered an explosion inside the plane.

Unable to take his gaze from the stricken airliner, Mike saw a large metal plate forming part of the underside of the forward cabin slowly separate from the fuselage. As it broke clear, a small figure—identifiable as a man and no doubt the copilot—tumbled into space. Flailing his arms frantically, he began to fall, looking uncannily like a sky diver maneuvering before opening his parachute—except that this man wore none.

Pulling his eyes away from the falling figure, Mike saw that, by some miracle, the plane was still holding together. Moreover, at the price of his life, the copilot, whose body had now disappeared beneath the tops of the pines, seemed to have lowered the wheels completely, although whether they were locked in place Mike couldn't tell.

"Six-twenty to Dulles Tower," came the frantic voice of the pilot over the radio, which, by some miracle, was still working, "we've had an explosion and my instrument panel's gone dead. Are my wheels down?"

"Roger, Six-twenty. Your wheels appear to be down and in place. You're cleared to land."

Through the controller's radio, Mike could hear the wailing sirens of emergency vehicles moving into place on the distant airfield, even as the sharp high tail outline of the 727 descended below his angle of vision.

"The wheels just touched the runway, so they're locked," he heard the pilot say over his radio.

"Just slow her down gradual—" The soothing tones of the tower controller were suddenly cut off by a frantic shout from the pilot: "My brakes won't work and I can't reverse the engines. We're going to hit the main terminal building!"

A moment of silence followed the dramatic announcement by the pilot of the 727, then a girl's voice came from the speaker of Mike's radio. High-pitched, hysterical, it screamed, "Master! Save!" before becoming a keening shriek of pure terror, rising in pitch until it was literally the howl of a banshee that could hardly be of this earth. The howl was suddenly cut off by the sound of a rending crash—then silence prevailed, during which Mike could hear, through the tower controller's radio, the whine of sirens as the airfield's emergency vehicles raced to the scene of the crash.

Quickly he switched to the state police channel, just in time to hear the dispatcher's announcement:

"An explosion and fire has just occurred at Dulles International Airport! All rescue units in the area proceed there at once. Other units control traffic until the nature and extent of the crash can be determined. Apparently an incoming plane has landed out of control and smashed into the terminal."

God help the people inside when those glass walls were shattered, was Mike's thought as he meshed the gears of the convertible into forward. Pulling out into the four-lane highway—mercifully clear of traffic for roughly a quarter mile in either direction—he stepped hard on the accelerator. As the powerful little car responded and the speedometer needle crept past fifty-five to seventy and then to eighty, he suddenly remembered the pilot's enigmatic words when he'd told the ground controller, "This is one cargo I'll be glad to get rid—" and wondered just what he had meant.

2

A half mile from the airport entrance, Mike came to a long line of stopped cars, obviously being held back by police somewhere ahead, probably at the gate. Without hesitation he sped past them, to the accompaniment of much gesticulating and cursing by the angry drivers, most of whom probably hadn't even heard of the accident when they were suddenly forced to halt. Almost at the airport entrance, he was stopped short by a Sheriff's Department car and the bullfrog-like face of a policeman who looked as if he wanted to eat Mike alive.

"Dammit, mister!" the officer snapped. "Where the hell do you think you're going?"

Mike reached for his wallet and identification. "I'm a doctor and a police reserve surgeon in Georgetown."

"I don't care if you're the Presi—" The angry tirade suddenly ceased. "You say you're a doctor?"

"Yes. Why don't you get on that walkie-talkie you've got in your hand and ask whoever's directing things whether he wouldn't rather have me inside, doing what I know how to do, than arguing with you outside?"

The policeman spoke into the walkie-talkie. "There's a doctor out here says he wants to come in and help. Do you want him let in?"

"Want him?" a harried voice answered. "*Escort* him in and take him to Dr. Smathers. He's swamped."

"They say it's okay, Doc," said the officer. "Just follow me so nobody else will stop you."

As he followed the police car along the curving approach road, Mike could see that the 727 had plowed through one of the spectacular glass-paneled walls of the airport terminal—for which the architect had won all sorts of kudos. The plane had been stopped when the wings struck the slanting metal columns that not only formed a framework for the massive panes of glass between, extending from floor to ceiling, but also supported the curving roof that gave such soaring beauty and grace to the building.

Through the panes on either side, which had not been smashed by the plane as it plowed into the side of the building, he could see inside the terminal an occasional leaping flame between clouds of smoke and steam as firemen sought to control the fire. The entire forward part of the airplane was apparently still burning, and even before Mike was ushered inside, he had time to doubt that anyone in that section could have gotten out alive.

The glass walls, whose wide slanting panes distinguished the Dulles Airport from any other in the world, had proved a handicap, Mike saw immediately. The floors were littered with shards of glass and smears of blood where the injured were being taken from the forward cabin, which made walking difficult.

Scarcely more than twenty minutes had elapsed since Mike had heard over the radio the anguished cry of the pilot, "We're going to hit the main terminal building!" so it was hardly surprising that a considerable degree of pandemonium still prevailed. The firemen, however, trained to handle crashes on or around the field, were functioning efficiently in handling this unexpected disaster, he saw. Long hoses ran through doorways from the engines parked outside and streams of water from them were playing on the smashed cockpit and forward cabin.

Flames were still licking from the cockpit and clouds of steam were pouring from the hot metal when the water struck it. Firemen wearing asbestos suits and masks were carrying out the dead, laying them in an orderly row at one side, where a police officer and an airlines clerk with a clipboard searched each body for identification.

Some of the shops and the lunch counter at the center of the departure level, where the crash had occurred, were still smoldering. Terminal employees with extinguishers were busy coping with these flames, however, leaving the firemen for the more important job of confining the fire to the forward cabin of the plane. At the far end of the terminal, a group of spectators huddled, held back by an airport security guard. Women were weeping and children, taking the cue from their elders, were screaming, but the sound could hardly be heard over the hiss of steam and the roar of the engines pumping outside.

Some of the vacation-bound spectators, Mike saw to his amazement, were busy photographing the scene of horror and death with small movie cameras. Almost equally bizarre, too, was the presence of a television film crew, busy with cameras, microphones and glaring floodlights, filming the scene around the nose of the still-burning plane, ignoring both the orders and the curses of police and fire fighters alike.

Near the row of bodies, Mike saw a tall, harried-looking man stop one of the asbestos-clad firemen carrying a still-smoking body, long enough to feel for a pulse and lift an eyelid to examine a pupil, before nodding for the victim to be laid out like the others. Moving gingerly with his medical bag across the open space made slippery with blood and burned tissue falling from the bodies being carried across it, Mike made his way to where the airport physician was standing.

"Dr. Smathers?" he asked.

"Yes. What is it?"

"I'm Dr. Michael Kerns from University Hospital. Anything I can do?"

"Excuse me, Doctor; thought you were another of those TV ghouls. Most of the people in the forward cabin are dead, the others were evacuated through the rear exit. Take a look at those women over there by the insurance booth if you will. One of them might still be alive."

"I'll see." Mike started across the some fifty feet of space separating the area of the crash from the booth where a thin-faced blonde always sold insurance.

"I didn't overlook them," Dr. Smathers called after him. "A MAST team from Andrews AFB is due here any second with the latest thing in rescue gear, so I left those two for the experts to resuscitate."

"I'll take care of them," Mike promised, knowing the other doctor was right in staying on the job of triage—sorting the possibly living from the certainly dead—leaving any questionable corpses to the skilled and splendidly equipped medical aid service team with its big helicopter from nearby Andrews airfield.

Two blanketed forms were lying near the insurance counter while the attendant leaned over it to look down at them with the fascination of a tourist watching a snake charmer.

"It was awful, Doctor," she said as Mike knelt beside the nearest of the two bodies and put his medical bag down on the floor. "I just happened to be looking across at the other side of the terminal when the nose of that plane came crashing through the glass wall. One of those metal frames smashed the Plexiglas front of the cockpit, and the next thing I knew, that other girl shot through it and landed on her face."

She shuddered. "When her face hit the tiles, it was like the sound when you drop a sopping wet towel on the bathroom floor."

Mike had been pulling back the blanket to expose the face of the girl nearer to him and the insurance booth attendant leaned farther over to look closer.

"Oh, my God!" she gasped. "That's Lynne Tallman! Talk about poetic justice!"

Miraculously, the dead girl's face had not been injured at all, although most of her clothing was burned off. The burns on her body were so extensive that the firemen, in dragging her from her seat and carrying her out of the burning plane, had peeled off patches of skin here and there. Oddly enough, though, Mike could see no sign that she had died in agony, as must have been true with such extensive third-degree burns. Instead, the immobile features were frozen in a strange look, an appearance of sly happiness that startled him. It was the insurance clerk, however, who put the feeling into words.

"Look at her face, Doctor. I saw that same expression on it last night when they showed her on TV, before the FBI brought her from Chicago. She looks like the cat that stole the cream."

The girl was right, Mike agreed silently as he made a quick examination and confirmed that Lynne Tallman was dead beyond any shadow of a doubt. Pulling the blanket back up over her face, he uncovered the other victim and shuddered involuntarily at what he saw.

The second girl had obviously struck the floor of the terminal full face, as the insurance clerk had said, smashing her features almost into a pulp but breaking the skin only to the extent of a small cut at the corner of her right eye. What she had looked like before the accident was impossible to tell from his brief examination—except that her body, which appeared to be uninjured, was lovely. Since no long bones were broken, he was able to estimate her height at perhaps five feet eight, with proportions to match.

Undoubtedly, by being thrown through the nose of the plane, before the cockpit and the forward cabin were engulfed by flame, she had escaped the burns which had killed the other girl. Nevertheless, the impact of her head against the tiled floor had reduced her face almost to a pulp, in addition to concussion and a possible skull fracture as well.

Her nose had been pushed into her face until it was flat and almost unrecognizable as such. The upper jaw—the maxilla—was caved in, where the front layers of bone forming the walls of the maxillary sinuses had been smashed. The lower jaw did not appear displaced though obviously fractured, but when he took her upper jaw between thumb and forefinger and moved it gently, the crunch of broken bones was audible.

The injured girl had lost a considerable amount of blood from her nose and mouth, too. The floor of the concourse was slippery with it and a pool had formed where her head lay on the floor, but the amount of hemorrhage, Mike decided in a quick mental evaluation, was probably not enough to cause death. The concussion and shock from hitting the marble-hard floor with her head, traveling at the speed her body must have attained to have been thrown clear through the shattered Plexiglas windshield of the cockpit, could easily have killed her, however.

A closer examination with his stethoscope over her heart elicited no sounds, but something about the feel of her muscles and the fact that the blood oozing from her nostrils was still bright red convinced Mike that some spark of life might still remain.

"I think this girl is still alive," he shouted to the airport medical director, who was using a walkie-talkie radio to direct the dispatch of the injured to waiting ambulances. "Any news of that MAST team?"

"A helicopter is landing at the front of the terminal right now," said a new voice and Mike looked up to see a man with a camera and strobe-light flash gun standing on the countertop of the insurance booth, focusing the lens straight down on the girl's smashed face and Mike's upturned countenance. The burst of light as the strobe unit fired almost blinded Mike and, angered at the callousness of the action, he half rose to slug the photographer, then dropped to one knee again, reminding himself that the girl needed his skill desperately, if she were indeed alive and could be saved.

He didn't need to be told what the Military Assistance Safety and Traffic system—condensed to MAST—was. In operation since 1970, the program provided the skilled help of medical corpsmen to civilian rescue situations within roughly a hundred miles of military organizations. He'd seen the teams from nearby Andrews Air Force Base operate more than once and their big helicopters were a familiar sight around Washington.

"What's your name, Doc?" the reporter asked, but Mike ignored him as he listened to the voice of the airport physician.

"They're coming right in with a respirator and a pacemaker," Dr. Smathers shouted. "You'd better go with the MAST crew to the hospital, Dr. Kerns. What about the Tallman girl?"

"She's dead."

"Take her body to the morgue in the 'copter, too, please. The FBI's breathing down my neck to get her out of here."

A burly Air Force sergeant in fatigues came running across the concourse, as Mike reached for the scalpel in the emergency tracheotomy set he always carried in his medical bag. The airman was pulling a stretcher of the wheeled basket type used in rescue squad work, with a respirator and a portable pacemaker-defibrillator resting on it. A corporal followed, carrying another kit, but the television team, alerted by the shouted conversation, was ahead of them. From a distance of a few yards the cameraman flicked the switch of his powerful floodlight and Mike blinked as the camera whirred.

"You're a bunch of damned ghouls," he snapped, "but leave the light on. I've got some surgery to do and for God's sake keep out of the way."

"Roger, Doc," said the cameraman and the light was held steady, revealing the damage to the girl's face in every gory detail but furnishing vitally necessary illumination for the delicate piece of surgery Mike was embarked upon.

"Sergeant Stone, Dr. Kerns." The Air Force medical corpsman was panting. "Tell us what you want us to do."

"Place your hand under this girl's neck, please, Sergeant. I'm going to do a tracheotomy."

The airman needed no further instructions: making a fist, he put it back of the injured girl's neck, arching it so the cartilages protecting the voice box—colloquially known as the Adam's apple —were thrust forward.

"You got a tube, sir?"

"A small one. I'm only going to do a coniotomy so we can connect the respirator to it."

Holding the scalpel between his index finger and thumb with less than half an inch of blade exposed, Mike made a neat cut across the bottom of the Adam's apple just below a prominent ring of cartilage. The pressure of his fingers upon the blade kept it from going too deep and damaging the voice box with the vocal cords inside. Then, pushing the point directly through the membrane that showed in the depths of the wound, he opened into the respiratory passage itself.

Holding open the cut he'd made directly into the trachea—or windpipe—by turning the knife, he picked up a small curved metal tube from the sterile pack and slipped it into the opening, with the curve pointing down. Next he taped the flanged outer end of the tracheotomy tube into place with adhesive to keep it from slipping out. Meanwhile Sergeant Stone had loosened a tube connected to a valve on the emergency tank of oxygen inside the respirator case and Mike attached the end to the tracheotomy tube. When the sergeant opened the valve to the oxygen tank, the respirator began to fill, forcing the vital gas into the girl's lungs.

"Let's get the pacemaker going, too, before we move her to the helicopter," said Mike, and Sergeant Stone handed him the two electrodes leading from the battery-operated machine.

"Do you bastards have to photograph *everything?*" he demanded angrily, but the TV camera was not turned off—and he stepped across the girl's body, so his own head and shoulders blocked the view of the camera lens. Then, tearing open the girl's blouse, he carefully placed the two electrodes directly on the skin of her chest about eight inches apart over the area beneath which lay the heart.

Fortunately, her breasts were small for her height and build, so he had little trouble placing the electrodes properly. And, when Sergeant Stone threw a switch on the machine, a sudden sharp jolt of electric current flowed from one terminal to the other, passing through the heart muscle and stimulating it to contract, even as her chest muscles jerked from the stimulus.

"You brought a pulse that time, sir," reported Stone, who was holding a finger on the girl's wrist.

"That means the blood hasn't started to coagulate, so she may have a chance, but it doesn't prove she's alive."

"When can you be sure of that?" the TV reporter inquired and, when Mike loomed up briefly to answer, he saw that a small crowd of people—airline clerks, the waitress from the smashed lunchroom, and a dozen others, plus one airport security guard in uniform—surrounded him.

"Disperse these people, Guard," he ordered, angry at being a player in what was becoming a small circus. "We're trying to save this girl's life."

"And doing a damned good job," said the camera-bearing reporter, shifting position as he took another picture. "In less than five minutes you've got both her heart and lungs working."

The cheer from the crowd that followed only angered Mike more.

"All right, Sergeant," he said. "Let's get her into your helicopter. And you," he added, motioning to the security guard, "make a path for us through these people!"

"You handle the respirator and keep the pacemaker electrodes in place while we put her on the strecher, Doctor," said Stone. "Grab her feet, Al."

The second rescue squad attendant, who had been standing by, now stepped forward and took the girl's feet while Stone lifted her torso. With the two instruments resting upon her abdomen, the pacemaker stimulated her heart and the respirator rhythmically inflated her lungs as they moved her to the basket stretcher. Meanwhile the body of Lynne Tallman, still covered with a blanket, had been transferred by other attendants to a second stretcher.

With the security guard moving ahead to clear away the curious crowd, drawn by a chance to see the infamous Lynne Tallman— even as a corpse—the little procession moved swiftly across the concourse and out to where the big helicopter stood waiting on the circle of grass inside the approach to the airport entrance.

The first stretcher was carried to the back of the cabin, so Mike would have room to work there. Next the blanket-covered form of Lynne Tallman was brought aboard on a second stretcher, and placed on the floor behind the pilot's seat. When a tall man wearing dark glasses and civilian clothes entered the cabin behind it, Mike looked at him sharply.

"What are you doing in here, buster?" he demanded. "We're crowded enough as it is."

Reaching into his breast pocket, the tall man opened a leather identification folder on which Mike read the words: "Federal Bureau of Investigation."

"Inspector Frank Stafford, FBI," he said.

"Why would the FBI keep watch on somebody who's already dead?" With the motor gunned, the conversation had to be carried on by shouting.

"Two of my best friends in the Bureau died guarding the Tallman girl on that flight from Chicago," said Stafford crisply. "Somebody in that Chicago cult wanted to shut her up before she could testify and wired a couple of sticks of dynamite to the landing gear assembly inside the plane so it would explode when the copilot started lowering the wheels for the descent to Dulles."

"Jesus!" said Sergeant Stone. "Whoever did it wanted to be sure it would happen where everybody could see it."

"If they could manage that," said Stafford, "they could hijack Tallman's body from an ambulance between Dulles and the city, then hold it until they found another girl who looked like her and claim she was resurrected or something. After all, she was the acknowledged high priestess of that devil worship cult in Chicago."

The small electronic picture of the heartbeat on the monitor screen of the portable pacemaker suddenly wavered and Mike quickly moved the electrodes, flat disks of metal partially covered by plastic, until the heartbeat resumed the former pattern of regular stimulation.

"We've had some trouble with those pacemaker electrodes, Doctor," said Stone. "Nowadays you can't depend on anybody to do things right."

"Do you have a transvenous catheter pacemaker aboard, Sergeant?" Mike asked.

"I believe so, sir, but I wouldn't know how to put it in."

"I do. By using it we'll get a lot better stimulation of the heartbeat."

Sergeant Stone had been rummaging in one of the cabinets on either side of the helicopter cabin. Now he took down a cloth-wrapped package. "Here it is sir. The cutdown set's inside."

"Strap the right arm to a board but leave me room to work in the antecubital fossa in front of the elbow."

Inside the sterile pack, Mike found a pair of surgical gloves and carefully slipped them on. Next he swabbed the depression in front of the patient's elbow, through which several large veins passed just beneath the skin, using a cotton pledget dipped in antiseptic. Then, taking a small sheet with a window some two inches square from the sterile pack, he placed it with the opening directly over where he planned to work.

"Mind telling me what you're doing, Doctor?" The FBI inspector had moved to the foot of the stretcher.

"We've got the girl's heart beating artificially by stimulating it with an external pacemaker, but the electrodes on her skin aren't working too well," Mike explained as he worked. "Her lungs are being inflated, too, with pure oxygen carried throughout the body by the bloodstream."

"Just as if she were alive."

"I think she *is* alive." Mike was making a small incision into the skin over a faint bluish swelling marking the course of one of the veins ordinarily used for obtaining blood for laboratory examinations or making intravenous injections. "Every time the pacemaker delivers a jolt to the heart, it also stimulates the muscles of the chest; you can see how they jerk. If I can slip a special catheter electrode up through a vein of the arm and into the heart so the tip touches the inside wall, we can stimulate just the heart muscle with the current and stop her chest from jerking."

"If you can do that, you're a magician."

Mike was looking at the veins in the girl's arm, which were barely visible, even with the heart contracting strongly under the stimulus of the electrical impulses fed to it by the pacemaker. "She's lost a lot of blood and her pressure is low from shock. These veins are almost collapsed and if we don't get some blood into her soon . . ."

He didn't finish the sentence but, using the tip of the scalpel blade, nicked the wall of the vein. The ooze of blood from the cut was easily controlled by the pressure of his index finger and, with his right hand, he picked up the catheter. Besides the electrode running through it to carry the current, the plastic tube with the Y-shaped outer end contained a second channel enabling air to be pumped into a tiny balloon surrounding the tip. With the balloon uninflated, he slid the catheter into the vein and began to push it along inside the ever larger venous channel toward the girl's trunk and the heart.

"The current of blood will start pulling the catheter up the vein as soon as we get the tip into the larger portion of the vein and can inflate the balloon," he explained.

Sergeant Stone had connected the tip of a sterile syringe to one of the Y-shaped ends of the catheter while Mike had been pushing it slowly up the vein toward the heart, noting the distance by markings on the plastic tube.

"Put in a little air, Sergeant," he directed. "We ought to be into the subclavian by now."

"What does that mean?" Inspector Stafford asked.

"The tip of the catheter is probably somewhere beneath the collarbone," Mike explained, "with perhaps six or eight inches more to go before it reaches the right ventricle of the heart."

"And then?"

"The metal-tipped electrode at the end of the catheter can send a current directly into the heart muscle."

"Neat! Very neat!"

"If we're lucky. Right now shock and brain injury are both working against us."

For almost a minute, the catheter kept on moving, before a sudden change of pressure was perceived by Mike's sensitive fingers, telling him that the tip had passed through the smaller right chamber of the heart—the auricle—and the tricuspid valve separating it from the thick-walled ventricle below, where he hoped the electrode would impinge against the muscular wall of the larger chamber.

"Connect the electrode, please, Sergeant," he said quietly. "This may be it."

Quickly the medical corpsman made the transfer, so the current that had been flowing in regular pulses through the flat electrodes on the girl's chest now passed along the wire inside the catheter and into the heart itself.

"You hit it, Dr. Kerns!" he cried when the pattern of the heartbeat reappeared on the small monitor screen of the pacemaker. "That was the slickest thing I ever saw."

"I'm not sure I understand just what happened, Doctor," said the FBI agent admiringly. "But whatever it was, you deserve credit for saving this girl."

"I still may have been wasting everybody's time," said Mike as he strapped the catheter electrode to the girl's arm. "Only the electroencephalograph can tell us whether or not she's really alive."

"I just notified the Emergency Room at University Hospital that we'll be landing on their rooftop helipad in five minutes, Dr. Kerns," the pilot reported from the front of the cabin. "Any special instructions?"

"Tell them to hold one of the high-speed elevators to Emergency and have O-type blood ready so we can pump it into her as rapidly as possible. If the EEG shows brain waves, she's still alive, with a chance to pull through, providing the brain injury isn't too great."

"What about her face?" Inspector Stafford asked.

"I can put it together later; plastic and reconstructive surgery is my special field."

"Get ready for a bump," the pilot called from the front of the cabin. "A breeze always blows across the tops of these high buildings, but I'll set her down as lightly as I can."

The landing was uneventful, and the special high-speed elevator connecting the Emergency Room with the rooftop helicopter landing pad dropped a wheeled stretcher to which the patient had been transferred, with the respirator and pacemaker still working, down to the ground floor of the big teaching unit hospital where Dr. Stewart Porter, the Emergency Room director, was waiting. The young surgeon was about Mike's age and an old friend from their house officer days in this same hospital.

"Take over, Mike," he said. "You've been with her from the start."

"We'll put her on the EEG, Stew, and see whether or not she's alive, while you're getting a transfusion of O-type blood started. She lost quite a bit of blood from the facial injuries but shock and concussion are what we have to fight."

Dr. Porter started working while Mike wheeled the stretcher into the first of a dozen cubicles in the Emergency Room, where swift and effective treatment could be administered as needed. This one contained a monitoring screen for the electroencephalograph that measured electric activity—the index of life or death—in the brain, as well as a connection by which to monitor heart action.

He didn't waste time pulling back the girl's reddish golden hair, now matted with blood, but began thrusting needle electrodes into her scalp in the pattern used for the test. As fast as he put in needles, Mrs. Saunders, the graying nurse supervisor who had coped in her time with about every conceivable emergency, connected them to the terminals of the machine. At the same time, another nurse attached small electrocardiographic electrodes to the patient's body, supplementing the information provided by the wire electrode inside her heart. Finally, the multiple insertions completed, Mike stood back and nodded to the older nurse.

"Turn it on," he directed. "We'll know in a minute whether we have to go any further."

Mrs. Saunders threw the switch and both of them leaned forward to study the monitor screen. At first they saw nothing and Mike had the sinking feeling that all during the past half hour he'd been trying to revive a dead body. Then, as the machine warmed up, a faint wavy line appeared on the screen, not as strong as a normal EEG pattern should have been, but nevertheless discernible. Moreover, they could distinguish the separate waves indicating different levels of brain activity. At the bottom of the monitor, too, the regular pattern of the artificial heartbeat was now appearing.

"You've brought her back from the dead, Doctor!" The nurse's voice, for all her experience, had a touch of awe in it, then she sobered. "But I wonder whether she or her fiancé will thank you when they see the mess that crash made of her face."

"What's this about a fiancé?"

"Don't tell me you haven't seen that diamond she's wearing on her left hand? Which reminds me, I'd better get it off and into the hospital safe before it disappears mysteriously."

3

By the time Mike had finished packing the injured girl's nasal passages with narrow strips of gauze in order to control hemorrhage from the crushed bones, Dr. Stewart Porter had exposed a vein with a small incision over the inner side of the left ankle and inserted a short nylon catheter. Connecting that to a transfusion apparatus, he started a transfusion of the O-type blood kept stored at all times for emergencies, since it matched the three other types and almost never caused a reaction. Meanwhile laboratory technicians had taken blood samples for exact matching and to determine the degree of shock and hemorrhage.

As he worked, Mike had sought to mold the badly crushed nasal bones into as near their normal shape as possible. More definitive reconstruction would have to wait, however, until she was conscious and shock had been combated by the transfusion to a point where a more thorough examination could be carried out to determine whether there were other injuries, and particularly whether the brain damage from striking her head would leave permanent effects.

"Once or twice I thought I detected some weak contractions on the cardiac monitor," said Mrs. Saunders, as Mike finished tying the ends of the postnasal pack's anchoring threads together over a small roll of gauze beneath the patient's nose.

"Stop the pacemaker and we'll see."

When the nurse switched off the pacemaker current, all eyes in the room were focused on the screen of the monitor. Seconds before, the regular procession of artificially created heartbeat waves had been moving across the screen, stimulated by rhythmic jolts of current from the pacemaker through the electrode inside the girl's heart; now the line was flat.

For a long moment nothing happened; then just as Mike was reaching for the pacemaker switch to start the stimulating current again, a low wave suddenly appeared. Its presence meant only one thing: the heart was reacting to the natural stimulus of its own pacemaker, a collection of special nerve-muscle tissue in the upper part of the right auricle. It strengthened on the second beat, then—as if sure of itself following that first tentative contraction— took up a regular rhythm.

"That's a miracle," said Dr. Porter, his voice hoarse with emotion.

"Miracle is right," said Mike. *"We* certainly didn't do it."

When Mike came out of the adjoining Intensive Care Unit, after supervising the transfer of the patient to one of its cubicles— where all the vital processes would be continually monitored and the nurse on duty at the central nursing station could watch all patients through the glass walls of the small compartments—a tall gray-haired man wearing thick-lensed spectacles was sitting in the small waiting room just outside.

"Dr. Kerns?" he asked.

"Yes."

"I'm George Stanfield, managing editor of the *Star-News*. Janet Burke—" He stopped at Mike's look of incomprehension. "You didn't even know her name, did you?"

"I'm afraid things have been moving too rapidly for that, but it looks now like Miss Burke may live."

"Thank God—and you—for that, Doctor," said Stanfield. "Janet's my niece, and also the best reporter we've got in the Chicago bureau. She's been on the Lynne Tallman case from the start; I guess you could say she was closer to the girl than anyone outside the cult."

"I'd call that rather a dubious honor."

"Not when you're the sort of reporter Janet is. She called me last night from Chicago to say the FBI was bringing Lynne to Washington this morning and she was coming with her. Janet said she was writing a story about why Lynne Tallman decided to cop a plea and would have it ready to turn in when she got here this morning. In fact, I'd be willing to bet Janet talked the Tallman girl into it."

"And got an exclusive story, I suppose."

"That she did—and don't think it wasn't smart reporting with every paper in Chicago, plus the wire services, trying to get it. I was waiting for her at the airport when the crash came, but the police wouldn't let me into the concourse while the fire was being fought. I saw somebody being put on the helicopter with Lynne Tallman's body, but had no idea who it was until the head of airport security told me. I came here as fast as I could, but from what they said at Dulles, I was sure she was dead."

"I guess your niece was about as near death as you can be and still have life, Mr. Stanfield," said Mike. "There's a coffee shop off the foyer. Why don't we have a cup and maybe a danish? I'm starved."

While they were eating, Mike brought the newspaperman up to date on what had happened since he'd knelt beside the girl Stanfield had called Janet Burke.

"Then you weren't able to do anything about her facial wounds?" Stanfield asked.

"First things had to be handled first, but I did pack her nasal passages to stop hemorrhage. As soon as it's safe, I'll go in and straighten out her face."

"Is it badly damaged?"

"Externally there is only a small cut at the corner of the right eye, but internally the structures of the upper jaw are quite badly crushed. The lower's broken, too, but there's no displacement, so it shouldn't be too hard to hold. By the way, would you have a recent photograph of her? It would help me to know what she looked like before the accident."

"I have one in color at home and the personnel office at the paper will have more. Will she be scarred?"

"I'd say very little, if any, judging by my first examination."

"Surely the surgery—"

"I hope to do most of that from inside the mouth. The only laceration I saw was a small one at the outer corner of her right eye. Was she very beautiful?"

"'Wholesome-looking' would be a better term, I suppose," said Stanfield. "But smart—and dedicated to her job. Lynne Tallman apparently trusted her and opened up more to her than to anyone else. Janet even made some tapes of her interviews with the Tallman girl and has already nailed down a contract for a book on that she-devil's life. My paper has the exclusive right to print parts of it before book publication—if Janet ever gets to finish it now."

"We should know the answer to that question tomorrow," said Mike. "I've asked Dr. Josh Fogarty to see her. He's the best neurosurgeon on the staff and also an expert on brain damage."

"I know him," said Stanfield.

"The most serious danger to her recovery, however," Mike continued, "is the fact that her heart stopped beating and her brain was without a supply of blood for at least a brief period."

"Is five minutes really the outside limit for lack of oxygen to the brain cells not to damage them permanently?"

"It's only a rule of thumb; I've seen cases that went longer without any evidence of damage to the higher centers."

"Don't let her end up without a mind, Dr. Kerns. Neither her fiancé nor I—nor Janet either—would want that."

"We're doing our best, Mr. Stanfield—and with the facilities of this hospital and the medical school at our disposal, our best is pretty good."

"She's in your hands, Doctor. I must go and call Gerald Hutchinson in Chicago. He's the *Star-News* religious editor for the Chicago area and he and Janet were to be married next month."

4

The prints George Stanfield had promised Mike were delivered to his office, about two blocks from University Hospital, by special messenger late that afternoon. As her uncle had said, Janet Burke had been a wholesome-looking, if not exactly beautiful, girl before the accident. Studying the photos, however, Mike could see that, in the hands of a skilled plastic surgeon, her features could be shaped to achieve real beauty. And the more he saw of the challenge they presented, the more certain he was that he could rise to it.

When Mike stopped by University Hospital for his evening rounds on the way home, he found that Janet Burke had started breathing spontaneously about an hour after leaving the Emergency Room. Her heart action was strong, too, and, with the transfusions, her blood pressure had risen to a normal figure.

With a pair of large calipers and a notebook, he recorded the measurements of the unconscious girl's face and head in a dozen places and took photographs with his instant-developing camera. Dr. Fogarty had not yet seen her but the neurosurgeon's office assured Mike he would when he made late afternoon rounds on his own patients, about six o'clock.

Shortly after Mike came into his Georgetown apartment at six-thirty, the telephone rang. The caller was Dr. Josh Fogarty from the Neurosurgical Service.

"Thought you might like to have my opinion on the Burke girl tonight, Mike," he said. "I just finished going over her and doing a spinal puncture."

"Anything significant?"

"She's still unconscious, but the spinal fluid pressure is within normal limits and there's no blood in it."

Both findings were good news; had the head injury been really severe, the pressure would probably have risen, at least somewhat. The absence of blood in the fluid surrounding the brain and spinal cord also meant none of the blood vessel network covering the brain surface had been injured by the blow to her skull.

"The only thing that worries me about her condition," Fogarty added, "is that her heart may not have been beating for over five minutes. Of course, she could come out of it mentally okay, but then again, she could turn into a human vegetable."

"Let's hope your first guess is right. Thanks for seeing her, Josh; you'll keep watching her, won't you?"

"Of course. Good night."

Going into the small bedroom he used as a den and studio, Mike began to prepare the armature, or frame, that would serve as the skeleton, so to speak, for the model he planned to make of

Janet Burke's head before planning the actual surgical reconstruction.

In the center of a five-ply board, ten by twelve inches in size, he nailed an inch-and-a-half-square upright, six inches high. Next he took a piece of half-inch lead tubing sixteen inches long and bent it roughly into the contour of a light bulb, with a rounded top and two straight sides. These he nailed to the upright on either side, thus forming a firm center around which he could begin to mold the head.

For the actual molding, he preferred to use plasteline because, having an oil base, it did not dry out so quickly as did clay and would hold its shape better during the several evenings required to make the model he had in mind. Opening several packages, he began to shape the doughy substance into rolls, each about six inches long, applying them to the armature to form a column for the neck, surmounted by a rough block that would become the head.

Before starting the model, Mike had placed two photos of Janet Burke from the *Star-News* personnel department, one full face and one profile, in racks on a small table where they were in bright light. Beside them, he'd also put a color print Stanfield had given him, taken apparently at some social function, for she was in an evening gown. Obviously healthy, intelligent and attractive, she'd no doubt been the kind of girl who never made beauty queen in high school or college but did become a cheerleader. Her hair, he'd already noted at the airport, was of a red-gold hue and light enough in texture to be easy to manage, whether tinted or not.

As his facile fingers began molding the plasteline, Mike became more and more convinced that his first impression had been correct: if she regained full consciousness, there was an excellent possibility of rebuilding the girl's features to make her a real beauty along classic lines. Imbued with that idea, he put down the two-inch section cut from the top of a broom handle he'd been using to smooth the rolls of plasteline and went to the encyclopedia to look for photographs of heads from the classic Greek period. He was searching for a particular Aphrodite, a copy of which he remembered seeing in the British Museum, but it took him about half an hour to find the one he was looking for. It was the bust of Aphrodite by Praxiteles, one of the loveliest specimens of Greek statuary ever created.

The longer he studied the lovely head in the encyclopedia, and compared it with the photos of Janet Burke, the more convinced he became that his memory had not served him false in suggesting that the girl's face was quite similar in proportions and shape to that of the statue, though not so perfectly formed, of course, as to create the rare beauty of the bust itself.

Taking the volume back to the table on which the blocked-out model stood and propping it beside the prints of Janet Burke, he began to work more intently, pausing every few moments to study the photos, the measurements, and the copy of the Praxiteles bust from the encyclopedia. By ten o'clock he was exhausted but had the satisfaction of seeing his model beginning to take on both the shape of the girl's face and the unique classic beauty of the Goddess of Love, as created by the most famous sculptor in Greek art history.

When he finally laid down the modeling tools, he was more than pleased with the results of his evening's work and, pouring himself a liberal drink of Bourbon, his favorite sipping whiskey, he switched on the TV and watched the eleven o'clock news before going to bed.

5

"Your patient's doing fine, Dr. Kerns," Mrs. Sheftal, the nursing supervisor of the Intensive Care Unit, greeted Mike when he came on the floor the next morning. "When do you think she'll regain consciousness?"

"Dr. Fogarty won't hazard a guess. Did she need the pacemaker during the night?"

"Not once. Her pulse is as regular as mine."

"I think I'll take out the catheter electrode this afternoon, then," said Mike. "You'd better have a cutdown set ready, in case I have to tie off the vein."

"I'll be glad to get her off that monitor," said the nurse. "We never know when we'll need them for coronary cases. What about the EEG?"

"I want to keep monitoring the brain currents until she's conscious."

In the cubicle of the ICU Janet Burke occupied, Mike made a brief check of her condition but found nothing to cause alarm, except that she still hadn't regained consciousness. That, however, could be an ominous sign in itself, growing more so with each passing hour.

As he was finishing the examination, he experienced the odd feeling that, even though the sleeping girl showed no other sign of consciousness, she was actually cognizant of everything he said and did. He was startled, too, when the nursing supervisor asked, "Do you sometimes get the feeling she's nearer consciousness than she wants us to believe she is, Dr. Kerns?"

"What makes you think that?"

"I guess I've been in this business so long I've begun to doubt that anybody's really what they appear to be."

"I had the same feeling just now," Mike admitted. "I can't think of any reason why, so I guess we're both wrong. Any change in her electroencephalographic pattern?"

"The brain waves are stronger, but once or twice I've seen a few I didn't recognize."

"I'm certainly no authority on brain waves, but Dr. Fogarty just came in. Maybe he can tell us."

"What are you two in a huddle about?" the tall blond neurosurgeon asked.

"The Burke girl is still unconscious, but Mrs. Sheftal and I both get the impression that she's closer to consciousness than she wants us to realize," said Mike.

"It's those waves we're wondering about," the supervisor explained. "When I'm working here at the station, I usually keep one eye on the bank of monitors; it's become sort of a habit."

"What's so special about these waves?"

"They're different from the regular brain waves, but I can't tell you exactly how." The nurse's voice suddenly rose on an excited note. "There's a burst of them now."

Both doctors turned quickly to watch the pattern of waves moving across the monitor screen as they registered Janet Burke's brain currents by means of the needle electrodes Mike had put into her scalp the day before. Mike saw at once what Mrs. Sheftal meant: during the space of perhaps five seconds, the regular, slow rhythm of normal alpha waves characteristic of complete relaxation or drowsiness was replaced by a smaller and much more rapid wave pattern on the screen.

"That's called the theta rhythm!" Fogarty exclaimed. "But it's particularly odd with an unconscious patient."

"Why, Josh?"

"I don't know; phenomena like this are more often connected with parapsychology—"

"ESP?"

"That's one aspect, but it's a pretty complicated subject, so most hard-nosed doctors steer clear of the paranormal. Still, we can't deny that some people are much more sensitive to mental imagery than others."

"I can understand that from my own small experience in sculpture," Mike commented.

"How much do you know about biofeedback?" Fogarty asked.

"Only that those working in the field claim to be able to teach experimental subjects to achieve voluntary control of autonomic functions like heart rate, blood flow and some other physiological processes we always thought were independent of consciousness."

"That's as good a description as any," said Fogarty. "Because the emotional state more or less controls the physiological state, many researchers are beginning to believe the latter can be changed—improved, if you will—by controlling the former."

"I'll buy that," said Mike. "Last summer I spent a few weeks in India for a seminar on plastic procedures used there as early as five to seven hundred years before Christ. Some of the things I saw the fakirs doing can hardly be explained any other way—if at all."

"One or two research programs in parapsychology found that biofeedback methods resulted in a sharp increase in the amount of imagery—imagination, if you will—reported by the subjects," said Fogarty. "What was more, it was accompanied by an increase in the theta rhythm of the EEG wave patterns in the subjects under study."

"Then Janet Burke may be experiencing imagination—dreams, if you want to call them that—at a subconscious level? Imagery that's sufficiently vivid to cause a change in her EEG wave pattern, with enhancement of what you call the theta rhythm, but perhaps not able to break through to consciousness yet?"

"Go to the head of the class."

"If her brain cells are healthy enough to be capable of initiating a dream, why don't they achieve consciousness?"

"I told you the whole subject is hard to explain."

"So what can we do?"

"If she'd been taught biofeedback, we might use it—though I don't at the moment see exactly how. But she hasn't—"

"That we know of."

The brain surgeon gave him a startled look. "What do you mean, Mike?"

"This girl was apparently so close to Lynne Tallman that the Tallman girl insisted on Janet's being on that plane. She apparently trusted Janet, too, and gave her a lot of information she didn't give to anybody else."

"I remember reading one story in the *Star-News,* maybe under the Burke girl's by-line," said Fogarty. "Lynne Tallman was boasting of conducting rites of Satan worship with members of her cult in Chicago. Do you suppose the Burke girl could have joined them?"

"Not a chance, from what her uncle tells me about her. Of course, she's a smart reporter and might have pretended—no, I can't believe that either. But she must have had an understanding —call it a kindred feeling—of Lynne Tallman's mentality to get so close to her."

"The kind of mentality that got its kicks from setting off bombs and killing innocent people?" Fogarty's eyebrows rose expressively. "Maybe when she becomes conscious, your patient can tell us a lot of things."

"Or more likely keep them to herself and put them into the book she's writing about the Tallman girl. One more thing: George Stanfield thinks Janet Burke persuaded Lynne Tallman to give herself up and testify for the prosecution against the cult members. If that's so and she's really conscious enough to know what happened, she's probably blaming herself for the Tallman girl's death and suffering the tortures of the damned inside."

"Which could account for the appearance of theta rhythm waves in her EEG and her reluctance to become conscious," said

Fogarty thoughtfully. "This parapsychology business must be con-
tagious; you're going a lot farther out with your theory than I ever
did."

"I can't really call it *my* theory," Mike admitted. "Two thou-
sand-odd years ago, Plato said, 'If the head and body are to be
well, you must begin by curing the soul.' But how do you relieve a
guilt complex in somebody who doesn't choose to become conscious enough for you to even communicate with her?"

"I can't tell you that but I know a man who might help," said
Fogarty. "Professor Randall McCarthy in the Department of Psychiatry took a Ph.D. in parapsychology while he acquired his
M.D. He likes to dabble in the paranormal and I've seen him do
some weird things in that field."

"He must have joined the faculty while I was in New York on a
fellowship last year," said Mike. "I don't seem to remember him."

"McCarthy came here about six months ago, after working at
the Stanford Research Institute, a think tank in California, and at
the Laboratory for Parapsychology at Duke, I believe. From what
I hear, he's remarkably effective in psychotherapy, even if some of
his methods are a bit far out."

"Such as?"

"Hypnotherapy, mild hallucinogenic drugs and the like; but I
suspect much of what we hear about him is merely rumor."

"I'll ask McCarthy to see her but I want you to keep on
watching her, too, Josh. We won't be out of the woods until she's
conscious."

"Can you put her face back together while she's still in coma?"

"I'd rather not, though I suppose George Stanfield could give
me permission. I've just about finished modeling the way she
could look when I finish the reconstruction, but I'd rather not
make some of the necessary changes until I've got her name on
the permission sheet."

"Even then you'd better be certain she knows *all* about what
you're going to do," the neurosurgeon warned. "The doctrine of
informed consent doesn't hold up very well in court as a defense
against a malpractice suit. Patients always complain that they
didn't really understand what the operation was to be and, since
the jury rarely understands either, even after the evidence is in, it's
liable to be sympathetic with the plaintiff."

6

Mike called Dr. Randall McCarthy's office at the medical school and, told that the psychiatrist was out of town at a seminar, left a request for consultation on Janet Burke the next day, when McCarthy was expected to return. George Stanfield called Mike about eleven o'clock.

"My reporter on duty at University Hospital tells me a rumor's going around there that Janet's never going to regain consciousness, Dr. Kerns," he said. "Any truth to it?"

"Hospitals thrive on rumors, Mr. Stanfield. I suspect the reporters may have started it themselves, just to get something to write about."

"You may be right. Since this 'death with dignity' business got so much publicity, it's become a pretty newsworthy question—but what about Janet?"

"I can't deny that it's a possibility, as I warned you."

"Is she okay otherwise?"

"I never saw such a severely injured patient do so well."

"Even so, if she doesn't regain consciousness . . . ?"

"Let's cross that bridge when—or if—we get to it," Mike said firmly.

"I just talked to the city editor at the *Post.* They're going to print a story tomorrow morning, saying Janet will have to be or machines to keep her alive and speculating that she may turn into another pull-the-plug or not-pull-the-plug case."

"You can put a stop to some of the rumors and also get ahead of the *Post,*" Mike assured Stanfield. "Just quote me as saying I'm going to remove the catheter electrode this afternoon because Janet's heart is now beating strongly and regularly under its own power and her breathing no longer needs any help. Also that I confidently expect her to become conscious in less than twenty-four hours."

"We'll run the story; there's still time to get it in the Wall Street Final; but aren't you going out on a limb, Dr. Kerns?"

"I went out on one when I decided she had a chance to live, Mr. Stanfield. Taking another perch there won't hurt me."

"Has the FBI been in touch with you yet?"

"No. Why would they?"

"In the wreckage of the plane they found a briefcase Janet was apparently carrying with her. It got thrown clear of the forward cabin where she was sitting, so its contents weren't damaged too much from the heat, I judge."

"Haven't you examined it?"

"Not yet. The FBI's holding the briefcase, claiming it's important evidence, but I learned from a private source that it contains some notes Janet had made for future articles on Lynne Tallman and some tapes of interviews with her. My lawyer's in Federal District Court right now with a petition to have everything turned over to me as her next of kin and we expect a decision in our favor before the day's over."

"Has anyone claimed the Tallman girl's body yet?"

"Not that I've been able to determine. Apparently nobody wants to even claim kin with such a she-devil. You'll keep me posted on Janet's condition, won't you?"

"Of course. The minute there's any change."

"By the way," Stanfield added, "Janet's fiancé, Gerald Hutchinson, is arriving on a late evening plane from Chicago. He edits a religious-philosophical page that we syndicate to a dozen newspapers from Chicago."

"Then he's a minister?"

"No, but he's a lay reader and very active in the Episcopal Church. He'll want to talk to you, but I'd appreciate your playing down any permanent disfigurement—"

"I don't expect any," said Mike. "In fact, by day after tomorrow I'll be finished with a model showing how she can look—if she wants to."

"Do you think trying to improve on nature would be wise, Doctor?"

"Let's leave that up to her," said Mike. "I think she'll like the changes I propose to make."

Mike was about to go to lunch just before one o'clock when his office nurse told him Inspector Stafford was outside asking to see him. He came out and shook hands with the tall, graying man from the FBI who'd ridden with him in the helicopter.

"I was just going out for a bite, Inspector," he said. "Had lunch yet?"

"No."

"Then how about joining me? There's a fairly decent restaurant around the corner."

Stafford glanced at his watch. "At three o'clock I'm going to talk to the controller at Dulles who handled Flight Six-twenty yesterday, but there'll be time for a bite while we talk."

"Any news yet about the cause of the explosion?" Mike asked as they walked the short block to the restaurant.

"The setup was simple enough, a few sticks of dynamite and a detonator attached to the landing gear. The controls for the wing flaps and the rudder, along with the brakes, were put out of action when lowering the wheels triggered the explosive."

"Whoever did the job had to know his business."

"Armand Descaux is an expert," said Stafford. "The U. S. Army saw to that before they gave him a Section Eight discharge in Vietnam."

"How could you know who did it?"

"We've known Descaux was kingpin, after Tallman, in the Chicago cult for quite a while, but couldn't get our hands on him. All the earlier bombings by the cult bore the same markings, so this was unquestionably a Descaux job, too."

At the restaurant they were shown to a table and gave their orders before the conversation continued.

"What about Janet Burke's briefcase?" Mike asked. "Are you going to let Mr. Stanfield have it?"

"We made a compromise; Stanfield let us make copies of everything in it and we surrendered the originals. Unfortunately, what we were looking for—the names of other people in the cult group —wasn't in either the manuscript or the tapes Lynne Tallman made for Miss Burke—"

"Just what do you mean by 'cult group,' Inspector?"

Stafford shrugged. "It's become a catchall word for radicals, screwballs, schizoids and religious fanatics, I'm afraid, so it doesn't really mean anything. Tallman seems to have headed a group of devil worshipers who used an alleged devotion to Satan as an excuse for the bombings and arson that were their specialty. We think the men are all probably veterans of the Vietnam war who were dishonorably discharged."

"If that's true, how could Descaux have flubbed the explosion on the plane?"

"He must have had to work very fast," Stafford explained. "The Chicago Bureau didn't get instructions to fly the Tallman girl to Washington until around midnight. After that she had to be convinced and, when she refused to come without Janet Burke, our people there had to rout Miss Burke out and tell her what was going to happen. During that time, a leak occurred."

"From Miss Burke?"

"No. We've checked the telephone in her apartment in Chicago and the only call she made was to Mr. Stanfield, which means the leak had to come from within the Bureau. It isn't a pleasant thing to face," Stafford added on a grim note, "but with a charge set to explode while Flight Six-twenty was in mid-air, as Descaux intended, anybody connected with the bombing would know that those of our own people guarding Lynne Tallman would be killed, along with a lot of other passengers."

"Could part of the purpose in blowing up the plane have been to shut Janet Burke up at the same time?"

"We think it was. That's why I want your permission to put around-the-clock guards on her."

"You have it, of course—if the hospital authorities agree."

"We can *make* them agree, Dr. Kerns."

"Then why ask?"

"For one thing, whenever we throw our weight around, someone usually complains to his congressman. Immediately, *he* sees a political advantage in delving deeper into FBI activities than's been done already, so he reports it to a congressional committee and we're off on another witch-hunt."

"I can see what's involved."

"Not quite all of it, Doctor; and here I need your promise that what I'm about to tell you will be held in strictest confidence."

"You have it, so long as it doesn't involve something that might endanger the welfare of my patient."

"This does."

"Then I'm afraid I shall have to insist on being the judge of what can and cannot be revealed."

Stafford nodded. "I was sure you would feel that way, so I discussed this beforehand with the Director. We're prepared to leave the decision up to you, with the proviso that you let us know if you decide to make anything I shall tell you public."

"That's not an unreasonable request. I'll buy it."

Over after-lunch coffee, Stafford said, "The real reason for all this hocus-pocus is that, while what Miss Burke brought from Chicago will undoubtedly be of value to her as a reporter and to her employer, it still didn't tell us anything at all about Tallman's associates, or what they plan to do next."

"Maybe they lost their touch when she was captured. After all, Descaux did bungle the bombing of the plane."

"Only because he was working under difficult circumstances. The plan was clever and the placing of the bomb was carefully selected, but the bomber had to get into the hangar and into the airplane, wire everything into place and get out again in a few minutes."

"How do you know that?"

"Several mechanics had been working on the plane all night, except for about fifteen minutes at seven o'clock when the change of shifts occurred, with the eleven-to-seven group going off and the seven-to-three shift of mechanics coming on. For roughly fifteen minutes, as far as we can tell, the plane was unattended and, during that time, someone wearing a mechanic's uniform of Tri-Continental Airlines could have carried what appeared to be a tool chest into the hangar. With his skill and experience, Descaux could have put the bomb in place and been out before the next crew came on."

"Sounds plausible."

"Not just plausible, Doctor—certain. After Flight Six-twenty took off, a mechanic's coverall was found stuffed in a trash container in the airport employees' parking lot, but nobody connected it with danger until the flight ended in disaster at Dulles."

"And nobody even remembers seeing a suspicious character?"

"With so many people coming and going at shift-change time, nobody would be likely to notice. We've got to smoke out the remaining leaders of Lynne Tallman's cult another way."

"But how?"

"Mr. Stanfield's agreed to include in the article he's putting into the Wall Street Final edition today an intimation that Lynne Tallman gave Janet Burke the names of people working with her and also places where their atrocities were carried out."

"My God! You're making the Burke girl a decoy."

"That's the general idea and, frankly, it worries us, too. Those fiends have already caused over fifty deaths, including the people killed on Flight Six-twenty, but Mr. Stanfield assures me that if Janet Burke were conscious, she'd co-operate in trying to destroy them."

"I suppose it finally comes down to a matter of statistics, then," said Mike. "You risk one life to save a lot of others, but it's still pretty tough on the one who's taking the risk."

"You can help us considerably, Dr. Kerns, by moving your patient off the Intensive Care Unit and into a private room," said Stafford as they were leaving the restaurant. "It will be much simpler to guard her there than on the Intensive Care Unit where she is now. She's not really in danger of a relapse now, is she?"

"Not nearly as much as she is from the spot you're putting her in," said Mike bluntly. "All we're doing is watching her brain waves on one of the ICU monitors."

"Will you have her moved, then? I've already spoken to Mr. Stanfield and he agrees."

"You think of everything, don't you?"

"Not quite everything, Doctor. If we had, that plane would have been guarded in Chicago from the moment we received orders from Washington to put Lynne Tallman on it."

7

When Mike stopped at the hospital for evening rounds, he found that Janet Burke had already been moved to a private room. The reporters were no longer hanging around but an alert-looking young man with a neat mustache was sitting in a small alcove, from which he had a clear view of the door to her room.

"I'm Dr. Kerns." Mike shook hands with the FBI agent. "Inspector Stafford and I had lunch together."

"Agent Jim McIvor, Doctor. Glad to know you."

"I'm going to be working with the patient for about half an hour—in case you want to run down to the lunchroom for a cup of coffee."

"No offense, Doctor, but my orders are not to leave this post for any reason, until I'm relieved by another agent at eleven o'clock."

A nurse named Ellen Strabo was in charge. She and Mike were old friends and had been, on occasion, somewhat more than that. She smiled warmly in greeting.

"How's it feel to be the most famous plastic surgeon in Washington?" she asked.

"I'll ask him when I see him."

"Look in the mirror tonight. If I'd known you were going to turn out so well, I'd have played for keeps on the few occasions when we made sweet music together." Her tone changed suddenly as another nurse came into the station. "Miss Burke is doing fine, Dr. Kerns. We had a monitor free, so we're still watching her EEG."

"Good. We'll take out the heart electrode while I'm here."

"The cutdown tray's ready; Mrs. Sheftal said you wanted one. Those theta rhythm waves in the EEG are coming more often and in longer bursts now. She's been moving her arms and legs, too."

Janet Burke didn't move while Mike freed her arm from the splint that had held it still. Working gently, he began to ease the catheter out of the vein and was almost finished when he was startled to hear a voice say, "Darn it! That hurts!"

He glanced up quickly and found himself looking into the loveliest pair of eyes he'd ever seen. The pupils were somewhat widened still from the effects of the injuries she had sustained and their depths were like smoky-dark pools, while the irises surrounding them were a lovely shade of violet. The whole gave a somewhat exotic effect he'd not expected in a girl who was essentially plain-looking in her natural state, as he knew from the photographs. Not even the color print George Stanfield had lent him had given any intimation of the beauty of her eyes.

"Decided to wake up?" Mike asked with a smile. "We've been wondering when you would."

"Mind telling me who you are and what's been going on?" Her voice had a muffled, nasal character, because of the packing in her nasopharynx, but preliminary X rays had shown no displacement of the fractures in her lower jaw, so she could move it enough to speak fairly intelligibly.

"Let me finish what I'm doing; it may hurt a little but I'll make it as easy on you as I can. Then we'll talk."

Completing the removal of the catheter took only a few minutes. Once or twice he heard her gasp with pain, particularly when the balloon at the tip was being pulled through the small opening in the skin of her arm, but she didn't cry out. There was only a little bleeding, and he controlled that with pressure before pulling together the edges of the tiny skin wound over the vein with small strips of adhesive called "butterflies."

"There," he said as he finished taping a dressing over the wound. "That scar will be so small, you'll never know it's there."

"My face feels like an elephant stepped on it."

"Something like that did happen when you landed on the floor of the concourse at Dulles." He turned to the nurse. "Thanks, Miss Strabo. I'll stay here and talk to Miss Burke for a while, but there's no need to hold you."

As the nurse departed, taking the cutdown tray and the catheter electrode with her, Mike pulled up a chair beside Janet Burke's bed and reached for the switch that controlled the movements of the bed.

"Talking will be easier for you with your head up a little," he suggested. "Let me know when you're most comfortable."

The head of the bed had reached an angle of almost forty-five degrees when he heard her sudden gasp of horror. Looking up from the switch with which he'd been raising the bed, he saw that the angle was great enough now for her to see her face in the small mirror placed in the middle of the bed table for the convenience of women patients when applying makeup or men while shaving.

"Is that my face?" she cried. "Or what's left of it?"

"It's all there," he assured her, as he raised the bed support beneath her knees to make her more comfortable. "You have only one small skin laceration." He touched the dressing opposite the corner of her right eye. "And when I get through fixing that, you'll never know the scar was there."

"What are you? A magician?"

"A plastic surgeon, but we sometimes need a magician's skill. In your case I can promise to put your face back together again like it was before."

"Nobody ever called me beautiful *then*, but *now*—" Her voice broke and she turned her head away.

"The situation isn't nearly as bad as it seems now," he assured her, as he closed the mirror so it wouldn't be visible. "I've fixed many faces that were damaged more than yours is."

"But you'll have to cut it all to pieces—and there'll be scars."

"That's where you're fortunate; almost all of the work can be done from inside the mouth at one operation." He took a tissue from the box on the bedside table and gave it to her to dab at the tears that filled her eyes.

"H-how could you do it at one operation?"

"It's a matter of raising the two bones that make up the prominence of the cheeks—the zygomatic arches. To get them even and symmetrical, the whole thing has to be done at once. I'll probably take a very small bone graft from the crest of your ilium, your hip-bone, too, and make a new bridge for your nose—"

"It had a little hump in it before. I broke it when I was ten, playing baseball."

"Do you want to keep that?"

"No."

"Then it will be gone when I've finished," he assured her. "Of course, your jaws will have to be wired together for a while and you won't be able to talk as easily as you do now—or as clearly."

"I don't sound like myself. Enough air doesn't seem to be coming through."

"You've been breathing mainly through a tube in your windpipe for the past thirty-six hours," he explained. "As long as it's there, part of the air from your lungs will be diverted below your vocal cords, but you'll be able to talk louder by holding a piece of gauze over the opening."

He held a small tissue over the outer end of the tracheotomy tube and her voice immediately became louder and clearer.

"Sounds like I owe you my life, Dr.—"

"Kerns. Michael Kerns."

"I guess I should be grateful, Dr. Kerns, but when I look in that mirror—" She broke off and shuddered. "It's just that I still can't believe I'll ever look the same again."

"If you'd rather look like someone else, I can give you a practically new face, too. We're doing it every day now with plastic surgery."

"The whole thing sounds fantastic. Last night I was asleep when the FBI called to say Lynne Tallman wouldn't come to Washington without me. Now here I am—all smashed up."

"Even then you were lucky," he assured her. "The front cabin and the cockpit of the plane were a mass of flames seconds after the nose crashed through those glass walls of the Dulles main terminal."

"It's all like a dream, a horrible dream." She shuddered again. "Did you see it happen?"

"Part of it. I was on the highway not far from Dulles International Airport yesterday morning—"

"Have I been unconscious that long?"

"Yes. For a while we were worried that you might never wake up."

"I almost wish I hadn't."

"Things will turn out all right, take my word for it. Okay?"

She looked at him appraisingly for a moment, then nodded. "All right. I guess I don't have much choice."

"As I was saying, I was on the way to Dulles when I saw this 727 making an emergency landing," Mike continued. "Are you sure you feel like talking about it? After all, you've also had a severe concussion."

"I'd like to, if you have the time. There's so much to learn."

"Go ahead, but stop if you get tired or feel a headache."

"I promise. The FBI got me out of bed in Chicago around midnight, when they decided to bring Lynne to Washington. I just had time to call Uncle George and throw a few clothes in a bag before going to the jail where they were holding her. The FBI took us directly to the plane from there."

"Mr. Stanfield told me that much; he's been very worried about you and will be pleased to know you're conscious. I'll call him when I leave the hospital. Please go on."

"When the stewardess served breakfast, I had a couple of glasses of that champagne they give you in first class on early morning flights, so I guess I dozed most of the rest of the way. As we were descending, I remembered the pilot warning the passengers that there was trouble with the landing gear but that the copilot was putting it down by hand. For some reason, Lynne was terrified and I remember loosening my seat belt so I could reach over and comfort her."

"That's one time breaking the rules saved your life. You were the only passenger thrown clear before the fire started."

"Then the explosion occurred, and afterward I remember feeling the wheels hit the runway and being relieved that the copilot had gotten them down."

"He lost his life doing it."

"Then the pilot came on saying he couldn't stop the plane and we would crash. The stewardess was busy getting everybody's head down and handing out pillows to crouch over. Lynne was screaming that we were going to be burned to death when the plane crashed and I was trying to comfort her. I was the one who persuaded her to come—"

"Your uncle says you'd become very close."

"As close as anyone ever got to her, I suppose. I did feel responsible for her, but she was practically berserk with fear of being burned and screaming—"

"Like a banshee's wail," he confirmed. "I was listening to the radio conversations between the pilot and the Dulles Tower and heard her."

"It was horrible." She shivered. "Then I saw the terminal coming at us like an express train and I guess I blacked out."

"The cockpit door apparently was opened by the crash and you were thrown through the smashed windshield and landed, face first, on the floor of the terminal concourse," he told her. "I saw the plane going down and drove to the airport as fast as I could. When I came into the concourse, you were lying beside the Tallman girl. The firemen had dragged her body out of the flames in the nose of the plane, which was sticking through the wall of the terminal, but she was already dead. When I got to you, there was neither respiration nor heartbeat but something convinced me you still had a chance, so I did a tracheotomy to let air into your lungs. Fortunately, a MAST team arrived from Andrews Air Force Base just then with a pacemaker and a respirator. We got your heart and respiration going immediately and I came to University Hospital with you."

"How was Lynne Tallman killed?"

"By the flames. When I got to both of you, there was no question of saving her, so I concentrated on you."

"Poor Lynne. I had finally convinced her she could still make something out of her life by pleading guilty to a lesser charge and testifying against the others."

"Do you know who any of them are?"

"No. She wouldn't tell me and I really didn't want to know. That sort of knowledge isn't safe to have in Chicago."

Or in Washington either, if the plans of the FBI bring results, Mike thought, but didn't voice his concern. Alive, Janet Burke had enough to worry about without being concerned for her life, too.

"It's sort of ironic, you know; I guess some would call it a grim form of justice," Janet added. "After she chose the one way of saving herself from life imprisonment or, at the worst, death, by co-operating with the government, the plane she was coming to Washington on had to crash."

"It didn't just crash—someone had wired a bomb in place so it would be detonated when the landing gear was lowered. The plan was for the plane to explode in mid-air when the pilot lowered the wheels as it was approaching the airport."

"With everybody aboard being killed, especially me—which means they probably think Lynne told me something about the others involved in the Chicago bombings."

"That's the way the FBI sees it. This room is being guarded twenty-four hours a day."

She shivered involuntarily. "It's all such a mess. . . ."

"You're alive," he reminded her. "And you can be far more beautiful than you were—if you want to."

"Who are you anyway—Superdoctor?"

He laughed. "Not quite. I specialize in plastic and reconstructive surgery, so I know how to make your face as good as new—if you want me to do it."

"Has Uncle George commissioned you to take care of me?"

"Yes . . . subject to your approval when you became conscious."

"I'd like to get this over as soon as possible. When can you operate?"

"With luck, day after tomorrow," he told her. "We've only been able to get temporary X rays so far because we didn't want to move you, but I'd like to get a more definite set tomorrow morning. Think you feel up to it?"

"I'll do what I have to do, but from the way my face looks now, I shudder to think of the result."

"We surgeons don't often have an opportunity to make over a patient's face completely, so I've been working at home on a model of what you can look like when the operation's all completed and the ecchymosis—black eyes, to you—has been absorbed. When you see it, I'm sure you're going to be pleased."

It was midnight before Mike went to bed, after calling George Stanfield and telling him his niece was conscious and, seemingly, rational. He slept with a clear conscience, for he was reasonably sure a duplicate of the model he'd completed that evening could be achieved on the operating table in living flesh.

He'd really had trouble with only one feature—the mouth. Somehow, it had almost seemed as if some perverse nerve impulse to the muscles of his right hand insisted on giving Janet Burke's lips—in the model he was constructing—a sarcastic curve, something, he was sure, even swollen and distorted as they were now, they didn't possess. Again and again he'd molded them until now he was sure that, after the operation and the healing process were complete, Janet Burke would be a great beauty—the greatest possible tribute to the genius and surgical skill of her creator.

And yet, taking a last look at the model before going to bed, Mike found himself disturbed by something about it, a feeling of familiarity with some person he'd seen—not Janet Burke—lately, but whom he couldn't exactly identify.

8

"The Burke girl's anterior facial structures are a mess, Mike," Dr. Thorndyke, the chief roentgenologist and an old friend, reported when Mike came into his office in the hospital X-ray Department the next morning. "I'm wondering how even you'll be able to give her anything except a *facies scaphoidea*."

"Dish face" was the literal translation of the Latin phrase, a distressing condition largely found as a birth deformity but also happening in severe facial injuries not treated expertly at the first opportunity for surgical manipulation.

"Her nasal processes are squashed," Dr. Thorndyke continued as he placed a series of X-ray films taken that morning on a long series of view boxes. "Her upper jaws are crushed, too, with the zygomatic processes flat against the maxillas, to say nothing of four fractures of the mandible, fortunately without much displacement."

"I figured that when she was able to talk fairly intelligibly." Mike was studying the films closely. "Is she still down here?"

"Yes. I wouldn't let them take her back to the ward until you were satisfied."

"Think you can show me how much of the anterior walls of the maxillary sinuses are left?"

"Sure," said Thorndyke. "A shot through the mouth upward should do it; I'll see to placing the tube myself."

While the roentgenologist was out of the office, Mike studied the whole series of films once again, working out in his own mind just how the reconstruction would have to be performed. The lower jaw was simple; all he had to do there was pull the chin forward and wire a curved metal bar with small hooks set on the outer curve in front of her teeth. Then, by placing a similar bar around the upper jaw and also wiring it to the teeth, he could splint the lower jaw against the upper by attaching tiny rubber bands to the hooks on the two bars. Thus the lower jaw would be immobilized while healing, yet the mouth could be opened quickly by cutting the bands, in case vomiting occurred and created the possibility of asphyxiation.

It was the upper jaw with which he was most concerned, however. That the cheekbones—in medical terms, the zygomatic arches—were flattened he'd been able to see for himself at the first examination. And even though the front walls of the maxillary sinuses—the mucous membrane–lined cavities in the upper jaws just above the teeth—appeared to be partially crushed, they could always be levered back into place from inside the sinuses themselves, a simple enough procedure.

"The front walls of the sinuses are caved in somewhat, as you suspected, Mike," Dr. Thorndyke reported as he came back into the office carrying the developed films. "But to nothing like the same extent that the zygomatic arches are squashed. I don't envy you the job of straightening it all out, without cutting her face to pieces and doing open reductions of the fractures."

"I'll do the major part from inside the mouth."

Dr. Thorndyke's eyebrows rose.

"How in hell do you plan to raise those zygomatic arches without putting hooks into her cheeks?"

"Did you see the small wound at the outer angle of the right eye?"

"Yes, but—"

"It's just about large enough to allow the insertion of a half-inch-wide elevator," Mike explained. "Using that from above the cheekbone, with another pushed up along the front of the maxilla through an incision inside the mouth at the fold of the gums just above the upper teeth, I can lift that zygoma into any position I want to put it."

"What about the other side where there's no cut?"

"I'll make a skin incision there in the exact position of the small laceration she already has beside the right eye. When the two are sutured, she may have just the slightest oriental cast to her eyes, but who said that can't be beautiful?"

"What about the flattened anterior walls of the maxillary sinuses?"

"I should be able to elevate them to a normal position from inside each sinus. If I can't do that, I'll take a piece of bone from her hip—the iliac crest is easy to get to—and graft it into place to bring her upper lip out to its normal level. In fact, because her nose fractures are so extensive, I'll have to make a new bridge for it anyway, so, while I am at it, I can give her whatever nasal contour she wants."

"How will you hold the bridge of the new nose in place?"

"I'll take out a piece of bone from the ilium through a small incision over the hip and divide it into two sections. One of them I'll shape into an L to form the bridge of the nose; the other into sort of a horseshoe and put a hole in the middle. The whole thing can be put into place through the incision into the gums above the upper teeth with only one tiny incision into the skin—at the tip of the nose—so I can slide the L-shaped graft into place. The long arm of the L will form the bridge and the short one will support the actual tip of the nose, by locking into the middle of the horseshoe-shaped graft."

"Don't tell me you already know what she'll look like at the end," said Thorndyke.

"I always make a model of these cases beforehand to show the patient the possibilities." Mike opened a box he'd brought with him into the radiology laboratory and carefully lifted out the plasteline model. "How about this?"

Dr. Thorndyke stared at the head Mike had spent two evenings modeling, using the photos of Janet Burke before the accident, the measurements he'd made from her face and skull while she was still unconscious, and the photograph of the Praxiteles Aphrodite bust from the encyclopedia.

"Are you going to tell her you can make her look like that?" Thorndyke asked incredulously.

"I'm certainly going to try if she'll let me. Think she'll like it?"

"Like it? Most women would give anything, including their virtue, to look like that. But don't do it, Mike."

"Why the hell not?"

"If you succeed, you'll make her into a modern-day goddess and they bring nothing but unhappiness to those who worship them. Leave her like she is now—"

"With her face all bashed in? She could sue me for all I've got —which isn't much."

"Then make her the way she was."

From a manila envelope he was carrying, Mike took one of the prints George Stanfield had given him.

"This?" he asked. "When she can look like Aphrodite?"

The old doctor studied the photograph, then examined the head once more. "I guess, with your conscience, you have to offer her the chance to be either," he said with some reluctance. "But I hope she was satisfied with what she looked like before and chooses that. Make her what you see her as in that model and she'll break a lot of human hearts—probably starting with your own."

9

Mike accompanied the stretcher on which Janet Burke lay from the X-ray Department back to the cardiac floor.

"What's in the box?" she asked after he had helped put her back to bed.

"You. Or rather a possible you."

She shrugged. "Might as well open it and let me have the bad news."

"Close your eyes."

Obediently she closed her eyes and he placed the model on the table across her bed, so she would look straight at it when she opened them.

"You can open now."

At the first sight of the model, he saw her eyes go wide with surprise, pleasure and finally disbelief.

"You couldn't—you can't really make me look like that," she said at last, then looked up at him with imploring eyes. "Could you?"

"I'm willing to risk my reputation as a plastic surgeon on it."

"Why?"

"I guess it's the challenge posed by the purely technical kind of surgery involved. Shall I explain what I plan to do?"

She shook her head. "I don't want to hear about it. But what if you fail?"

"You won't look any worse than you did before. Which," he hastened to add, "wasn't bad."

"You don't have to be less than frank with me, Dr. Kerns. Every time I saw Lynne Tallman, even in prison, she made me feel like the Ugly Duckling. But I long ago decided to make the best of what I was born with, so I didn't let it get me down."

"When your book about Lynne and the Chicago atrocities comes out, you're bound to become a celebrity, too."

"If you make me into what you obviously think I could be, I'll be even more of a celebrity in my own right."

"I don't think that's bad, either."

"I won't claim I've never dreamed of what it would be like to have great beauty, every girl does that, whether she admits it or not. But what you're offering almost takes my breath away."

"You don't have to make the decision now, I'll leave the model here and you can study it. Let Mr. Stanfield see it, too, and you can decide together."

"Gerald Hutchinson, my fiancé, arrived from Chicago late last night—after visiting hours, so I haven't talked to him except by phone. They'll be over after breakfast but I almost wish he didn't have to see me until after the surgery."

"That's understandable. Fortunately he can see from the model what the final result will be."

She looked at him thoughtfully. "Would you want your wife to look like the Goddess of Love?" she asked finally.

"Yes—particularly if I had fashioned her that way myself."

She smiled, as best she could with her battered features. "I wonder whether Gerald is going to be as broad-minded as you are, Dr. Kerns, he's pretty much of a stickler for the *status quo ante*. Tell me again what piece of sculpture you used as a model."

"The Aphrodite of Praxiteles; a copy is in the British Museum."

"I've never been there."

"I brought along the encyclopedia." He opened the large volume to the page showing the bust of Aphrodite, as the most famous of Greek sculptors had seen her, and propped it on the dresser where she could easily see it. "Here she is."

She studied the photograph, then looked at the head once more. "I can see where you've changed things somewhat in the model and still kept the beauty of the statue intact. Did you realize that you're going to make me look a little like Lynne—particularly about the mouth?"

"I had trouble there," he confessed. "For a while, it was almost as if the plasteline insisted on taking another shape under my very fingers than the one I wanted."

She frowned. "I don't understand."

"Neither do I, but somehow my fingers seemed to be trying to give something like a cynical—almost a sarcastic—curl to the lips, which you don't have."

"Lynne did. Where did you know her?"

"I never saw her but once, lying dead beside you on the floor of the airport concourse, but I'll never forget the look on her face. At the time I remember thinking it was almost like I imagine she might have looked when alive, if she'd succeeded in putting something over on somebody."

"I saw that look more than once, in the months I studied her in Chicago."

"Do you have any objection to looking just a little like her?" he asked.

"Not really—especially considering how beautiful I'll be, if you re-create me in the image of the model. But do I really need the slightly oriental cast to my eyes?"

"That dressing at the outer corner of your right eye covers a small laceration," he explained. "It's less than an inch long but some tissue was avulsed—torn out. To suture it so there'll be only the faintest possible scar, I'll change the shape of the eyelid just a little, and naturally I'll shape the other one to conform."

"You sound like a tailor."

He smiled. "Successful plastic surgery involves a lot of the tailor's art."

"When can this tube in my throat come out?"

"As soon as you're over the effects of the light anesthetic we'll have to give you, mostly sodium pentothal intravenously. I'd rather leave the tube in as an extra airway, just in case you have any breathing difficulty as an aftereffect of the concussion."

"By all means leave it, then," she said. "You resurrected me once but the next time neither of us might be that lucky."

10

George Stanfield called Mike's office about ten o'clock. "Gerald Hutchinson and I are just leaving the hospital after seeing Janet," he said. "He's very anxious to talk to you; I wonder whether it would inconvenience you if we dropped by the office, since we're so near."

"I don't have an appointment for another half hour," said Mike. "By all means come by."

The two men appeared in ten minutes. Gerald Hutchinson was stockily handsome and wore his hair long in the back, with a pronounced wave that Mike judged could only have been put in by artificial means. His eyes were gray behind gold-rimmed glasses, his manner completely assured, and his handshake crushing—until Mike used muscles from tennis and handball to equal it.

"I might as well tell you I went to the medical library at Cook County Hospital before I left and looked you up in the Directory of Medical Specialties, Dr. Kerns," he said. "According to the directory you were only certified by the board of your specialty last year."

"That's right." Mike could see from Hutchinson's manner what was coming but, if the stocky newspaperman was genuinely in love with Janet Burke and planned to marry her, as George Stanfield had said, he had a right to be certain she would receive the best treatment possible.

"Then you haven't been in private practice long?"

"Less than a year," said Mike. "I took the boards while I was in the second year of a fellowship in cosmetic surgery at Bellevue, after completing the residency in plastic and reconstructive surgery here at University Hospital."

"I believe Dr. Elmo Sebastian, one of the leading experts in that field and author of the definitive text, is chief of the department at University Hospital."

"You're quite right, Mr. Hutchinson. I am an Assistant Clinical Professor in Dr. Sebastian's department."

"Gerald," George Stanfield interposed, "is this inquisition really necessary?"

"I'm only thinking of what's best for my fiancée," said Hutchinson, a bit sharply. "Nobody denies that Dr. Kerns's prompt action at the airport saved Janet's life and I'm naturally grateful, but a great deal more skill is required to correct the kind of facial injuries she sustained than is needed to do an emergency tracheotomy."

"If it will make you any happier about Miss Burke's future, I'll be glad to ask Dr. Sebastian to see her in consultation," Mike offered.

"I think that is indicated," said Hutchinson.

Mike reached for the telephone and started dialing. When Dr. Sebastian answered, he pressed the switch of the conference phone so the others could hear the conversation.

"What's on your mind, Mike?" the department head asked.

"I have a patient in the hospital who was injured when that 727 crashed at Dulles a few days ago—"

"I know. From what I hear, if you hadn't been there at the time, she wouldn't be alive."

"We were both lucky," said Mike. "The reason I called is that Miss Burke's fiancé is here and seems to doubt that I'm qualified to operate on her."

"Qualified?" Sebastian's voice boomed over the conference phone speaker. "After those two years you spent at Bellevue, you

know a damned sight more about the cosmetic side of reconstructive surgery than I do."

"I think everyone would be happier if you saw her, sir."

"Sure. I'll drop by on the way to lunch and give you a ring."

"I hope you won't mind calling Miss Burke's fiancé, Mr. Gerald
Hutchinson, at the Washington *Star-News.*"

"Right," said Sebastian. "Tell him not to worry. His fiancée is
in the hands of the best young plastic and reconstruction specialist
in the country."

"Come on, Gerald," said George Stanfield when the telephone
clicked off. "When do you plan to operate, Doctor?"

"Tomorrow morning, if Miss Burke signs the permission sheet.
The hospital is holding an operating room and the chief anesthesiologist for me. If everything goes as planned, she should be back
in the recovery room by ten or ten-thirty. I'll see you both, I trust,
after it's over."

11

It was two o'clock when Mike's office nurse ushered out his last
appointment of the day, but she came back into the office immediately.

"A Dr. Randall McCarthy's been waiting outside to see you,"
she said. "Shall I bring him in?"

"McCarthy? I don't remember—"

"He's a psychiatrist. Says you requested consultation on a patient at University."

"Oh yes. Please show him in."

Dr. Randall McCarthy was about Mike's own size, impeccably
dressed and, Mike surmised, about fifty. He walked with the stride
and had the trim body of an athlete but his face somehow didn't
fit the rest of him.

The eyes were deep-set, but bright, reflecting an intelligent
mind, yet the face from which they looked out was ravaged, either
by age or by a dissolute life. Large bags hung under his eyes, too,
and his cheeks sagged heavily, all of which gave him an oddly

debauched appearance, like that of a man who'd packed two or more lifetimes into one. Nor did his small pointed beard, giving him somewhat the appearance of an overaged and overactive rake, plus a rather prominent nose, do anything to dispel the first impression.

"I was downtown for a civic club meeting, Dr. Kerns, so I thought I'd drop by and give you an oral report on your patient, Janet Burke," McCarthy said as they shook hands. "I also dictated one on the chart, of course."

"I hope you didn't go to any trouble, Doctor." Mike gestured toward the chair on the other side of the desk. "When Miss Burke didn't regain consciousness as soon as we'd hoped and we saw those bursts of theta waves on her EEG, Dr. Fogarty and I had an idea she might be more conscious than she appeared to be."

McCarthy smiled, making him look oddly like a leering satyr. "In other words, fudging?"

"Something like that. Of course, now that she's conscious and apparently completely rational, I'm afraid I wasted your time."

"Not at all, Doctor. Not at all. Miss Burke is a very intelligent young lady; I enjoyed talking to her very much, particularly about the Tallman girl. That type of psychopathic personality has always fascinated me and Miss Burke was very close to Lynne Tallman for several weeks in Chicago."

"Did you find anything psychiatrically wrong with her?"

"She's redheaded, which automatically makes her a bit schizoid—"

"I doubt that many redheads would agree with you there."

"On the contrary. Most women like to think they have more than one personality—and they do. There's the one that watches the soap operas every afternoon and lives each incident as it occurs. And there's the one that gets her husband off to work in the morning, drives the children to school, to music lessons and to Boy Scouts for years, then one day packs her suitcase and leaves to take up a life of her own. As a rule, redheads are perfectly normal women, Dr. Kerns, except for being a little on the hyperthyroid side. Which, when you come to think of it, makes them such fascinating creatures. Well, getting back to your patient, Miss Burke. I found her to be a perfectly normal young woman—"

"That's good news."

"I didn't see her until this morning; got in late last night from a seminar on parapsychology at my former university, Duke."

"How did you get interested in ESP?" Mike asked.

"Please, give us our due, Dr. Kerns: the scientific name is parapsychology. I worked one summer while in med school with a traveling magic show, where I learned a lot of the standard tricks —you know, levitation, disappearances, hypnosis and the like. One woman with the magic show had a mind-reading act and I worked with her a lot."

"Aren't those acts faked?"

"Usually, but some things that happened neither she nor I could explain. So, when I went back to Duke at the end of the summer, I combined my M.D. studies with those necessary to get a Ph.D. in parapsychology. By the way, that model of how you expect Miss Burke to look after tomorrow's operation was in her room. It's a beautiful job of sculpture, Dr. Kerns."

"Thanks. I dabble a bit in it but I'd never want to make it a career."

"Believe me, you could be a success. Still, if you can do for Miss Burke what that model promises, you're worth a lot more to humanity as a plastic surgeon than as a sculptor."

"I feel much the same way."

"I stopped by to ask whether you would have any objection to my studying Miss Burke psychologically, Dr. Kerns. After you finish your work and she recovers, of course."

"Once I discharge her from the hospital, I'll have no control over what she does or does not do, Dr. McCarthy. She's the only one who could give you that permission."

"I think she will, but I want to be certain first that you would have no objection to my looking in on her every now and then while she's in the hospital."

"I can see no reason why you shouldn't, but I can't order it and have the charge on her bill."

"I had no idea of charging her for my visits," McCarthy protested. "It's just that I shall be very much interested, as a psychiatrist, in seeing how becoming one of the most beautiful women on earth will affect her life from now on."

"Do you think the change will be for the better?"

"She's intelligent. She's a gifted writer. And she's ambitious. How could the change be anything but for the better?"

"I was just wondering."

McCarthy stood up and held out his hand. "Thank you for inviting me to see Miss Burke in consultation; I think she's going to make a very interesting case study. How lucky for her that you happened to be on the way to Dulles that morning."

Mike walked out into the small waiting room with the visitor and saw him out. His nurse, a shapely mother of two, was filing the case records for the day and looked up when the door closed behind the visitor.

"What do you make of him, Doctor?" she asked.

"I was about to ask you the same question."

"He's a strange one, all right—but all male. He was here in the waiting room for maybe ten minutes while you were seeing the last patient, and all that time I felt like he was undressing me with his eyes."

12

Dr. Sebastian called just after McCarthy left. "I saw Miss Burke after lunch, Mike," he said. "Do you really think you can make her look like that model when you finish the surgery?"

"I was pretty sure of it when I completed the model, but so many people seem to doubt it today that I'm not sure any more."

"Don't let their doubts stop you. If you come anywhere near succeeding, it will be a remarkable accomplishment."

"Was the fiancé there?"

"Waiting for me," said Sebastian. "He learned pretty quickly that he wasn't going to get me to admit you weren't capable of doing the job, though, so he tried to get me to agree that she's not rational enough after a severe concussion to sign the permit sheet for surgery. I cooled him down on that, too."

"I can't understand why he took such an antipathy toward me. Before Miss Burke and her uncle mentioned him yesterday, I never knew he existed."

"Hutchinson is handsome and comes on strong, so I suspect he's been pretty dominating where their relationship was concerned. Then overnight the possibility arises that his fiancée can become a rare beauty and a lot of other men will be attracted to her. My bet would be our friend is afraid that, once you've turned the girl into a modern-day version of Aphrodite, he'll be out of the limelight."

"Dr. Randall McCarthy also saw her, this morning. He just left the office."

"Quite a guy, isn't he?"

"First time I ever saw him, but I was impressed. He agrees with you that Janet Burke is rational enough to make her own decisions."

"She made one this afternoon: signed the operative permission sheet in my presence, with Hutchinson standing by chewing his nails," said Sebastian. "Don't sell Randall McCarthy short because he looks like the roué he probably is, Mike. In his own field of parapsychology he's very highly regarded. I can tell you confidentially, too, that the Psychology Department of the university and the Department of Psychiatry in the medical school are setting up a joint research project for him, particularly in the area of what they call 'remote viewing.'"

"Never heard of it," Mike admitted.

"It's a form of ESP and precognition they've been specializing in out at the Stanford Research Institute. I've seen some of McCarthy's experimental results and they're fantastic."

"Those two years on the Cosmetic Surgery Service at Bellevue kept me working so hard, I hardly ever got to read a newspaper."

"Talk to McCarthy sometime," Sebastian advised. "He'll leave you wondering about a lot of things you used to take for granted. Oh, by the way, mind if I kibitz from the gallery occasionally tomorrow? The way Charlie Thorndyke says you're going to handle those smashed zygomatic arches intrigues me. If it works, I'd like to include it in the new edition of my text I'm writing."

"Be my guest," said Mike. "Maybe that will give me confidence."

"We gave you that with your M.D.," said Sebastian. "Good luck."

13

Janet Burke was propped up in bed when Mike made rounds shortly before five. She didn't, however, seem pleased to see him. "Whatever made you send that shrink to examine me?" she demanded.

"I requested the consultation while you were still unconscious and we couldn't tell how much your brain might have been injured by concussion. After you came around and it was obvious you were pretty rational, I forgot to cancel. Didn't you and Dr. McCarthy get along well?"

"Oh, he was all right. I guess I'm just worn out from arguing with Gerald. He doesn't want you to operate on me?"

"That's the understatement of the year," Mike said with a smile. "He'd already looked me up in the Directory of Medical Specialties before he left Chicago and decided Dr. Sebastian should do the job."

"He was here, too."

"I know. As soon as I learned how your fiancé felt, I called the Chief and asked him to see you. He's quite intrigued with my plan of operation and also with the model."

"Gerald says the model is a con, to persuade me to let you operate."

"What do you say?"

She smiled then. "I told him if you could make me look half as good as the model, I'd still be twice as beautiful as I was before. Apparently Gerald took a dislike to you even before he saw you and it really burned him up when Dr. Sebastian recommended you so highly. We had one hell of a row afterward and, if my ring hadn't been locked in the safe, I might have thrown it in his face."

"Wait till after the operation before you decide something as important as breaking off an engagement," he advised. "I wouldn't want to have *that* on my conscience."

"Actually, I think the reason why Gerald is raising so much hell is because he's afraid you really will make me look like the model.

He never could stand playing second fiddle and with a wife as beautiful as the Aphrodite of Praxiteles—"

"He'd be upstaged wherever you both appeared."

She gave him a keen appraising look. "Would that bother you, if you were in his place?"

"Not a bit; after all, you'd be a walking advertisement for my skill as a plastic surgeon. But getting back to Dr. McCarthy. Why didn't you like him?"

"I've got nothing against him. He's really a very stimulating person to talk to, but he wasn't nearly as interested in me as he was in Lynne Tallman. The way he questioned me about her, you'd think he was trying to psychoanalyze her through me."

"He's a specialist in parapsychology—ESP—besides being a psychiatrist. Before you became conscious, you were showing bursts of odd waves on your EEG, as if your consciousness was trying to break through. Dr. Fogarty thought Dr. McCarthy might be able to tell us something from them."

"That reminds me," she said. "Do I still need these needles sticking in my head? I'd like to wash some of the blood out of my hair."

"No reason why you can't," he told her. "I'll leave an order when I go out."

"Did the shrink tell you anything about me?"

"Only that, being a redhead, you're mildly schizoid, but he considers that normal."

"Dr. McCarthy did ask how far I'd gotten with my book, but I couldn't tell him because I don't know whether my briefcase was destroyed in the fire when we crashed."

"It wasn't. Your uncle has it."

"Why didn't he tell me?"

"I guess because he and the FBI have put out a story that the papers and tapes you had in the case tell a lot about Lynne Tallman's Chicago operation."

"But they don't! I tried to get details out of her but she always clammed up on me."

"We already know that, but the FBI wants to leave the impression, in Chicago at least, that a lot was revealed. They're trying to smoke out Lynne's associates."

"With me as bait?"

"That's the general idea, but there's an FBI agent on duty outside your room twenty-four hours a day, so you're really not in any danger."

"I still don't like it," she said firmly. "Lynne died because of me and now the FBI is using me, hoping to lure her associates into some sort of shootout. Doesn't that strike you as being a bit immoral?"

"Considering what Lynne and her crowd have done, no."

"I guess you're right."

"By the way," he told her, "Dr. McCarthy wants to study what effects the change in your appearance will have on you in the next month or two."

"Do you approve?"

"If you don't object."

"I guess it should be interesting—and he does have a sense of humor. Tell him it's okay with me."

"I'll call him after the operation. Anything else you want to ask about tomorrow before I go?"

"Won't I see you before you start it?"

"You'll see me but you may not remember it. Dr. Petrie, the anesthesiologist, will premedicate you fairly heavily so he won't have to use as much anesthetic during the surgery."

"Tell him to put me out completely before they take me to the operating room. I don't want to know what's happening."

"You won't remember a thing," he promised as he started toward the door.

"Dr. Kerns!" He paused with his hand on the doorknob and, for an instant, wondered whether anyone could have come in without his seeing her. Another woman's voice had spoken his name, yet when he turned back from the door there was still no one else in the room except him and Janet Burke.

The voice was definitely not the same, however. Instead it had a hoarse, brassy note and, when he moved back toward the bed, he saw that the expression on what he could see of her face had changed, too. When before her manner had been concerned and a little anxious about the operation, it was jaunty now, challenging, even a little provocative. And, when he looked at her eyes, he saw an odd mocking light burning there he'd never seen before. In fact, except that he knew perfectly well the girl in the bed was still

Janet Burke, he could easily have believed another had taken her place.

"What is it?" he asked.

"I remember seeing that statue of Aphrodite now—in the British Museum, wasn't it?"

"Yes."

"Well, if you're going to make a goddess like that model out of me when you operate, how about giving me a bosom worthy of a goddess, like the bust in London has?" It was the same mocking tone—and utterly unlike the normal speaking voice of Janet Burke.

"What size brassiere do you wear?" he asked.

"Thirty-two A—when I wear one, which isn't often."

"What size would you want to be?"

"You're the doctor. What do you prescribe?"

"How about a thirty-six B? That's about right for your build and weight."

"Sounds okay—if you can do it." The voice still had the brassy ring with the odd, almost seductive note. Hearing it, he could hardly bring himself to believe the same girl was speaking, although he could see her lips move as they formed the words.

"I can't promise to do your breasts tomorrow; that will depend on how long it takes me to make your face over," he told her. "But if not tomorrow, I can do them a few days later. The operation is simple and the incisions are in the axilla, the armpit, where they won't show—even topless."

"I'll sign the permission sheet—and, Dr. Kerns?"

"Yes?"

"You won't regret it, *I promise you that.*"

There was no mistaking the significance of those final four words. With the voice, and the manner, of the girl who spoke them, they could only mean one thing and Mike felt his pulse spurt in spite of himself.

"Is it a deal?" she asked.

"Like you said," he told her. "I'm the doctor."

As he was turning away, Mike glanced at the EEG monitor and what he saw there startled him more than had the sudden change in the girl's voice and manner. The regular pattern of the brain waves that had characterized the EEG tracing since she'd become conscious was now largely replaced by a burst of the strange theta rhythm seen occasionally while she was in coma from concussion.

Halfway from the hospital to his apartment he suddenly remembered her reference just now to the bust in the British Museum, although only that morning she'd denied ever having been there. It was yet another in the odd sequence of events concerning Janet Burke: her having been thrown through the Plexiglas nose of the plane cockpit at the time of the crash; the theta waves visible in the EEG while she was unconscious and again just now; the changed voice and manner, when she'd asked him to enlarge her breasts through the operation of mammaplasty; and the reference to having seen the Praxiteles bust in the British Museum.

Most startling of all, however, was Mike's own realization that he'd heard Janet Burke's second voice once before—from the speaker of his VHF radio as the stricken 727 had been carrying Lynne Tallman to her death.

"Master! Save!" the same voice on the radio had begged, as if in a prayer, before rising to a banshee howl of fear that had sent a chill through him then, as if it had come from the throat of a denizen of another world.

14

When Mike came into the operating theater from the adjoining scrub room the next morning, Dr. Hal Petrie was inserting into Janet Burke's arm vein the needle through which he would inject sodium pentothal solution and produce anesthesia. Tying the strings of his mask, Mike walked over to the table and looked down at the girl lying there.

The nurses had shampooed her hair, after taking out the needle electrodes from the EEG circuit. It was even a lighter red tint than he had thought, more like a reddish gold.

"This is Dr. Kerns," he said almost in her ear. "Can you hear me, Miss Burke?"

She opened her eyes and once again he was startled by the deep violet color. There was none of the burning light he'd seen there last night, however, when she'd summoned him back from

the door of her room and challenged him to give her the breasts a
goddess should have.

"Hello, Doctor." Her tone was slurred from the drugs but still
that of Janet Burke.

"Everything will be okay," he assured her. "Dr. Petrie will give
you something to make you sleep."

The anesthesiologist had inserted the needle and was ready to
begin the injection. "I want you to start counting, Miss Burke," he
said, "as slow or as fast as you like."

"One . . . two . . . three . . ." Her lips moved as Petrie
pushed gently on the plunger of the large syringe, injecting the solution. "Four . . . five . . . six."

Mike was moving back to the adjoining scrub room to complete
his own preparation for starting the surgery, when the soft, slurred
tone of the voice doing the counting changed suddenly to the
harsh, brassy note he'd heard briefly the day before. Except that
now the tone was loud and the words were enunciated clearly in a
torrent of obscenities and cursing that brought all activity in the
white-tiled operating room suddenly to a halt.

Startled by the spewing torrent of foul words, Dr. Petrie's hand
tightened on the plunger of the syringe, sending a spurt of the
sodium pentothal solution—a bolus—into her circulation. And, as
the heavy dose of anesthetic took effect, the flow of obscenity was
immediately shut off.

"Jesus!" Petrie's voice had a note of awe. "What was that?"

"She has interviewed some pretty unsavory characters, notably
Lynne Tallman," Mike said quickly. "Your anesthetic must have
loosened some of the material from her memory for an instant,
Hal."

"I've given sodium pentothal plenty of times in psychiatric cases
and what the public likes to call 'truth serum' for the police, but I
never heard anything like that before."

The preparations for the surgery, brought summarily to a halt by
the burst of profanity and obscenity, were resumed. But as Mike
started scrubbing, he found himself wishing Janet Burke had still
been connected to the monitor of the electroencephalograph just
now. For he was pretty certain that, if she had, he would have
seen again the same burst of waves in the odd theta rhythm that
had startled him yesterday.

Mike had brought the model up from Janet Burke's room and it now stood on a table where he could see it easily as he worked.

"Do you really think she'll end up looking like that?" Hal Petrie was looking at the model while Mike was putting on his gloves and gown, with the help of the circulating nurse.

"That's what I promised her."

"Not in writing, I hope."

"Before witnesses. Don't you think I can do it?"

"If you're that confident, you probably can," Petrie conceded. "But you've left yourself wide open to the possibility that the girl may wake up and decide she doesn't want to look like a new person—even somebody as beautiful as that model is—and sue you for false representation."

"She's got a fiancé who'd like very much to do just that," said Mike.

"I know," said the anesthesiologist. "He came to the O.R. with her, and her FBI guard is in the gallery."

Mike looked up and recognized Agent Jim McIvor, sitting inside the glass-enclosed cubicle that formed the upper half of one side of the operating theater. "What about Lover Boy?" he asked and Hal Petrie laughed.

"Hutchinson heard me give Agent McIvor permission to watch but didn't say anything; guess his stomach isn't made of brass like the rest of him seems to be. Do you think there really is any danger that the late Lynne Tallman's gang from Chicago will try to get Miss Burke because of what they think she may know about their identities?"

"The FBI takes the threat seriously enough to have her guarded, even in the O.R.," said Mike as, gloved and gowned, he moved up to the table.

"Even if you do succeed," Petrie reminded him, "the girl's bound to have psychological reactions, too. And in one of those, that fiancé could persuade her to make trouble for you with a malpractice suit."

"That leaves me no choice except to make her the most beautiful girl in the world, does it?" said Mike as he took the scalpel handed him by the instrument nurse. "So stop being so damned cheerful and watch her vital signs."

"They're perfect," said Petrie. "A robot could give this anesthetic."

"Don't let it get around or you might find yourself replaced by one."

Lifting Janet Burke's upper lip, he made a U-shaped incision through the mucous membrane of the gum just below the fold where the upper lip began, cutting through to the bone underneath. Dropping the knife and picking up a shaft of stainless steel with a flattened end called a periosteal elevator, he began to push back the membrane until the walls of the maxillary sinuses were thoroughly exposed. At the same time the hospital photographer took up a position on an elevated stool where he could shoot down upon the operating field with a telescopic lens. Like the two circulating nurses not involved in the operation itself, he wore cap, mask and gown.

15

"Are you going to do the mammaplasties today, too, Mike?" The voice of the anesthesiologist intruded itself into Mike Kerns's thought patterns, which had been concentrated upon the task at hand during the hour and a half of delicate surgery that had preceded it.

"I'd like to. Is she okay?"

"What you've done so far hasn't bothered her at all," said Petrie. "But it still bothers me."

"Why, Hal?"

"Have you really made her look like the head you modeled? With all that hemorrhage under the skin around her eyes and over the cheekbones, I don't see how anybody could tell."

"We won't know for sure until the bandages come off and the hemorrhage has been absorbed—maybe six to eight weeks in all," said Mike. "But I'm betting a stiff surgical fee that the result will be as planned."

From the very first incision into the gum margin just above the roots of the upper row of teeth, Mike had known exactly what to do. With the anterior surface of the upper jaw exposed, revealing the crushed and depressed front walls of the sinuses inside the spongy bone, he had drilled an opening just above the roots of the teeth into each of the maxillary sinuses.

From inside the sinuses themselves, he'd had little trouble levering the depressed walls of bone back to a nearly normal position. He couldn't hope to restore completely bones so severely crushed by the pressure of the girl's face against the floor of the terminal at Dulles. Nor did he waste time trying, especially when a solid foundation was needed upon which to build the entire nasal structure so it would fit the pattern of the head he had so confidently modeled from plasteline.

Leaving the front walls of the sinuses in approximately their normal position, he'd next inserted an elevator—shaped roughly like a blunt screwdriver—downward through the small laceration in Janet Burke's face at the corner of the right eye. Next he slid a second elevator upward from the incision in the gum inside her mouth across the front of the maxilla. Then, by using the two instruments, one in each hand, as levers, he'd managed to work them under the smashed cheekbone, the zygomatic arch on the right side, and lift it into its former position, raising it a little to give more prominence to her cheekbones and thereby elevate just a little the entire facial structure.

On the left side, he'd made an incision through the skin in exactly the same position as the corresponding laceration on the right and repeated the process. Satisfied that her cheek structures were now close to what he desired, he'd trimmed the edges of the laceration and closed it carefully so as to promote healing with the least possible scar, then also closed the incision he'd made beside the left eye.

Before starting to rebuild the badly flattened nose, he'd made an incision over the left hip, the iliac bone that formed a perceptible crest to the pelvis on either side, and cut out a block of bone from it. While the resident assisting him closed the small incision over the ilium, Mike carefully shaped the block of bone into two pieces. One he made boat-shaped but flat, roughly a U. The other he trimmed until it was L-shaped, the pattern he had described to Dr. Thorndyke in the X-ray room.

Now he worked the boat-shaped graft into place through the incision in the mucous membrane of the mouth until it lay against the fractured front of the upper jaw, restoring its normal outline.

A small incision was then made at the tip of her nose and, after freeing the bony structure of the smashed nasal bridge, he worked the L-shaped bone graft into place, restoring the pristine lines of the nose once more.

When the short end of L was then locked into a tiny depression in the center of the boat-shaped graft that served to rebuild the general structure of the upper jaw, the outline of a somewhat higher-bridged nose than Janet Burke had possessed before was easily created by molding the crushed nasal bones he'd freed into the desired pattern. A few tiny stitches of gossamer-light silk had closed the small incision at the tip of the nose and a dozen sutures brought the cut edges of the gum margins beneath the upper lip into position.

Before proceeding to the lower jaw, Mike carefully molded a splint by immersing a sheet of plastic in hot water. Then, shaping it into the final outlines in which he wanted the nose and cheek structures to remain while healing, he taped the plastic mask-support into place over the dressings covering the wounds, in somewhat the same shape and position as the butterfly mask worn at masquerade balls.

The lower jaw had proved quite easy to correct. Fortunately the patient's chin pattern had been lovely enough in itself, so he had simply placed hooked bars, as he had described to Dr. Thorndyke, on both the upper and lower jaws, wired them to the teeth and secured the bars together with rubber bands to make traction and lift the lower jaw into a position where it was splinted against the upper.

"I always shudder when I see you plastic men working inside the mouth the way you do, but your wounds never seem to get infected like so many clean surgical wounds do," said Hal Petrie. "How come?"

"For one thing the whole face area has a plentiful blood supply," said Mike. "For another we'll give her an intramuscular injection of penicillin daily for the next five days or so, just in case."

"That was a beautiful job of reconstruction, Dr. Kerns." Dr. Sebastian's booming tones came through the microphone in the gallery whereby observers could ask questions while watching. "I'm certainly going to use it in the new edition of my book."

"Thank you, sir," said Mike as he stepped back from the table to change gown and gloves. "She wanted augmentation mamma-plasties done, too. Would you combine them with what I've al-ready done?"

"If Dr. Petrie says she's in good shape, there's no reason why not," said the department head. "Are you going to use the axillary approach you brought back with you from New York?"

"I'd planned to."

"You'll save her the trouble of two other operations, then. Thanks again for letting me watch."

"Since Dr. Petrie and Dr. Sebastian have given us the go-ahead, we'll do the mammaplasties today, too," Mike told the operating team and the small group of medical students and nurses observing from the enclosed gallery, while the resident who had assisted him twisted the last rubber band into place, holding Janet Burke's jaws snugly shut. "We'll need a new setup, of course, and a complete change of gloves, gowns and drapes."

"They're ready, Doctor," said the supervising nurse. "Do you want the table jacked up?"

"Please." Mike was pulling off his gown as he spoke, being careful not to contaminate his hands when he stripped off the surgical gloves he'd worn during the first part. "The nearer you can elevate her to a forty-five-degree angle, the quicker we'll be finished."

While the changes were being made and the operating team put on fresh sterile gowns and gloves, Mike studied the breasts revealed when the supervisor removed the sterile towel that had covered the surgically prepped operative area. They were small, as he'd noted at his first physical examination, but they were well formed and high, with darker-skinned areolae around the nipples.

"Breasts like these are ideally suited for an axillary approach," he told the staff as they moved busily to prepare for the last part of the operation sequence. "Even under local anesthesia it's easy to expose the edge of the pectoralis major muscles beneath them, open a space by blunt dissection and insert the prostheses, thrust-ing the nipples forward and augmenting the size of the breasts to what the patient prefers."

"If you can do those the way you just did her face," said Petrie, "this gal won't even need to wear a brassiere."

"She'll wear one, or she'll catch hell from me." Mike looked at the photographer, who had just finished taking the "before" shots of the small but quite symmetrical breasts. "Ready, Joe?"

"When you are, Doctor."

"Everything's okay," said the nurse supervisor. "We've got two sizes of the prostheses sterilized, like you ordered, Dr. Kerns."

"The approach with a transaxillary incision—through the armpit, to those in the gallery who may be laymen—is frequently done under local anesthesia and is the simplest form of augmentation mammaplasty," said Mike. "We will make the incision in the long axis of the axillary hair pattern where it will be practically invisible when healed. Incidentally," he added, "barring accidents, we do not cut through any breast tissue and future lactation is not affected."

As he spoke, he was making an incision downward just back of the front fold of the axilla formed by the edge of the large muscle beneath the breast, the pectoralis major. While the assistants busied themselves clamping skin bleeders and closing them with ties of fine catgut, Mike was opening a space between the breast and the large flat muscle beneath it. Spreading the jaws of a blunt clamp, he enlarged the space and, using now the instrument, now his gloved fingers, steadily increased the size of the pocket thus created.

"You will note," he told the watching gallery, "that I do not open a space higher than the level of the second rib, or nearer to the midline than three or four centimeters—about two inches or slightly more. Nor should the dissection extend lower than the sixth rib, else the prosthesis might slip down and distort the final shape of the breast."

The preparation of a bed for the artificial breast finished, he stopped and carefully inspected the cavity he had created to receive it for any sign of bleeding, which was carefully controlled.

"Breast prostheses are made from silicon gel with an outer skin of silicone, to which patches of Dacron have been attached, allowing them to be sutured into place and thus avoid the possibility of migration," he said, holding up the round plastic sac. "Incidentally, from a strictly esthetic point of view, the feel of the silicon gel inside the sac is fully as soft as normal breast tissue."

Lifting the edge of the incision with his fingers, he began to slide the bag, with its silicon gel contents, into the pocket. "You will see that the prosthesis completely fills the cavity I have dissected out in the fascia overlying the pectoralis major muscle of the chest. However, we have not entered mammary tissue at any point during the dissection, thus ensuring that all functions of breast tissue remain. Anchoring sutures will hold it in place and the wound can be closed."

Leaving the assistants to insert the dozens of tiny sutures closing the several layers of skin and subcutaneous tissue revealed as the incision was made, Mike moved to the other side and quickly repeated the hollowing-out procedure under the opposite breast. By the time the resident assisting him had completed his sutures on the right side, Mike was starting the closure on the left.

When he stepped back from the table, a cheer broke out from the gallery, and the photographer moved in for a close-up of the lovely final result.

"That's a real work of art—and what a lovely canvas!" said Dr. Petrie. "One thing's certain, whether she likes her new face or not, she'd never sue you over those mammary appendages."

16

George Stanfield and Gerald Hutchinson were waiting in Janet's room.

"She's fine," Mike reported. "They'll keep her in the recovery room until she regains consciousness, but only as a precaution, in case she should have any nausea and they need to get the rubber bands off her jaws in a hurry."

"She'll be all right, then?" Stanfield asked.

"No doubt of that. Dr. Sebastian was watching from the gallery and gave the whole procedure his unqualified approval. In fact, he's going to include the method I used to elevate the fractured cheekbones in the new edition of his textbook."

"That's wonderful, Mike," George Stanfield said.

"The mammaplasty procedures didn't bother her at all, either," Mike added.

Gerald Hutchinson was staring out the window and had made no commentary until Mike mentioned the breast operation. Now

he turned suddenly to demand, "What the hell do you mean—
mammaplasty?"

"It's an operation—to augment the size of the breasts—"

"I know what mammaplasty is—a slick way of taking advantage of women's vanity. Who the hell gave you the authority to do
that?"

"When I came by last night making evening rounds, she asked
me if I could do an augmentation mammaplasty, after I finished
reconstructing her face this morning," Mike explained. "Her rea-
soning was that, if I was going to make her into a goddess, I
should give her a bosom like one."

"That's the first I've heard of it," said Stanfield.

"What time were you two here yesterday?" Mike asked.

"I came by about three o'clock," said Stanfield.

"I was here until about four," said Hutchinson. "I had a lecture
engagement last night."

"Apparently she must have decided she wanted the mammaplasties done after you left," said Mike. "She signed the permission
form just after I left here about five o'clock, so she obviously
knew what she was doing. Besides, the surgery is really quite
minor; a lot of plastic surgeons now do it in their offices. She was
in good condition when I finished with the reconstruction, so I
went ahead and did the mammaplasties. I'm sorry you didn't
know about it."

"Janet used to joke sometimes about wearing falsies," said Stanfield. "But I didn't realize she was actually that sensitive about it.
I guess it just occurred to her after we left that you might be able
to correct that, too."

"Surely you're more intelligent than that, George." Gerald
Hutchinson's tone was that of an adult humoring a child. "Janet
probably told Kerns that neither you nor I would be back yesterday afternoon to stop him, so he took advantage of her irrational
state to talk her into another expensive operation and earn an ex-
orbitant fee." He wheeled on Mike. "Surely you can't claim any
longer that the concussion left her in her right mind."

"She did seem excited and not quite her normal self," Mike's
innate honesty forced him to admit. "Even her voice sounded like
that of somebody else when she asked if the breast operations
could be done."

"What do you mean by her voice sounding like somebody else?" Stanfield asked.

"Just that. I put it down to embarrassment at asking to have her breasts done, but some other odd things have happened in connection with your niece." Mike went on to describe the strange waves on the EEG screen, which had led him to call Dr. Randall McCarthy into consultation.

"McCarthy?" Gerald Hutchinson frowned. "Wasn't there some scandal in the news about him just after he came to the university here to teach?"

"I wouldn't know," said Mike. "I was working in New York at the time."

"I'll look it up when I get back to the office," said George Stanfield, "but I don't remember a scandal."

An idea suddenly struck Mike. "Did you say the FBI let you have duplicates of those tapes that were in Janet's briefcase? The ones of the interviews with Lynne Tallman?"

"I've got the originals," said Stanfield. "The FBI made copies and kept them."

"Could I hear some of them?"

"Of course." Stanfield gave him a probing look. "Why don't you come by the office around five o'clock? By that time I should have located that story about Dr. McCarthy, too."

"Another quack?" Gerald Hutchinson sneered. "No wonder you were able to get him to certify Janet as rational when she obviously was not."

Mike ignored the thrust—it was either that or sock the other man.

17

"We can play the tapes you wanted to hear in our audio laboratory," George Stanfield said when Mike came into the newspaperman's office that afternoon. "Meanwhile I found some material on Dr. McCarthy you might want to look at."

Gerald Hutchinson was in the office but didn't speak when Mike came in. The material on McCarthy dealt with some rather flamboyant experiments in parapsychology he'd carried out shortly after coming to the university, and Mike remembered now that Dr. Sebastian had apparently been rather impressed by the ability of the psychiatrist in the psychic field. He had barely finished reading the newspaper accounts when the phone rang and Stanfield answered.

"They're ready in the audio lab when you are, Mike," he said.

"Fine. I still have evening rounds to make at the hospital."

They took comfortable chairs in the small audio laboratory. "Roll the tapes when you're ready," Stanfield told the technician and there was a click, followed by the voice of Janet Burke from the loudspeakers.

"Tape number three, Lynne Tallman interview. All right, Lynne, will you tell me how you came to get mixed up with the crowd that carried out the bombings?"

A stream of obscenity came from the loudspeaker and Mike stiffened suddenly. He recognized that voice, with its hoarse, brassy tone, almost from the first word, having heard it yesterday afternoon in Janet Burke's hospital room when she had requested the mammaplasties, and again this morning when Hal Petrie had started injecting the anesthetic solution.

"Anything wrong, Doctor?" George Stanfield asked.

"No, why?"

"You look like you'd just seen a ghost."

"Heard, not seen." Mike recovered his aplomb quickly. "The first—and last—time I saw Lynne Tallman, she was lying dead on the floor of the airport concourse; hearing her voice now sort of got to me."

He didn't tell the newspaperman or Gerald Hutchinson—who was staring at him suspiciously—that, although he'd heard the same voice twice in the past twenty-four hours, both times from the lips of Janet Burke, there'd been still a third occasion. And that was through the speaker of his VHF radio tuned to the pilot's broadcast on the morning of the disaster when the agonized voice of a woman screaming, "Master! Save!" had risen above even the tumult just preceding the crash.

That time it had come from the vocal cords of Lynne Tallman while she was still alive, but the power she was begging to save her could be none other than Satan, Master of Evil. Which left only one conclusion, a conviction, Mike realized now, he'd been evading from the moment he'd first seen those strange bursts of theta waves on the monitor of the electroencephalograph connected to the brain of Janet Burke.

Although her corpse was still in the morgue refrigerator, the evil spirit—perhaps demon was the better word—that had driven Lynne Tallman to initiate and direct acts of terror which had already killed more than fifty people was alive and well.

Moreover, in a true Devil's gamble, the demonic presence of Lynne Tallman had somehow seized possession—no doubt at the moment the plane had crashed—of the body of Janet Burke. And worst of all, transfigured only that morning by the skill of Mike Kerns's own fingers into one of the most beautiful women in the world, Janet herself was capable, conceivably, of the greatest possible evils because nobody else would believe what was to him now an inescapable truth.

BOOK TWO

THE SECOND IMPOSSIBLE

The concept of an evil and
criminal presence or spirit gaining
ascendancy in a hitherto benevolent
person can scarcely be presented
without arousing in the human heart
some echoes or stealthy overtones
of witchcraft and demonology.

Corbett H. Thigpen, M.D., and
Hervey M. Cleckley, M.D.: *The Three*
Faces of Eve (McGraw Hill Book Co., 1957)

1

In the lobby of the newspaper building, Mike Kerns looked up a number in the telephone directory before going into a telephone booth and ringing it.

"Dr. McCarthy's office," a male voice answered.

"Who's speaking, please?"

"This is Randall McCarthy. Is that you, Dr. Kerns? I was just thinking about you."

"Ditto. Maybe we don't even need the telephone but, since we're already connected, we might as well use it. Will you be there for the next half hour, Doctor?"

"Sure. I'm grading some quiz papers that piled up while I was in Durham for the seminar. My office is in Building 13D, room 304 of the old medical school quadrangle. How long will it take you to get here?"

"Fifteen minutes or so. I'm just leaving the *Star* Building. I've been talking to George Stanfield about his niece."

"Doing all right, isn't she? She certainly looked like she was coming around when I stopped by the room after lunch."

"Then you've seen her since I have. Be there in fifteen minutes."

The medical school was in the midst of a huge building program and Mike had a little trouble locating Building 13D and room 304. When he opened the door he was startled to see, attached to the wall above the chair behind Randall McCarthy's desk, a shrunken human head, with long hair hanging down past its ears. The eyes had the vacant stare of the long dead but the rest of the head, though barely a fourth normal size, was dried until the skin lay on the face in ridges and deep clefts, with the appearance of old leather.

"Come in, Dr. Kerns." McCarthy looked up from the desk whose top was piled high with test papers, and held out his hand. "Don't let these things disturb you. I spent one semester with the Jivaro Indians of the Upper Amazon; they have a barbarous custom of eating the bodies of victims slain in the hunt or in combat but preserving the heads as evidence of their prowess."

"It's a bit startling."

"The rest of this stuff I collected on an expedition to Central

Africa and also in Haiti." The languid wave of a long-fingered left
hand, ornamented by a large seal ring set with a glowing emerald,
indicated a weird accumulation of what Mike Kerns immediately
labeled mentally as junk.

"That looks like a voodoo doll." Mike pointed to a small figure
on the desk, through whose abdomen several large needles had
been thrust.

"A *used* voodoo doll; I bought it off a witch doctor in Haiti
after it had fulfilled its purpose—the death of his client's enemy.
A strange death too, by the way; not a mark on him, yet his bowel
was punctured in a dozen places, causing a fulminating peritonitis.
The diagnosis was verified at an autopsy; I saw the local medical
examiner perform it last May."

"Surely you don't believe in voodoo, Doctor!"

"No, but I noticed that voodoo doctors always make sure word
of their spells—like making a doll and thrusting needles through
it—gets to the intended victim. Once that's done and the credulous doomed person knows of it, is a perforation of the bowel
wall any more difficult to understand than the way worry and
emotional tension can create a stress ulcer of the stomach that
eats its way through the wall in a perforation?"

"No. I suppose not."

"Of course, it's a little difficult to explain how, in this case, with
six needles in the doll, there were exactly twelve perforations of
the bowel."

Mike shrugged. "I guess where things like that are concerned,
you need to be like the Queen in *Through the Looking-Glass*,
who could believe six impossible things before breakfast."

"Believing what we considered impossible things as recently as
ten years ago is my bailiwick, Doctor, not yours. Surgeons are
supposed to be the most pragmatic people in the whole field of
medicine, so what's troubling you this afternoon?"

Mike gave McCarthy a quick summary of his conversation with
George Stanfield and a list of the odd things that had happened in
connection with Janet Burke lately. The psychiatrist listened intently until the account was finished, then nodded, his small beard
wagging, Mike thought, like that of a wise and mischievous old
billy goat.

"This time you don't need to be even a literary Queen like the one in *Through the Looking-Glass* to believe what happened, Dr. Kerns. The answer is simple."

"To you—maybe; certainly not to me. Every answer I dream up turns out to be impossible—in the light of logic. Right now, I'm almost willing to believe the demon of Lynne Tallman has possessed the body of Janet Burke."

"That impossible you *can't* believe, Dr. Kerns. Demons and evil spirits have no being, except in the minds of the credulous, or the imaginations of authors who know a good sales gimmick when they see it. Instead, try believing your patient has a multiple personality. We see those in psychiatry all the time, especially in cases of schizophrenia, but it's much more common in the general population than you'd think."

"Are you telling me you don't really believe in demons at all?"

"Why create something out of thin air, when there are more than enough people with mean streaks to furnish all the evil the world needs, and then some? Lynne Tallman was a prime example of that."

"What about the change in Janet Burke's voice to where it resembled Lynne Tallman's on the tape?"

"When a second—or third—personality makes its appearance for the first time, it always uses a different voice and manner from the original individual's. If the patient is imitating someone you know, the effect is sometimes startling—as it was to you yesterday and this morning."

"But why Lynne Tallman?"

"My guess would be that Miss Burke secretly envied her—"

"Surely not her criminal instincts."

"Probably not. When I talked to your patient before the operations, I detected a note of envy in her voice as she described how beautiful Lynne Tallman was and how she boasted of being able to have any man she wanted. Janet Burke wasn't beautiful, though she probably is now, judging by your model that was in the room when I stopped by today. So when she got a knock on the head in the plane crash that shook up the cells of her cerebrum enough to allow a second personality to emerge, it was a natural thing to pattern at least part of that personality, unconsciously, on somebody as beautiful as the Tallman girl."

It was an ingenious and, Mike supposed, a logical explanation of the enigma, making him wonder why he couldn't accept it as easily as the urbane psychiatrist apparently did.

"How long is the condition likely to last?"

"Not long would be my guess," said McCarthy. "If nothing goes wrong with her postoperative course, she'll end up being an extraordinarily beautiful young woman—even more so than Lynne Tallman. Men will certainly be pursuing her in droves—in fact, I find the idea very attractive myself." He gave Mike a quick, probing look. "That is, unless you plan to play the part of Pygmalion and keep your creation for yourself."

"Don't worry about that," said Mike firmly. "When I went to New York for the fellowship in cosmetic surgery, I knew most of my practice would be made up of women wanting to improve their appearance in order to attract men—husbands, lovers, or what have you—so I'm always careful to keep my social and professional lives completely separate."

McCarthy shrugged. "If more husbands did their full duty as lovers, neither of us would be very busy. Outside of pure psychoses, a psychiatrist's practice is largely made up of women wanting to be loved—often by the doctor who's trying to get them straightened out."

"Knowing that about cosmetic surgery," Mike agreed, "I made up my mind not to get romantically involved with my female patients."

"That's a lot more than many of your colleagues do. Some of the cosmetic surgeons around this town—and a lot more on the West Coast—make Casanova look like a callow youth."

"Will you see Miss Burke again and take charge of treating the personality disorder—if that's what it really is?"

"Of course. Actually, if you'll take me for a patient, I plan to be in the hospital awhile. That way I could see her practically every day."

"What could I possibly do for you?"

"My summer vacation starts tomorrow and I was considering having a face-lift. Does that surprise you?"

"Not at all. A lot of men are having them these days, but they're usually older than you appear to be."

"I'm forty-seven but, to use a cliché, I've packed a heap o' livin' into these forty-seven years and my face shows it, though fortunately the rest of me has held up rather well. Do you think you could manage to give me a more youthful appearance?"

Mike moved closer and focused the desk lamp on McCarthy's face so he could study him for a few moments.

"It's a mess, isn't it?" the psychiatrist asked with a wry grin.

"I've seen worse. Mind telling me why you wear the Vandyke beard?"

"If you must know my shame, it's to hide a slightly receding chin."

"I thought as much." Mike turned the light back to its former position. "Are you particularly fond of that beard?"

"No more than I am of the bags under my eyes, the sagging cheeks and receding chin."

"In that case, I'd advise a full face-lift, removal of the fat pads under the eyes, dropping the bridge of your nose to a straight line and using the bone from that hump you have in the middle of it to supplement the chin."

"Can you do all that at one sitting?"

"Easily. Using the nose hump is the easiest way to obtain bone for a chin build-up but I can't tell whether I'll be able to get enough from the nasal ridge to bring the chin out to where it will be in proportion with the rest of the face until you've shaved off the beard. But if we need any more, I can easily take some of the ilium or even some cartilage from one of your floating ribs."

"You've got yourself a patient, but I'll have to think about the nose part a little while. I've become sort of attached to it—like Cyrano."

"Keep the nose if you like," said Mike. "I can easily get some bone for the chin from your ilium."

"When can you do the operation?"

"As soon as you're free. I haven't developed much of a practice in cosmetic surgery yet."

"How about Monday morning?"

"I'll see about a room and also reserve an operating theater when I stop by University Hospital a few minutes from now to see Janet Burke," Mike promised. "Don't you want to hear what the fee will be?"

"Somewhere in the Bible it says the laborer is worth his hire. I'll leave that detail up to you."

"My usual fee for such an extensive job is five thousand," said Mike. "With a professional discount to a fellow physician, I could pare it down to three."

"That's agreeable to me," said McCarthy.

"You'd better plan on checking into the hospital for the preanesthetic work-up Saturday afternoon," Mike told him. "I'm going to be in the city over the weekend, so I'll stop by Sunday morning and get some photos of what you look like without that beard."

"I shudder to think of it," said McCarthy jocosely. "See you Sunday, Doctor."

2

Janet Burke was awake when Mike came into her room at University Hospital the next morning. The chart showed that she had needed only one hypodermic during the night.

"You look wonderful," he told her.

"Liar! I look like the Man in the Iron Mask. How long do I have to wear this contraption?"

"About two weeks, until the broken bones start to heal."

"Did everything go the way you wanted it?"

"Perfect. I'm going to take out the tracheotomy tube."

"When I saw this morning that the model was gone, I was afraid you'd taken it away because I wouldn't really look like her when it's over," she admitted as he was taping a dressing over the small throat wound.

"I left the model at the foundry on the way to the hospital this morning to be cast in bronze."

"Are you always that certain of your work?"

"I promised to make you as beautiful as you wanted to be. Any complaints so far?"

"Only one. Why do I have an elastic bandage around my chest? Every time I take a deep breath I can feel it stretching and sometimes there's a pain under my arms."

"That's to prevent any accumulation of serum or blood around the prostheses—"

"What prostheses?"

"The silicon gel implants I put under both of your breasts."

"I know all about breast implants from a story I did on what you plastic surgeons call augmentation mammaplasty in Chicago. Are you telling me you did one—two—on me?"

"At the end of the facial operations, you were in excellent condition, so I went ahead and inserted a silicon gel implant underneath each of your breasts—exactly as you requested."

"I don't remember asking you to do anything to my bosom, Doctor." Her voice was taut with anger.

"As I was leaving the afternoon before your surgery, you called me back and said, 'Since you say you're going to make me a goddess, Doctor, how about giving me the bosom of a goddess?' You also signed the permission form for the operation."

"Let me see it." Her tone was a shade less indignant, or at least he hoped his ears weren't betraying him. "I still don't remember."

Mike pushed the call bell. When the nurse at the desk answered on the intercom, he said, "Would you bring me Miss Burke's Permission for Surgery forms, please—both of them."

"Yes, Doctor. Right away."

A moment later there was a tap on the door and the nurse handed Mike a clipboard with the two printed forms at the front. He gave the chart to Janet and, after she had studied it for a moment asked, "Are those your signatures on the two permission sheets?"

"They look like mine, but I still don't have any memory of saying anything to you about any breast operation." She gave the clipboard to the nurse, who left the room. "Or signing a permission form authorizing you to do it."

"You'll be glad you did when the bandage comes off and you find yourself with a bosom worthy of Aphrodite herself."

She shrugged—and grimaced momentarily with pain. "I guess I should be grateful to be alive, even though I have to eat baby food strained through my teeth and a network of rubber bands. I had too many pounds, anyway, so things could be worse."

"By the way," he said, "I'm operating on someone you know Monday. Dr. McCarthy's having his face lifted."

"With the face he's got, anything could be an improvement," she said. "Am I going to bring you good luck, Dr. Kerns?"

"It's already started. When you're back in public circulation and people see how beautiful you are, men will be falling all over themselves trying to get a date."

3

A call from George Stanfield came late that afternoon; the publisher sounded perturbed. "Can you meet Gerald and me in my office at five o'clock, Mike?" he asked.

"Sure. What's up?"

"It's about Janet but I'd rather not discuss it over the phone."

"I'll be there at five. I'm seeing my last patient for the day now."

When he had hung up the phone, Mike looked at it thoughtfully for a long moment, wondering why the newspaper editor had been so concerned when his niece was doing so well. He'd expected Gerald Hutchinson to make trouble, but not Stanfield. Then, obeying a sudden impulse, he called University Hospital and rang the floor where Janet's room was located. Ellen Strabo answered.

"This is Dr. Kerns," he said. "Did Miss Burke have any visitors today?"

"Only her uncle, Mr. Stanfield, and that fiancé. You'd left word that they could see her whenever they wished, but I started to call you just the same."

"Why?"

"After he talked to Miss Burke, Mr. Stanfield came out and asked if I could have the Permission for Surgery sheets on her chart Xeroxed. He's listed on the hospital record as being her nearest relative and responsible for her bills, so I saw nothing wrong in having the Record Room make copies for him."

"Did seeing them appear to upset the patient?"

"I think it did—a little. After they left, she asked for the PRN hypo you ordered and we gave it to her. She's slept most of the afternoon."

When Mike came into George Stanfield's office, he wasn't surprised to find Gerald Hutchinson there. What startled him was the presence of a small plump man wearing thick-lensed spectacles.

"Professor Leibowitz, Dr. Michael Kerns." The newspaperman's voice was more terse than it had been over the telephone and his manner even a little hostile. Gerald Hutchinson's eyes showed only pleased anticipation, however, such as, Mike thought, a spectator at the Roman gladiatorial games must have exhibited when he gave the thumbs-down verdict of death for a fallen combatant.

"I met Professor Leibowitz some time ago when we were both testifying in a court case," said Mike, shaking hands with the handwriting expert.

"Before we go any further," said Stanfield, "I have a confession to make."

"About Xeroxing the Permission for Surgery forms?"

"Yes. How did you know?"

"After you called earlier, I telephoned the hospital to ask if there was any change in Miss Burke's condition. Miss Strabo, the charge nurse, told me you'd asked her to have the sheets Xeroxed."

"I guess I should have called you before I made the request," Stanfield admitted. "When we visited Janet early this afternoon, the nurse had left her chart hanging on the foot of the bed and Gerald started leafing through it."

"I noticed that the signatures on the two Permission for Surgery forms were different." Hutchinson took up the narrative. "Obviously one of them was a forgery, so I insisted that George have them Xeroxed and shown to a handwriting expert."

"Naturally I thought of Professor Leibowitz," Stanfield added. "As you probably know, his opinions on handwriting have been accepted as authoritative, even by the Supreme Court."

"I would like to hear the professor's opinion," said Mike quietly. "But in spite of any differences he finds in the two forms, I can assure you that they were both signed by Miss Burke."

Gerald Hutchinson gave a snort of derision but did not comment.

"Please go ahead, Professor," said Stanfield.

Leibowitz arranged three Xeroxed sheets on top of Stanfield's desk and turned a gooseneck lamp to shine directly upon them.

From the pocket of a baggy sport coat, he also produced a large hand lens.

"I have marked these Exhibits A, B and C." His tone, Mike thought, was exactly as if he were giving evidence before a jury. "Exhibit A is a letter written by Miss Janet Burke to Mr. Stanfield and dated two weeks ago. Exhibit B is a hospital form, 'Permission for Surgery,' apparently signed by Miss Burke and witnessed by Amanda Sheftal, R.N."

"Mrs. Sheftal is the morning-shift charge nurse on the floor," Mike explained.

"This document gives Dr. Kerns permission to perform whatever surgical procedures are necessary upon Miss Burke and appears to have been signed by her, since the signatures on it and a letter to Mr. Stanfield are identical."

"Are you implying that the second form was not signed by her?" Mike demanded.

"It certainly was not, as Professor Leibowitz is prepared to testify," said Gerald Hutchinson on a note of triumph.

"Please, gentlemen," said the handwriting expert. "Let me continue with the analysis and then we will discuss what it all means."

"I apologize, Professor," said Mike. "Please continue."

"Exhibit C is a similar permission form, purporting to authorize Dr. Kerns to perform an operation called 'bilateral augmentation mammaplasty.'"

"And signed by her that same afternoon," Mike interposed firmly.

"It was signed with her *name*," said Leibowitz with equal firmness. "But not by the same hand that wrote the letter to Mr. Stanfield that is Exhibit A and also signed the first Permission for Surgery form that constitutes Exhibit B."

"That's impossible!" Mike exclaimed. "Absolutely impossible!"

"You overlook the real possibility, Doctor," Gerald Hutchinson snapped. "Forgery."

"That's a lie!" said Mike flatly. "And you may well have to answer for that accusation in court."

"Which we most certainly expect to do," said Hutchinson with equal conviction.

"Please, gentlemen," said George Stanfield. "There's no question at this time of anybody suing anybody else. What I'm trying to do, as Janet's nearest relative, is to get at the truth of what this all means. Go on, Professor."

"The second signature is witnessed by a different person," said the handwriting expert. "The name is difficult to read but it looks like Strabo, Ellen Strabo."

"Miss Ellen Strabo is the three-to-eleven charge nurse on the floor," Mike explained. "The request for mammaplasty was made to me by Miss Burke about five o'clock on the afternoon before surgery, as I was leaving her room. I asked Miss Strabo to prepare the form and witness the patient's signature, which she did. It's part of the usual hospital routine, but what's this business about Miss Burke not signing the second sheet herself?"

"The evidence is quite conclusive, Dr. Kerns," said Professor Leibowitz. "Whoever did sign for Miss Burke tried to imitate her signature but there are subtle differences in calligraphy between the last signature and the two preceding ones."

"Why don't you ask Miss Burke herself?" Mike demanded.

"We did," said Gerald Hutchinson. "I showed her the second permission form and she has no memory whatever of having signed it."

Taken aback by this turn of events, Mike had no explanation for it at the moment. "When I told her this morning that she'd had mammaplasty operations on both breasts, she *was* surprised," he said thoughtfully. "But she didn't seem to be upset."

"She was later," said Gerald Hutchinson. "Very much upset."

"In any event," said Mike, "the first permission form she signed authorized me to do whatever was indicated."

"I'm not at all certain that argument would be valid for the second operations in a court of law, Dr. Kerns," said Professor Leibowitz.

"Why not?"

"Was mammaplasty really indicated?"

"Cosmetically, it certainly was."

"Did it have any connection with repairing the damage to Miss Burke's body caused by the accident?"

"No. I only did the mammaplasties because she requested them. Wait a minute," he added, "this whole business can be settled by calling Miss Ellen Strabo at the hospital." He reached for the telephone on George Stanfield's desk. "Can I use this?"

"Certainly."

"Connect the conference phone, please. I want all of you to hear her," Mike said as he dialed the number of University Hospital and asked to be connected to the nurses' station on the floor where Janet Burke was a patient.

"Miss Strabo," he said when the connection was made, "I want you to tell me exactly what happened when you took in the second Permission for Surgery form, the one for the mammaplasty operations, to be signed by Miss Burke the afternoon before surgery."

"I filled in the name of the operation and the patient's name like I always do, when it's requested by a doctor, and took it into the room," said the nurse.

"Did she hesitate at all about signing it?"

"No, Doctor. But she did seem excited. She was laughing to herself and, when she looked at the form, her eyes were bright, with a strange light in them."

"Strange in what way?"

"We—ll, I guess you could call it devilish."

Mike had been hunched near the conference telephone speaker when he asked the question. Now he sat erect suddenly, a startled look on his face.

"Did you say devilish?" he asked quickly.

"Yes. You know, excited—like she was putting something over on somebody. Her voice was different, too, sort of hoarse. And her hand shook a little as she signed the form."

"But she didn't object to signing it?"

"Oh no; in fact she hardly bothered to read it. While I was signing as witness she laughed and said, 'Nurse, I'm going to have the finest pair of tits the world has ever seen.'"

"That's absurd!" Gerald Hutchinson snapped. "Janet would never say such a thing."

"Was that all she said, Miss Strabo?"

"Well, no. She made me promise, if her uncle or her fiancé came by that evening, not to say anything to them about the breast operations."

"Did you ask her why?"

"No. She was rather small-bosomed for her height, so I figured maybe the new ones were to be a wedding present."

Gerald Hutchinson looked as if he might have a stroke. Leaning close to the phone, he said, "This is Mr. Hutchinson. Are you sure it wasn't Dr. Kerns who asked you not to mention the operations?"

"Oh no," Ellen Strabo answered without hesitation. "Dr. Kerns had already left the floor. I did notice one thing, though. The patient was still connected to the EEG and Dr. Kerns had asked me to be on the lookout for more of those theta waves we'd seen occasionally. There were a lot of them on the monitor just then."

"Thank you, Miss Strabo," said Mike and switched off the conference phone.

"What was that business about the theta waves?" Gerald Hutchinson demanded suspiciously.

"We've noticed some abnormal waves on the electroencephalogram from time to time. Apparently they're a residue from the severe concussion she sustained." It was an explanation he hoped the other two men would accept, but far from the one that had already taken form in his mind.

"Obviously the nurse is in cahoots with you," said Hutchinson.

Mike held his temper but only with considerable effort. "You heard her say Miss Burke appeared to be excited. That could account for any differences in the two signatures."

"I don't agree," said the handwriting expert unexpectedly. "The differences are much more pronounced than that."

"You'll have to show me," said Mike firmly. "An accused person is entitled to see the evidence against him."

"I'm not accusing you of anything, Mike," said George Stanfield. "As far as I'm concerned, your explanation is adequate."

"It's not adequate for me," said Gerald Hutchinson. "Please proceed, Professor."

The handwriting expert placed the three exhibits close together and handed Mike the hand magnifier.

"Study the first Permission for Surgery sheet, Doctor," he directed. "You will note that the signature is firm and certain. The capital *J* is smooth and symmetrical, the little *a* and the little *n* are well formed and the little *e* and little *t* are made without a break. The same is true of the letters in *Burke,* especially the little *k,* which is often slurred when part of a signature."

"I can see that."

"Now look at the signature on the last operative permit. Notice that the capital *J* is printed, not written out in script, as it is on the first sheet. A break can also be seen between the little *n* and the little *e*, while the little *t*'s are crossed differently. In Miss Burke's letter to Mr. Stanfield and also in her signature on the first Permission for Surgery form, you can see that the little *t* at the end of her name is crossed almost horizontally with a rather short bar, while in the second form, the little *t* is crossed with a slanting stroke that is almost twice as long."

"And your conclusion is that the two forms were signed by different people?" Mike asked.

"In a different handwriting, at least. The evidence is indisputable and I'd be willing to go into court on it."

"I hope you won't take offense, Mike, but there's one question any smart lawyer would be certain to ask in a malpractice suit," said George Stanfield gravely.

"I'm liable to be on the receiving end of a lot of such questions," Mike said resignedly. "Shoot."

"How well do you know Ellen Strabo?"

"I've had a few dates with her. If you're asking whether she'd help me falsify a Permission for Surgery form, so I could perform an extra operation for a larger fee, the answer is no. If two people did sign two different forms that day, they were occupying the same body—" Mike stopped suddenly. "That has to be the answer, of course." Turning to Professor Leibowitz, he asked, "Did you ever see such a case, Doctor—two persons, so to speak, inhabiting the same individual?"

"Once I testified at a sanity hearing in a case of schizophrenia —split personality. The patient existed sometimes as one person, at others as another."

"Were the handwritings of the two at any time the same?"

"No. They were quite different—as these are."

"There!" Mike exclaimed triumphantly. "That explains the whole thing."

"Except that Janet has never shown any signs of a neurosis or other personality disorder," Gerald Hutchinson objected. "I think you'd have trouble proving that in court."

"Not after a severe injury with concussion like the one she survived. Dr. Randall McCarthy thinks she is definitely showing signs of a multiple personality."

"McCarthy!" Gerald snapped. "Here we go again."

"What in the world are you talking about, Mike?" Stanfield asked.

"I told you I'd asked McCarthy to see her—"

"Yes, I remember, but he said there were no sequelae from the original injury that would make reparative surgery inadvisable."

"There were no signs of multiple personality at the time, either," said Mike. "But this morning, I asked him about her strange behavior in requesting mammaplasty and he said a temporary case of double personality could explain everything."

"Then what we need is further study by McCarthy—and a report for the record."

"What good would that do?" Gerald Hutchinson demanded. "He'd only agree with Kerns; you know doctors won't testify against each other."

George Stanfield spoke before Hutchinson could say more. "Will you ask Dr. McCarthy to examine Janet again as soon as possible?"

"Of course. He can probably see her in the morning."

Gerald Hutchinson started to object but stopped at Stanfield's terse command. "Break it up, Gerald. We've caused Dr. Kerns enough trouble for one day."

4

Ellen Strabo was working at the nursing station when Mike came on the floor shortly before six o'clock. A tall blonde, she was vivacious and very popular with the staff—particularly the male contingent.

"What was that business just now about my witnessing Miss Burke's signature on the permit sheet?" she asked Mike. "Any trouble brewing for you?"

"A handwriting expert says the signatures on the two sheets aren't the same."

"I saw Miss Burke sign the sheet myself and I knew it was her. But at the same time it was like you were looking at somebody and knew perfectly well who they were, then suddenly they were somebody else."

"In what way?"

"It's hard to explain but the tone of her voice, her movements, the look in her eyes—"

"On the telephone you used the word 'devilish.'"

"That's exactly the way she looked—with her eyes glowing and everything about her somehow different."

"I noticed the same thing when she called me back, as I was leaving the room that day, and asked me to do the mammaplasty."

"Lord knows she needed that second operation, so what's she got to gripe about?"

"I'm not sure *she* will. Did you make a note on the chart that day about her manner and appearance?"

The blond nurse shook her head. "There didn't seem to be any reason to, especially when she asked me not to say anything about it to her uncle and that pompous bastard of a fiancé. Besides I was looking straight at her when she signed the permission form and I certainly knew who she was."

Maybe neither of us knew who she was just then, Mike thought as he picked up the chart and moved down the hall to Janet Burke's room.

She was propped up in bed and had just finished brushing her hair, using the small mirror in the over-the-bed table and an ivory-handled brush. A comb with the initials *JB* in gold lay on the table beside the mirror.

"Feeling better?" he asked.

"I guess so, but I'm weak as a kitten. Miss Strabo was in just now and helped me to the bathroom; I'd never have made it under my own power."

"You lost more blood than we replaced with transfusions, but it will come back fast when you're able to eat something else beside baby food."

She looked at her wristwatch. "You're late making rounds."

"I've been attending a conference about you at your uncle's office."

"About me?" She seemed genuinely surprised. "Why?"

"Your fiancé is trying to prove you didn't give me permission to do the mammaplasty operations."

"Poor Gerald. Whenever we're together, he always tries to keep me in the background, but if I'm going to look the way you told me I will, I suppose he thinks he'll have to play second fiddle."

"Doesn't that worry you—as a basis for marriage?"

"I never considered it before; I guess because he's so dynamic, I just naturally assumed that would be my role. But now . . ." She paused, then added, "What difference does what I signed or didn't sign make, now that you've done the operations and I'm happy with the results?"

"Miss Strabo witnessed your signature on the second form but didn't notice at the time that it was quite different from the first one."

"In what way?"

From the large manila envelope he was carrying, Mike took the Xerox copies of the permit forms and also Professor Leibowitz's report that George Stanfield had let him keep for Dr. Randall McCarthy to see in the morning.

"Look over the report of the handwriting expert first," he advised. "You can see the differences more easily if you know where to look."

"I already see them; it looks like somebody was trying to forge my signature. Did a good job on it, too; except for a few things, I'd be fooled myself."

"For instance?"

"The *J* in Janet. One is script, the way I write it, the other is printed, with a little curlicue—the kind of *J* poor Lynne Tallman used to make—at the top. The *a*'s, *e*'s and several other letters are different, too."

"The handwriting expert pointed out all those things in his report."

Janet looked up from the printed forms. "So what does it mean?"

"If you really don't remember requesting me to do the mammaplasty procedures—"

"I didn't even have any idea you'd done them until I asked about the elastic bandages this morning and you told me."

The note of concern in her voice seemed genuine but, while he was looking at her, a startling change occurred—almost, he thought, as if she'd suddenly become another person. The bright, provocatively bold light he'd seen in her eyes the day before her operations was suddenly there again. When she spoke, the voice, too, had changed, taking on the same hoarse, slightly brassy note, while her manner was as different from what it had been when he came into the room as night from day.

"Hey!" she cried on a note of sudden excitement. "I could sue you, couldn't I?"

"If you want to," Mike said, rather stiffly. "Though I don't—"

"Man, I could take you to the cleaners!" she chortled. "There must be some pictures somewhere showing how flat-chested she— I—was. If I introduce them as Exhibit A and then display the new bust you made for me to a jury as Exhibit B, they'd convict you without leaving the box."

"You haven't seen the results of the mammaplasty operations yet," he reminded her.

"Those artificial pads you put in under the skin, what do you call 'em?"

"Prostheses."

"Well, whatever they are, they're bound to look and feel like I'm wearing a pair of breastplates."

"Silicon gel has the same consistency as breast tissue," he assured her. "Unless you pressed hard enough to distinguish the plastic skin that holds the gel in place from breast tissue, you'd never know the prostheses are there."

"What size did you make me?"

"Thirty-six, B cup."

"Generous, weren't you?" Her voice still contained the same brassy note, but now the cutting edge of sarcasm had been added. "If I sue you, it would still be my word against yours and a jury would always believe a woman—especially when I showed them the bags of silicon you hung on me."

"You're forgetting that Miss Strabo witnessed your signature and will testify that you signed the Permission for Surgery form," he said sharply, but she only laughed—in the same cynical tone.

"A smart lawyer could tear her testimony apart. All the time she was giving me evening care before you came this afternoon, she was talking about you. The girl's crazy about you, Mike; she'd jump into bed with you the first chance she gets—that is, if you aren't laying her already. And if you aren't, take my advice and go to it, she ought to be plenty pneumatic."

Mike's sudden flush betrayed the truth before he could deny it, and the brassy laugh of the girl in the bed rang out again. It was a jarring sound with an odd quality that made him shiver.

"There!" she exclaimed in triumph. "I've shocked you, haven't I?"

"Of course not." He made no effort to curb the irritation in his voice. "I'm not that naïve."

She looked at him speculatively for a moment, with the boldly provocative manner that made the hackles along his back and neck rise in a reflex as old as man.

"No, I don't think you are, but you don't look like the kind of man who turns down something as luscious as that, either."

"If you're through discussing my sex life—"

"Don't get huffy, darling, just because I accused you of having normal male instincts."

Turning on his heel, Mike left the room, followed by her mocking laugh until he slammed the door shut. But though he was seething with anger he still couldn't bring himself to believe the words he'd just listened to had actually come from the mouth of the Janet Burke he'd known before the surgery.

At the nurses' station, he scribbled a note on the chart that the patient appeared to be doing well, but made no mention of the change in her appearance or manner that had been apparent during the last few minutes of his conversation with her.

"You don't look exactly happy," said Ellen Strabo as he was putting the clinical chart back into its rack.

"I can't understand how she can be two different people while you're looking at her, even while you're talking to her."

"Once every week or so I substitute for the night super on the psychiatric ward," said the nurse. "They've got a couple of cases over there that are real dillies. One minute they're as sweet as pie and the next you're talking to an entirely different personality—when you aren't trying to keep from being garrotted. If your patient's liable to go psycho, maybe you'd better move her to the psycho ward before she does something really crazy."

"Just watch her a little more closely than you would normally and let me know if the second personality takes over again."

"Shall I note her behavior on the chart?"

"I'd rather you didn't."

"Sure, Mike." She smiled. "You're the doctor."

But as Mike drove to his apartment through the busy afternoon traffic he knew that, although McCarthy's diagnosis of probable double personality had satisfied Stanfield and the newspaper publisher could probably persuade his niece not to sue, it didn't satisfy him any more than it had Gerald Hutchinson.

Having eaten a pizza he'd bought at the corner pizzeria, with a bottle of beer from his refrigerator, Mike went into the den-studio to look at TV. Before he turned on the set his eyes fell upon the encyclopedia, which was still open at the plate of the Praxiteles Aphrodite. And as he studied the lovely statue, he fancied for a moment that he saw appear briefly in the sightless eyes the almost demonic light that had been in the eyes of Janet Burke at the hospital.

Then suddenly the imagined light was gone and only the lovely face and bosom of the Goddess of Love, chiseled from cold marble, met his gaze. She was far from cold, however, when she came into his arms in a dream later on that night. Nor was she any longer a marble statue but now a living breathing woman who looked exactly as Janet Burke would look, he was certain, when she finally recovered from the effects of the sculpture he had performed with the scalpel in the operating room at University Hospital. With the added fact that—in the dream—her naked body was warm and responsive to his touch upon it as he caressed her and her lips avid against his own, demanding the only act of homage that could properly be rendered by worshipers to the Goddess of Love.

5

"With a chin like that, no wonder this guy always wore a goatee," said Dr. Hal Petrie when Mike looked into the operating theater from the adjoining scrub room at seven o'clock on Monday morning. "Think you can get enough bone off that beak he's got to build him a chin, Mike?"

"He prefers to keep the nose. Says it gives him individuality."

"It's a noble proboscis all right," said Petrie. "With that nose and those bushy eyebrows, he could double for Satan himself!"

Startled, Mike dropped the brush he'd been using to scrub his hands. The day after the conference in George Stanfield's office, Dr. Randall McCarthy had examined Janet Burke and made a diagnosis of a temporary case of multiple personality following concussion, effectively taking Mike off the hook as far as Gerald Hutchinson's accusations were concerned.

Hal Petrie's comment raised a new, and troubling, question, however. If Janet was really possessed by the demon that had driven Lynne Tallman to murder innocent people by planning and directing the Chicago bombings, and the patient he was about to operate on was of the same ilk, so to speak, then McCarthy would hardly have made any diagnosis other than the one he had. One demon to cope with had been more than enough; now, it seemed, he might be dealing with two.

Scrubbed, gowned and gloved, Mike approached the table where Randall McCarthy was lying, his body almost hidden by sterile drapes. Only two areas were exposed, one the face and the other a rectangle of bare skin over the left hip, where the bone graft would be removed and used to build up the patient's chin.

When the instrument nurse handed him a swab dipped in gentian violet he began to mark out carefully the incisions he planned to make. First, he drew a pattern shaped somewhat like a quarter moon beneath each of McCarthy's eyes, including most of the baggy skin there. Then, moving over to the region of the patient's ear, he began to mark out the incision he planned to use for the face-lift, keeping it close to the hairline so, when McCarthy's rather long hair was combed down slightly after healing was complete, it would cover the almost invisible scar.

Starting above the ear and about two inches along the forehead at the hair edge, he drew a line of violet color down to the upper angle of the ear at the front. Continuing on, he carried the line down across just in front of the ear and, lifting up the lobe, curved it around that, to follow the hair line about two thirds of the way across the neck.

Next he took a slender needle attached to a strand of black silk and thrust it through the lobe of the ear. Moving up to the middle of the ear, he placed another suture there, both to be used for traction while he was working—and removed when he was through. Turning McCarthy's head, he did the same on the opposite side before making a small incision over the hip and removing a section of bone about an inch long from the crest of the ilium.

This he shaped very carefully before pulling down McCarthy's lip to make an incision through the mucous membrane at the base of the teeth in the lower jaw.

Using periosteal elevators, he very carefully pushed the tissues back until they could be folded down over the receding chin and the point of the jawbones exposed where they came together to form the chin. This done, he fixed the section of bone he had removed from the graft in place across the receding ends of the jawbones to give the patient something he'd not had before, a normal-sized chin. A few stitches closed the wound in the mucous membrane and the operating crew then changed gowns and gloves for the major part of the surgical procedure, the face-lift.

Moving back to the table now, Mike first made two incisions on the right side beneath the eye, following the quarter-moon-shaped pattern of lines he'd drawn there. Dissecting away the skin inside the markings with the fatty tissues beneath it, he teased out the fat pad that had herniated through the muscles under the eye. When this skin was carefully sutured with tiny stitches of very fine black silk, the bag under McCarthy's right eye was removed, and only a few minutes were needed to do the same on the left.

"I removed the excess tissue and fat from beneath the eyes first," Mike explained to the crew and a few observers in the elevated gallery, "because, when we finish the rhytidoplasty—the surgical name for face-lift—and begin suturing, there will be a certain amount of tension along the suture line and we would have trouble closing those incisions."

Taking a fresh scalpel, Mike started on the right side and, following the violet line he had drawn around the ear, cut through the skin along its entire length. Working swiftly, he and the resident assisting him placed about ten traction sutures along the edge of the skin wound. Using them to lift the skin edge toward the nose with his left hand, Mike then began to undermine it with a pair of small scissors, searching for one of the normal fascial planes beneath the skin. When he opened into this space, he took a somewhat larger and narrower pair of scissors and began to undermine the skin across the cheek, almost to the outer corner of the eye and halfway up across the lower temple in front of and above the ear, until he reached the area where he had just removed the fat pads.

As Mike freed the skin from the muscles and the fascia beneath, the resident quickly caught any bleeding points with small artery forceps. Whenever as many as half a dozen hemostats were in place, he closed the small blood vessels with the coagulating current from the electric knife system. Moving swiftly but always on the watch for nerve branches and larger blood vessels that must be left in place, Mike continued to undermine the skin across the face almost to the fold from the corner of the mouth to the opening of the nostril.

Next he moved down and across the jaw into the upper neck, being careful here not to injure nerves, which would result in loss of feeling in this area. This dissection was carried down almost to a line even with the Adam's apple and also along the neck beneath the jawbone back as far as the lower end of the incision itself and the region where he had just placed the bone graft.

"Rhytidoplasty, as practiced by experts like Dr. Cardoza at Bellevue in New York, where I spent the last two years, is quite extensive," Mike explained to the watchers in a running comment. "Originally, undermining was carried out only for a short distance across the cheek from the front of the ear and down along the neck. Besides, no reefs or tucks were taken in the tissues beneath the skin and, as a result, the original benefit often disappeared after a year or two—sometimes less."

"How long will it last using this technique?" the anesthesiologist asked.

"About ten years on the average, sometimes longer."

The dissection finished on the right side and all bleeding points carefully coagulated, Mike next teased out a fat pad that had accumulated under what Randall McCarthy had possessed of a chin, giving it a slightly double appearance. Then, while the resident who was assisting him lifted up the now undermined skin, he very carefully reached beneath it and took a number of small tucks or reefs across the tissues from which the skin had been separated. He tightened the sutures before tying them, being very careful not to create lumps or swellings that would give the patient an uneven appearance after healing.

"Now comes the hard part, deciding how much skin to remove," Mike commented.

With a large forceps inserted beneath the loose skin, he drew the edge across the ear. When it was snug, but not too tight, he began to trim off the redundant skin, before finally closing the entire length of the hockey-stick-shaped incision with tiny black silk sutures. Only when the last skin suture was in place did he look up at the clock.

"Forty minutes," he said. "Cardoza does it in twenty-five."

"When you've been at it as long as he has, you'll be that fast, too," Petrie assured him.

"Maybe the other side will go faster."

The second side of the face took only thirty minutes and, when Mike stepped back from the table, a faint cheer came from the observers' gallery where about a dozen students and house staff were now watching.

"Give him about six weeks, say three for the healing and another three for the ecchymosis to clear up so the skin looks normal again," Mike said as he started to pull off his gloves, "and he'll look at least ten years younger—maybe even more."

"That will just about jive with his personality," said the student nurse who was handling instruments. "I took one of his courses last year and any girl who got out of his office without a feel was lucky."

"Or unlucky," a second nurse volunteered. "It's no secret that the extent of the feel had a lot to do with the grade you got on the course."

"By the way, Miss Scarlet," Petrie asked the first student with a look of complete innocence, "how was your grade?"

"I got a B+," she confessed, then laughed. "If I hadn't been ticklish, I'd have gotten an A."

6

Mike left the necessary orders on the patient's chart, then showered and dressed before going to Janet Burke's room. He almost hesitated to enter it after the dream and a weekend out of the city, but found her sitting in a chair beside the bed reading. Her hair was tied back with a ribbon, and he was pleased to see that she was herself instead of the sarcastic, cynical creature with the strange glow in her eyes, which were growing more and more beautiful as the swelling of her face above the plastic mask subsided.

"I just finished a face-lift on our friend Dr. McCarthy," he told her.

"I know, he's on this floor. Last night he came in and told me about how you first wanted to take off part of his nose and put it on his receding chin."

"He decided to keep the schnozzle, so I had to do a bone graft to give him a chin."

"Like the one you did on my upper jaw?"

"Roughly the same. How does he strike you?"

"He seemed very nice last night. We talked mainly about Lynne and he explained why she was like she was."

"So? What did he say?"

"He thinks she was a psychopath, born without a sense of conscience or morality, and that her personality was made worse by her childhood. What he says does fit what I already knew about her, too—from things she'd told me about herself."

"I guess she really didn't have a chance to be anything but what she was, then—sort of a rebel without a cause."

"Oh, Lynne had a cause all right; she hated everybody who didn't think like she did."

"*You* obviously don't think that way. Why do you suppose she trusted you?"

"Actually we were alike in some ways."

He gave her a startled look. "Come again?"

"My parents were killed when I was only three, and even though Uncle George couldn't have been kinder to me, I still felt a sense of resentment toward them for leaving me alone. When I got older, I understood that the feeling wasn't really rational, but it took me a long time to get over it and not have a grudge against them and the world because I was an orphan and didn't have real parents like the rest of the kids. Lynne just didn't try to get over her original hate, I guess. Anyway, she was always trying to get back at the world by making each new bombing bigger and more destructive to life than the one before."

"Do you say that in your book?"

"Yes."

"Ever think she might have been doing a snow job on you?

Using you to tell her story the way she wanted people to think of her?"

"I'm sure she was—at least at first." She didn't seem to have taken offense at the question, which rather surprised him. "But as our relationship progressed while she was in jail, I think she finally came to understand that I was really interested in her as a person and not just as a wild animal needing to be kept in a cage. That's when she really started opening up to me. By the way, when will we know how successful you've been in making me over?"

"Tomorrow morning, when I take out the stitches on the fifth postoperative day. You'll be black and blue and there'll still be some swelling to distort the final picture, but we ought to be able to get a general idea of how near you come to the ideal woman I modeled."

"Your ideal—or Praxiteles'?"

"A little of both, I guess. A lot of what I put into the model, and into reconstructing your face, certainly came from an artist who was probably the finest sculptor in history. Every time a plastic surgeon does this sort of a job, I guess he unconsciously molds the tissues into some resemblance of an ideal of his own, too."

"Considering the beauty of the model you made, that's quite a compliment."

"Then you feel differently about me from the way you did when I left last Friday afternoon?"

"What do you mean?"

"After you saw the different signatures on the operation forms, you were talking of suing me."

She frowned. "I remember looking at the forms and noting the differences in my signature, but after that, I don't even remember your leaving. I guess you actually did me a favor by doing the second operations; I've never been happy about having to buy pads for my bras."

"You won't have to any more," he assured her.

"I can tell that, even through the elastic bandages."

"Sometimes it seems to me that there are two of you," Mike confessed. "One is the person I'm talking to now, a very friendly warm girl whom everybody likes; the other is a rather brassy and cynical and even unpleasant sort of person."

She gave him a startled look. "Are you saying I'm a multiple personality? I studied a case like that once."

"Professor McCarthy says there's something of that in all of us."

"I've never seen it in myself, and none of my friends ever mentioned it."

"Perhaps you'd better ask your uncle when he comes by; he knows you a lot better than I do."

"I'm not sure I'd be happy about being two people. Particularly if one of them threatened to sue you when you saved my life after the airplane crash."

7

Mike had promised Janet to remove the few skin sutures that would need removal on the fifth postoperative day. He arrived at the hospital that morning to find her in a state of considerable apprehension.

"I hardly slept a wink last night," she confessed when he came in with a nurse and a dressing cart, "wondering whether the incisions might break open and leave me with a lot of scarring, like a patient I saw in Chicago who'd had a face-lift."

"Nothing like that will happen," he promised, as he began to remove the dressing over the small wounds at the corners of her eyes.

They were healing beautifully and, after taking out the stitches, he carefully removed the plastic mask and the cotton padding beneath it. Loosening the dressing over the tiny incision he'd made at the very tip of her nose, in order to insert the L-shaped bone graft that formed a new bridge for it, he removed the two sutures that closed it.

"Want to have a look?" he asked, adjusting the tilting mirror in the middle of the across-the-bed table.

"You haven't taken the stitches out of my mouth."

"They're absorbable and will drop out in a few more days."

"Ugh! In the middle of my food?"

"They're also digestible, so don't worry about them." She still hadn't opened her eyes and he added, "You really should take a look before I put the mask back on. Your new face is quite a work of art."

She reached out to grasp his hand tightly before opening her eyes. Then, as the image in the mirror grew clearer, she caught her breath in a gasp of surprise, pleasure and disbelief.

"You really did make me look like the Aphrodite of Praxiteles in the encyclopedia," she cried. "I was sure you couldn't do it with the smashed-up mess my face was in."

"Satisfied?"

"Oh, Mike, yes. I feel like Eliza in *My Fair Lady.*"

"I know another part for you. You'd be singing, 'I feel pretty! I feel pretty.' "

"It's much more than that. Even with the ecchy—"

"Ecchymosis."

"—you warned me about, I can see that my new face is going to be lovely, not just plain Jane like before. Do you have to cover it back up?"

"For about a week; if you bumped against anything or fell, you could smash all that delicate work I did on your beautiful nose."

"You're a miracle worker. When I first became conscious and realized how badly I was smashed up, I wished I could die. But now—"

"A whole new life as a raving beauty is ahead of you. Have you thought about what that's going to be like?"

"I've dreamed of being beautiful—all girls do. Every time I looked in the mirror I told myself I was wasting my dream, but now you've made it come true." She squeezed his hand. "I hope you charge Tri-Continental Airlines a big fee for this job. It's worth it."

"I'd better put you back in the plastic mask but, now that you know what's beneath it, you won't have to worry."

He worked swiftly, covering with small dressings the wounds at the corners of her eyes that gave her the slightly oriental look he'd warned her about. Then he taped the padded plastic mask back in place to support her cheekbones and the cleanly straight profile of her new nose.

"Now if you'll sit up and let the nurse take off that bedjacket," he told her when the mask was in place, "we'll see if the rest of the surgery turned out as well as the first part. You can hold a towel in place over your breasts with your right hand after we get the elastic bandages off."

"What's that for?"

"I'm old-fashioned enough to think a woman has a right to be modest, if she likes, even before her doctor."

Janet Burke laughed. "That's really being old-fashioned, considering what swimsuits are like these days, but I'm sure you're as anxious to see how your work turned out as—"

The last bandage came off just then and, since the dressings over the incisions themselves were in her armpits, the resculptured breasts were fully exposed in all their lovely symmetry. No ecchymosis disturbed the appearance of the skin, as had been the case with her facial structures, and her ecstatic gasp of surprise and pleasure was all the reward he needed.

"You did give me the bosom of a goddess, didn't you?" she cried.

"Try the softness. I doubt that you can even detect the presence of a prosthesis at all."

She squeezed each breast gently and her eyes widened even more. "I can't tell where *me* ends and the silicone begins."

"You're symmetrical, too," he told her as he started removing the stitches from the two incisions. "Thirty-six, twenty-five, thirty-six. Not quite the proportions of the Venus de Milo but good enough for nowadays. One more thing," he added as he taped a small piece of gauze over the last incision, which was now completely hidden by the fold of the armpit. "I want you to wear a bra. It doesn't make any difference how skimpy the bra is, just so it puts the minimum of support under the breasts to keep the prostheses from tending to slide down."

"Don't worry; I'm not going to let anything change what you've made of me. Can you tell yet how much longer I'll have to be in the hospital?"

"Your jaws need to be wired together for about four weeks but you won't have to stay here for that. I'd say another two weeks of hospitalization would be enough. When did you plan to have the wedding?"

"There isn't going to be any wedding; apparently I sent Gerald packing."

"Don't you know?" he asked, startled by this development.

"It must have been the other me, the one Dr. McCarthy says takes control at times." Her voice was suddenly troubled. "But I can't have someone else inside me running my life without my knowing what she—it is going to do."

"Dr. McCarthy thinks the second personality is a product of the concussion and will soon fade away."

"What if it isn't?"

"Do you have any reason to think it might not be?" he asked.

"I don't know, that's the whole trouble. So far it's all worked out for the best. I mean, I have my new face and a lovely bosom and I was considering breaking off with Gerald anyway. But no matter what the other me does, I'm still responsible for it, aren't I?"

"I'm afraid so, unless there's another explanation."

"What do you mean?"

"I'm not sure enough to say," he told her. "But I do have a theory and, when it's developed to where it seems logical, I'll tell you about it. What are you going to do when your injuries have completely healed? Go back to Chicago?"

"Not for a while, anyway, and maybe not at all. Uncle George has been wanting me to move to Washington and, now that I'm here, I think I'll stay. Besides, I know he feels Chicago would be a dangerous place for me to be just now with the rest of the Lynne Tallman gang presumably still there."

"He's probably right. The FBI's still guarding you."

"Uncle George thinks it would be a good idea for me to go into hiding somewhere until I finish the book, but I don't like the idea of being shut up in his apartment."

Mike had a sudden inspiration. "I've got a cottage in Maryland on the east bank of the Potomac south of I-495. I was on the way from there to the airport when I saw your plane going down. It's isolated and very comfortable; you'd have all the time you need to work or just to loaf, and hardly anybody would know you were there."

"That sounds wonderful." She was putting on her bed jacket again. "But only if you let me rent it."

"If you insist. I hardly ever get down there except on weekends, anyway."

"Skin sutures removed, wounds healing well," Mike wrote on Janet Burke's record before leaving the hospital, but he wasn't nearly as pleased with her possible future as he was with her medical present.

If the demon that had driven the acknowledged queen of the Chicago devil worship cult to such destructive excesses had indeed transferred itself to the body of Janet Burke—as he half suspected —no one could tell when the second personality, if it could be called by such an innocent name, might change. So far it had shown itself only as "devilish," to use Ellen Strabo's description, and inclined to harmless mischief like breaking up an engagement Janet Burke had admittedly been ready to break off anyway. The danger point would come when, or if, it took complete control of the lovely girl, with all its capacity for vicious depravity intact.

8

From his office, Mike called George Stanfield at the publisher's office.

"I'm glad you called," said Stanfield. "I should have called you several days ago and apologized for Gerald Hutchinson's rudeness."

"Fortunately he couldn't prove anything," said Mike. "I didn't know until this morning, when Janet told me, that she'd given him the heave-ho."

"And not a minute too soon."

"Did you know it was the second personality that sent him packing?"

"No." Stanfield's tone was grave. "Could that mean it's starting to take over Janet's life?"

"I hope not. She admitted that she would have done it herself if the other one hadn't, so I may be making a mountain out of a molehill."

For a moment there was silence at the other end of the line, then Stanfield said, "That's a strange expression to use, Mike. Mind explaining what you mean?"

"I'm not sure in my own mind, perhaps because what I think I believe is so clearly impossible."

"Tell me anyway," said Stanfield. "I've seen enough strange things happen during my career as a newspaperman not to shut my mind entirely to anything."

"I've become obsessed with the idea that, in the moments before Lynne Tallman's death, the demon that possessed her somehow managed to move into Janet's body," Mike confessed.

"But that's impossible."

"A patient of mine, Father Julian O'Meara, is chief exorcist for the diocese. We have discussed some of the cases he's treated—if you can call exorcism therapy—and from what Father O'Meara tells me, it's a contest between the exorcist and the demon to see which one is the stronger."

"That business went out with the Middle Ages," Stanfield protested.

"According to Father Julian, the demons want you to think just that. But if you'd read some of the official transcripts of exorcisms carried out by him and his staff, and listened to the tape recordings, you'd find that it's all pretty believable."

"Surely not of Janet. I've known her all her life, Mike."

"Don't forget that you've seen her only briefly since the possession occurred, if indeed it did."

"Have you told her of this belief of yours?"

"No. I'm not going to without more proof, but I think she has some inkling. She's probably shut the portals of her unconscious mind to it, except on rare occasions, like the first part of the anesthesia induction period—"

"What are you talking about, Mike?"

"I guess I didn't mention it to you at the time, perhaps because I didn't want to admit its significance to myself." He went on to describe to Stanfield the stream of obscenities Janet had voiced briefly during the induction of anesthesia with sodium pentothal.

"Was that why you asked to listen to the tapes?"

"Yes. The voice and the words were the same, too. It was as if Lynne Tallman were speaking through Janet's mouth."

"I'm stunned," Stanfield admitted. "I can't believe it and I can't ignore it."

"I think the demon is gaining strength," said Mike. "Janet admits that it was the other personality who sent Gerald Hutchinson packing."

"That time whoever, or whatever, it was did us a favor. But what do we do now?"

"For the moment, nothing. I may be entirely wrong and, if I am, I'll be glad to admit that McCarthy's right and the simpler diagnosis of multiple personality is correct."

"Pray God that's true."

"I agree fully. I told Janet this morning that she'll be able to leave the hospital in two weeks, but she should stay in your apartment for another week at least. That way I can watch her and make sure there's no serum accumulation beneath the armpit incisions where I implanted the breast prostheses. After that, I've suggested that she isolate herself for a while and have offered my cottage on the Potomac just north of Indian Head."

"It's a lovely area. Sheriff James Knott of Charles County is an old friend and has a place along the river. We often go fishing there when the shad are spawning."

"I'm sure she'll be safe there while the swelling and hemorrhage beneath the skin of her face is being absorbed."

"When the tissues are all back to normal I'm planning a feature on your marvelous job of reconstruction," said Stanfield. "But how are you going to prove or disprove your theory about possession by the evil spirit of Lynne Tallman?"

"I operated on Dr. McCarthy yesterday morning—a face-lift. He and Janet will be on the same floor in the hospital for another ten days or so; perhaps in that time he can give us a final answer."

9

As the June days passed, Mike found his two prize patients making rapid progress in the healing of their wounds. At the end of the second week after the surgery, he removed the plastic protective mask from Janet Burke's face. He was gratified to find that the skin beneath it was already losing its dark color and that she was even more beautiful than the model from which he'd worked.

On a Monday morning Mike brought a bronze cast of the model from the foundry. Janet was sitting in a wheel chair in the sun parlor at the end of the porch, talking to Randall McCarthy, who had been up and around since the third day after his operation. He still wore a pressure bandage around his face below the eyes and his large nose projecting from it gave him a rather striking appearance.

"Beauty and the Beast," McCarthy had labeled the two when they first started sitting on the porch together, away from the constant going and coming of patients, nurses and professors, each with his queue of students in attendance or discussing the case just examined in low-voiced colloquy. No other patients were up at the moment, however, so Janet, Mike and McCarthy had the porch to themselves.

"The professor and I are planning to collaborate on another book as soon as I finish up the story of Lynne Tallman," Janet told him.

"We're going to tell the whole truth about the psi phenomenon that makes extrasensory perception possible," McCarthy explained. "Both the charlatanry and the real thing."

"Dr. Peters, 157. Dr. Peters, 157," the voice of the paging operator said over a nearby loudspeaker and Mike grimaced.

"Develop a system of ESP to replace a hospital paging system and you'll earn the gratitude of both patients and staff," he said.

"I'll start working on that as soon as you let me out of here," McCarthy promised.

"With so many quack cults springing up all over the world, you could use your experience and talent as a magician to create still another one," Mike commented.

"That would be easy, now that you've made a combination of Adonis and Cyrano de Bergerac out of me."

"Cyrano's noble proboscis didn't help him as a lover," Janet commented.

"That was because he only wanted Roxane, my dear. Me, I always play the field, and many women appreciate a noble proboscis like mine, as I already know. Why else do you think I made Mike here leave it like it is?"

"I've done stories on some of those crackpot cults you mentioned, Mike," said Janet. "For my money, they're just that—crackpot."

"How about the one Lynne Tallman was high priestess of?"

"I'm not wholly convinced that Lynne was a fake, but then she didn't claim to be anything except an earthly form of evil incarnate, a bride of the devil himself."

"Is there such a thing?" Mike asked. "A devil, I mean?"

"According to what Lynne told me, she had possessed several other bodies besides the one she was using then. Remember those four murders back in Alabama, when race conditions were in such a turmoil there?"

"Vaguely."

"Lynne claimed to have been responsible for them. She said she was working as a waitress in a hash joint and egged the men on who actually did the murders, by promising to sleep with them."

"Why didn't she stay?"

"She claimed to have the power of going from one body to another, but I never really believed her."

"Could she make the change at will?"

"I'm not sure whether the recipient of her spirit had to be willing or not, but Lynne was a very strong-willed person. I imagine she usually got her way—even in something like that."

She turned to McCarthy. "You're an authority on the paranormal, Randall. Do demons really exist?"

"My dear, we can't be sure of anything in this screwed-up world," said McCarthy indulgently. "If I believed in God—which I don't—I'd probably also believe that absurd story about God creating the world and then giving a rebel angel named Lucifer the right to do battle with Him for possession of the souls of men."

"In one theory," said Mike, "God sent Jesus of Nazareth as His Son to fight against Lucifer for those same souls, evening the odds a little bit. At least, a priest I talked to believes that."

"Balderdash!" said McCarthy. "There are no such things as evil spirits, only good and evil influences battling together inside men for control of their souls."

"Then you do admit there's such a thing as a soul, even though you don't believe in God," said Janet triumphantly.

"Soul is essence, sort of an electric charge. At best, it's able to galvanize—to use an electrical term—a group of cells into becoming a living and functioning body instead of just some chemicals lumped together. When that body is used up, or destroyed, however, the charge, soul or whatever you want to call it, must go into the earth—or flames—with the rest of the chemicals that make up the human body unless it finds an even more suitable body to inhabit."

"Spoken like a true fundamentalist," said Mike with a smile. "I must admit I never expected to hear that from you."

"In advanced parapsychology we're not concerned with what the soul—or anything else you want to call it—does after death. Once we can identify the source from which it gets the electric charge or whatever it is that makes human cells function, then we can free ourselves from the cage that is the body. Through the secrets of things like astral travel, we can let our ethereal bodies go wherever they wish."

"And do whatever they wish?" Mike asked.

"Naturally. That's the best part."

"Do you really believe this balderdash, as he called it?" Mike asked Janet.

"When I hear him talking, I can believe practically anything he says," she confessed with a smile. "He's a very convincing person; I only wish I'd had professors like him when I was in college. But when I'm away from him, the whole thing seems to float away of its own accord."

"Janet tells me she's going to be staying at your cottage near Indian Head on the Maryland side of the river, Doctor," said McCarthy.

"She's renting it while she's finishing her book," Mike confirmed.

"Two friends of mine, Roger and Rita Coven, have been looking for a place to rent during July and August over on Chesapeake Bay and wanted me to convalesce there until my face looks like something besides a blackamoor, but haven't found anything. Are any of the cottages in your area along the Potomac for rent?"

"I don't know, but I can give you the name of the agent who rented mine for me while I was on a fellowship in New York. It's Maggie Persons and she has an office in her home at Indian Head."

"I'll call Rita at their apartment and she can contact your agent. Roger is with the Atomic Energy Commission and Rita's a stenotype operator. They both worked with me at Duke years ago."

"I'd better be going," said Mike. "Want to go back to your room with me, Janet, and show me where to put this head?"

"Sure." She stood up. "See you in a little while, Randall."

"Don't rush, I'm going to take a post-breakfast nap," he said cheerfully. "Unless my psi power is strong enough to lure a particularly pneumatic nurse I've got my eye on into an empty room."

"You didn't like the idea of Dr. McCarthy's being down on the Potomac near your cottage, did you?" Janet asked as they moved toward the room.

"Why do you say that?"

"It was obvious in your voice; you see, I'm getting to know a lot about you."

"And I know almost nothing except what your uncle has told me about the Janet Burke who existed before the plane crash."

"You certainly know practically all there is to know about the one who has existed since."

"I'll try to spend more time with you when you go down to the cottage—unless you require complete solitude when you work."

"Oh no. I'm counting on you to come down weekends and whenever else you can."

"I was hoping you would invite me. With McCarthy down there, too, I can check on both of you until the ecchymosis clears up. Besides, I've never been exactly sure I trusted him, though I can't exactly say why."

"I felt that way at first, but nobody could have been nicer than he's been since we've been on the same floor here at the hospital, so maybe my first impression was wrong. Before the operation, he looked a lot like the sort of person you'd expect to go around pinching waitresses and looking through the windows of women's washrooms."

"I changed his face, but I didn't change anything else."

"Why don't we give him the benefit of the doubt and wait and see," she suggested.

Mike had just returned from a quick lunch when Maggie Persons, the real estate agent at Indian Head, called.

"I want to thank you for recommending me to the Covens, Mike," she said. "I've rented them the Lane cottage through Labor Day. Mrs. Coven asked for a place as near yours as I had available, so they'll be less than a quarter of a mile away."

"Did you rent it by phone?"

"Mrs. Coven called me first but she came down right away and brought a check for the first month. Quite a looker, too."

"I've never met them. A patient of mine, Dr. Randall McCarthy, will be staying with them while convalescing from surgery."

"Did you say McCarthy?"

"Yes. Why?"

"The check she gave me was signed by Randall McCarthy. I guess he wants to be near you for a while on account of having had an operation."

"I don't see why. All I did was a face-lift."

"So you're doing 'em on men, too. I'll have to take a look at him; been thinking about having one of those jobs myself. If you can make a man look good, maybe it'll be worth trying."

"Any time, Maggie," said Mike. "I'll even give you a discount. By the way, Miss Janet Burke will be taking the cottage for a while about ten days from now. She's finishing up a book and wants plenty of solitude."

10

On a Friday afternoon in July Mike and Janet drove to the cottage. She'd rented a car and he was following her in the Porsche, as they turned south on Maryland State Road 210, following the course of the Potomac. The sun was still a couple of hours high when they stopped at a crossroads store about two miles from the cottage. Mike went inside to buy the extra groceries they would need for the weekend and enough to supply Janet's needs until he came down again the following Wednesday afternoon.

There had been no sign of the other mischievous personality since she'd given Gerald Hutchinson his walking papers, and Mike dared hope it was gone forever. When they came, at the end of a private road, to the clapboard cottage sitting on the very bank of the river, with the back porch extending out as a short deck to where a powerful runabout was moored, Janet exclaimed with pleasure, "You didn't tell me the place was anything like this, Mike. It's absolutely beautiful."

"I love it," he said as he took a bag of groceries from the trunk. "This was the family summer place and, after my parents died, I kept it. The woods adjoining my land are part of a state forest and the next cottage is over a hundred yards away, so there's plenty of privacy."

"How can you bear to rent it?"

"I don't—usually. When I was on the fellowship in New York, it was rented to help pay expenses. Since I came back, I've spent nearly every weekend here."

"I hope you'll keep coming."

"Did your Uncle George have any reservations about our being alone together here this weekend?"

"Where my uncle is concerned, you can do no wrong," she assured him. "Besides, I'm quite able to defend myself. In high school the curriculum included a class for girls in self-defense— plus a few judo and karate tricks."

"I'll remember that and behave," he promised.

"From what the nurses said at the hospital you don't have any trouble finding female companionship."

"You can't believe hospital gossip, but don't trust me too far," he warned. "After all, I'm only human and you once promised to sleep with me—"

"What?"

"It was just after you called me back the evening before your operation and asked me to do the mammaplasties."

"I don't remember that either, but considering the results, I'm certainly glad I did."

"I told you I'd do them if you were in good enough condition after I'd finished the really important part of the surgery. Your reply was, 'You won't regret it, I promise you.'"

"Didn't it strike you as strange that I would say something like that?" she asked.

"I could hardly believe it was you; but when we played the tapes you brought from Chicago of your interviews with Lynne Tallman, her voice sounded exactly like yours did when you told me I'd never regret operating on you. And also when you suddenly let loose a lot of obscenities while Hal Petrie was injecting the sodium pentothal before surgery."

Janet sat down suddenly. Her face was pale, and when she gripped the chair, he saw that her hands were trembling.

"See if there's anything cold to drink in the refrigerator, please, Mike," she begged. "You're telling me things I can hardly believe, but I know they must be true, and they scare me. Especially when I recall how Lynne sounded on those tapes."

He hurriedly opened a Coke and handed it to her. "I guess I made a mistake in telling you all of this," he confessed.

"You said my manner and my voice were different when I asked you to do the breast operations. How about the obscenities you spoke of?"

"It was the same voice; you even used many of the words that were on the tapes."

"But how could I—?"

"Your uncle thinks you picked up Lynne's mannerisms and her peculiar voice from having been so close to her in Chicago. When your brain got shaken up by the concussion, small bits of memory probably popped out from time to time and you put them into words without remembering them at all."

"If that's true, how long could it go on?"

"I think it's over," Mike assured her. "When your brain settled down after the concussion and your strong will was able to take over again, those memories weren't able to surface any more."

"Let's hope so," she said fervently.

"I haven't noticed anything out of character about you since you threatened to sue me after the operation, and that was several weeks ago," he assured her.

"If you find me crawling into your bed tonight," she said, laughing now that she had regained her composure, "just remember I'm not myself and throw me out. I'd love a swim before supper if it's all right to use my arms that much. Do we have time?"

"Time doesn't count down here," Mike assured her, "and your axillary incisions healed long ago. I'll put on my swim shorts and set the crab traps so we'll have some supper by the time we finish the swim. You can change in the guest bedroom, it's the one where my clothes aren't hanging."

He was lowering the crab trap over the end of the dock, having baited it with some fish heads he'd bought at the crossroads store, when Janet came out of the cottage. She was wearing a white bikini and, at the sight of her, Mike caught his breath.

"Wow!" he said. "Venus herself!"

"I don't feel like I've got much more on than Venus usually

wore," she confessed, her skin pink from his admiring gaze. "When I called a swank sport clothes shop in Washington and gave the saleslady my measurements, she said she had exactly what I needed in swimsuits, so I had her send out a white and a blue. I hadn't tried them on before, so I didn't realize she'd sent what is popularly known as *le string*."

"Sheriff Knott promised your uncle to have a deputy check on you once a day, but you'd better not wear that suit when the policeman comes by or he's liable to arrest you for indecent exposure."

The incredible loveliness of her face with the crowning glory of her light golden-red hair, even tucked beneath the rubber swim cap. The lovely outthrust breasts. The beautiful symmetry of her arms and shoulders, the gentle curve of her waist and the swelling of her hips. The prominent thrust of the *mons Veneris* in front of the pubic bone barely covered by the bottom of the bikini. The slender but well-muscled thighs, calves, ankles and feet. Everything about her was enough to take away the breath of an artist —or a lover.

"Better not dive," he warned. "The water's plenty deep at the end of the dock but I don't want you to flatten that beautiful nose job I did on you."

"I'll be good," she promised as she came out to stand beside him. "Can you really catch crabs in that trap?"

"All we'll need. Tomorrow I'll show you how to make a casserole that will melt in your mouth."

He tied the cord attached to the trap on the bottom of the river to an upright. "The ladder's over there, you can slip in without endangering that lovely profile. It's a little slick, though, from lack of use, so I'd better swim over and steady you as you come down."

He dived in and swam to the ladder, hooking a foot around one of the rungs, and reached up to steady her as she descended it. In so doing, she was practically in his arms and he looked up to see her smiling down at him.

"Nice trick, that, Doctor," she said as she came down the ladder until her head was on a level with his. "You deserve a reward for figuring it out."

Before he realized her intention, she turned her head and kissed him on the lips in a moment of brief but stimulating contact, before sliding out of his arms as they were about to close about her. Kicking out, she shot away from the ladder and started to swim with a strong, practiced crawl toward a float anchored about fifty feet from the end of the dock. Mike followed her but by the time he reached the float she had pulled herself up on it to sit with her feet hanging over the side in the water, laughing down at him.

"Slowpoke! Aren't you ashamed to let a girl beat you?"

"I'm out of shape," he said a little breathlessly.

They swam for half an hour, then took the boat out for a run on the river, cruising past the headland that obscured the view of Mount Vernon, on the west bank of the river, from the cottage. It was almost dark by the time they returned and Mike emptied the crab trap of a dozen fine blue and yellow prey. While Janet changed into slacks and a blouse and rubbed her hair dry from the shower, he set water boiling in a pot to scald them in.

"It always seemed brutal to drop crabs into boiling water," she said, "but Uncle George assured me they're killed the moment they hit it."

"I'll back him up," said Mike. "Are you hungry?"

"I could eat 'em—claws and all."

"That might not be good for a healing jawbone, but unless you bite down on a piece of shell, you ought to be safe."

He picked up a wooden object shaped like a baseball bat but smaller and shorter. Tapping a large claw against the table with it, he broke the claw open easily and handed her the tip to use as a handle in eating the large chunk of succulent-looking white crabmeat projecting from the broken end. It took some forty-five minutes to consume the crabs and beer and afterward Mike dumped the shells off the dock.

"Helps to bring in the fish," he explained. "You haven't lived until you've dined on soft-shell crabs, Maryland terrapin, Ocean View spots and a lot of other Potomac and Chesapeake delicacies, including lime pie."

The night was rather warm and the moon bright outside, so they sat on benches on the dock after Mike had dragged out some sunning pads to cover them and sprayed on mosquito repellent to discourage the nightly visitors in the area.

"When I get too old to practice, I'm going to live down here," he said. "My grandmother left me an old-fashioned rocker—it's in your bedroom—and I'm going to just sit on the dock and watch the boats go by."

"It's absolutely beautiful. When I finish my book, I'll hate to leave."

"You can stay as long as you like, just so I get to come down on Wednesday afternoons, when I can make it, and weekends."

"I have to work, too, you know. The publisher wants my book as quickly as I can finish it and Uncle George plans to start serializing parts of it soon in the Sunday edition of the *Star-News*."

"How long before it will be finished?"

"A month—maybe two. I've got to write the section beginning with Lynne's capture and trial in Chicago and give it the final editorial revisions."

"Most of my reading is confined to medical journals, so I don't remember much about that story. How did they ever catch her?"

"Lynne thought someone in the group was jealous of her leadership and betrayed her. She occupied much the same position with the others as Charles Manson did in his 'family,' so everyone was supposed to obey her unquestioningly. She did mention that some of the men seemed to resent her being the leader, though, and it may even have been her lover, Armand Descaux."

"What was he like?"

"I never saw him but I know he and Lynne had been lovers for a long time. She said he considered himself the high priest of the cult, so he may have become tired of being prince consort and betrayed her. Anyway, he would have known she often went walking by the lake late at night and occasionally frequented a bar where she would pick up men who particularly attracted her."

"Perhaps Descaux was jealous."

"I never managed to get much out of her about the group itself, but she did tell me it wasn't supposed to be monogamous. From what she said, they were planning something big, too, and the others are to carry it on."

"Do you have any idea what their next project was?"

"She wouldn't tell me, but she boasted that she expected to be elevated to another level of power and responsibility in what she called the Kingdom of Darkness—"

"What did she mean by that?"

"In her mind, at least, she was an acknowledged high priestess of Lucifer—the devil—on earth."

"And you believed it?"

"I neither believed nor disbelieved," Janet admitted. "But some of the things she told me make it hard to deny that she was at least possessed by a demon. Nowadays a lot of people believe in things like that."

"A friend of mine, a priest, is the official exorcist of the Washington diocese. He always insists on having a doctor present when he carries out the rites of exorcism and has asked me more than once to help with one of them, but I never did."

"Why didn't you? Obviously you have a considerable curiosity about whether or not there is an underworld around us we can't see."

"I wasn't particularly curious about it until I got involved in the Lynne Tallman case," Mike admitted. "One thing I don't think I'll ever forget is the look on her face, in spite of the agony she must have suffered just before she died. It was almost as if she had put something over on somebody and was gloating about it."

Janet got to her feet. "Do you mind if I go to bed now? I still haven't gotten back all my strength."

"Forgive me for forgetting." He was instantly contrite. "Do you want to get up early or sleep late?"

"By habit, if not by choice, I'm an early riser, but let's get up when we wake up. Good night, Mike."

"I'll leave my door open in case you hear anything during the night and get disturbed," he told her. "There are some big frogs along the riverbank that go 'Baroom! baroom!' Every now and then you may hear a friendly raccoon scratching at the doors, too, trying to get to any food that might be available inside."

"I don't think I'll hear anything," she said. "Thanks for letting me rent your beautiful cottage. I love it."

"You can transfer some of that affection to the cottage's owner any time you wish."

"That wouldn't be hard to do." Her tone was warm, though serious. "But don't rush me, Mike. It's hard enough just getting used to the new me."

11

Mike awakened with his body bathed in perspiration, even though, as always at the cottage in summer, he slept nude. A glance at the illuminated dial of the bedside clock told him it was only about a quarter after twelve, but the breeze from the river that usually kept the cottage cool at night had evidently stopped, perhaps as a prelude to a storm, the distant thunder of which he could hear muttering far away. Ordinarily he slept very soundly, and he wondered what had awakened him, until he heard a splash from the river and, getting up, went to the window.

The moon was still bright, its face not yet covered by clouds massing to the southwest. At first he thought the splash had been made by a fish jumping, then, as he continued to scan the area beyond the end of the dock, he saw two white arms cleaving the water in a graceful crawl stroke toward the diving float. While he watched, the swimmer reached the float and the lovely body of a girl, easily recognizable even at that distance as Janet, climbed the ladder to the surface of the float. With a sudden spurt of his pulse, he saw that she was completely nude and surmised that, waking as he had and uncomfortable from the sticky heat, she'd simply pulled off her nightgown and gone for a swim to cool off.

She seemed perfectly happy as she sat there, a breath-taking picture of loveliness, pushing her hair back from her face, for she wore no swim cap, and splashing her feet in the water. Momentarily he debated joining her, then, exciting though the prospect was, gave it up.

She remained on the float for perhaps five minutes, then slipped down the ladder into the water again and began to swim toward the dock. He waited for her to reach the ladder and climb to the surface of the wooden planking, an even more lovely figure seen at closer range than she'd been on the float. Picking up a towel she'd dropped on the floor of the dock, she began to rub her hair dry as she crossed toward the back door, so he moved back to his bed, leaving her undisturbed.

Lying there, he heard the back door close and the soft pad of her footsteps along the short hall separating the two bedrooms. But when she entered the room and, still rubbing her hair, walked across to the side of the bed and stood looking down at his nude form, he had to hold himself rigid to keep from moving and betraying the fact that he had been spying on her.

For a breath-taking instant, he thought she might be going to join him on the bed, then he heard a deep chuckle in her throat that he recognized as the same he'd heard the afternoon when she'd called him back and asked him to do augmentation operations on her breasts. She left the room, however, and moments later he heard the bed creak in her bedroom, indicating that she'd gone back to bed.

For perhaps a half hour, Mike lay there, thinking about the scene he'd just witnessed and debating its significance. That the other one had been in control, he was certain; the deep-throated chuckle was unmistakably that of the strange personality—or demon, as he'd almost convinced himself—inside her that could apparently take control whenever and wherever it wished. And that, considering the possible source of the other being, was the most frightening prospect of all.

Mike awakened to the fragrant aroma of frying bacon and the sound of feminine humming from the kitchen. Putting on swim trunks, he went into the kitchen and Janet looked up with a smile. She was wearing shorts, a bra top and sandals.

"Good morning," he said. "If you don't mind, I'll just take a quick swim to wake me up."

"Take your time. How do you want your eggs?"

"Over light. I won't be long."

Mike swam to the float and back, then climbed the ladder and went in for a quick shower. When he came out, dressed in shorts and a polo shirt, Janet was just sliding the eggs onto a plate where four slices of bacon already reposed. The toaster was on the table with bread inside and a glass of orange juice was beside each plate. Both of them were hungry, so there was little conversation until Janet had poured a second cup of coffee for each of them.

"What else do you do well besides write, swim, cook superbly—and look beautiful even at this hour of the morning?" Mike asked.

She laughed. "The last part I owe entirely to you; I hope you're sending the airline a proper size bill. Uncle George says I'll have quite a settlement coming out of it myself, but when I look in the mirror and see what I look like now compared to what I always saw before, I feel guilty about even suing them."

"Don't forget how close you came to losing your life, or the pain you suffered."

"For my life, I have only you to thank."

"In the Orient that could mean I have to be responsible for you the rest of our lives." He spoke on a bantering note, but, when he continued, his tone was serious. "And the more I consider the prospect, the more convinced I've become that I want to do just that."

She reached across the table to cover his hand in a sudden gesture of affection. "Dear sweet Mike!" she said. "I guess the greatest gift any girl could want would be to have you fall in love with her."

"Why resist, then?"

"Who's resisting? But let's not go too fast. After all, I just got rid of a fiancé I thought I wanted to marry—until I knew you. Besides, I'm not at all sure you're ready to tie yourself down to one girl, either."

"I just told you, I've fallen in love with you—something I'd promised myself not ever to do where a patient was concerned. What other proof do you need?"

"Maybe a period of probation, to prove you're ready for monogamy. After all, you've already got everything a handsome bachelor could desire."

"Except you."

"You can get along. I found a pair of pantyhose under the lining paper in my bureau drawer—and a half-full container of birth control pills at the back of the medicine cabinet in the bathroom."

"They must have been left here by the last renters."

She laughed. "Maybe, but I doubt it. I've got a book to finish, plus a case against the airlines to settle, and besides, we need to know each other longer. I thought Gerald was my ideal, remember? Although right now I can't imagine how I could have ever been that dumb. Let's just settle for knowing each other a few months longer; that way we can be sure outside factors aren't rushing us into decisions that ought to be made more slowly."

"Like what?"

"Don't forget that I'm really your creation, which naturally makes you feel responsible for me. You'll make other women beautiful, too; and as handsome as you are, a lot of them will be eager to give you anything you want—without marriage."

"With Aphrodite herself for a wife, how could I want any other woman?"

"Don't forget that I might be as much of a failure at the physical side of marriage as I'm a success in the purely decorative side —and that only because of you."

"We can easily settle that question."

"Not so fast, young man," she said, laughing. "Doctors' marriages are notoriously unstable, probably because so many of their patients fall in love with them, and want to prove it. Besides, until I'm sure just who I am, I couldn't very well saddle you with less than a whole wife."

"So what do we do?"

"What we're doing—enjoying each other's company, sharing pleasures less exciting than going to bed together."

"About twelve-thirty this morning, I thought we might be much more intimate than—"

He saw her eyes go wide, with surprise—and fear. "What are you talking about?"

"Don't you remember a midnight swim in the nude? Or standing beside my bed as if you were debating joining me?"

"So that's why my hair was still wet this morning?" The color had drained from her cheeks and she reached out to support herself by holding on to the table. "What happened?"

"Nothing," he said, on a note of regret, "but from the way you've just been talking, you want me as much as I want you, so what would have been wrong with our being together last night?"

"Mike, I don't know anything about what you're telling me."

"Are you saying I'm lying?"

"Of course not, darling." She was quick to apologize. "But even if we had made love it wouldn't really have been me. Tell me all about it."

He gave her a graphic account of his being awakened by her dive from the dock and watching her swimming nude in the moonlight, climbing the ladder to the dock once again and re-entering the house.

"You say I came into your bedroom?"

"You were within two feet of my bed. The moon was still shining and I could see you plainly. I lay still, thinking perhaps you were walking—or rather, swimming—in your sleep, though I had never heard of that before. For at least a minute you stood there, looking me up and down—"

"Were you . . . ?"

"As naked as you were, I always sleep that way in summer. You looked me over like a horse you were thinking of buying, then took a step toward me. I was sure then you were going to come into my arms, but you turned away and, as you did, I heard that same chuckle deep in your throat."

"Same? When did you hear it before?"

"The day before your operation when you asked me to do the mammaplasties. I'll admit that I was really hot and bothered by that time and ready for whatever you chose to do. But you just walked out and the next time I saw you was when I woke up and found you already up and cooking breakfast."

"I never believed it before," she said almost with a sob, "but how can I deny any longer that I really am two people, the one I know and a wanton besides?"

"Don't be so upset." Mike reached out to capture her hand—and was not surprised to find the palm wet with perspiration. "Someone once said the ideal wife is a grande dame in the parlor, a graduate of the Cordon Bleu in the kitchen—and a wanton in the bedroom."

"But I'm none of those!" He saw that she was close to tears. "I'm two people—and neither knows what the other does when she's in control."

He moved around the table quickly to take her in his arms. "If you're ever a wanton," he said softly, "just be sure it's with me."

"That's the whole trouble! I have no control over my alter ego."

"You did last night, although I'm not too sure I'm happy about the whole thing."

"Don't joke about it, Mike. When these things happen—and I'm myself again—I wonder whether I'm not losing my mind."

"Nothing's wrong with your mind—as Janet Burke," he assured her. "You had a severe concussion and your brain cells were receiving little, if any, oxygen for several minutes at least. Because of the oxygen lack some possible disturbances of function could be expected afterward, but you've been normal ever since."

"Except last night."

"Let's put that down to sleepwalking as the simplest explanation. It was hot and you already knew the water at the end of the dock was cool and pleasant, so you simply enjoyed it."

"And the latter part, when I came into your room?"

He grinned. "Maybe you've got a greater sex drive than you credit yourself with. Masters and Johnson proved most women do, if they can ever break through their repressions from childhood, largely instilled by their mothers, and free themselves from inhibition. I'll certainly not deny that, when I saw you out there on the float looking like Venus herself rising from the waves, I was strongly tempted to join you. And, when you stood by the bed in the moonlight, so beautiful that you practically took my breath away, I had to grip the mattress to keep from jumping up and taking you into my arms. But you went to your room, so your will power is under your own control, not that of some other personality—temporarily created by a few damaged cells—that will disappear in time."

"I guess you're right," she conceded. "Besides Randall McCarthy has promised to help me, since we're almost going to be neighbors down here on the river. You know his friends the Covens have rented a cottage nearby, don't you?"

He nodded, a little glumly. "I'm still not sure I like the idea, especially with him hanging around here every day, while I'll only be able to see you on Wednesday afternoons and weekends."

"If Randall can help me get rid of a bête noire while we're both recuperating, so much the better."

"Speaking of bête noires," he said, "do you know how to handle a gun?"

"Fairly well. Why?"

"Sheriff Knott's men will only drop by once a day on weekdays, so it's a good idea for you to be able to protect yourself between times. Wait a minute and we'll have a little target practice."

He went into the bedroom and came out carrying a .22 caliber target pistol and a box of cartridges.

"I keep this mainly to shoot turtles that scare away the fish," he explained, "but thieves sometimes raid these riverfront cottages—particularly in the winter when a lot of them aren't occupied—looking for radios, TVs and the like. I come down a lot of weekends in winter, just to get away from town."

"But not alone, the way I heard it. When I told Ellen Strabo I was renting the cottage, she said it was a lovely place."

"Let's go out on the dock and see how well you can shoot."

On the way out he dug some beer cans out of the trash container inside the back door. "That reminds me," he told her, pointing to a red fire extinguisher on the wall just outside the door to the kitchen. "If some grease catches on fire or anything, just grab this down and pull the pin with the chain attached, squeeze the handle and direct the stream of CO_2 at the base of the flame."

"I'm familiar with that type of extinguisher, I had one in my apartment."

On the dock he slipped a loaded clip into the pistol and handed it to her, before tossing an empty beer can out into the river. "Think you can hit that?"

"I can try; Uncle George taught me to shoot before he sent me to work in the Chicago bureau." Raising the pistol, she fired and the floating beer can flew several feet above the surface.

"Good shot! I'm not sure I could have done as well."

She handed him the pistol and he fired, sinking the can.

"I'm going to leave the gun in the bureau drawer in your room, along with the ammunition and a full clip," he told her. "You can help keep down the scavenging turtle population, if you like. And, if anybody suspicious appears, a shot into the air should scare them off. It would probably only be some young people from the neighborhood looking for a lovers' lane, anyway."

"What do you want to do this morning?" she asked.

"You name it."

"If you can find something to occupy yourself with, I'd like to start back on my book—at least for a few hours."

"I'll get a rod and reel and catch us a mess of fish for dinner."

"Sure you don't mind?"

"Not at all, I've been neglecting my fishing lately anyway. And don't worry about lunch, I'll call you about one, when the sandwiches are ready."

Janet stopped work at four o'clock that afternoon, by which time Mike had caught a fine mess of fish, cleaned and fileted them, and put them in the refrigerator. They took the powerful outboard downriver for a fast run as far as the bridge where U.S. 301 crossed a narrow section of the river, a distance of about thirty five miles. Coming back, the sun was just setting over Mount Vernon on the west bank of the Potomac, a fiery red ball that promised a clear day tomorrow.

"Sometimes I feel like this is all a dream," Janet confessed as they were tying up the boat back at the dock, "the accident and you happening along to make me beautiful."

"And all because you happened to get the assignment to interview Lynne Tallman in jail after the FBI captured her."

"I didn't just happen to get it. The chief of the Chicago bureau, Paul Mast, gave it to another and more experienced reporter, but Lynne had read some of my articles and refused to talk to anyone but me."

"How long had you known her when the request came?"

"The first time I ever laid eyes on her was on the TV news, when she was being hustled into the jail by the FBI after her arrest. Her asking for me was as much a surprise to me as it was to Paul Mast. It's strange but she seemed to know all about me, too: my connection with Uncle George, my journalism training at Northwestern, almost as much as I knew about myself."

"I read some of the articles you wrote on her. Is your book a rewrite of them?"

"The same material, but handled better, I hope. When you're writing for a newspaper, everything has to be done in a hurry to meet a deadline. Would you like to read what I've done—in manuscript?"

"I'd love to—but I should warn you that I'm no literary critic."

"This isn't a literary book but more a straight reporting of what Lynne herself told me. Of course, I checked the facts separately but they all stacked up."

"I'll be ready to start reading as soon as I can get a shower and change," he said as they went into the cottage, "if you don't mind getting us a snack later on."

"I'll do better than that, though I can't promise that it will be prepared according to the Cordon Bleu technique you said you demanded in a wife—"

"I didn't say I demanded that, only that some people do."

"Oh yes," she said, laughing. "It was the last part you wanted—about being a wanton in the bedroom. Go on and get your shower but don't use all the hot water."

The length of the manuscript surprised him. It was over two

hundred pages—with the story of the decision to turn state's evidence, the flight from Chicago, and its tragic ending, still to come. Mike read continuously with only a brief stop for dinner and, as he moved deeper into it, he could appreciate why Janet had risen so quickly to a high place in her profession.

From the typed pages, Lynne Tallman emerged as a complex human being, ruthless, unconcerned for the opinion of others, even a murderess when it came to heading a movement that was evil by every standard he had been brought up to believe in. When he put down the last page of the manuscript, Mike was startled to see by the clock on the mantel over the fireplace that it was after 1 A.M. Janet had been sitting in a chair across the room reading most of the evening, and he hadn't even realized she had gone to bed until he saw that the chair was empty.

When he tiptoed to the door of her bedroom, he saw that she'd left it open so the breeze from the river could cool the room—a gesture of trust and confidence that made him love her even more, if that were possible. She was wearing a filmy white nightgown and her bare shoulders were like marble in the moonlight, her hair a dark fan against the pillow. But he knew she was actually utterly beautiful and lovable human flesh, which the very thought of not owning for himself one day made painful beyond measure.

Obeying a sudden impulse, he tiptoed into the room and, leaning over the bed, kissed the sleeping lips. They softened beneath his own and her arms went around his neck briefly to hold him against her, but then sleep erased any hint of passion and she released him.

12

The next day being Sunday, Mike and Janet both slept late and woke about ten for a breakfast of pancakes, sausage, butter, syrup and coffee, which Mike prepared while Janet was showering after their morning swim.

"You can give me the verdict on the manuscript," she said when, satiated with food, they pushed their plates back and Mike poured the second cups of coffee. "I'm strong enough to take it now."

"I've never read anything so interesting in my life. You're going to be rich and famous! The way you write, you can easily make a success free-lancing after the Tallman story comes out—if you decide that's what you want."

"That's the trouble, Mike," she confessed. "Before I knew any better, I thought I was content with what I was and the prospect of marrying Gerald. Now I'm not sure of anything and, to make things worse, I don't know who I really am."

"A severe concussion could do that."

"You and Randall McCarthy assure me of that, and you're both tops in your fields so I ought to be convinced, but—"

The telephone rang, a jarring sound.

"Damn!" he said, getting up from the breakfast table and going into the bedroom to pick up the phone. "Must be my answering service; they have this number for emergencies."

"Are you up yet over there, Doc?" the booming voice of Randall McCarthy asked.

"Sure. We've already had a swim and breakfast. When did you come down?"

"Friday night. We were busy Saturday getting settled but came by late yesterday afternoon in Roger Coven's boat. Yours was gone, though, and nobody answered when I called."

"We took a ride downriver as far as the 301 crossing. Got back about dark."

"Well, don't worry about lunch today; you're both invited for an al fresco meal, plus swimming and skiing if you feel up to it. Come in bathing suits, that's our uniform for the day."

"I'll have to ask Janet."

"Sure, but don't let her say no. I want her to meet the Covens, since we're all going to be down here awhile together. I've been telling them about the fantastic job you did on her and, even through the ecchymosis, they can see what you did for me. They're dying to meet you both."

Mike put his hand over the telephone and spoke to Janet, who had come to the bedroom door.

"It's McCarthy. The Covens are inviting us over for a swim and lunch. How about it?"

"Fine with me if it suits you."

"I'd much rather be alone with you, but I'd also like to see what kind of neighbors you're going to have." He uncovered the telephone. "Janet says okay. We'll be over in about an hour."

"Whenever you say. We'll be expecting you."

Three handsome people were sunning on the deck of the Lane cottage, less than a quarter of a mile away from Mike's hideaway, when he maneuvered the boat in close to the dock and Janet tossed a mooring line to a lean handsome man in swim trunks. Randall McCarthy got up from a beach chair and came out to reach a hand down to help her from the boat.

"Your host is Roger Coven and the voluptuous blonde over there is Rita, his lovely spouse," said McCarthy. "This is Mike and Janet, folks; suppose we dispense with last names from the start."

Randall McCarthy had used the right word about Rita Coven, Mike decided when he reached down to the beach pad where she had just risen to a sitting position, her left hand holding the straps of a very small bra across her bosom but failing to cover much of it. Blond, blue-eyed and just enough on the plump side to fit the term McCarthy had used, she was wearing a bikini that was, if anything, skimpier than Janet's. Her husband was broad-shouldered and craggy-featured, with eyes that startled Mike with their almost flinty gray tint while showing no warmth at all, though he greeted them cordially.

"Randall's been telling me how Mike remade you into the image of the Aphrodite of Praxiteles, Janet," said Rita Coven on a note of envy. "I remember seeing a copy of the bust in the British Museum a couple of years ago and told him he had a hole in his head, but now that I see you in the flesh, I take it all back." She turned to Mike. "You're an artist, Mike—an artist in the flesh and of the flesh."

"I had some fine material to work with. Even though Janet's bone structure was all smashed up, it was basically good, all I had to do was put it back together with a few changes here and there."

"And the job you did on Randall! All these years I've been accustomed to seeing him as a leering and slightly aging goat, but you've turned him into a cross between Adonis and Cyrano de Bergerac. I can't get over it."

"His rhytidoplasty did turn out rather well."

"Whatever that means," Rita said with a smile. "Only one thing's wrong."

"What's that?"

"He was vain enough before; now he's become impossible. I guess he told you we were together at Duke a long time ago."

"Roger and Rita are two of the best subjects for research in extrasensory perception I ever had," said McCarthy. "Once, when I was in England for a seminar, we tried an experiment where Roger transmitted a picture of a rare kind of orchid blooming in the Duke Gardens. I sketched it perfectly from the picture I received."

"You must feel naked much of the time," said Janet to Rita Coven, "having men around who can read your mind."

Rita laughed. "It isn't so bad; much of the time I'm thinking about the same thing they are." Her meaning was perfectly clear.

"Don't let Rita's directness startle you, Janet," said McCarthy. "She's actually quite psychic herself—and a damned good stenotype operator into the bargain. By the way, how's the book coming?"

"I'm starting the final chapters tomorrow morning, after Mike leaves," said Janet.

"Which will be pretty early; I've got a hair transplant scheduled for ten o'clock," said Mike.

"Thank God I didn't need that, too," said McCarthy.

"Mike read what I've finished of the book last night," Janet volunteered. "He said it's pretty good."

"Pretty good, nothing!" Mike exclaimed. "It's absolutely fascinating."

"I'd like very much to read it when you finish." Roger Coven had hardly spoken during the badinage and the note of intensity in his voice startled both Mike and Janet. "I'm pretty sure Lynne Tallman was in a first-year physics class I taught at the University of Chicago, when I was a graduate assistant out there."

"Tell me all you remember about her," Janet said eagerly.

"While you two are talking ancient history, I'm going water skiing." Rita got to her feet and started pulling on a swim cap. "Unless both of you other males are so ungallant as not to want to tow me."

"We can use my boat," said Mike.

"I'll drive," McCarthy volunteered, "and you can ski with Rita, Mike."

"Maybe Janet would like to go," said Rita.

"I'm not very good at it and Mike's afraid for me to ski yet," said Janet. "He says if I hit the water at full speed on my face, he'd have to make me over again. Besides, I'd rather talk to Roger about Lynne."

McCarthy was an excellent driver and they took a long run downstream, then circled back. When they came in for the landing Roger and Janet were still in earnest conversation, Mike presumed about Lynne Tallman and the time he'd known her.

"Where'd you learn to ski so well?" Mike asked Rita as she was climbing the ladder to the dock, while McCarthy pulled the double ski line back into the boat idling about fifty feet away from the end. "You could do credit to the Cypress Gardens chorus line."

"I did a lot of water skiing on the TVA lakes down in Tennessee, while we were at Oak Ridge. You know Roger is with the Atomic Energy Commission, don't you?"

"I think Randall mentioned it when he told me you'd taken the Lane cottage and he was going to recuperate here as your guest."

"Roger's an engineer—and dedicated to his work. I could be out of the house all day—all night for that matter, except maybe Saturday—and he wouldn't even know it."

The implication was obvious and Mike had enough primordial male instincts to realize it.

"I hope to be down here quite a bit over the next few months," he said. "There's a local pub just beyond the crossroads called the Taverna Milano. Maybe all of us can have a drink together there sometime."

"All?" Her eyebrows rose into twin quotation marks. "I didn't exactly have in mind a convention."

Mike changed the subject. "I've never been to Oak Ridge. What's it like down there?"

"Dull. A lot of needless security measures and wives trying to occupy themselves without taking lovers—at least when they're first buried down there. After that they learn the ropes. The social life is typical of what used to be called the Lockheed Syndrome: tired unromantic husbands, dull bridge games, driving the kids back and forth to school, club meetings—you know the bit."

"You don't have any children, do you?"

"No, and frankly I'm happy with the whole thing. Roger's satisfactory enough as a lover, when he puts his mind to it, which isn't very often."

"I'm afraid Lane Cottage is going to be even duller than Oak Ridge, when it comes to diversions."

Rita laughed. "You're underestimating our friend Randall McCarthy. Don't forget that a psychiatrist wrote *Games People Play*. Randall knows a few games the author of that book never even heard of."

Lunch at three o'clock was delicious. Janet and Mike left soon afterward on the plea that Mike had to leave very early in the morning.

"You and Rita certainly hit it off," said Janet as they were driving the boat homeward. "She's very attractive, too."

"If you like voluptuous blondes who are practically panting to jump into bed with you."

She gave him a startled look. "I got the impression you weren't too unwilling—under other circumstances."

He grinned. "A man has to hedge his bets; it's foolish not to. Besides, I'm sure you're going to be seeing a lot of the erudite Professor McCarthy while I'm in Washington laboring in operating rooms or running an office."

"At least he paid some attention to me," she said rather testily. "Which is more than you did much of the afternoon."

"I was trying to find out a few things. Rita is inclined to be talkative after a few hours and a few drinks."

"What could you possibly need to learn from her?"

"Maybe it's just curiosity, but I'm wondering why the Covens would set up housekeeping down here on the Potomac on such short notice, just to accommodate an old friend."

"Didn't you say Randall is paying the rent?"

"I wonder about that, too. As an engineer and a high-level federal employee, Roger Coven makes a good salary, probably even better than Randall's. There has to be another reason for this setup besides the one she gave me."

"You mean you asked her about the arrangements?"

"No. She made no bones about the fact that the three of them find a lot of pleasure in being together—and I do mean pleasure."

"A *ménage à trois?*"

"Something like that."

"I've read about them but I've never known anyone who really belonged to one. How does it work?"

"If you don't know, I'm certainly not going to tell you; I'd prefer for my fiancée to be ignorant about such things."

"I'm ignorant about a lot of things, Mike," she said. "Once when Lynne referred to the 'missionary position,' I had to ask her what it was. She never stopped kidding me about it after that."

"Do me a favor," he said as they made the boat fast to the dock and snapped on the canvas cover. "Don't have any more to do with those three than you have to."

"Does that mean you're jealous—of Randall McCarthy?"

"Of course, but it isn't all that simple. From the start I've been convinced that something about him and the Covens doesn't ring true."

"Then why did you operate on him?"

"Who can afford to turn down three thousand bucks, especially since I plan to get married as soon as the girl I love makes up her mind? By the way, could Roger tell you anything you didn't already know about Lynne?"

She frowned. "What do you mean?"

"He did say he knew her in Chicago, and you two were talking intently about something."

"It's strange," she said on a troubled note, "I remember him saying he had her in a physics class he was teaching, but nothing else he said about her after that. Do you suppose—?" She broke off and looked at him imploringly. "What's the answer, Mike?"

"I don't know," he admitted. "The other personality may have taken over just then, but I can't imagine why. Just keep your eyes and ears open and call me if anything unusual happens."

"How can I be on the lookout for something sinister—at least, that's the way you make it sound—when even you don't know what it is?"

"If my suspicions are right and we're both vigilant, maybe we'll discover the answer—and the question. When we do, I'm pretty sure it's going to involve you, which is the reason why it bothers me so much. By the way," he added, "I keep a drum filled with gasoline in the shed over there on the waterfront corner of the lot, in case you want to go anywhere in the boat."

"I probably won't even use it before you come back," she told him. "Rita Coven offered to buy whatever groceries I'll be needing from the crossroads store so I can concentrate on my work."

"I'll call you every night or two," he promised, as they were eating an early breakfast the next morning before he left for Washington. "But don't greet Sheriff Knott's deputy, when he stops by, wearing *le string*. He'd be sure to mention it in town and you'd have libidinous males all over the place."

"I'll take my swims after the deputy has called," she promised. "After all, I don't want to damage your reputation down here as a solid citizen with impeccable morals."

Driving along the I-495 beltway west of Washington through the rolling Virginia countryside on the way to Georgetown and University Hospital, Mike passed the access road leading to Dulles Airport. Nor could he help wondering just how much different his life might be, if he'd been fifteen minutes earlier or later that Monday morning, when he'd looked up and seen the crippled 727 stumbling in for a landing at the big airport.

Now, however, some sixth sense warned him of danger to Janet, but he could think of no source beyond the possibility that a member of Lynne Tallman's cult might still seek to destroy her and her manuscript because of what it might reveal about others in the group. And with the county patrol watching for suspicious characters, that eventuality hardly seemed likely.

13

For the next two weeks, Mike was in seventh heaven. He drove to the cottage Wednesday afternoons and weekends and spent the time falling more in love with the beautiful girl he'd helped create than he could have believed possible. And she, he was sure, was equally as much in love with him. They saw little of the Covens or Randall McCarthy, preferring to be alone together. Then on Wednesday afternoon of the third week, when he would usually have left for the cottage at lunchtime, an emergency at one of the hospitals kept him busy until the afternoon was gone.

It was after nine when he came out of the operating room, after doing a tedious débridement—cutting away damaged tissue—and placing immediate split-thickness skin grafts on a large burn sustained by a boy who'd been constructing a rocket to be launched in his back yard. A relatively new technique for burns, it obviated, if successful, a series of several skin graft operations and diminished sharply the amount of scarring that would follow. When he rang the cottage before changing into street clothes, the line was busy and only about a half hour later was he able to get through.

"I was wondering what happened to you, Mike," said Janet.

"I've been tied up with a severe burn case and just finished the skin graft."

"Ugh! Don't remind me how close I came to having some of those."

"Are you making out all right?"

"I'm fine, working ten hours a day and falling into bed at eleven o'clock without even listening to the late evening TV news. Uncle George phoned this morning to tell me the publisher is panting for copy so they can start setting type, and at this rate the book will be finished in another ten days. A story like this one has to get on the bookstands before the public can forget a dramatic event like Lynne's death."

"Have you seen much of Dr. McCarthy?"

"He knows better than to bother me when I'm working and it's just as well he doesn't try." She laughed, a happy sound over the telephone. "It's stifling hot down here and I've been working in the bottom half of a bikini."

"Try sleeping in the altogether on a pad on the deck, if it gets too hot at night. I often do, when the mosquitoes will let me."

"I did last night. Felt real sensuous."

"If I'd even suspected that, I'd have come down."

"You're still coming Friday afternoon, aren't you?"

"Unless hell freezes over. Why?"

"I was going to fix a Bourbon highball tonight before dinner to ease my disappointment at your not coming and discovered that we're almost out of liquor."

"There's a cocktail lounge and package store out on the highway, I'll stop by on my way down Friday afternoon. Well, I'd better let you get to bed; don't work too hard."

"I won't. When Rita Coven brought the groceries I ordered on the phone this afternoon, she invited me to go jooking—that's what she called it—tomorrow night with them. I'm not sure I want to go, though."

"It might do you good, but watch that guy McCarthy. He's got designs on you and I'm not sure they're completely honorable."

She laughed. "I told you I had a course in self-defense in high school. If Randall tries anything funny I'll kick him in the groin, our teacher said that's the best way to disable a would-be attacker."

"Those new neighbors of yours are something, Dr. Kerns," said Jake, the barman at the Taverna Milano, when Mike stopped there Friday afternoon to pick up a new supply of liquor. "They were in here the other night with Miss Burke. Now, there's a doll, if I ever saw one."

"She's very beautiful."

"Looks like one of those statues I used to see in Greece, when I was on duty with the Army over there. But man, was she full of life the other night! And the professor! He told me you took ten years off him."

"Just about."

"Everybody was talking about how you made the professor over and gave Miss Burke a new face after that accident. Is she really writing a book on the Tallman girl?"

"Yes. She rented my cottage to finish the book. It's going to be published soon."

"That's one book I want to read. If there ever was a triple-plated bitch, Lynne Tallman was it."

Janet came out of the cottage when Mike drove into the yard. She was wearing a light summer dress, carried a bag to match and to Mike was the most beautiful thing he ever remembered seeing before. The discoloration of her face, he saw, was almost completely hidden by the dark pancake makeup he had advised her to use.

"Uncle George wants us to meet him in Alexandria for dinner," she told him. "We've just got time to make it."

"What's the rush?" he asked, kissing her.

"Might as well admit I've been a bad girl. Apparently, when I was night-clubbing the other night with Roger, Randall and Rita, I had one over the eight—as the British say. Whenever I do that, I always talk too much and somebody spoke to Uncle George about it."

"I stopped for a supply of booze at the package store and the barman told me you were really whooping it up with our friend McCarthy and the Covens. But don't you remember?"

"I don't even recall getting to the Taverna Milano—"

"It's a shame to have so much fun and not even remember having it, but you were there all right. The barman said you were the life of the party."

"And you're jealous?" She kissed him again, this time so warmly that he said, "Let's go into the house and do this for a while," but she only laughed and pushed him back into the car.

"That's all you get for now and, if you don't behave, there'll be no necking when we get back. You don't have to be jealous of Randall McCarthy, either; all he wants to do is seduce me."

"Isn't that enough?"

"I told you I'm able to take care of myself, darling. If Randall gets too physical, I'll just tie him in a knot. But he does keep me amused when I'm tired and depressed from working, so I owe him something."

"What about Roger and Rita Coven?" Mike asked as he turned the car around and headed for the main highway again.

"Roger's a deep one; Rita told me he's got a graduate engineering degree in atomic physics from the University of Chicago but he doesn't talk much about it."

"He didn't seem very loquacious to me, either."

"You could be right about that *ménage à trois* business, too, because I get the impression Rita's on the make for Randall. There's obviously been something between them for a long time and Roger doesn't seem to mind—whatever that means."

"I can see why you're a demon reporter, if you learned all that while three-quarters lit in a jook joint—"

"I told you I don't remember even being at the place. Rita told me most of it, when she brought my groceries from the crossroads the other day. Incidentally, she hasn't called to ask if I needed anything since."

"You must have really turned Randall McCarthy on, then."

"I love you when you're jealous, darling." She put her hand over his on the steering wheel and gave it an affectionate squeeze. "I guess the main reason I've been holding back on admitting just how I do feel about you is because I'm afraid you might look on me as somebody you created and therefore have the prior right of ownership."

"Do I? Have the prior right of ownership, I mean?"

"Not quite, but I'll let you know when you do—maybe as early as when I finish the Lynne Tallman story and it's no longer so fresh in my mind, along with the accident."

"When will that be?"

"Another ten days. Rita has asked me about the story every time I've seen her."

"Maybe Roger and Lynne had something going in Chicago. I remember that he mentioned knowing her the Sunday afternoon we were at Lane Cottage." A sudden warning bell rang somewhere in Mike's brain. "Has he said anything about it?" he asked casually.

"Come to think of it, while we were having a drink here before they took me to the Taverna Milano, he asked me to describe, in as much detail as I could remember, everything that happened between the moment the pilot announced he was having trouble lowering the wheels and when I was thrown from the plane and lost consciousness. Do you think that's significant, in the light of his having known Lynne in Chicago?"

"Perhaps, but it could also simply mean he has a normally morbid curiosity."

She shook her head. "I don't think the answer's that simple, Mike. My guess is Roger may have known Lynne a long time ago —probably even before he and Rita were married. He spoke of concussion, too, now that I think about it. Said he had one while playing football in college that left him with blackouts for months afterward."

"What kind of blackouts?" Mike asked, suddenly alert.

"Times when he'd suddenly come to—that's the way he described it—but couldn't remember how he got to be wherever he was. Or even how long he'd been without knowledge of what had been going on—exactly like what's happened to me several times."

14

At a Howard Johnson's Restaurant on the Beltway across the Potomac, Mike and Janet found George Stanfield pacing up and down the parking lot.

"What's the emergency?" Mike asked as the newspaperman waved them into an empty slot and they got out of the car.

"Come inside; we can have hamburgers and coffee while I explain, but I'm afraid that's all the dinner you're going to get for a while."

"If it's connected with what happened the other night at the Taverna Milano, Uncle George," said Janet, "I'm sorry I got a little tight and apparently talked too much."

"Don't sweat it," said Stanfield. "I should have known better than to try to keep you under wraps so long, but I was hoping to combine the announcement of your manuscript delivery with the announcement of the new Janet Burke."

"I don't remember anything after I had two drinks at the cottage. Liquor always did have that effect on me."

Stanfield beckoned to a waitress. "Hamburgers and coffee for three; we're in a hurry," he told her, then turned back to the other two.

"Our stringer for the Western Shore area was at the tavern the other night and phoned our gossip columnist this morning about your being there and causing quite a sensation. Since we don't know who else from the newspapers, radio or TV could have been there, too, I decided to unveil you, so to speak, in Sunday's edition before you find a TV news crew on your doorstep at the cottage. How much information could you give us from the hospital records, Mike?"

"You won't need them. The hospital photographer covered the entire operation and I have color prints of everything he shot in my office file on Janet, with permission from the hospital to use them."

"Good! That will save us a lot of trouble in putting the story together as a lead feature. We're going to print a detailed account of

the surgical miracle that not only saved Janet's life but also made
her over into a remarkably beautiful woman." Stanfield leaned
forward to study her face for a moment, then nodded approvingly.
"That dark makeup you're using now hides most of the remaining
discoloration, dear. The makeup artist I've hired to work with us
tonight at the newspaper studio can probably hide all of it."

He turned back to Mike. "What about the casting you had
made from the model you did before the operation?"

"It's at my apartment, with the rest of the material on her case.
I've been working on the beginnings of a case report and exhibit
for the fall meeting of the local society of plastic surgeons."

"Suppose you go to your apartment from here, then, and get all
that stuff, while I take Janet to the newspaper office, where the
makeup artist is waiting?" said Stanfield. "Did you bring that
bathing suit I asked you to bring with you, dear?"

"Yes. But it's pretty bare."

"The barer you are, the more newspapers we'll sell Sunday
morning," Stanfield assured her. "We'll be in the *Star-News* photographic studio when you get there, Mike. Just tell the guard who
you are and he'll help you carry up the material. Don't forget to
bring that casting model you made, either."

"I'll also bring a color photo of the Praxiteles Aphrodite from
the British Museum," Mike promised. "I called a friend in London right after I got the idea for using it and he sent me a color
print. It came too late for the operation, but it's a very handsome
picture."

"Fine," said Stanfield. "Molly Walker is our best human interest
feature writer. She's waiting for us and will start interviewing
Janet for the story while we're getting the 'after' pictures. That
snapshot I lent you when you were making the model will have to
be the 'before,' Mike, so be sure and bring it too."

"Hey!" said Janet. "Don't I have any say in all of this?"

"Of course," said Stanfield. "What do you object to?"

"Nothing, I guess. It seems I'm the cause of it all."

Janet was posing in the white bikini when Mike came into the
brightly lit photographic studio about an hour later. He'd brought
the bronze bust that had been cast from the model he'd made before Janet's operation. The security guard behind him also carried
a couple of boxes containing reproductions of her X rays and

prints of the photos taken in the operating room during the surgery.

"You made good time, Mike," Stanfield said as he came into the studio from the darkroom. "The first black and white prints are perfect. Did you find the color print of Janet I gave you before the operation?"

"Right here." Mike took it from the envelope and handed it to the photographer, who had followed the publisher. He studied it for a moment before nodding approvingly.

"This was made from a Kodacolor snapshot, wasn't it?" he asked Janet.

"Yes. Is that bad?"

"It's exactly what we need for contrast with the full-length color shots I'll be making of you." He saw the casting from the model and also the plates from the encyclopedia. "You know what would be sensational? A photo of that bust from the encyclopedia, the cast from Dr. Kerns's model and a shot of Miss Burke, side by side in a three-column spread." He whistled softly. "A beauty over two thousand years old, a model by Dr. Kerns before surgery to show what he planned to make you into and the final results, *à la* Aphrodite."

"But wearing at least the bra I have on now," said Janet.

"Okay, if that's the way you want it," said the photographer with a shrug.

"A bare shot of that gorgeous bust would make Dr. Kerns a rich man," said Molly Walker. "Monday morning, women would be queuing up outside his office begging him to give them bosoms like that."

"The lady said no and no it is," said Mike, firmly. "Besides, I'm already doing pretty well."

It was after midnight when Mike and Janet drove through the silent streets of Washington, down Constitution Avenue with the lovely mall to the south of it that, a hundred years earlier, had been an open sewer, past the White House and the towering dome of the Capitol. Turning beyond the vast spread of the old Union Station, they headed for the new I-295 leading southward into Maryland.

George Stanfield had suggested that Janet spend the night in his apartment and that Mike take her back to the cottage in the morning. She'd been anxious to get started early on the final chapter of her book, however, so she and Mike had decided to drive back to the cottage after midnight.

It was a beautiful night and, once they reached Highway 210, the traffic thinned out considerably. She curled up in her seat belt with her head on his shoulder and promptly went to sleep. Only when he pulled the car to a stop in the yard of the cottage and shook her gently did she wake up.

"You were certainly bushed," he told her. "Went to sleep as soon as we got out of the District of Columbia and into Maryland."

"I'm still bushed, but I wonder if I'll be able to go back to sleep, now that I've waked up."

"I'll fix you a highball while you undress for bed," he told her. "It'll leave you so relaxed you'll probably fall asleep on the floor."

He finished the drinks and knocked on the bedroom door but found her fast asleep sprawled across the bed. Her dress was already rumpled from the car and he couldn't see much point in not letting her sleep on in it. So leaving the door open for ventilation, he went back to the kitchen, downed both highballs himself, and crawled into bed.

He woke to the smell of coffee perking and the sound of a typewriter engrafted upon the normal bird sounds of early morning and the gentle wash of the Potomac against the dock. When he looked out his bedroom window to the back porch and dock outside, he saw Janet busy typing with the machine on a card table so the electric cord could connect with an extension leading through the open window of her bedroom to an outlet within the room. She was wearing shorts and halter and, as usual, was a picture of loveliness.

"Good morning," he called. "Any of that coffee left?"

"Look in the kitchen on the bar," she told him. "When I saw that you drank both those highballs last night, I figured you'd have a hangover and would need some, so I made a percolator full. There's plenty of aspirin in the medicine chest, too."

"I'll take a plunge first and then have coffee." Pulling on swim trunks, he went outside and leaned down to kiss her.

"Go on and get your swim while I make breakfast." She

pushed him away after kissing him back. "I waited to eat with you but I can't even type a word without my morning coffee so I just had to have a cup while you were asleep."

When he came into the little dining alcove about fifteen minutes later, wearing old jeans and a T shirt, breakfast was on the table.

"I figured you'd be working today, so I put on some working clothes, too," he explained as he tackled bacon and eggs. "Thought I'd better clean the yard up a bit."

"It's going to be hot out there."

"If the going gets tough, I can always hop into the water and cool off," he assured her. "I keep a small garden tractor in the shed along with gasoline for the boat and I can at least cut the weeds and high grass and rake them into a pile near the riverbank. Tossed into water, they make a fine bed for bream and crappie and those fish will come in handy as food in our retiring years."

"You think of everything, don't you?"

"Not everything. The prospect of spending the rest of my life with the most beautiful girl in the world, watching her grow fat with pregnancy, then produce a couple of small deities like herself, pretty well boggles my mind and shuts out everything else."

"If I do decide to marry you, I wouldn't mind the girl looking like me, but I would certainly want our son to look like you and be a fine surgeon like his daddy." She carried her dishes to the sink. "But if I don't stop looking into the future and get the book finished, somebody else is going to beat me to it."

"Why don't you stop resisting what you really want to do and marry me right away?"

She was rinsing her plate before putting it into the dishwasher but stopped suddenly, staring at the backboard. When she spoke, her tone was strained.

"I told you the other night, I've got to find out who I am, Mike. The trouble is I can't escape the conviction—maybe I'd better say the fear—that I'm also somebody else besides who I am right now. I'm not too sure that somebody else is really very nice, either."

He was surprised to see that she was trembling and quickly circled the table to take her in his arms.

"You're still worrying about the other night, when you don't even remember being the belle of the ball at the Taverna Milano, aren't you?"

"Not just that. One morning last week my hair was damp when I woke up, as if I'd gone swimming again during the night, like I did the first night we were here."

"Wish I'd been here."

"It's nothing to joke about, darling. First the swim and then not remembering what I did or said at that jook joint. What am I going to do if these strange things keep happening?"

"Marrying me would be one solution."

"I can't do that, never knowing when I'll turn into somebody else—and maybe be unfaithful to you."

"I've an idea this other personality"—he wished he could believe it was simply that—"isn't strong enough to make you do something your personal moral code wouldn't let you do. What worries me most is that you might drown while swimming alone, or take the car out and have an accident. Why don't you come back to the city where your uncle and I can watch over you?"

She shook her head firmly at that suggestion. "I'm making too much progress with the book and, besides, I love the cottage, the river, and everything about it. Whatever this other me is—and I'm not as convinced as you and Randall seem to be that it's simply another personality—I've got to lick it myself."

"But—"

"You just said my moral code is strong—and it is. Even during the blackouts, no man is going to take advantage of me."

"They may try—especially after tomorrow, when the *Star-News* will carry that feature story about you. Is that pistol where you can get to it easily?"

"It's in the dresser drawer, where you left it."

"Maybe I'd better put the clip in before I leave, just in case."

"I already did. The other night I put out one of the set lines you had in the shed and baited it to get some fish for dinner. When I got up I'd caught two fine spots—but a damn turtle had eaten both of 'em right down to the heads. He kept swimming around there with his head out of the water like he was daring me to resent what he'd done, so I went inside and got the pistol. When that soft-nosed bullet hit him, he exploded like a balloon."

Mike laughed. "I'll have to make a note to announce myself by telephone from the service station on the highway when I'm coming here from now on. I sure don't want one of those bullets tearing a hole in me."

15

Mike was cutting weeds with the tractor near the water's edge later that morning when the Covens' motorboat idled to a stop at the dock. Only Randall McCarthy was aboard.

"Roger and Rita have gone into Washington and I can hear Janet typing inside," the psychiatrist called. "Since we've both been deserted, how about going fishing with me."

"Haven't got the time. As soon as I cut down the weeds around the cottage, I've got to rake them up and dump them in the water to make a fish bed."

"I'll help you; fishing alone is no fun anyway." McCarthy made a line from the boat fast to one of the supports. "How about a beer? I've got two six-packs in the cooler."

"That I can take." Switching off the tractor, Mike came along the bank of the river to where a tree grew over the edge along the side of the dock, shading it at that time of the morning. Sitting on the dock, he took the can McCarthy opened for him and drank deeply before putting it down. "That's good." He couldn't quite keep the grudging note from his tone when he added, "Thanks."

"Something's eating you and it obviously concerns me." McCarthy looked at him over the top of the can he was holding. "Want to get it off your chest?"

"You can start by explaining why you chose to recuperate here so close to where you knew Janet was planning to stay."

"That's easy. I'd spent some time down here on the Potomac once before and loved it. Janet's a lovely girl and any man would be attracted to her for physical reasons alone, as you are. But she's also quite intelligent and sincere—something you don't find in pretty young girls very often any more. I enjoy Janet's company and I hope she enjoys mine, so, since we're both to be in isolation, so to speak, for maybe a month or more, there was no logical reason why we shouldn't be in fairly close touch."

"To the extent that you're paying the rent for the Lane cottage?"

"You *have* done your homework and I don't blame you for it."

McCarthy's tone was still cordial. "The Covens and I are old friends from Duke; we worked together at the parapsychology laboratory there for several years. Rita and I had quite a thing going, too, while she was single, but she realized I wasn't the marrying kind and chose Roger. When they came to Washington we got in touch, but Roger often works late on some secret project the Atomic Energy Commission has got him on, so Rita and I spend a good deal of time together—very pleasantly, too."

"Does Coven know?"

"Really, Mike, you're not that naïve. Arrangements of this sort, where a passionate and desirable woman is concerned and the husband has neither the time, nor the desire, to satisfy her needs, are quite common, though more often the other way round in Washington."

"I'm afraid I'm too old-fashioned for that sort of thing."

"Stay that way; you're much too good a surgeon to be mixed up in divorce, keeping mistresses and the sophisticated techniques that are often called sexual perversion by the great unwashed. Besides, too, Janet's midwestern upbringing has left her with far too high standards for anything less than marriage. Anyway, as I was saying, the Covens and I have been friends since college days, so, when I needed a place to recuperate and they wanted a vacation, I rented the cottage and they treat me as a guest—at no other cost."

"Sounds cozy."

"We like it. Now that you know all about what you no doubt consider a sordid story, what's bugging you, friend?"

"I guess I need your advice as a psychiatrist."

"Surely not for yourself. I never saw a more normal man."

"It's Janet. As you already know, ever since the airport accident she's been subject to what she calls blackouts like the one that brought on the hassle about whether or not she signed the permission sheets."

"Spells of unconsciousness are not uncommon after severe concussion—I don't have to tell you that. She was unconscious for nearly thirty-six hours, too, so some cells in her brain could have been damaged."

"The thing that worries me—and Janet, too—is the blackout periods."

"Maybe you'd better explain what you mean by the term, Mike. It does cover a lot of medical conditions, you know."

Mike gave McCarthy a quick rundown on the morning Janet discovered she'd gone swimming alone during the night and also the disturbing fact that she didn't remember going to the Taverna Milano with McCarthy and the Covens.

"The other night I can easily explain," said McCarthy. "As Janet told you, we stopped by to see if she wouldn't go with us jooking, as Rita learned to call it down in Tennessee. She didn't want to, so we all had a drink of that potent—and delicious— Bourbon you stock. What is it?"

"Wild Turkey, 101 proof."

"A nectar for the gods, however plebian the name. Anyway, we all had a couple of rounds together and, if I might say so, your girl friend's tongue got pretty loose. Janet then decided to go with us, and, believe me, she was the life of the party."

"Didn't you think her behavior was a bit out of character?"

"A lot of people are considerably different under the influence of alcohol, my friend, and she had enough to do the trick, considering that she wasn't accustomed to drinking. I'll admit to being surprised at how much she did loosen up, but then girls who've been pretty inhibited before often do."

"She doesn't even remember going with you. How do you explain that, if not by one of what she calls 'blackouts'?"

McCarthy frowned. "You say she remembers nothing?"

"Not a thing after all of you left the cottage."

"That is odd; she seemed to be in full possession of her faculties at the tavern. We danced a little, and she talked to Roger while Rita and I were dancing, but she made sense."

"What worries me most," Mike admitted, "is the possibility of sexual involvement—"

"There wasn't any that night, take my word for it. I'm no prude but I don't go around seducing girls when they're too loaded to know what they're doing."

"What about Roger?"

"Not a chance; the only thing of that kind that turns Roger on is something kinky. Janet can be very provocative when she's loaded but she's a teaser—the kind that takes you right up to the threshold, then suddenly turns on you in anger. That's all right, as long as she stays with the right people when she's loaded, but in other company she could wind up being raped."

"That worries me more than anything else."

"In your place I'd advise her to play down the wanton act, if she's not prepared to go through with it, else she might wind up the victim of a gang bang. I've seen a few of those in consultation afterward—as a psychiatrist. What happens to the mind is even worse than what happens to the body, if that's possible."

"Could we be dealing with a true case of multiple personality?" Mike asked.

"Possibly. I couldn't be sure without a complete psychiatric examination, and even then, maybe not. A number of bona fide cases have been reported, though, with two or more personalities occupying the same body and in control at different times. They're often almost exact opposites, too, like the difference between Janet's normal actions and the way she was at the Taverna Milano the other night."

"While one personality is in control, doesn't the other one know what's going on?"

"Often there's a complete memory blank, but I happen to believe some restraints from the submerged personality are still in operation. Certainly, watching Janet's behavior the other night, I would say that's the case."

"What do you mean by that?"

"Well, if *you* had been there, granted that Janet's in love with you, the ending might have had quite a different character. Generally speaking, however, the change from one personality to another is sudden and the second personality knows nothing about how she—they're more common in women than men—got to where she finds herself. In fact, the abnormal personality—if you can ever tell which one is normal and which one is abnormal—often decamps when it gets into a hot spot, like the possibility I've referred to in Janet's case."

"Then you're unwilling to diagnose Janet as being a multiple personality?"

"I just finished telling you I'd have to make a complete study," said McCarthy. "Until I stopped by this morning, I would have diagnosed Janet as a lovely girl who isn't accustomed to drinking and got loaded the other night without really knowing what was happening. Fortunately she was with friends, so when we came back, Rita put her to bed."

"Thank God for that."

"I'm not surprised either that Janet doesn't remember what

happened," said McCarthy. "An alcoholic neophyte on the first binge frequently doesn't—or at least is so anxious not to remember that the mind shuts down a curtain before the memory."

"What about those other happenings? Not remembering asking for the mammaplasties and such?"

"Put them down to a brain shaken up by concussion that hasn't quite settled down yet. Satisfied?"

"No. But I appreciate your being frank with me—also the reassurance about what happened that night."

"Mike, my boy, I'm a self-admitted rake and not at all ashamed of it," said the psychiatrist. "I deal in what are often called occult phenomena by those who don't know much about legitimate paranormal psychology, but I'm not in league with the devil."

Janet came out as Mike was piling up the cut grass and weeds with the rake attachment of the small tractor after the psychiatrist had left.

"Ready for lunch?" she asked. "You and Randall were having such a deep conversation I didn't want to interrupt. Besides, we only have ham enough left for two."

"I'll catch some crabs for dinner," he promised as he cut off the ignition. "And I'll bring you a supply of ham from the convenience store at the crossroads when I go to get the Sunday papers tomorrow morning."

"I'll be afraid to look at them," she confessed.

"You don't need to be. By this time tomorrow the world will know you're one of the most beautiful creatures in it."

"Incidentally," he said as they were sitting down to a lunch of ham sandwiches, cottage cheese and applesauce, "you don't have to worry about anything that happened at the Taverna Milano the other night. McCarthy says you were the life of the party and provocative enough to give every man there a case of the hots, but that's as far as it went. In spite of his free-wheeling sex habits, the guy's a gentleman and assures me that you came out of it with your virtue intact."

"What else of an intimate nature did you two discuss about me?" she asked, a little stiffly.

"Nothing. He did say I ought to warn you against what might happen if you're the way you were the other night around other men, but what bugs me is why you're never like that with me."

"Just think what you've got to look forward to," she told him and leaned over to kiss him. "Please forgive me for being snippy, I guess the real truth is that I got drunk and made a fool of myself. It won't happen again."

He grinned. "If it does, just make sure it happens when I'm around."

"Would you have been as noble as Randall McCarthy was?"

"Frankly, I doubt it, but fortunately this two-girls-in-one-body phase won't last, as lovely as both of them are. It's bound to be only a temporary thing due to the concussion."

"I wish I were as sure of that as you are," she said soberly.

When Mike woke Sunday morning at eight Janet was still asleep so, pulling on shorts and a T shirt without bothering to awaken her, he drove to the convenience store at the crossroads, where he bought a pound of ham, getting some quarters in change. Dropping them into the newspaper vending machine, he took out several copies of the *Star-News*. When he opened the newspaper at the second section, devoted to local news, he gave a soft whistle of admiration.

Andy Stoltz, the photographer, was undoubtedly an artist with his camera; the quarter-page photo of Janet in color, poised in the white bikini, was breath-taking. So, too, were the three smaller black and white photographs bracketed in a row in the other corner of the page. They included the plate of the Praxiteles bust, Mike's own model, and Janet's lovely silhouette, fully as beautiful as the goddess whose image had been carved over two thousand years ago.

Beneath the three photos was the question in heavy type:

"WHICH IS THE REAL APHRODITE?"

Molly Walker had done her job superbly, too, he saw. The story filled the rest of the page, with a small photo of Mike himself in a lower corner. In the interview Janet had given him full credit, both for saving her life and for turning what she'd called a plain Jane into a striking beauty.

Janet was still asleep when he got back. Knocking on her bedroom door, he called, "I went for the newspapers. We're the talk of the town."

"One moment," she called, then, "come in."

As she sat up in bed, holding the top of the sheet across her breasts, her eyes still somewhat dewy from sleep and her hair tumbled upon her shoulders, Mike thought she was the loveliest thing he had ever seen.

"Your Uncle George really went all out for you," he said, spreading the pages out on the coverlet before her. "By now you're the envy of every woman who's opened her Sunday paper."

"Oh, Mike!" she exclaimed after the first glance. "I'm really beautiful!"

"No doubt about it; you're going to have to accustom yourself to having men worship you—including one hard-working doctor."

"My creator, you mean! Everything on that page is your handiwork."

"Not below the waist. You had all that before but were so convinced you were plain that you didn't dress to emphasize your good points."

"I'll know better from now on," she promised.

"I only wish there was some way I could take a scalpel and cut out that other you, the one who doesn't remember what she does."

She nodded soberly. "That worries me, too. How do I know she won't make me do anything she wants—maybe even—" She broke off and didn't finish, but he knew what was troubling her.

"I'm not sure even the other one could take you all the way to the sex act with just anybody," he assured her. "At least I'm praying she can't."

"How can we be sure?"

"You love me even though you won't admit it yet and deep down inside you that love could keep the other one from taking you off the deep end, but any way you look at it you need psychiatric advice. Randall McCarthy has an appointment in the office Monday afternoon for me to do a little final trimming; he's seen you as the other personality and I'm sure he would like to study you from the purely psychiatric point of view."

"But if the other one seizes control again, can we trust him?"

"I think so. Short of shutting you away in a mental clinic, it seems to be the best answer, at least for now. I'll ask Randall to drop by the cottage occasionally in a professional capacity, but steer clear of Roger and Rita Coven, I don't trust them."

She smiled crookedly. "You don't have to worry. After the per-

formance I must have put on that night at the Taverna Milano,
Rita won't want to be in the same room with me, if any other men
are there. And she says Roger spends all his time either in Washington or working in that laboratory he's set up in the Lane garage."

"I've got to take emergency calls at the hospital the next two
weekends, but you won't have to be alone," Mike told her as he
was leaving the next morning. "I'll ask your Uncle George to
come down and spend them with you."

"I'd like that," she said. "We haven't spent much time together
in years."

16

"You've made a conquest," Mike told McCarthy when the psychiatrist was ushered into his office Monday just after lunch. "My
office nurse."

"The vibrations out there were good. Mind if I invite her for
lunch—and lust?"

"Lunch, if you want to, but no lust," said Mike firmly. "She's
happily married and the mother of two. Let me see about that tag
of skin just below your right ear. My scissors must have slipped
when I was cutting off the excess."

It took hardly ten minutes to inject novocaine into the base of
the tag, cut away the excess and close the wound with a few
stitches.

"Got a few minutes to spare?" Mike asked as he was applying
the dressing.

"Sure. Rita's having her hair done and Roger's at the Atomic
Energy Commission. I'm to meet them in front of the Union Station at five."

"They're an interesting pair. I believe you said you'd known
them quite a while."

"Over ten years. Like I told you, Rita and I had something
going and she's still a superb lay, double or triple."

"She mentioned Oak Ridge once."

"They went there from Duke, stayed several years until Roger took some more special work at the University of Chicago last year. It's been a center for atomic physics since the first test explosion under the stadium during World War II."

"Sounds like they get around."

"Talented people usually do in the academic world. Roger and Senator Magnes were boyhood friends, too, and with Magnes a big wheel on the Atomic Energy Commission since he got defeated for re-election two years ago, Roger can get practically any assignment he wants and chose Washington."

"I remember something about that election," said Mike. "Magnes was pretty bitter about it, wasn't he?"

"He had a right to be; losing by eight votes and all of them, plus some others, questionable. But Magnes was a Republican and, with a Democratic Congress in control, he didn't have a chance at getting the seat. He did deliver his state to Nixon, though, and was rewarded with a seat on the commission. But I'm taking up your valuable time and I have to stop by the university for a little while, too, so what's your problem?"

"This second personality that seems to take control of Janet's body at times: is it really possible that it could have been there all the time and didn't surface until now?"

"As far as we know, that's what happens, but I'll admit it's hard to explain. Just as it's hard to explain how one can be in control and the other have no memory of what happened, when the shift is reversed."

"That's what's got me buffaloed."

"Janet and I talked a lot at the hospital while we were both patients. From what she said, I gather that she's always been a strong-willed girl where her own work and interests were concerned, the very antithesis of the social butterfly type that is typical sorority material. It's not surprising, then, that the organizations she belonged to, in both high school and college, included the top scholars. She didn't do much dating, either, because she wasn't what is conventionally considered beautiful, which goes to show you how stupid men are in evaluating beauty. Except for the small bosom, which you fixed so beautifully, she's built like the proverbial brick privy. Actually her lack of popularity, I gather, came from the fact that, unlike a lot of college girls these days, she wasn't ready to flop on her back for any guy who wanted a roll in the hay."

"More power to her."

McCarthy grinned. "Spoken like a potential husband. Anyway, Janet knew perfectly well that she could be popular if she really wanted to, and one side of her emotional self, she says, kept upbraiding her because she was a prude. But her will kept that side under control by concentrating her energies on making a career as a top-rank newspaperwoman, which she was well on the way to becoming, even before the Lynne Tallman affair thrust her into the spotlight."

"Limelight is a better word."

"Anyway, there she is, making a career and secretly envying other girls, when Gerald Hutchinson comes along. He's the first man to really make a play for her and the first thing she knows, she's engaged to him."

"What I can't figure is why she didn't spot him as a phony from the beginning."

"Maybe she did, but she got bowled over because he was handsome and selected her. Then she gets thrown through that cockpit windshield into the middle of a severe concussion and Prince Charming comes along to make her into a raving beauty, with the added knowledge that now she can have practically any man she wants—including you. Naturally she's torn between being what she was and what she can easily be, a public idol in almost any field she chooses to enter, whether show business, the Washington social circus, or you name it."

"I name it being a wife and mother, but the way you've been talking I don't see much chance of that," said Mike glumly.

"With the second personality, no. That one may merely have been shaken loose when her head hit that terminal floor, however. Once we get rid of it, Janet's too sensible a girl deep inside not to know what she's got in you."

"Are you willing to help her expel the other one? As a psychiatrist, I mean?"

"Of course; she's one of the most fascinating problems I've ever tackled. But can you trust me?"

"Oddly enough, considering your reputation in the classroom and out, I do," Mike assured him. "But I'm also banking on the real Janet's love for me to keep her from letting the other one go overboard with somebody else."

"Maybe, but if you'd seen what you call the other one in action—" McCarthy stopped suddenly and, when he spoke again, it was on a note of excitement. "But that's the answer to your problem!"

"What the hell are you talking about?"

"You're worrying about some man seducing Janet Two, so the logical thing is to be the guy yourself."

"But how—?"

"Two drinks of Wild Turkey did the trick the other night and you've got all the trappings for a romantic interlude built in right here."

"It won't work."

"Why not?"

"I've already suggested it—and was turned down."

"But not by Janet Two?"

"No."

"Then you owe it to yourself—and to her, for that matter—to try with Janet Two. And all my experience with women says that will be something you'll never forget."

"It doesn't sound fair to trick her—"

"Believe me, Mike, to trick a woman who wants to be made love to into dropping her scruples with her pantyhose, is to do her —and yourself—a favor."

"What's the alternative?"

"Nothing I know of—chastity belts went out of style centuries ago and, even then, I'd bet there were plenty of clever locksmiths around." McCarthy got to his feet. "Does Janet know you're going to ask me to treat her professionally? So far I've only been dabbling around a little with hypnotism, mainly to impress her."

"I talked to her about it before I left. By the way, George Stanfield is coming down for the weekend; I called him early this morning. He isn't convinced that the second personality exists."

"He will be when he sees it."

"How are you going to do that?"

"I'll try hypnosis and, if that doesn't work, I can always give her a couple of drinks. That Bourbon you stock would bring out the sexy side of a snowman."

17

George Stanfield called Mike's office on Monday morning a week later, inviting him for lunch at the Gridiron Club at twelve-thirty. The publisher was at the bar having a drink when Mike came in.

"Glad you could make it," he said as the headwaiter ushered them to a table. "How about a drink? I could use another."

"Bourbon and ginger," said Mike and Stanfield took a second scotch and water.

"From the way Janet talked when I called Saturday afternoon, it sounded like you were all going to have a gala evening at the cottage," Mike told the publisher as they were waiting for their drinks and studying the menu.

"It was delightful. Janet's obviously very happy there and she's making fabulous progress on her book. I got a chance to talk to Dr. McCarthy, too, and I have to admit that I seem to have been wrong about him. He's got quite a sense of humor and, although I gather that he doesn't bother much about morals where sex is concerned, he's smart and immensely entertaining."

Their drinks came and they gave their orders: a small K.C. steak for Mike, with a baked potato and coffee; Stanfield, who was inclined to be a little portly, settled for a julienne salad.

"What did you think of the Covens?" Mike asked when the waiter had departed.

"She's obviously on the make, even for an old guy like me, and her husband doesn't seem to mind. In my youth that would have made them social pariahs but it seems to be accepted nowadays. Roger Coven's either a deep one or rather sour on the world, I'm not sure which. Anyway, something about him repels me, but I can't exactly put my finger on it."

"I felt exactly the same way, but they've been very nice to Janet."

"She seems to like them, too, and she's the one who's down there."

"Did the other personality appear while you were there?"

"No, and I wonder if you aren't jumping to too many conclusions just because Janet never could hold her liquor very well. Actually, I think she drank hardly at all in Chicago, so she naturally wouldn't have acquired much tolerance. A couple of drinks can make a lot of women pretty kittenish and that could easily be mistaken for something else."

"I hope you're right."

"McCarthy's been trying some sort of experimental treatment on Janet, using hypnosis, but I don't think he's gotten very far. Said he would report to you on it."

"I'm seeing him in the office on Tuesday to remove some stitches from where I had to trim off several small redundant tags of skin. I'll talk Janet's progress over with him then."

"I must say that was a remarkable job you did on him; I never would have recognized him. By the way, when I saw those Police and Fire Department telephone numbers you have posted on a card over the kitchen sink, I called my friend and fishing buddy Sheriff Knott from the cottage. He says there's been no sign of anybody in the area the police don't recognize, but I asked him to keep on having one of his men drop by every day to make sure Janet is okay. Even though Inspector Stafford doesn't think there's any possibility of that Tallman crowd from Chicago trying to shut her up, I'm not entirely happy about her being down there alone."

"I asked McCarthy and the Covens to sort of look after her, too. We haven't had much trouble with prowlers but some hippie types do camp out in that state forest next door. I lose a radio or a small TV every year or so and I often find evidence that young people have been using that dead-end road into the cottage as a lovers' lane."

"Janet plans to have the manuscript of her book on Lynne Tallman ready for delivery to the publisher by next weekend and I'm going to have a press reception to announce its completion on Friday afternoon in time to meet the deadline for material to make the Sunday edition," said Stanfield. "We're also using a feature on Lynne Tallman by Janet on Sunday as sort of an introduction to the series of excerpts from the book we'll be running several Sundays prior to book publication."

"Good!" said Mike. "That will bring her into town next weekend, when I'll have to stay in the city on emergency call."

"You're invited to the press conference, of course. I'm sure the reporters will want to ask you some questions about how you came to choose the model for rebuilding Janet's face. I don't imagine the publicity will hurt your practice any, either."

"It's growing every day already, thanks to the operation on Janet. I think half the bosoms in the District must be sagging."

18

When Mike returned from a fast lunch at the McDonald's around the corner on Tuesday, he found Randall McCarthy entertaining Mrs. Fenters, his office nurse, with the tales of his carnival days. Only a few minutes were required to remove the stitches from the small skin wounds. When the task was finished, Mike took the psychiatrist into his office.

"I suppose George Stanfield told you I failed to produce your girl friend's alter ego by hypnosis," said McCarthy.

"Any idea why the second personality wouldn't appear?"

"As long as Janet is the dominant personality, she can probably hold back the other one—unless she takes a couple of drinks and temporarily weakens her will."

"What do you mean by 'as long as she's the dominant personality'?"

"When I left here the other day I stopped by the medical school library and took out several books and journals, so I could refresh my memory. The emergence of a second personality in susceptible subjects usually means a lack of satisfaction on the part of the subject with her status. Most such patients hesitate for quite a while to let the second one appear—usually for reasons of conscience or even fear of consequences. When Number Two is finally allowed to emerge, however, the situation is often happier for them than when Number One was entirely in charge. Under such circumstances, the first often fades slowly into the background and lets the second one take charge."

"You mean the patient—I suppose by then you have to use that term—figures all this out?"

"Not at all. Changes like these are always unconscious."

"Always?" Mike's eyebrows lifted in a quizzical expression.

"They have to be, else one would be conscious of the presence of the other."

"One of the first things I learned in medicine is never to say 'never,'" Mike reminded the psychologist.

"Oh, I suppose, if you could study the memory patterns in the brain substance, you'd find some kind of evidence of the forgotten material," McCarthy conceded. "Particularly since we believe nothing a person thinks or does is ever really forgotten. That's why I was trying hypnosis on Janet, but I could never get her to a deep enough level to explore such patterns."

"What were you hoping to gain?"

"In an unusually sensitive subject—which she isn't—deep hypnosis frequently brings up memories of past existences."

"Like the Bridey Murphy case?"

"That one got a lot of publicity but there've been others. I think the reason Janet One, as I call her, refused to become Janet Two while her uncle was at the cottage was because she didn't want him to know there's a side of her nature that can be as deliberately provocative as we know the second personality to be."

"But if we could somehow bring Janet One face to face with Janet Two, possibly by making motion pictures of her while she's in the second phase, wouldn't that cure her?"

"Perhaps—if you really want her cured."

"What do you mean by that?" Mike demanded.

"You hope to marry the girl, don't you?"

"Of course. The only thing holding us back now is her insistence that she can't marry me as long as there's a possibility of Janet Two emerging and embarrassing me—or even being unfaithful."

"Why not convince her you want both of her, like I suggested the other day? That way you'd have what most men are looking for but rarely get—a conventional wife for business, you might say, and a very unconventional one for pleasure."

"Don't be absurd."

McCarthy shrugged. "Me, I'd settle for Janet Two any day. She's exciting enough for any man."

"By now you should understand the real Janet well enough to know she'd never be happy, knowing she might turn into another person of whom she'd be ashamed."

"What a pity she's not really two people, instead of just two personalities with one body. When I think of destroying that exciting creature I first saw at the Taverna Milano, it breaks my heart." McCarthy stood up to go. "At that she's lucky to be living today instead of three hundred years ago."

"Why?"

"In those days multiple personalities were considered to be witches, or possessed by demons, and cured by fire."

The reception for Janet, announcing the start of serialization of the Lynne Tallman story in the *Star-News* prior to book publication, was held in the *Star-News* building at five o'clock Friday afternoon. With free drinks and food, the turnout by the media, including television, was large. Mike stayed in the background, until Janet insisted upon pulling him out and crediting him fully, not only with saving her life, but with making her the beauty she had become. She did not drink during the reception, however, except to sip from a glass of ginger ale occasionally.

McCarthy attended the reception at the invitation of Janet and George Stanfield. The Covens had been invited, too, but had begged off. As usual, the urbane psychiatrist was surrounded by a jovial group whom he regaled with what appeared to be an endless supply of witty and rather scandalous stories. Finally the reception was over and the manuscript, which had been on display under guard during the party, was returned to the vault.

"How about letting a would-be fiancé take you and your uncle to dinner at some quiet place?" Mike asked when Janet had said good-by to the last of the guests.

"You two go out and enjoy yourselves; I've had it for the day," said Stanfield. "You still have your key to the apartment, don't you, Janet?"

"It's in my purse. Are you sure you don't mind, Uncle George? It's not like you to turn down a social invitation, especially when you're so fond of Mike."

"Just don't wake me up when you come in. I'm a heavy sleeper but, once I'm awake, I have a hard time getting back to sleep."

"I'll take good care of her, sir," said Mike. "Where would you like to go, Janet?"

"How about Wolf Trap Farm Park? I used to watch their taped folk music programs on Chicago ETV and loved them."

"I'll call and see what's on the program for tonight," said Mike. "They serve an excellent buffet dinner out there, too, before the performances."

"We're in luck," he told her when he came back from telephoning. "We can have a whole evening of country music under the stars. I made reservations for dinner and seats in the covered area, in case there are showers, but you'd better change into something less formal than a long dress."

"I won't be but a minute," she promised and disappeared into the bedroom she used in the apartment.

By the time Mike and George Stanfield had finished a quiet drink together, she came out, looking even more lovely than usual in a yellow pants suit and with a kerchief over her hair. By using the Washington Beltway, they made good time and were at the famous performing arts park, located actually near a small town in Virginia called Vienna, by seven, in time for the buffet. The food was good, the twanging of guitars, banjos, even a zither, and the nasal tones of the performers singing folk melodies both old and new were delightful. The crowd was mostly young and enthusiastic, as was Janet.

"I've never enjoyed myself so much in one evening in my whole life," she told Mike as they were walking through the vast parking area to his car shortly after ten-thirty.

"Are you going back to the cottage, now that the book is finished?"

"Monday, I think, if I finish shopping before dark. Uncle George wants me to take off another month before I begin working as a feature writer here in Washington, and I'd rather spend the month at the cottage than anywhere I know. Besides, Randall McCarthy wants to try another week or two of treatment to see if he can't straighten out the jumble that concussion made in my brain processes."

"How much has he told you so far?"

"Only that he calls the other one Janet Two and that she's very unlike the real me. What I can't understand is how *she* can exist and do things without my actually remembering them." For the first time that night, her voice had an anxious note. "Does she really exist, Mike? Or am I going off my rocker?"

"She exists, all right; I'm convinced of that, although I differ with McCarthy about the exact mechanism."

"I asked Rita Coven about the night they took me to the Taverna Milano, but she says all that happened was I got a little tight. She says liquor does the same thing to her, you know—it makes her sexy."

"With the difference, I'm sure, that Rita doesn't stop at merely *feeling* sexy."

"If I have no memory of what I'm doing when Janet Two is in control, how can I keep her from doing something I wouldn't do as Janet One?"

"The real *you* wouldn't let the other one do anything you have very strong feelings about," he assured her but she shook her head slowly, obviously not quite happy with his explanation.

"I wish I could be sure of that," she said, then her face brightened. "But there's a way to prove whether you're right."

"How?"

"I remember seeing a cocktail lounge on the road. . . ."

"There's a very popular one—called the Purple Pussycat."

"Let's stop there and have a nightcap. You haven't asked me whether I wanted a drink all evening."

"For a reason," he admitted. "I'm perfectly happy with Janet One but whiskey seems to let the other one out of her cage."

"As long as I'm with you, I'm safe, even if I become Janet Two."

The cocktail lounge was dim lights, soft music, and discreetly sequestered banquettes. They were shown to one and Mike ordered drinks. Janet's eyes were sparkling as she looked around the room.

"This is nice. Everybody seems so engrossed in each other that it makes you feel romantic."

"I don't need any encouragement to feel romantic when I'm with you," Mike assured her as they touched glasses.

"I wonder if an ancient Temple of Aphrodite wasn't something like this."

"The general idea was the same," said Mike with a grin, "but I've an idea the ritual of worship was a bit more advanced."

"I must read up on that ritual so, now that you've made me a goddess, I'll know what goddesses did."

"What the particular goddess you're patterned after did, I'd just as soon you didn't do—at least not with anybody but me."

He hadn't noticed her glass was empty until the waiter appeared at their booth with two more tall glasses on his tray. "Compliments of the management to the lovely and famous Miss Burke," he said before Mike could protest.

"He must have been reading my mind; I was just going to ask you to order another for me," said Janet. "They're delicious."

"And also potent."

"Who cares?" Too late Mike heard the throaty note in her voice and saw the bright gleam in her eyes that signaled the sudden appearance of her alter ego. "Are you operating in the morning, darling?" she asked.

"No-no," he said a little reluctantly, knowing what was coming and wondering whether he wanted to hear it or not.

"Then let's make a night of it." Her eyes challenged his with a fire that stirred him from his scalp to his toes. "If you're game enough to take me to your apartment."

"What will your uncle think?"

"That we made love—what else? Everybody does it nowadays." Her voice took on a coaxing note. "Don't you want me?"

"Of course I want you. But I'm not going to seduce—"

"Seduce!" Her laugh rang out, so loud and brassy that the couple at the next table smiled knowingly and the man even lifted his hand with thumb and forefinger joined in the universal sign of success and approval.

Mike realized then that he had to get Janet out of the crowded cocktail lounge before, as drunk and amorous as she was rapidly becoming, she created a scene.

"Okay, we'll go to my apartment," he told her. "I have to stop at a drugstore on the way, though."

"You innocent darling," she cooed. "Wouldn't think of being prepared when you're with that other straight-laced me, would you? Still, it would be a good joke on her to wake up in the morning pregnant and not remember how she got that way."

Before he could stop her, she'd downed the rest of the potent drink and gotten to her feet. She was already decidedly unsteady and he had to catch her arm to keep her from falling against the table. With his arm around her, while she leaned against him, laughing and rising on tiptoes every now and then to kiss him passionately, he managed with some difficulty to get her out to the car.

It was only a short drive to an all-night drugstore he knew of and his purchases were quickly made, but Janet was already asleep when he got back in the car. He was half afraid to wake her lest she would be herself again: the girl he loved, instead of this strange, though exciting, creature he was almost beginning to hate.

Driving slowly with one hand, while Janet slumped against him, he took the route to George Stanfield's apartment, instead of his own. Only when he brought the car to a stop did she awaken enough to look at the building. But when she suddenly stiffened, he knew she'd realized the truth.

"What the hell?" Janet Two snapped. "This isn't your place."

"You went to sleep so quickly, I figured you were too soused to make out, so I might as well bring you home."

"Well, I'm wide awake now, so come on up," she said with a shrug, then laughed as she got out and staggered against him. "You got me so drunk you'll probably have to carry me but, once we get up there, I'll show you how well I can make out—as you call it. And don't worry, Uncle George told us he's a sound sleeper."

Putting an arm about her, Mike managed to half drag her into the apartment building and into the elevator, praying no one else would be coming in late. At the door of George Stanfield's apartment, she fumbled in her bag and handed him the key.

"It's Lynne you're with now, lover." The words were slurred but perfectly understandable. "With the kind of body you and Janet gave me, I can make the real Aphrodite look like a schoolgirl gettin' laid for the first time in the back seat of a car—like I once did."

Having no other choice, Mike half carried her into the apartment, closing the door behind them.

"Be quiet," he admonished. "Don't wake your uncle."

Putting her finger to her lips in a gleeful gesture of conspiracy, she nodded. "Fix us 'nother drink while I get into something more comfortable," she said as she staggered through the door to her bedroom and shut the door behind her.

At the bar off the living room, Mike poured a jigger of Bourbon, ice and ginger ale into each of two glasses and carried them to the coffee table in front of the sofa. When Janet came out of the bedroom a few minutes later without bothering to close the door or switch off the light in the room behind her, Mike promptly forgot any intention his conscience had forced upon him to get her so drunk that she would fall asleep.

She was wearing only a nightgown of sheerest white nylon and, silhouetted in the light from the bedroom, might as well have been garbed in a will-o'-the-wisp. Crossing the room, she took the glass he handed her and emptied it like a thirsty man on a hot afternoon.

"I'm glad you brought me here, darling," she said in the tone that always set the hackles rising along his spine and made his pulse beat faster. "This way you won't have to sneak me out of your apartment at dawn to keep from compromising your reputation."

He had risen when she came in, and when she put her arms around him he would needed to have been made of stone to resist —and felt no desire at the moment to do so. Finishing his drink in one gulp, he swept her up in his arms as she pulled his head down so their lips met. The warm fragrant cavern of her mouth promised ineffable bliss, as her tongue explored his own avidly for a long kiss that did not break until he was forced to turn in order to carry her through the door to the bedroom.

"That's only the antipasto, lover," she said, laughing up at him. "Just wait till you see what the main course is going to be like."

At the sound of a key grating in the lock, her body suddenly went rigid and she slid out of his arms to stand momentarily in the doorway to the bedroom. Then as the door opened and George Stanfield stepped inside, she retreated into the bedroom, pushing the door shut, and leaving Mike to stand with his back to the bedroom door while he faced the startled eyes of her uncle.

"Hello, Mike!" said Stanfield. "When did you two get back?"

"Just now." Mike was conscious of a hoarse note in his voice and wondered whether Stanfield noticed it and would guess what had been about to happen when he opened the door. "We had a drink and Janet went—" He stumbled, then came out with: "—to the bathroom."

"Don't call her. I'll just go to bed; I'm bushed."

"Anything wrong?" Mike managed to ask in a more normal tone.

"One of the main presses broke down and I had to go to the plant to arrange for the *Post* to print our City Edition tomorrow morning. Tell Janet good night for me."

"I'll be happy to," said Mike. "Good night, sir."

When George Stanfield disappeared into the other bedroom, Mike leaned against the bar and mopped his face with his handkerchief. He didn't think the newspaper publisher had seen Janet before she closed the bedroom door but it had been a close shave, nevertheless.

When the door to George Stanfield's bedroom had closed and he heard water running in the other bathroom, Mike knocked softly on the door through which Janet had disappeared. There was no answer, so he opened the door wide enough to see that she was lying across the bed, still in the gossamer nightgown and with the light on, but apparently sound asleep. Stepping inside, he straightened her body out on the bed and shook her by the shoulder, with no effect. Even when he shook harder, she didn't awaken and he understood now what had happened.

When Randall McCarthy had tried to bring out the other Janet —the one she herself had called Lynne earlier that evening for the first time—while Stanfield had been spending the weekend at the riverfront cottage, everything the psychiatrist had tried failed. Which could only mean that the second personality refused to reveal herself in Stanfield's presence, with the obvious corollary that she had changed when Stanfield stepped into the room tonight. And not knowing what had happened, the real Janet had stumbled to the bed and fallen across it, out cold from the drinks they'd had since they'd stopped at the Purple Pussycat.

For a long moment, Mike stood looking down at the lovely girl in the white gown, sleeping quietly but with almost no likelihood now that she would resume the exciting personality and the promise of the night which had been so near fulfillment until her uncle had opened the door. Finally he shut off the flow of water from the faucet she'd left running in the bathroom and, leaning down, kissed her. And when the lips beneath his, though soft and warm, gave no sign of response, he left the room and the apartment sadly for his own quarters and a lonely bed.

19

Mike finished morning rounds by ten-thirty and stopped by George Stanfield's apartment, figuring Janet might be awake by then. He had to ring twice before she opened the door, looking utterly lovely with her hair down, her eyes still foggy with sleep, and a thin robe gathered around her superb body.

"Go 'way, I just woke up," she wailed. "I don't want to see you again—ever."

She tried to shut the door, but he put his foot inside and pushed it open far enough to take her in his arms. For a moment, her body was stiff, then all resistance left her and she collapsed against him, her face buried against his neck while her shoulders quivered with sobs. Finally, when she'd had out her cry and was quiet, he lifted her chin to kiss the somewhat puffed lips before wiping her eyes dry with his handkerchief.

"I—I woke up wearing only a nylon gown, so you must have undressed me. What happened?"

"You undressed yourself before practically raping me," he told her. "You'd had two drinks at the Purple Pussycat, plus another after we came back here, which is why you've got such a hangover."

"How could you ever look at me again, after the way I must have behaved?"

"Not you—it was the other one. Now go take a shower and brush your hair, while I see what I can find in the refrigerator for your breakfast. What you need now is loving care, coffee and food —in that order."

"But—"

"No buts. Scoot!"

She obeyed and he went into the kitchen where, after some searching, he found instant coffee and put water on to boil in a Pyrex flask. Next he started six strips of bacon frying while he set the table in the breakfast nook. When Janet came back in, looking considerably more like herself after the shower, he was ready to cook the eggs.

"That's my girl," he told her as he poured coffee for her. "You look like every wife wishes she could look in the morning, or any time for that matter."

"I guess you know now what the wanton you're always talking about every man wanting in his bedroom looks like—and does."

"Only what she looks like. Your uncle had to go to the plant last night and got back just in time to keep me from finding out what you could be as a lover."

"What am I going to do, Mike?" she asked miserably as he slid two eggs from the skillet onto her plate. "You saw last night what the other one can do."

"Marry me. It's still your best bet."

"I couldn't do that to you."

"Let me worry about that. I'm willing, even anxious, to take on the responsibility."

"Answer me one thing—I want the whole truth. Last night at the Purple Pussycat—I remember our going there but not much more—suppose I'd been alone and some man, or men, had invited me—her? Do you think she would have gone?"

"I—" He stopped, not wanting to answer the question.

"Tell me the truth, Mike; it's very important."

"I'm afraid the answer is yes," he admitted. "But if we were married—"

"You could never be sure where I was, or what I was doing, when I wasn't with you. And you couldn't watch me all the time; she's got a will of her own and I'm afraid it's getting stronger than mine."

Randall McCarthy had raised exactly that same question, Mike remembered, and the eggs he was eating suddenly lost their flavor.

"I'm going back to the cottage," she said. "It's the only place I feel safe—from her."

"That might be a good idea; Randall McCarthy still thinks he can help you get rid of her. By the way, you—or rather she—gave herself a name last night."

"What was it?"

"Lynne."

Her eyes opened wide in a sudden look of surprise and fear. "Why would she—I—do that?"

"McCarthy thinks you secretly envied Lynne Tallman."

"That's absurd."

"What was she like? Around men, I mean?"

"The guards told me she almost drove them crazy flirting—if you could call it that. She was always inviting them into her cell at night after lights out and I'm not sure some of them didn't go."

"Do you say that in your book?"

"Yes. Why?"

"My guess is that some part of you has always fantasized about being a femme fatale, with men at your feet; I understand that a lot of young girls do. So when the second personality finally emerged after the crash, she naturally took the name of Lynne, because her actions are patterned after Lynne's. I know that's what Randall McCarthy thinks."

"Then why didn't she go to bed with him?"

"He thinks your love for me would keep you from letting her carry you that far, but—" He stopped and did not go on.

"You were going to say that, after last night, you're not sure any more, weren't you?"

"I'm afraid so."

"What am I going to do, Mike?" The pain and desperation in her voice twisted his heart. "Last night proved I really can't control her."

"Last night you were with me and I hope that was why you were willing. But I still say marry me and let me worry about the future."

"I couldn't put that burden on you," she said firmly. "This is something I've got to lick myself."

"Then psychiatric treatment may be our only hope."

"Are you saying I'm psycho? Maybe even another Lynne Tallman?"

"No!"

"How can you be sure, when I can't?"

"In the first place, not even the worst part of you, the part that calls herself Lynne, could ever be like she really was. The real *you* has too strong a moral fiber to let Janet Two—I like that better than Lynne—take over your life completely to the point where you'd set off a bomb, for example, just for the thrill of destroying property and killing people."

"Darling, it's hopeless." She pushed her plate away, the breakfast half eaten. "I'm going back to the cottage, I'm safer there."

"I can't be with you for two weeks," he objected. "It's my turn to be on emergency call for the hospital."

"Getting away from you will give me time to think, and perhaps come up with a solution. I'll be safe from Janet Two down there; Randall McCarthy won't take advantage of me and I'm sure Roger Coven wouldn't. Rita says she hardly ever sees him from early morning weekdays until dinnertime."

"What does he do?"

"Something for the Atomic Energy Commission in Washington and, when he isn't there, he's working in the garage at Lane Cottage, making something. Even Randall doesn't know what this is and, anyway, I don't think even Lynne, as she calls herself, would go for him. Meanwhile, I'm going to do everything I can to keep her from escaping by cutting out drinking, since that seems to be the escape route she prefers."

"I've got some ideas of my own about what's going on inside you," he told her. "If my hunch works out, we may be able to get rid of the Lynne character once and for all."

"Oh, Mike!" She leaned forward to kiss him. "If you do, I'll love you to death."

"Try to stop a little short of exitus," he told her with a grin. "But up to that point, you've got carte blanche."

Before Mike could make any move in his plan to drive out the personality called Lynne, however, the roof—figuratively, at least —fell in. He was nodding over a medical journal in his apartment shortly before ten-thirty Wednesday night, when the telephone rang. Going into the bedroom, he picked it up.

"Mike!" The note of near-hysteria in Janet's voice brought him instantly awake. "Can you come down here right away?"

"Sure." He was still technically on call for the hospital, but her obvious anxiety was enough to make him decide his presence in the city wasn't that important. "Is anything wrong?"

"I just shot a prowler with your twenty-two." Her voice broke and he heard her sob. "He—he's dead."

BOOK THREE

THE THIRD IMPOSSIBLE

Evil Spirit is personal, and it is intelligent. It is preternatural, in the sense that it is not of this material world, but it is in this material world.

MALACHI MARTIN: *Hostage to the Devil* (Reader's Digest Press, 1976)

1

"Do you have any idea who the dead man is?" was Mike's first question.

"Nobody I ever saw." Janet had her voice under control now. "He pried off the lock on the back screen door and slipped in while I was watching TV. He—he tried to rape me."

"Where's the pistol?"

"On the floor. I dropped it after I saw him fall."

"And you're sure he's dead?"

"He has to be. There's a hole in his forehead and blood and brains all over the rug where he fell. I didn't have any choice, Mike." Her voice was approaching hysteria again. "When he saw me pull the twenty-two out of the dresser drawer, he drew a small pistol. It's on the floor, too, where it fell out of his hand."

"Don't touch it, and don't change anything," he told her. "Remember the card over the sink with the telephone numbers of the sheriff's office and the Fire Department?"

"Yes."

"Call the sheriff's office and tell them what happened. Then give Randall McCarthy a ring at the Covens' and ask him to come over and stay with you until your Uncle George and I can get there. Okay?"

"Y-yes. But please hurry."

"Don't panic, you're doing fine. Whoever he was, he was attacking you with a weapon, so you had every right to shoot him. Everything will be all right."

"I—I hope so. I'd better hang up and call the sheriff."

"That's my girl. See you in forty-five minutes."

It was only forty minutes since Janet's call, Mike saw by the dashboard clock as he drove into the yard at the cottage with George Stanfield and parked. A hearse from a funeral home at the county seat was also parked there, along with three police cars. As Mike and Stanfield got out, a uniformed deputy switched on a powerful flashlight, silhouetting the two men against the darkness.

"It's all right, officer," Mike called to the deputy. "I'm Dr. Kerns and this is Mr. George Stanfield, Miss Burke's uncle and a friend of Sheriff Knott."

"Go on in," said the deputy. "The men from the funeral home

just got here and are going to take out the body as soon as Deputy Thornton finishes taking pictures."

Inside the cottage, Janet ran to Mike, and started sobbing. He held her until she could gain control of herself. Glancing around the room, he nodded to Randall McCarthy and the Covens, who were standing in the corner; meanwhile, George Stanfield was greeting the sheriff, a burly man with a stetson hat and a badge pinned to his shirt front.

"What happened, Jim?" he asked.

"If your niece wasn't as brave as she's pretty, George," said the sheriff, "there could have been an even worse tragedy here tonight than a hippie prowler getting shot. Fortunately Dr. Kerns kept a pistol in the bedroom and Miss Burke knew how to use it."

"Do you have any idea who the man is—or was?"

"He's a stranger to these parts," said Sheriff Knott. "Probably one of the vagrants that camp in the state forest adjoining the cottage. They often prowl around at night, looking for a closed-up cottage to rob—or a woman alone."

"Why do you think he was just passing through?" Stanfield asked.

"We found a motorcycle with an Illinois license plate in the woods. When we get a make on it in the morning, the Illinois authorities can probably tell us who he is—unless he stole the bike."

"Mind if I take a look at him?" Stanfield asked.

"Not at all. Deputy Thornton should be about through getting the photographs and we'll hand the body over to the funeral home to hold for the coroner."

The corpse, Mike saw when he went into the bedroom with Stanfield, leaving Janet in the living room, was a man about thirty-five, with a scraggly beard and greasy blond hair tied at his neck in a pony tail. He wore faded Levi's, a khaki shirt and sandals without socks.

The cause of death was easily apparent, a round hole nearly an inch in diameter in his forehead. The soft-nosed .22 caliber bullet had obviously exploded the brain inside the skull as effectively as Mike had exploded the body of many a turtle inside its shell.

"I never saw him before," said Mike.

George Stanfield had been carrying on a low conversation with a deputy, who was holding a camera with a flash attachment. As it ended, Mike saw a bill change hands, then Stanfield came over to look down at the dead man more closely.

"Stranger to me, too," he said and went out into the other room. "Is there any need to hold Janet?" he asked the sheriff. "This looks like an open and shut case of self-defense and I'll be responsible for bringing my niece to the inquest, if you need to hold one."

"The coroner will probably be satisfied with that hole in his forehead and the larger one at the back," said Sheriff Knott. "Why do you use those soft-nosed bullets, Dr. Kerns?"

"For shooting turtles, so they won't eat up all my fish."

"That's an idea. The guy was carrying a Saturday night special and Miss Burke says he pulled it on her, so she was lucky to reach the bedroom where you kept the twenty-two."

The funeral home attendants came through, rolling the blanket-hidden form of the victim on a stretcher, and the sheriff's party followed, leaving Mike, Janet, Stanfield, Randall McCarthy and the Covens in the living room.

"I guess we'd better be going, too," said McCarthy. "When Janet called, we jumped in Roger's boat and were here in no time."

"It—it was horrible with all that blood and brains on the floor." Rita Coven's voice had a note of hysteria, and she swayed against her husband. "I need a drink."

"You can have that at home." Roger Coven's voice was curt as he took her by the arm. "Coming, Randall?"

"Sure," said the psychiatrist. "Good night, all."

"Since you got here first, the coroner may want the three of you to testify if he holds an inquest, but I imagine Sheriff Knott will let you know," said Mike. "Good night, and thanks for coming to Janet's aid so quickly. This has all been pretty rough on her."

"She stood up fine," said McCarthy. "A lot better, I suspect, than I would have done under the same circumstances. Good night."

"How about it, Janet?" George Stanfield asked her as the others were leaving. "Don't you think you'd better go back to town with us?"

"I'll go anywhere," she said with a shudder. "Anywhere except into that bedroom again. Rita was right, all that blood—"

"You won't have to look at it again," Mike promised. "I'll come down early Sunday morning with a strong cleaner and scrub the floor boards. Do you have any nightclothes at the apartment?"

"All I need. Let's go right away, please."

While George Stanfield took Janet outside, Mike got her purse from the bedroom, but made no attempt to do anything about the mess on the floor. Putting out the lights, he locked the door and went out to where the cars were parked.

"I'll drive Janet's car and follow you two, but don't worry if I turn off toward the county seat," said Stanfield. "I slipped the deputy who took the photographs a fifty and he'll have some glossy prints waiting for me in the developing laboratory at Jim Knott's office. Then I'll have to go by the newspaper and dictate an account of what happened down here to a rewrite man, so it will be a couple of hours before I get home. The morning edition of the *Post* will already be in the presses, so the *Star-News* will have a clean beat with the story for our City Edition shortly before noon."

"Oh, Uncle George!" Janet exclaimed. "Do you have to print the story?"

"I'm a newspaperman, dear, and so are you. The story will make the wire services before noon; you'll be a heroine all over the world."

2

Mike Kerns drove back to Washington much more slowly than he had during his eighty-mile-an-hour sprint from his apartment in Georgetown to the cottage on the Potomac. For almost half the way, Janet didn't speak but lay back in the sleek Porsche with her head against the headrest. He was hoping she was napping, until she finally spoke—and what she said startled him.

"Mike, there's something funny about what happened tonight. When that man—whoever he was—came into the cottage, he acted as if he'd been invited."

"Why do you say that?"

"He called me by a name—"

The realization of what she was saying hit him like a blow on the head. "Was it 'Lynne'?"

"Yes." She turned to face him and her hand reached out suddenly to grip his arm with a force that made the car swerve a little. "How could you know that?"

"Before I try to answer, maybe you'd better describe exactly what happened."

"Like I told the sheriff, I was watching TV and didn't hear any noise—except the frogs and the night things I love so much. Then I happened to look up and there he was, standing inside the room."

"Did he act as if he recognized you?"

"Maybe not recognized, startled would be the word I would use. It was almost as if he'd expected me to look like somebody else. I remember him saying, 'Baby, those newspaper photos didn't even do you justice,' before I asked, 'What do you want?'"

"'You, baby—all of you,' he said." She shivered. "I never heard real lust in a man's voice before, but I guess I recognized it by the instinct every woman must have when she's about to be . . . ?"

"Raped. Violated."

"No, his tone wasn't really like that. Actually, I'd almost swear he expected me to welcome him with open arms, as eager for him as he obviously was for me."

"You underestimate the effect your beauty has on men, darling. If you'd been listening to me the other night after I brought you home from the Purple Pussycat, I suspect you'd have heard something of the same tone."

"No, Mike. He almost growled, like an animal—as if he couldn't wait to get his hands on me. When I started backing toward the bedroom to get the pistol, he said, 'Don't play hard to get, you tormenting devil. Your name's still Lynne, no matter what you call yourself now. I rode all night and all day for this and I'm going to have it.'"

"Are you sure he said 'Lynne'?"

"Yes. That's what I didn't understand—even though you had told me I—the other me—had called herself Lynne the other night. How could a total stranger know that?"

Mike didn't answer, not wanting to admit, even to himself, the horrible thing that was taking shape in his mind. "What happened next?" he asked.

"I kept backing toward the bedroom and he followed. He was laughing, too, like we were playing a game he enjoyed because he knew he'd be the winner in the end. By the time I backed against the dresser in the bedroom, he was maybe ten feet away, coming through the door.

"'So this is where you're leading me, you little minx,' he said. 'Getting up in the world, aren't you? The floor used to be good enough for you when you were really in heat.'

"'That's what you think,' I managed to say, while I was fumbling in the drawer for the twenty-two," she went on. "When I finally pulled it out and snapped off the safety, he must have realized I wasn't really who he thought I was, for he jerked out that little pistol. I knew then he would shoot me if I didn't get him first." She shuddered. "When I pulled the trigger, he wasn't six feet away."

Suddenly she collapsed against him. "Oh, God! It was awful— seeing that hole suddenly appear in his forehead and hearing the bullet explode inside his skull, like an echo of the shot."

"Don't think about it any more," he urged as he stopped the car in front of George Stanfield's apartment. "I'm going to give you a sleeping pill and put you to bed."

"Don't you dare leave me until Uncle George gets home," she said as they rode up in the elevator. "I've had enough trouble for tonight."

"All right, I'll tuck you in and hold your hand," he promised. "It'll be quite a change from the last time I was in that bedroom."

While she was changing into nightclothes, Mike poured himself a stiff shot of Bourbon at the small bar and sat down to think. No matter where he started, however, the sequence of events recounted by Janet on the way into Washington kept giving the same answer. It was an answer he wasn't prepared to admit, but he could see no other solution, no matter how horror-provoking it was.

"You can come in now. I'm in bed," Janet called to him.

When he went into the bedroom, she was wearing pajamas, and a light robe was across the foot of the bed. When he kissed her good night, her lips were soft and warm from approaching sleep.

"That was a powerful pill you gave me," she said sleepily. "I—I felt so soiled after what happened tonight that I took a shower and almost collapsed in the stall. That tablet gives you a wonderful feeling of floating on air."

"Float away to dreamland, then," he told her. "I'll stay till your uncle gets here."

She was almost asleep before he finished pulling up a chair beside the bed. "You'll call me tomorrow, won't you?" she murmured drowsily. "I'll need help in straightening all this out in my mind."

"About eleven," he promised. "Maybe we can have a quick lunch together, if the newspaper reporters and TV people get through in time. You're front-page news again."

"I'd rather be on the society page, with the announcement of our wedding," she said as she drifted off to sleep.

Mike finished the drink and poured himself another but it didn't dull his mind to the fact that the girl sleeping so peacefully a few feet away from him, the girl he loved more than anything else in the world, was under attack by a malignant force he found almost impossible to understand, much less guard her against.

George Stanfield came in shortly after three, looking very tired. He poured a drink for himself before dropping into an easy chair.

"Anything new on the shooting?" Mike asked.

The newspaperman shook his head. "The deputy who took the photographs at the cottage says Sheriff Knott hopes to identify the corpse in the morning."

"From the motorcycle license?"

"If it wasn't stolen. He authorized release of the photographs to the newspapers, hoping someone who sees them will recognize the dead man, and took fingerprints that will go to the FBI as soon as their laboratory opens. If the prowler had a criminal record or was ever in the armed forces or held a government job, the computer will finger him in a few minutes. Did Janet tell you anything we don't already know?"

Mike briefly considered repeating the story she had told him, then decided Stanfield—conscientious newspaperman that he was —might feel obliged to print it, and gave up the idea.

"Nothing important," he lied. "I gave her a pretty strong tranquilizer, so she'll probably sleep till noon."

"Good! That will give me an excuse to keep the *Post* reporters from bothering her. I'll tell them she's had a harrowing experience and her doctor—meaning you—has put her under heavy sedation."

As he drove across a sleeping Washington to his apartment, Mike was still puzzling in his mind over the strange fact that, according to Janet, the intruder she had shot apparently thought he was expected at the cottage. But only as he was driving to his office in the morning, after making hospital rounds, did he think of a possible way to find out for sure.

At the office, Mike rang the number of the telephone company business office and was connected with a pleasant-voiced young woman who was in charge of his telephone account for the Potomac cottage.

"This is Dr. Michael Kerns," he told her. "I think someone may have been making unauthorized calls from my cottage on the Potomac off Indian Head Highway. Could you look up this month's bill so far and tell me if any long distance calls were made outside the Washington area?"

"Certainly, Doctor. What's your number?"

"Seven-seven-four, two-seven-oh-one."

She was gone only a few moments before she came back on the line. "There was a call on Monday, Dr. Kerns. Direct distance dialed, station-to-station after 8 P.M.—to Chicago 555-7677. The call lasted ten minutes and the charge was $3.65 before tax."

"Thank you." Mike hung up the telephone but stared at it unseeingly for a long moment before picking up the Metropolitan Washington telephone directory and looking up the number for FBI headquarters. When he was connected, he gave his name and asked to speak to Inspector Stafford.

"Dr. Kerns." The hearty voice of the FBI man sounded in his ear. "I was just reading Sheriff Knott's report on last night's events that came with his request for fingerprint identification of the corpse. Sorry to hear Miss Burke was inadvertently involved in another painful incident."

"That's what I'm calling about," Mike told him. "I'd like to ask a favor of you."

"Certainly, if I can do it."

"First, an unauthorized telephone call was made on Monday from my cottage on the Potomac—the number is 774-2701—to

Chicago 555-7677. I want to find out where and in whose name the phone is listed."

"That's easy enough. Did Miss Burke make the call?"

"Possibly, I can't be sure."

"I'll take care of it this morning, but unofficially as a favor to you."

"One other thing: is it true that there's a central computer here in Washington with a complete dossier on anyone who ever worked for the government, was under investigation, or was in the armed forces?"

"That's classified information, Doctor. Even if such a central computer tape bank exists, I couldn't reveal it."

"You don't have to tell me anything that doesn't have reference to Miss Burke, Lynne Tallman, the man who was shot last night, or maybe three other people."

"That's still a tall order. Who are they?" Stafford's tone was all business now.

"An employee of the Atomic Energy Commission named Roger Coven; his wife, Rita, who was once a stenotype operator at Oak Ridge; and a professor of psychiatry and parapsychology here at the medical school named Randall McCarthy. No matter what you discover, though, I'm not asking you to reveal anything that isn't pertinent to the Tallman case or the man who was killed last night by Miss Burke."

"We have no official connection with that case, as yet, except Sheriff Knott's request for a fingerprint check."

"Unless I miss my guess, Inspector, when that identification is made, you'll be in the case up to your ears."

There was a moment of silence, then the FBI man's voice came crisply over the line. "In that case, Doctor, I think you and I may want to talk some more, but privately. I'll put your several requests through—"

"Make them 'Urgent,' please. Miss Burke's life—or her sanity —may be at stake."

3

Shortly before noon, Mike's office nurse brought in a copy of the City Edition of the Washington *Star-News*.

"Mr. Stanfield sent this over by special messenger, Dr. Kerns," she said. "It looks like you had a busy night."

The account of the shooting was on the break page, with photos of the dead man, of Janet in the white bikini, and of Mike himself. In the story, however, George Stanfield had avoided sensationalism as far as possible and told it straight: another prowler and potential rapist had been killed by a brave young woman, who hadn't been afraid to use the weapon any homeowner, or renter in this case, had a right to keep inside the house for his or her protection. It was powerful and hard-hitting, nevertheless, an earnest plea for the forthright destruction of bands of lawless vagrants who were fast becoming a menace to every home and every peace-loving citizen.

The telephone rang shortly before twelve; Inspector Stafford was on the line.

"You're almost getting to be another Jeane Dixon, Dr. Kerns," he said crisply. "The prowler Miss Burke shot last night has been identified as Armand Descaux—"

"The man who probably put the bomb in the plane and killed Lynne Tallman?"

"He's also one of the ten most wanted criminals on the FBI list —for bombing, arson, rape, grand-theft-auto and you name it. Incidentally, the motorcycle he rode was stolen in a small town just south of Chicago two days before he was killed. Descaux was a known associate and lover of Lynne Tallman before her arrest, as well as high priest of that devil cult she was in."

Mike felt his heart sink, although actually he'd been half expecting to hear exactly what he had just heard. "What about the phone call?"

"We only know what telephone was called and the address, not who the caller talked to. But since the call was station-to-station and direct distance dialed, the caller obviously knew the number. Moreover, she—"

"Aren't you jumping to a conclusion, Inspector?"

"Perhaps. . . . I was going to say that the caller almost certainly invited Descaux to come to your cottage, which is a pretty damning piece of evidence, Doctor, any way you look at it. Acting on a request from me, the Chicago Bureau raided the address where the phone was located early this morning. It was an abandoned warehouse and only one member of the gang was caught, but it had obviously been headquarters for Descaux and a number of other known terrorists who were associated with Lynne Tallman."

"You say you caught one?"

"Only a small-time ex-con and addict named Frelinghausen, but he sang like a drunken canary. The cult was warned of Armand Descaux's death late last night or early this morning by telephone from the Washington area and advised to get out before the first call could be traced. In fact, the call last night appears to have been so urgent that they decamped in a hurry, leaving some of the stuff they'd been smoking still warm."

"Good work."

"But not good enough, Doctor," said the FBI man dryly. "Do you remember who was at the cottage last night when you were around—besides Sheriff Knott and his deputies?"

"Dr. McCarthy and Mr. and Mrs. Coven came by boat from the next cottage, as soon as Janet called them. When Mr. Stanfield and I arrived, two attendants from a funeral home were there, too."

"Just a minute, Doctor, while I make a call on another line. Will you hold or can I call you back?"

"I'll hold," Mike told him. "I'm as anxious to get this business of the telephone calls straightened out as you are."

The FBI man came back on the line in less than five minutes. "The telephone company has no record of long distance calls from the Coven cottage last night, so we're up against a blank wall."

"I'm glad you don't suspect Janet—"

"Certainly not of making the second call, but the big question is, who made the first? I heard on TV this morning that she's remaining in her uncle's apartment under sedation on her doctor's orders, which probably means you. Is there any chance that I could talk to her today?"

"A reporter from the *Post* called me this morning; they're pretty hot over there about the beat George Stanfield stole on them, so I'm sure newsmen are watching the apartment," said Mike. "If you appear there, they're sure to smell a rat and decide the Tallman case is involved."

"I'd just as soon avoid leading the press to that conclusion, too."

"Let me handle it, then," said Mike. "I haven't talked to Janet this morning; she may still be asleep but I'm sure she'll be as anxious to settle this business as I am. If I can sneak her out of the apartment early this afternoon through the service entrance to the building, where would you want to see her?"

"Here at the office where what she says can be recorded. She can bring a lawyer if she likes."

"We're co-operating a hundred per cent, so what need does she have of a lawyer?"

"None, since she undoubtedly killed Descaux in self-defense. Can you have her here at two o'clock?"

"We'll be there, but go easy on her, please, Inspector. There are aspects of this case—medical aspects—I don't understand myself."

"Don't worry if you feel that you're being followed on the way here," Stafford told him. "Since the Chicago Bureau raided the warehouse and learned about the second telephone call warning the gang, Miss Burke has been under full surveillance—and protection—by the Federal Bureau of Investigation."

"But—"

"The small fish we caught in Chicago told us the entire Tallman-Descaux cult is on the way to the Washington area, Doctor. Knowing them, they may decide to take a shot at Miss Burke for killing their high priest and noble leader, Descaux, or they could have some other mischief in mind. We won't know which it will be for some time, maybe not even before it happens; but we'll try to protect Miss Burke."

4

It was just after two when Mike, George Stanfield and Janet entered Inspector Stafford's office in the FBI building.

"I felt that Mr. Stanfield should be here," Mike explained as Stafford greeted them courteously. "He's Miss Burke's legal guardian, as well as representing her employer, the Washington *Star-News.*"

"Of course. Please sit down," said Stafford. "First, however, it is only fair to warn you that this conference will be taped for our records and also to make sure that Miss Burke is apprised of her rights."

"Am I being charged with any crime, Inspector?" Janet asked and Mike was impressed by the way she had regained complete control of herself, after a good night's sleep following the ordeal at the cottage.

"Not by the Bureau, Miss Burke, but the shooting happened in a neighboring county and we never know when an overzealous county attorney—"

"May intervene, hoping for publicity to help build his own political reputation," George Stanfield interposed dryly. "As reporters, my niece and I are both quite familiar with the type, Inspector, but what would he have to go on?"

"There is a possibility that local officials in Maryland might decide to lay charges against Miss Burke of luring a wanted criminal into a trap that resulted in his own death."

"What trap?" Janet demanded indignantly. "I never saw that man before in my life."

"Nevertheless, on last Monday evening a telephone call was made from Dr. Kerns's cottage, in which you are staying, Miss Burke. It was to a telephone in Chicago, located in an abandoned warehouse known now to have housed Armand Descaux and the cult he headed with Lynne Tallman before her death. As a result of that call, Descaux left Chicago immediately and stole a motorcycle somewhere in the suburbs, using it to come directly to Dr. Kerns's cottage, where you were staying."

"Oh, my God!" Janet groped for Mike's hand and dug her nails into his palm. "Then what he said was true; she *had* called him."

"What's all this?" George Stanfield demanded.

"If we listen to Janet's own account of what happened last night, I'm sure the picture will become clear," Mike suggested.

"Are you saying you knew of this and didn't tell me?" Stanfield demanded angrily.

"Janet told me about Descaux's behavior, as we were driving in from the cottage last night," said Mike. "When I recognized that it would only involve speculation and possibly create unpleasant publicity, I waited until this morning to check on possible phone calls from the cottage. And when I found one had been made to Chicago Monday night, I asked Inspector Stafford to try to find out who was called."

"You'll still have the whole story, Uncle George," Janet promised. "That is if Inspector Stafford is going to record it."

"With your permission, Miss Burke?"

"You have that, Inspector; I've been telling the truth and I expect to keep on telling it."

"You may begin, then." Stafford reached for a switch on his desk. "Let the record show that Miss Janet Burke is making this unsworn statement of her own free will and accord. Please proceed, Miss Burke."

Speaking slowly and distinctly, Janet recounted the story she had told Mike last night, describing again, in detail, the actions and words of Armand Descaux when he broke into the cottage.

"Thank you, Miss Burke," said Stafford, when she finished. "Did you make any telephone calls to Descaux before he arrived? Or to his Chicago headquarters afterward?"

"I made no such calls," she repeated in a firm voice. "And I am quite willing to swear to everything I have said."

"Nevertheless," said Stafford, "telephone company records show a call was made from Dr. Kerns's cottage on Monday night to the headquarters of Descaux's gang."

"I didn't make it."

"Were you alone all Monday evening?"

"Yes."

"Yet, from your own account, Descaux was obviously expecting to be welcomed by you with open arms—"

"Don't answer that, Janet," George Stanfield interposed sharply.

"I can't lie about it, Uncle George. He even stated that he'd been invited to come to the cottage."

"How do you rationalize that with your statement that you made no telephone call to Chicago, although you were the only person in the cottage on Monday night?" Stafford asked.

Janet looked at Mike, who had carefully coached her while on the way to the FBI building against just such a question. "I'm under the care of Dr. Kerns," she said. "I'd prefer that he explain."

"Can you, Doctor?" Stafford asked.

"I think so, if you'll let me recap a little."

"Of course."

"Miss Burke is under my care as far as the physical injuries she sustained in the crash at Dulles are concerned," Mike began. "One of those injuries was a severe concussion that kept her unconscious for about thirty-six hours. It made me suspect a possible permanent brain injury, so I requested consultation with Dr. Josh Fogarty, a neurosurgeon, and with Dr. Randall McCarthy, a psychiatrist."

"Why a psychiatrist, Doctor?"

"Dr. Fogarty identified some unusual wave patterns in Miss Burke's electroencephalographic picture before she became conscious, Inspector. Since serious personality disturbances are not at all uncommon following severe concussion, we wanted to be on top of them, so to speak, should they occur. And now that they have—"

"Wait a minute, Mike!" George Stanfield exclaimed. "There's nothing wrong with Janet."

"That's something else we didn't want to trouble you with, before Mike and Dr. McCarthy could be sure what happened, Uncle George," said Janet quietly. "It's hard for me to understand myself but it seems that I'm two people."

"Multiple personality!" Stafford exclaimed. "We had a case like that when I was in charge of the Birmingham office."

"Then you know something of what's involved," said Mike on a note of relief. "In Dr. McCarthy's opinion, Janet's concussion disturbed her brain function to the point where her body now harbors two distinctly different personalities. One is the Janet Burke you see now, but the other, a mischievous hoyden who calls herself Lynne, occasionally takes control of Miss Burke's body."

"Have you seen this other personality, Doctor?" Stafford asked.

"Yes, I have. Her actions correspond very closely to Janet's description of Lynne Tallman's behavior in Chicago."

"Good God!" Stanfield groaned. "It's unbelievable."

"Are you saying that the personality called Lynne made the call to Chicago on Monday night, Dr. Kerns?" Stafford asked.

"There doesn't seem to be any other explanation."

"But how could you know the telephone number?" he asked Janet. "Unless Lynne Tallman had told you where the gang was living before you left Chicago?"

"She didn't. Actually, I never saw Lynne before I started interviewing her in jail, and every time I tried to question her about the others in the cult, she clammed up."

"Can *you* explain her knowing the right number to call, Doctor?"

"I think I can, but I can't tell you why—at least not at the moment."

"Mike!" Janet cried. "What are you saying?"

"Just that I have a theory about all this, but until I prove it, I can't reveal it."

"When you *have* proved it, you'll let me know, won't you, Doctor?" Stafford's tone was suddenly sharp.

"Immediately."

"Very well, Doctor. You mentioned just now that you had seen Miss Burke when the other personality was in control. Would you describe what she is like?"

Mike quickly described the incident at the Purple Pussycat, but not Janet's behavior at the apartment until the unexpected arrival of George Stanfield had forced the Lynne personality to give up control, leaving Janet out cold from alcohol.

"Two people in one body and one of them imitating a murderess." George Stanfield wiped sweat from his forehead with a handkerchief.

"Suppose we accept Dr. McCarthy's double personality theory for the time being, Dr. Kerns," said Stafford as the tape recorder on his desk whirred softly. "If the Lynne personality made the call last Monday night, as we think it did, why doesn't Miss Burke remember it?"

"That's another thing about multiple personalities," said Mike. "None of them can remember what the other said or did."

"Can the other personality, the one called Lynne, emerge at will?" Stafford asked.

"Not *my* will," said Janet firmly, "but apparently at *hers.*"

"What difference could that possibly make?" George Stanfield inquired.

"Perhaps a great deal," said Stafford. "The crook we caught in the Chicago raid, Frelinghausen, said the second call, telling the members of the cult that Armand Descaux was dead, came shortly before midnight last night. The reason the whole gang, except him, was able to escape was that, because of the Monday night call, Descaux had ordered them before he left Chicago to follow him at the end of the week. In fact, according to Frelinghausen, he'd even given them directions for finding a meeting place, although they were to remain scattered in the Washington area until he called for them."

"Was that meeting place my cottage?" Mike asked.

"Frelinghausen was too drunk to remember much about the directions but what he did remember fits your location."

Janet shivered. "Then that man came to the cottage expecting to be welcomed by someone there—"

"Probably by the Lynne personality, who must have been planning to take the place in the cult that Lynne Tallman had occupied before her death," said Mike.

"Mike!" Janet protested. "How could you think such a thing?"

"We've got to be realistic, darling. You've never seen that side of you in action and you can't remember her, so you don't know how dangerous she can be. If she has decided to take over the small empire Lynne Tallman built when alive, one of the first things she'd do would be to get rid of Armand Descaux, her only rival for the leadership."

"By luring him to Washington with a telephone call," Inspector Stafford observed, "and setting up a situation where Miss Burke would be repelled by Descaux's advances and would probably shoot him, leaving her to lead the cult. It's a logical theory, Doctor."

"Well, it isn't logical to me," said Janet indignantly. "You're practically making me a murderess."

"Not you—Lynne," said Mike. "The evidence is still clear that you acted in self-defense, so you can't be guilty of killing Descaux. Am I right, Inspector?"

"Technically, yes."

"Do you see a jury accepting the theory I have just outlined and punishing Janet for something she didn't do, as herself?"

"No." Stafford reached over and switched off the tape recorder. "But I still have trouble believing Miss Burke could possibly harbor another personality capable of the evil that characterized Lynne Tallman."

"You forgot one thing." Janet's voice broke and Mike instinctively reached out to comfort her, but she pushed his hand away. "How can I go on living as what amounts to two people, knowing one of them lured a man to his death because he trusted her?"

5

Mike dropped Janet at George Stanfield's apartment and took the publisher by the newspaper building.

"I guess I'm like the inspector was, when it comes to believing your theory that Janet is actually two personalities in the same body," said Stanfield. "I just can't buy it."

"Neither do I," said Mike and Stanfield gave him a startled look.

"But you said—"

"I was merely repeating Dr. McCarthy's theory and his explanation of Janet's behavior in order to keep Stafford from thinking she's really responsible for Descaux's death. My personal conviction may be even more impossible for you to believe, although to me it's more logical than the first."

"What do you mean?"

"I'm convinced that Janet is possessed by a demon."

"I can't believe that now any more than I could when you first mentioned the possibility about six weeks ago. Things like that just don't happen."

"That's what I thought, until I talked to a very special patient about a year ago, Father Julian O'Meara—"

"Never heard of him."

"On Catholic Church records he's the priest of a small parish on the outskirts of Washington but his official position is exorcist for this diocese. He says possession by demons is always on the increase in troubled times like these, perhaps because people are so emotionally disrupted that they don't have the moral fiber to fight off the agents of Satan."

"Janet's my only niece. I raised her like a daughter, Mike." The agony George Stanfield was suffering twisted his features into a mask of grief. "Don't ask me to believe she could turn into the sort of she-devil the Tallman girl was."

"Janet couldn't, but the evil spirit that now possesses her could. That's the thing we have to fear most."

"But why?"

"Lynne Tallman was no fool, everything Janet has written about her proves that. Which means she was perfectly capable of seizing possession of Janet's body when Janet's will power couldn't prevent it. And what better time than when Janet was unconscious from the crash and Lynne herself faced destruction in the flames."

"Would a demon from hell be afraid of fire?"

"You've forgotten your Dante. The ninth circle of hell, the worst and probably the one from which come evil spirits like the one that controlled Lynne Tallman, is bitterly cold. Father O'Meara says, too, that during exorcisms the temperature inside the room often falls rapidly, even though the weather may be swelteringly hot outside."

"I don't pretend to understand—or believe," said Stanfield. "But I do know that Janet loves and trusts you, Mike. And since you love her, too, it looks like only you can protect her from the she-devil inside her."

"I intend to, but first we have to prove that an evil spirit does exist in Janet's body. Fortunately, Father O'Meara will know how to do that."

6

It was twelve-thirty Monday afternoon when Mike and a guest came into the Falstaff Room of the Sheraton-Carlton Hotel and were guided to a table he had reserved in a secluded area. The guest was tall, with graying hair and the broad shoulders of the famous Notre Dame halfback he'd been. He had a lean, intelligent face and warm friendly eyes, and was wearing slacks and a sport coat over a tan turtleneck.

"Miss Burke should be here any minute, Father," said Mike. "Mind telling me how you intend to go about this test?"

"These demons have the power to read minds. If you knew, your fiancée would also know immediately and be warned, but I have learned how to keep thoughts out of my mind when dealing with suspected cases of possession."

"When will the test itself take place?"

"I can only promise you that, if she *is* possessed, there'll be no question in your mind." Father O'Meara's eyes widened suddenly. "That must be her now; what an incredibly beautiful girl!"

The sudden stir among the male patrons in the restaurant would have heralded Janet's arrival, even if Mike hadn't seen her across the room and moved to meet her, lovely in a summer dress. The color in her cheeks was a little high from running the gantlet of the frankly admiring gazes from every man in the room and the envious ones of every woman.

"Hello, darling," said Mike, taking her elbow and guiding her to the table. "This is an old friend, Father Julian O'Meara."

With his hand on her elbow, Mike felt her body stiffen at the realization that O'Meara was a priest, but then she relaxed and held out her hand.

"How do you do, Father?" she said.

"Very well, thank you," said the priest. "Like you, I have been under your fiancé's knife, but with nothing like the effect he achieved in your case."

They ordered drinks: sherry for O'Meara and Janet, Bourbon

for Mike. Nothing untoward happened during a pleasant meal, however. O'Meara had a typical Irish charm and entertained them with tales of his experiences as a football player for Notre Dame during four years of college and then for several years in professional football before he'd become a seminarian.

It was nearing time to leave, and Mike was beginning to be worried, when the priest said casually, "I have a small parish in one of the older sections of the city, Miss Burke—I guess you could call it a slum. We concentrate on interesting young people in sports of all kinds and we're having wonderful results. Being a reporter, perhaps you'd care to stop by sometime and see what we're doing or maybe even do a feature on it."

"I'd love to."

"Last Monday was my birthday. Look what the boys' basketball team in my parish gave me." From his pocket O'Meara took a crucifix perhaps six inches long: of highly polished gold, it was set with a number of gem stones and, turning it over in his hand, he pointed to an acrostic, roughly shaped like a fish, with letters that Mike recognized as Greek but whose symbolism he did not know.

"The Sign of the Fish, an ancient symbol of the name of the Son of God," said O'Meara casually, as he put the crucifix down in front of Janet, almost touching her wineglass. "Are you familiar with that story, Miss Burke?"

Mike had glanced at the crucifix when O'Meara placed it on the table. Now, warned by something in the priest's voice that this was the test he'd been anticipating all through the meal, he raised his eyes to Janet's and what he saw there froze him momentarily into immobility.

At the sight of the crucifix, all color had drained from her cheeks, although her eyes had taken on a glare with which he was familiar. Only for an instant did she remain seated, then in a sudden gesture of flight she pushed her chair back, ignoring it when it turned over and a nearby waiter rushed to put it back in place.

"Excuse me. I have to go to the powder room," she said in a voice harsh with both fear and anger, but still unmistakably that of the Lynne personality.

She was ten feet away before Mike had time to rise from his chair; moving almost at a run, she brushed against people at other tables without stopping to apologize. And in the perhaps half minute it took the fleeing—no other word could accurately describe it—girl to reach the door to the lobby and disappear, Mike was conscious of a silence in the room.

"That was the test, wasn't it?" he asked Father O'Meara, as conversation was resumed.

O'Meara nodded and now there was a light of compassion and deep concern in his fine dark eyes.

"There can be no doubt any more, Mike," he said. "Your beloved is possessed by an evil spirit."

"The third impossible." Mike's tone was harsh because, although he'd suspected the truth almost from the beginning, this final proof could still break his heart.

7

"What can we do?" Mike asked the priest hoarsely.

"Right now you'd better stop her before she leaves as Lynne—else you may never get her back as her real self."

"Are you absolutely sure it's the same evil spirit that drove Lynne Tallman before her death?"

"Another agent may have been directed by Lucifer to continue what the Tallman girl and her cult of devil worshipers had already begun, but that makes no difference." Father Julian rose and, picking up the crucifix that had caused such a startling change in Janet, slipped it into his pocket. "If Miss Burke doesn't see me before she leaves the restaurant, you may be able to help her become herself again and explain what happened to her. My guess would be that she'll have no memory of it—or none she'll admit."

Mike had paid his check and was waiting in the foyer when Janet came out of the powder room. She passed within a few feet of him without giving any sign of recognition, but in the brief moment when she faced him, he saw in her eyes something he'd never seen there before. It was a look of almost pure terror which could only mean that, however self-assured and confident Lynne-Janet might appear to be, she feared the crucifix, the presence of the priest and the Power he represented more than anything else. And realizing that, Mike felt a surge of hope that somehow the evil spirit that had transferred itself to Janet in those final moments during the airport fire could be driven out forever.

She was almost at the door when he took her arm. For a moment, he thought she was going to struggle to free herself of his grip—even in the lobby of the busy restaurant—then the tension went out of her muscles and he felt the gust of icy cold air he'd noticed before when the demon called Lynne gave up its control of her actions. And when she turned to face him, the look of pain, almost hopelessness, in her eyes made him want to take her in his arms and comfort her.

"What happened inside the restaurant, Mike?" she asked, almost in a whisper.

"I'll tell you when we get outside. It—she's gone, isn't she?"

"Yes. But I still don't understand."

In the parking lot outside, Mike helped Janet into the Porsche and hooked her seat belt before sliding under the wheel. The car had been standing in the sun and was like an oven but quickly cooled when he started the engine and turned the air-conditioning blower up to full.

Janet leaned back against the headrest and shut her eyes so, without disturbing her, he drove in silence northward along the Rock Creek and Potomac Parkway past the National Zoological Park and into Rock Creek Park itself, before pulling the car to a stop off the road in the shade of a spreading oak near the winding creek. Cutting the motor, he pressed the button in his door that controlled the windows, lowering them so the breeze rustling the leaves of the giant oak could blow through the car.

He thought Janet might be asleep; the change from Lynne sometimes left her almost in coma for a while. Then she asked, but without opening her eyes, "Who was the man we had lunch with, darling? I don't seem to remember his name."

"Father Julian O'Meara. His parish is a small one in a slum area here in Washington but he's actually on the staff of the bishop of the diocese. I've known him since I was a resident at the University Hospital."

"He's very nice; I remember that much. Then something happened and I—" She broke off and did not speak for a moment, then added, "The other personality must have taken over. I hope she didn't behave badly to your friend."

"Actually I played a trick on you," he confessed, "but I didn't know any other way to learn the real truth—"

"About Lynne?" Her voice was little more than a whisper.

"Yes. From the start, I've found it hard to believe this theory of Randall McCarthy's that you're actually suffering from—or maybe a victim of is more like the truth—a multiple personality. But I was even less willing to believe the other possible answer, even though in my heart I was almost certain it was the real explanation of your seeming to be two people."

"One reasonably good—the other terribly evil?"

"One the girl I came to love; the other someone I'm very much afraid of because of what she can do to the real you. I was at my wits' end, until I thought of asking Father Julian to help me."

"But you're not a Catholic and neither am I."

"In this case it makes no difference, because Father Julian really wears two hats, so to speak. Being a parish priest is a cover-up for his real job—as chief exorcist for the diocese."

He heard her catch her breath and knew she understood his meaning.

"So I arranged this luncheon to bring you and Father Julian together, although he wouldn't tell me beforehand what he planned to do."

"Why?"

"Evil spirits can read minds even better than Randall McCarthy. If I'd known what he had in mind, Lynne could easily have learned from me who Father Julian actually is and even what he planned to do at the luncheon as a test. Then she'd never have consented to come."

"I *was* afraid," she confessed. "I even tried to get you at your office about eleven o'clock this morning to break our date for lunch, but your nurse said you wouldn't be back until this afternoon and I decided to go through with it anyway. What did the priest do just now that upset Lynne so? I don't remember anything about what happened after we had dessert."

"Father Julian's quite a conversationalist and you seemed to be enjoying yourself. Then he casually took from his pocket a jeweled crucifix the young people in his parish bought for his birthday."

She shivered, although the breeze was warm. "I remember the

crucifix; it was set with some kind of stones and, when he turned it over, there was an emblem on the back—"

"An ancient acrostic—the Greek initials for 'Jesus Christ, Son of God, Savior,' forming the outline of a fish. Father Julian says it was a sacred symbol in the primitive Church."

"I guess it was when I saw the acrostic that I blacked out."

"That was when Lynne took over but she was deathly afraid of the crucifix, or perhaps more particularly of the acrostic. She pushed her chair back and practically ran for the powder room."

"The first thing I remember after seeing the crucifix was the feel of your hand on my arm in the lobby of the restaurant, bringing me back." Her voice broke momentarily. "To sanity, I suppose."

"To your real self instead of the demon from Lynne Tallman that has almost seized control of your body."

"Not almost; she *did* seize control."

"I don't agree—entirely."

"How else could she make me lure Armand Descaux to Washington by telephone so I would kill him when he expected me to welcome him?"

"You didn't talk to Descaux, Lynne did," he corrected her. "And she doesn't control you entirely—at least not yet."

"How can you say that when she makes me do anything she wants me to?"

"You didn't leave without me just now, as Lynne evidently intended to do."

"But only because you held me back."

"From what I've read and things Father Julian has told me about what happens during exorcisms, demons are powerful beings, even if they don't possess corporeal bodies. If Lynne had been in complete control just now and had really wanted to leave, she could easily have tossed me halfway across the foyer, but the real Janet wouldn't let her do that. Which means that although part of you has undoubtedly been possessed by the demon of Lynne Tallman, the other you that loves me can still foil her."

"She's getting stronger. Each time she seizes control, it's harder for me to get it back."

"We're going to remedy that soon," he told her confidently.

"How?"

"By exorcism."

"Nobody believes in that any more, Mike. It's like witchcraft."

"Father Julian believes—and so do the people he's rid of possession by evil spirits. I've talked with some of them, and a book written recently describes at least five documented cases of exorcism."

"Documented?"

"With tape recordings, witnesses and, in some cases, even motion pictures."

"You don't know how strong she can be, Mike." She shivered and reached for his hand. "She might even kill me, if I try to stop her in anything she wants to do. Or kill you because I love you enough to resist her."

"Then you do accept that Father Julian is right in his diagnosis and that you are possessed by an evil spirit?"

"Accept? I've been sure of it since I killed Armand Descaux and you proved later that I had lured—"

"Not you. Lynne."

"We're two parts of the same body, even the same mind now—"

"Fortunately with neither able to remember what the other does."

"I'm not even certain of that any more." She shook her head slowly. "It's true that I have no memory of what *she* does, except fragments that seem like parts of a dream without any connection to each other. But sometimes I believe that Lynne knows much of what's going on in my mind, when she isn't in control—and that her knowledge is increasing all the time as she grows stronger."

"That's all the more reason why the exorcism must be carried out soon," he urged. "The important thing is, are you willing to go through with it?"

"I'll do anything to be myself again—even if she kills me."

"If she kills you, she loses your body and *that* she needs badly, at the moment anyway, for whatever atrocity she's planning next."

"How can you be sure of that?"

"The trick of luring Armand Descaux—who was probably Lynne's only threat to leadership of the cult in Chicago—to Washington so he'd be killed, plus having the rest of the cult come here, too, seems to indicate that she's planning some new act of terror."

"Using my body," said Janet bitterly. "And I can't stop her, short of killing myself."

"Don't even think of that," he said sharply. "You have one important advantage in that she needs your body to carry out her plan, whatever it is. And when we drive out the demon that's the only part of the real Lynne Tallman left now, she'll be helpless."

"Until she possesses someone else?"

"From what Father Julian has told me, when the rite of exorcism is successful the demon is not only dispossessed but also crippled or weakened in some way. What's more, during exorcism, an evil spirit often boasts of further atrocities it plans to accomplish, so it could just happen that we would not only get rid of the Lynne side of Lynne-Janet, but also foil whatever plan she's working on now."

"Ask Father Julian to start right away, please," Janet pleaded. "If we don't drive her out soon, I've got a premonition that it's going to be too late."

8

"Janet's ready," Mike told Father Julian when he called him at the parish rectory that evening. "We'd like to start immediately."

"Let me look at my calendar. I know several cases are already scheduled before Miss Burke."

"Could you possibly change the order?"

"Exorcism is something that cannot be hastened, Mike. Just the necessary preparations would make the week following Labor Day the earliest we could make the attempt."

"Preparations? What kind of preparations?"

"We never undertake an exorcism without a complete physical work-up; the strain on the patient's heart and, in fact, the entire body is often dangerous to life in any but a healthy individual."

"You saw her at noon. She's the picture of health."

"I agree—now. But she was nearly killed in the plane crash only a few months ago. Couldn't there still be sequelae that haven't yet appeared?"

"Possibly," Mike admitted reluctantly.

"Besides, we never undertake exorcism without a thorough psychiatric observation, too."

"Dr. McCarthy has been doing that. I'm sure he could wind up the study in a few days."

"By all means have the preparations made, then. I'll schedule her tentatively for the middle of September."

"She'll not want to wait, but perhaps I can persuade her."

Persuading Janet proved far easier than he had expected, however. When he called her the evening after his talk with Father Julian, she was bubbling over with enthusiasm, although he had left her depressed at the prospect of the forthcoming exorcism only the afternoon before.

"Why so happy?" he asked.

"The most wonderful thing has happened, Mike. Remember the feature I did a couple of weeks ago on distant viewing? Randall McCarthy was involved in some experiments with it at the Stanford Research Institute before he came to the university here."

"Yes. It was very good but hard to believe."

"If you'd read the reports Randall showed me of the work at the institute—it's a big think tank in California—you'd believe it. Well, I've been trying to break into the big-circulation magazine field ever since I took my master's in journalism at Northwestern, but without much luck. Then early this morning, the editor of the *Ladies' Home Journal* called from New York and asked if I would be interested in doing a piece with Randall on remote viewing for the *Journal*. Naturally, I jumped at the chance."

"That's wonderful, darling, but what about the exorcism? I've already made arrangements with Father Julian for it."

"That can wait, can't it? The *Journal* wants this piece right away."

"Well, I suppose . . ."

"When does Father Julian want to do it?"

"The easiest would be the middle of September."

"I'll be through with the *Journal* article before then. The deadline is Tuesday after Labor day."

"He insists on a thorough medical and psychiatric work-up, too."

"Randall has already done most of the psychiatric part and I'm as healthy as a horse now. A couple of days going through the Private Diagnostic Clinic at University Hospital should take care of the rest."

"You've convinced me," he told her resignedly. "Only one thing worries me about the delay."

"What's that?"

"The Lynne side of you has developed an almost uncanny ability to imitate your voice and even your manner. I only hope she never gets good enough at it to fool me."

"*You* I'm not worried about. I guess you think I'm brazen but I sometimes find myself wishing Uncle George hadn't come in when he did the night you took me home from the Purple Pussycat."

He laughed. "It looks like I'm going to get the hussy in the bedroom I once told you every man wants, whether it turns out to be Lynne or Janet in the end."

"Don't let it be Lynne, darling. Just don't let it be Lynne."

9

The office day was finished, and Mike was making some last-minute notes on the records of the patients he'd seen that day, when the telephone rang. It was Inspector Stafford.

"I've got a few facts at last on those people you asked me to check on, if you'd still like to hear them," said the FBI agent.

"I would. I'd also like to talk to you about something else, but with the way things are here in Washington, I don't think it had better be over the phone."

"I'm leaving the office in half an hour. Can you meet me at Hennesy's?"

"I'll be there."

Mike was in a booth at the far corner of the famous old tavern when Stafford came in. With its paneled walls of dark wood, its cushioned seats and chandeliers made from old wagon wheels—said to have rolled many a mile on the Wilderness Road across southern Pennsylvania ·to Pittsburgh, when George Washington was still only a young surveyor for Lord Fairfax—Hennesy's was a favorite spot for an end-of-the-day drink. The hour was somewhat early yet, so the tavern was only half filled.

Stafford stopped to pick up a scotch and soda at the bar and eased himself into the niche where Mike was sitting. "I don't have much time," he said. "Forgot that I promised to take my wife to a wedding tonight." From his pocket he took a typed sheet. "Your friend Dr. McCarthy's in the clear. He has an understandable flair for publicity and apparently some psychic powers—though I couldn't be sure since I don't believe in them."

"He's demonstrated them at Duke, the Stanford Research Institute, and at the university here. Janet's doing an article for the *Ladies' Home Journal* with him on what's called remote viewing—"

"That's the business Jack Perkins reported on for the NBC Evening News a few nights ago," said Stafford. "It's fantastic."

"This whole business of parapsychology is fantastic, but there's no longer any doubt that it's a science in itself."

"Anyway, McCarthy's in the clear," said Stafford.

"What about the Covens?"

"They're an interesting pair. The woman's a tart, but high-class, she's had innumerable affairs with other men since she married Coven, apparently with his encouragement. At least one of them is in a pretty high position here in Washington, too, so our hands are somewhat tied when it comes to investigating them."

"Senator Magnes?"

Stafford nodded. "Apparently Roger Coven doesn't mind; in fact, it would appear that he's moved up about twice as fast in his field as would ordinarily be the case because the Chairman of the Atomic Oversight Committee sleeps with his wife."

"The way I heard the rumor, it's sort of a *ménage à trois*," said Mike with a grin.

"Everything we learned bears it out, but as far as I'm concerned, or the Bureau, that's their constitutional right. I guess you know Roger and Rita Coven were in McCarthy's classes at Duke, too, don't you?"

Mike nodded. "I gather that's where the three of them met."

"What you probably don't know is that they were both involved in those student riots that almost tore Duke University apart some years ago. For a while Roger's diploma was in question but he was such a hot guy in atomic research that he finally got it. He took a Ph.D. in the same field at the University of Chicago."

"Did you know he knew Lynne Tallman in Chicago?"

Stafford appeared startled. "Yes. But how did you learn it?"

"Roger mentioned it one day at the cottage, said she was a student in one of his classes."

"But a student willing to stay after class," said Stafford. "He and Rita almost broke up over it, until Roger got a job at Oak Ridge shortly afterward. Rita dropped out of college to become a stenotype operator, a damned good one, in fact. She had no trouble getting a job at the Oak Ridge laboratories of the Atomic Energy Commission and was usually seen a lot with Magnes, when he went down there on tours of inspection."

"Which happened frequently, I'll bet."

"Usually on weekends," Stafford's tone was dry, "although Magnes apparently saw much more of Rita during those visits than he did of the laboratories."

"Sounds cozy—even for the Washington establishment."

"And even cozier for the Covens. While they were at Oak Ridge, small amounts of fissionable material started disappearing from time to time. At Magnes' suggestion, Roger was given the job of discovering who was involved and how."

"Why him and not the FBI?"

Stafford grimaced. "The Bureau's not quite as powerful now as it was under Hoover. Besides, Roger Coven's major field of study was the detection of small amounts of radioactive materials, mostly in the air as part of the watch on other countries, but also around atomic reactors producing electricity. He was the logical man for the job and pinned the theft on a technician in the isotope laboratory. The accused claimed foul, of course; swore the stuff was planted in his locker and he knew nothing about it."

"What happened to him?"

"He got fired."

"Was that all?"

"Prosecuting him would have caused a lot of publicity and people are already worked up over the fear of atomic accidents, so the whole thing was hushed up."

"I suppose Roger Coven was furious."

"Not so you'd notice it. He emerged as a full-fledged expert on the detection of fissionable materials and the commission sent him to Chicago to study the laboratory there. It took him about six months to nail a spy who was selling small amounts of plutonium to an agent for a South American dictator."

"I don't remember reading about that."

"Nobody does because the news that a Yanqui-hating nation to the south of us had the capability of producing an atomic bomb would scare the pants off half the country. So Coven winds up as head of that section here in Washington—"

"And Senator Magnes gets cozy with Rita again?"

"Not again—still. I'm afraid the only thing we have to Roger Coven's possible discredit, though, is that little affair down at Duke in the sixties. But like most of the young radicals of the Weathermen era, he's grown tamer and grayer." Stafford stood up. "Sorry I couldn't help you more."

"It was just a hunch, anyway. Any news from the Tallman-Descaux gang?"

"They probably came East but it's not hard to melt into a hodgepodge of a city like Washington. My guess is that losing both their leaders in a few months left them demoralized."

Unless they've found another leader, Mike thought as he watched the tall form of the FBI agent moving through the press of people beginning to fill the room.

Mike finished his drink, then signaled the waiter for another. He drank the second slowly, while his mind raced through a replay of events since he'd watched the small figure of a man tumble from the 727 on the approach to Dulles Airport, it seemed now years ago.

Every time he added up the facts he knew, they all came out to the same answer—the demon residing in the body of the girl he loved. He could see but two ways of evicting it, either through exorcism or by exercising the right a man had to shoot a sick dog he loved to save it from further misery.

10

Randall McCarthy came into Mike's office the next afternoon and received his final discharge from surgical treatment. Healing of the operative incisions was now perfect and his deep suntan hid most of the dusky hue of ecchymosis still apparent under the chin, where Mike had been forced to dissect rather more widely than in the average face-lift in order to put in place the small bone graft that had given the patient a normal chin outline.

"I think you'll be getting some business from the faculty," McCarthy told him. "Three doctors' wives of my acquaintance are trying to make up their minds. If you'd combine your work with a little plastic gynecology, I'm sure you'd make a fortune. Did Janet tell you we're doing an article together on remote viewing for the *Ladies' Home Journal?*"

"Yes. Is it for real?"

"Absolutely."

"She says you have a gift for it."

"I guess all psychics do; it's just that heretofore we've concentrated mostly on extrasensory perception, telepathy—"

"Why not combine the two and see things before they happen?" Mike asked facetiously but McCarthy was not amused.

"They've been doing some of that, too—at Stanford. Taken seriously, the way a real parapsychologist does, precognition is a pretty awesome responsibility."

"Perhaps you could tell when a real tragedy was about to happen—in time to prevent it."

"I don't think so, Mike. You see, that would be playing God and, whether you believe in a divinity or not, everyone I know of who ever tried it came to grief. Remember the Greek tragedies? Medea, Oedipus and the rest?"

"A little; I never had much time for the theater."

"All you have to do today is turn on your TV set any afternoon. They're being replayed endlessly in the soap operas—and to a far bigger audience."

"Speaking of tragedies," said Mike, "Janet's still brooding over the Armand Descaux affair."

"I know," said McCarthy, "and I'm not sure this latest caper of yours in persuading her she's possessed by a demon is going to help her get over it."

"You wouldn't doubt possession if you'd been there when Father Julian showed her the crucifix. She scared the hell out of me."

"Unfortunately it didn't scare the other personality out of herself. It's taken me several months to convince Janet that she's really a double personality and can get rid of the other one, if she works hard enough at it. Now you and an amateur psychologist with his collar on backward have almost convinced her she can get rid of the other one merely by being prayed over and having some holy water sprinkled on her head."

"Father Julian has exorcised other demons—"

"I've been to those performances. Give me a few days to practice with the necessary magician's equipment and I can still duplicate everything an exorcist does."

"Then you won't make the psychiatric evaluation Father Julian requires?"

"I didn't say that. Actually all I have to do is give her a few more psychometric tests and write up an extensive summary. I wouldn't do even that, though, if you weren't the sort of stubborn cuss who'd talk her into going to another psychiatrist."

"I'm not sure I'd trust her to anyone else," Mike admitted. "Especially the Lynne side."

"One more thing," said the psychiatrist unexpectedly, "I want to be present at the exorcism. Can you fix it?"

"I don't know, but I'll find out." Mike opened the small directory of frequently called numbers on his desk, found that for the rectory where Father Julian lived and had his office, and dialed it. The conversation lasted only a few moments but, when he hung up, he was smiling.

"Father Julian says he always insists on having a physician present at an exorcism and will be glad to have you. In fact, he says he's very much interested in your work and would like to meet you."

"I won't be there for that," said McCarthy. "My job will be to protect Janet."

"Come now. If anyone does her physical harm, it will be the demon of Lynne Tallman."

"I'm not concerned with physical harm, it's her mind I'll be protecting. If you'd seen some of the effects of this craze about demon possession that's sweeping the country since *The Exorcist* was published and filmed you'd never have taken her to that priest in the first place. But now that you have, I've got to protect my patient from further emotional trauma that might turn her from a simple case of multiple personality into a full-blown case of schizophrenia I'd probably never be able to cure."

"Surely exorcism isn't all that dangerous."

"It is in my book. Janet was just fantasizing unconsciously when she first turned herself into the hoyden she patterned after Lynne Tallman."

"Why would she do that?"

"Who knows exactly why these things happen in a patient's psyche? Maybe when Janet became conscious after the accident and found herself with a handsome young doctor, who was obviously interested in her, the unconscious mind decided to give free rein to her otherwise sublimated sexual interest in you and get rid of a nuisance from her past named Gerald Hutchinson at the same time. So she simply let the part of her unconscious that envied Lynne Tallman her freedom to go after any man she wanted take over. That way Janet could salve her middle-class, midwestern conscience while having the fun it had been denying her. . . ."

"That's the screwiest tale I ever heard."

"I told you we can't explain these things, but I can give you a piece of advice, as a psychiatrist and as a lover of many women in my day. When opportunity knocks, seize it—and her—or she's liable to get the idea implanted in her unconscious that you don't really want to make love to her."

"Of course I want to, but not when she isn't in her right mind."

McCarthy grinned, looking, Mike thought, even more like a satyr than before the face-lift. "When they're ready to be laid, women are in their right minds—take that from an old roué."

"You're talking about the woman I love," Mike protested. "The one I intend to marry—but as Janet, not Lynne."

"I'm telling you that they're really the same person. One's the woman she is—largely because of you; the other's the person she thinks she'd like herself to be. In either case, marry her and convince her she's the best lay—whether as Lynne or Janet—any man could want and she'll bury the other one, forever."

"But she refuses to marry me as long as Lynne exists."

"That's *your* problem," said the psychiatrist. "I'm trying to help you by doing my best to give her an understanding of the two aspects of her personality so she can merge them into the perfect woman."

"I'll do anything I can to help you," Mike assured him. "But if she really is possessed and Father Julian fails to drive out the demon . . ." He didn't go on.

When McCarthy gave him a thoughtful look, Mike wondered if

the psychologist was reading his mind—and discovered he was. "Were you going to say that, having given Janet life there on the floor of the terminal at Dulles, it would be your duty to destroy her, if you're really convinced the demon of Lynne Tallman has taken control of her body?"

"Something like that."

"It looks like my work is cut out for me if I'm to save both of you, then." The psychiatrist's tone was now one of deep concern. "But I can't get anywhere if you keep cutting the ground from under my feet—"

"Are you saying I shouldn't see Janet?"

"As little as possible, yes."

"But she'll think—"

"I'll explain the whole thing to her when she comes to the office tomorrow afternoon to work on the *Journal* article. One thing I do know—she's as anxious to become her normal self again as you are to have her in that state. Then, if I haven't cured her of the double-personality fixation in the four weeks between now and the middle of September, I'll let your Father Julian take over."

11

True to his promise, Mike avoided contact with Janet, but he couldn't very well refuse when she called about two weeks later and asked him to take her to dinner.

"How about the Harbour House on the old City Dock in Annapolis?" he asked.

"Sounds perfect, I remember Uncle George taking me there when I was in high school. By the way, I've taken Apartment 257 in Uncle George's building. How about six-thirty?"

"Fine. I'll pick you up in the foyer."

There'd been a summer shower that afternoon and the drive through the verdant Maryland landscape was relaxing and delightful, with the green fields of tobacco now half harvested and the smell of curing leaves from the barns along the way giving a pungent aroma to the entire countryside. At the old restaurant, they dined on terrapin à la Maryland, with a bottle of Liebfraumilch from German vineyards.

"I wish we were cruising up the Rhine on our honeymoon, and this unpleasant business was over," said Janet as they were finishing the bottle.

"Late September is lovely in Germany and Switzerland. I followed the route of Constantine the Great through Trier across northern Europe on a bicycle between my junior and senior years in college, stopping at hostels. I couldn't afford the Rhine cruise then, but I can now and we'll take it on our honeymoon."

"Whenever that is." Her tone was depressed, and when she reached across the table for his hand, he felt her nails dig into his palm, much as they had done at the cottage the night she had shot Armand Descaux. "Tell me that it will happen, darling," she pleaded. "Make me believe it."

"What's wrong? Has Lynne been troubling you again?"

"I don't remember; that's what troubles me most. When I checked the mileage on my car Saturday at noon, after going to Baltimore on a story, then again before I started to the office Monday morning, there was fifty miles difference on the speedometer."

"The distance to the cottage and back."

"Just about—but Randall says he didn't see me or my car there Sunday."

"Are the Covens still down there?"

"Randall says he rented it through September. Roger was away somewhere last weekend, so he and Rita were there alone."

"That should have been cozy."

"I gather that it was. When I went to the office on Monday afternoon to show him the first draft of the article on remote viewing, he still looked like the morning after the night before."

"I haven't talked to him about your progress lately."

"I'm convinced that Lynne's getting stronger all the time. Sometimes I'm not even sure which one I am any more."

"What does Randall say about that?"

"He thinks it's a sign that I'm approaching a point of emotional crisis where I'll settle for being one person."

"We're all working toward that."

"But suppose it's Lynne I finally choose to be?"

"Deep down inside, you're yourself. If the double-personality business is really a postconcussion syndrome, your brain cells will eventually return to normal. And if it's possession, the exorcism will drive Lynne out."

"I wish I could be as sure as you are."

"I didn't save your life and turn you into one of the most beautiful women in the world to desert you now. After we're married—"

"You mean *if* we're married," she said dolefully. "You don't know what it's like, living in limbo and not knowing who you are or what you're liable to do next."

"How's the *Journal* article going?" he asked, hoping to turn her thoughts in another direction.

"It's finished. I never realized what a remarkable person Randall really is until I read the results of his experiments and actually saw some of them happen."

"I don't understand what it's all about."

"Let me give you an example of how what's coming to be called remote viewing works. Last week Randall stayed in his office, while I drove around at random until exactly three o'clock, the time we'd agreed upon beforehand. When I stopped, I was in front of a store in Oxon Hill, roughly ten miles away from his laboratory. I stayed long enough to look at a dress on a mannequin in the window and took a Polaroid color snapshot. When I came back to the lab he'd sketched a rough outline of a storefront I went to, with the name of the store across the front and the evening dress I looked at on a mannequin."

"Randall's an accomplished hypnotist. He could have implanted a posthypnotic suggestion in your mind that would have sent you to that particular storefront."

"I thought of that, too, so we did another experiment. This time I picked an address from a phone book hanging in a booth several blocks away from the university."

"Selected by McCarthy?"

"No, by me—and wholly at random. I went to the new Space Exhibit at the Smithsonian entirely without Randall's knowledge, yet he actually sketched the Apollo capsule I was looking at. He's got the results of a lot of other experiments catalogued, too, and I also saw the article written by the researchers at Stanford who began it."

Her voice had lost its note of depression and was now alive with interest, making him hesitate before asking the next question: "Has he ever watched, viewed, you when you were Lynne?"

"Once, during the time I can't account for over last weekend. Randall called me and, when I wasn't at home, tried to 'see' where I was and what I was doing." She hesitated, then continued: "He could tell I was with a man somewhere but couldn't recognize the place."

"Or the man?"

"Randall never saw his face, he says. But he was about the size of Roger Coven and had gray hair like Roger."

"You and Roger Coven?" Mike's voice echoed his astonishment.

"I don't think so. You see, I don't even like Roger, though he's always been very nice to me. When Randall called Lane Cottage, Rita told him Roger had gone to the crossroads for some beer and, when Roger called Randall back about a half hour later, he confirmed it."

"Does Randall have any explanation?"

Janet shook her head. "He says the man I—Lynne—was talking to must have just happened to look like Roger from the back."

Mike frowned. "I don't like your meeting with strange men and not remembering."

"But it wasn't me—Janet. It was Lynne."

"Yet you have no memory of such a meeting?"

"The only thing that hangs in my mind is the conviction that Lynne's getting ready for some more mischief. And this time it's something really important, maybe even dangerous."

"I don't like this, darling. I don't like it at all."

"What can we do?"

"Will you go with me to see Father Julian?"

"Now?"

"Yes. I have the odd conviction that we can't afford to waste time."

"In doing what?"

"I don't know," he admitted as he signaled the waiter for the check. "Just that we ought to be doing something."

Father Julian, Mike discovered when he called the rectory from the restaurant, would be glad to see them, in spite of the lateness of the hour. His parish occupied an area of run-down tenements in Northeast Washington, and Mike and Janet drove there in only a little more than half an hour. The priest was wearing slacks, a black turtleneck and carpet slippers when he let them in and directed them to comfortable chairs in his study. He listened in silence to Janet's account of how Randall McCarthy had "seen" her with an apparent stranger.

"Those of us in the priesthood realize that many aspects of human experience are not capable of logical explanation by either medicine or religion," he admitted. "As for me, I was too concerned with seeing a sphere of pigskin while at Notre Dame to dabble in the parasensory field, beyond trying to perceive what play the opposition was going to use before it happened."

"I tried to develop that form of precognition in high school, too," said Mike, "but I never had any conspicuous success."

"Dr. McCarthy was kind enough to send me a report of his study on your emotional state, my dear," O'Meara told Janet. "I must admit that in your case he makes out a convincing case for what psychologists call a double personality."

"Please call me Janet, Father." She was obviously much more at ease than she'd been at the restaurant, now that she was convinced the priest had no desire to play tricks on her.

"Then you're not convinced that she is pos—" Mike started to say.

"I'm not convinced of anything except that Janet here is a very lovely and fine young woman who needs help—probably from both medicine and religion."

He turned a page in the report. "By the way, the first time we met, I wasn't exactly fair to you, Janet, but I had to use the only method at my disposal to be certain of something."

"That I am possessed by a demon?"

"Yes, but before we go any further, perhaps I had better give you a brief and simple explanation of possession by an evil spirit, as my Church sees it."

Seeing Janet stiffen in her chair at the priest's words, Mike reached for her hand and squeezed it tightly. The strength in her fingers, as her nails dug into his hand, almost made him cry out from the pain, as it had several times before. After a moment, however, as the priest began to speak in a quiet, matter-of-fact tone, her fingers relaxed. Nevertheless, that moment gave Mike enough evidence of the purely physical power of the evil spirit fighting to seize complete control of Janet's mind and body to convince him that it was indeed present in the room, although the now familiar signs of a change from Janet to Lynne had not appeared.

"In the sight of God, every person is capable of both evil and good," Father Julian began. "Or to put it another way, both a potentially evil and a potentially good spirit reside in us all. To the extent that the two are in harmony, the individual is in a state of spiritual and emotional balance and therefore capable of accepting God's beneficent grace and living a life that can gain divine approval. When good predominates wholly, we find a saint, though unfortunately not very often. Where evil is in full control, we find a person without conscience bent on destroying the meaning and purpose of life."

"Which is?" Mike asked quietly.

"An ancient prophet named Micah said it better than any words of mine could when he wrote: 'He hath shewed thee, O man, what is good; and what doth the Lord require of thee, but to do justly, and to love mercy, and to walk humbly with thy God?'"

"That's simple enough."

"It would seem to be, but unfortunately even the angels in heaven are not perfect. One of them fell from grace eons ago, taking many other weaker spirits with him. Rather than destroy him who was in the beginning the most beautiful among angels, God banished Lucifer and his minions to earth. There they seek constantly to gain followers by possessing the souls of those unfortunate enough to fall into their hands—as, for example, the girl who was called Lynne Tallman."

Watching Janet, ready to seize her if she tried to bolt, Mike felt her nails dig into his palms once again. This time, however, he was prepared and gripped her hand tightly, when she tried to pull away. He was startled, however, when a gust of cold air swept through the room and an odor that reminded him of his dissecting room days in medical school assailed his nostrils. It was the rotting scent of human flesh that often occurred when the embalming mixture injected into veins and arteries under pressure failed to reach and preserve completely the ends of fingers and toes. It was gone in an instant, however, and neither Janet nor Father Julian seemed to notice.

"Go on, please," she whispered through lips pale from the tension of the muscles that controlled them.

"The Spirits of Evil—a world of them in various forms and with varying strength—surround us all," said the priest. "They seek constantly to control our bodies and our minds, using both for purposes of evil. When we do not accept the buttressing power of God's indescribable grace and love, some of us succumb to evil and are destroyed, while others become agents of Lucifer in the flesh. In either event, those who do yield are destroyed, condemned to death and eternal damnation in the fires of hell."

"Is there no way to destroy a demon completely?" Mike asked.

"Only if the evil spirit—call it demon or what you wish—cannot leave the body it inhabits just before death and seize another. Like a carnivorous animal, it must possess a human soul and body as flesh and blood to go on existing. In ancient times the bodies of those possessed were destroyed by burning in the mistaken assumption that fire in the open could destroy the Evil One."

"Then fire cannot destroy them?" Mike asked.

"Dante described the lowermost level of hell—the ninth—as being cold, although the fires of hell forever torment the souls of those who die possessed. No, Mike, the only time a demon can be destroyed completely is when it is shut up with the body of its victim in a holocaust of fire and both are denied any route of escape."

"What of those you drive out in the rite of exorcism?" Janet asked, still in the strange, whispering monotone.

"Alas, they join the teeming hordes of their brethren that infest the spheres. We do know, however, that in the rite of exorcism, when the possessed is imbued with his or her own strength as a child of God through accepting His saving grace, immunity is granted to further attack from the Evil Ones."

The priest put his hand upon her head in a gesture of blessing. "Have no fear; I can see the real you in your eyes and it is strong. The ordeal of exorcism is always severe, but you will come safely through it and be made whole again in spirit, just as the skill of the man you love made you whole and lovely again in body."

12

In accordance with his promise to Randall McCarthy, Mike did not see Janet again that week. Instead he spent the evenings at home, hoping she would call, as she had the evening he'd taken her to dinner in Annapolis. But no call came until late Saturday afternoon, and then it was the voice of Father Julian O'Meara that came to his ears.

"Have you seen Janet lately, Mike?" There was a note of urgency in the voice of the priest.

"Not since we came to the rectory nearly a week ago. Why?"

"I came back from Baltimore a few minutes ago and found a note from my housekeeper by the telephone, saying Janet had called this morning and canceled the exorcism."

"She can't do that! Did you try to call her?"

"Yes, but no one answered."

"She's moved from Mr. Stanfield's apartment. Are you sure you had the right number?"

"Yes. It was listed on the psychiatric report Dr. McCarthy sent me. I also called Mr. Stanfield at his apartment but he doesn't have any idea where she could be."

"Don't take that cancellation as the last word, please, Father," Mike said urgently. "I may be able to find her and convince her to go through with it."

"She has to agree without reservation, Mike. We never force a person into exorcism the results could be too dangerous for both mind and body."

"Hold on until Monday, please. That will give me two days to try and convince her."

"I hope you succeed." There was a moment's hesitation. "Did you notice anything strange while we were talking here at the rectory the other night?"

"Only a blast of cold air and an odor like that of a mortuary."

"They're indisputable signs of possession. It was the demon's way of warning me not to try exorcism, and now it's gone a step further."

"Then it had to be Lynne who called, Father, which makes it all the more important that Janet go through with the exorcism."

"Be sure and call me early Monday morning. I have a conference with the bishop at ten; if you haven't convinced her by then, I'll have to tell him it's been canceled."

"Thanks for giving me that long. If what I think happened really did, her sanity and her life may depend on it."

"I agree. Good-by."

When the telephone clicked in his ear and the dial tone was resumed, Mike rang the number of Randall McCarthy's apartment, but received no answer. He cursed the psychiatrist silently as a traitor while he dialed the laboratory number, expecting it, too, not to answer, but McCarthy's brisk "Hello" sounded in his ear.

"All right, you Judas," Mike snapped. "Why did you stab me in the back?"

"What the hell are you talking about, Mike? Besides, that's lousy English; you've got your metaphors screwed up."

"Never mind the metaphors. Why did you persuade Janet to cancel the exorcism?"

"When did she do that?"

"This morning—in a telephone message taken by Father Julian's housekeeper. He was out and found it when he came back."

"I swear to God I don't know anything about this, Mike, though medically I'm not sure it isn't the best thing for her to do."

"Did you suspect she was considering it?"

"She never mentioned it to me. She was due to spend the afternoon here, working with me on the final draft of that *Journal* article. I called her apartment when she didn't show up but she didn't answer, so I figured maybe she decided to go to the cottage with you."

"I think she's down there now—as Lynne."

"That's it, of course. When the treatment of a double personality goes into the stretch, the second one often seizes control, in a final gesture of defiance."

"Or a resident demon takes over?"

"If you grant the presence of such things—which I don't. What are you going to do?"

"Go to the cottage and persuade her not to destroy herself, of course."

"Did you call to tell her you're coming?"

"No. I had to be sure she's not in Washington first. Besides, if I warned her, she might run."

"Got any idea where?"

"No, but she told me, when we had dinner at Annapolis one evening, about your using that distant-viewing gimmick, and seeing her somewhere with a man during the time she can't account for over last weekend."

"It isn't a gimmick, Mike." McCarthy's voice was dead serious now. "I almost wish it were."

"Then you suspect the man was really Roger Coven?"

"No. I'm convinced that it only *looked* like Roger."

"How can you be so sure?"

"Roger and Rita often get their kicks with kinky sex; in fact I'm not wholly innocent there myself. But when I took Janet as a patient, I warned them that she's *noli me tangere* and they wouldn't risk taking advantage of her disturbed emotional condition. You see, I know too much about their relationship to certain people."

"Senator Magnes, for example."

"Good God, man! Don't you know half the phones in Washington are bugged?"

"All right. I'll take your word that it wasn't Roger you saw, but can you give me any idea where the place was?"

"None. Except that it looked something like a tunnel. There were spots of light along the walls and something peculiar about the floor that I couldn't make out."

"Keep on trying," Mike advised. "Meanwhile, I'm going to the cottage."

"Promise me one thing, Mike." McCarthy's concerned tone stopped him before he could hang up the phone. "If Janet's there, and I think she is, play it the way she wants to play it."

"What does that mean?"

"If she's Janet, well and good; treat her gently and don't lecture her on exorcism. Just play along and let her talk it all out, if she wants to."

"And if she's Lynne?"

"The same—and let nature take its course."

"What the hell do you mean by that?"

"You just might make a discovery not many men ever make—that two lovers in one body are far better than one. And God, how I envy you the chance."

He saw the yellow bathing cap far out in the river when he came out on the dock after parking the car and noting that Janet's car was already there. Nor did he need the binoculars to recognize that graceful crawl with which her lovely body began to cleave the surface of the water, after she threw up an arm in a gesture of recognition. He stood on the dock at the ladder and reached down to take her hand and lift her as she came up the ladder, like a goddess rising from the sea.

"Darling!" Her tone started hackles rising all along his spine as she came into his arms, wet and lovely. And even before her lips parted beneath his own and he felt her tongue moving to meet his inside the warm cavern of her mouth, he knew for certain that, although the body was unquestionably Janet's, the personality controlling it at the moment was equally unquestionably Lynne's.

"Whoa, lover!" she cried, laughing as she pushed him away after a long, tremendously exciting embrace. "Now that you're here, we'll have plenty of time for *that* later."

"Why?" Just in time he remembered Randall McCarthy's advice about not lecturing her, but letting her take the lead.

"Why what?" she asked, pulling off the yellow cap and shaking her hair loose to fall to her shoulders.

"Why not now—*and* later?"

"You *are* horny, aren't you?" she said in the same throaty tone. "What time is it?"

"Almost seven. Go dress and I'll take you to the Taverna Milano for dinner."

"Not tonight, darling," she said as he followed her across the dock toward the door into the cottage. "I've got a couple of hours of work to do on that *Journal* article still; came down here so I could be free from interruptions." She turned in the doorway and kissed him again. "Not that you aren't the kind of interruption I love to have."

For an instant he thought Janet was in control again, so much did the voice and actions resemble hers during those first few weeks at the cottage earlier in the summer.

"You didn't put your name in the pot for tonight," she continued, "so you'll have to make do with pimento cheese sandwiches and applesauce for dinner—plus some elderberry wine I found at a roadside shop at Potomac Heights. It has the most wonderful bouquet. Why don't you take a quick swim while I shower and put on some slacks and a blouse? With the Labor Day holiday only a week away, it's already getting a little brisk down here at night. Supper'll be ready by the time you finish your swim."

"Sounds great. I'll change."

He heard her humming in the shower as he came out of his bedroom after changing. Running across the dock, he dived far out into the Potomac, swimming strongly until the bank was a hundred yards away, then treading water while he considered the way things were going. That Lynne was in control, he did not doubt, even though she'd managed to act, and almost sound, like a happy and sexually stimulated Janet. Which meant that, as he had suspected, it had been Lynne who had called the rectory and left the message for Father Julian. He couldn't see anything to be gained at the moment, however, by trying to make her change back to Janet, and felt only a little guilty about the rising excitement within him at the thought of what the weekend with the other person who occupied the body of the girl he loved might bring.

A flash of color came from the back door of the cottage as she waved to him, and he swam back to the ladder with a racing crawl and came up it to catch the terry-cloth robe she threw him.

"Put that on and take your shower later," she said. "I've already poured the wine and we don't want it to lose its chill."

Wrapping the robe around his body, he stepped out of his swim shorts and left them on the dock. The small table in the kitchen was set with two paper plates of pimento cheese sandwiches, a jar of applesauce and two tall glasses of red wine.

"To us." She lifted her glass as he slid onto the bench across from her in the breakfast nook. "And an exciting weekend."

"Is that a promise?" His glass was half empty, although the wine had an odd taste, somewhat like the almond flavor found in some Italian cordials.

"It is made by an Italian family near here, they flavor it just a little with almond oil." With a sudden shock, Mike remembered what Father Julian had said at the luncheon about evil spirits being able to read other people's minds. "But I love it, and when you've had it a few times, you will, too." She lifted her glass again. "Sorry to rush you, darling, but if you don't eat so I can go to work, there'll be no time for fun and games afterward."

The sandwiches were delicious, the wine even more fragrant and tasty when he started in on the second glass. Afterward he helped her clean up in the kitchen but they kept bumping into each other in the small space, as Mike felt the wine he'd drunk rushing to his brain with a swiftness he'd never known such a drink to do before. Finally, when dizziness made him start to stumble, she put her arm about him and guided him laughingly to his bedroom.

"Lie down while I finish in the kitchen and work on the manuscript," she said, helping him stretch out on the bed and pulling the sheet up so his fumbling fingers, with considerable help from her, could remove the somewhat damp terry robe. "Imagine passing out from only two glasses of elderberry wine."

The words penetrated Mike's fogged brain just deep enough to make him push himself up on his elbows to where he could see more clearly the smiling face of the girl standing at the foot of the bed.

"You gave me a Mickey," he accused her, but she only laughed and pushed him back down on the bed, leaning down to give him a kiss that sent a sense of warmth all the way to his toes.

"Only a little hash in the wine," she confessed. "I promise to make that up to you, before the weekend's over."

She was gone but, when Mike tried to get up and follow her, his arms and legs wouldn't work, so he had no choice except to sink into a pleasant sea of languor where he disported with a lovely nude goddess, who had somehow managed to come to life and make the journey from the British Museum in London.

Mike's drug-fogged eyes couldn't quite bring the numerals of the illuminated clock dial on the bedside table into focus when he drifted back to half consciousness, but he thought it was around one o'clock. One thing he could distinguish: the sound of voices from the living room of the cottage, with every now and then the remembered throaty laugh that always marked Lynne's presence.

Pulling back the sheet that covered his nude body, he tried to get up but managed only to crawl, reaching the bathroom in time to be briefly, but thoroughly, sick. Crawling back, he got a glimpse of the living room reflected in a mirror. The lights were low but he could see that Lynne appeared to be presiding over a gathering of about a half-dozen people.

The one voice was vaguely familiar, that of a man who seemed to be giving directions, for Mike distinguished the words "fifteen miles." But with his vision blurred and his brain fuzzy from the effects of the drug she'd given him in the wine, he couldn't tell whether the things he was seeing and hearing were hallucinations or reality. And since even the reflections in the mirror kept wavering and fading, he finally gave up and crawled back to bed, just before unconsciousness claimed him once more.

Mike was awakened again by the sudden sharp prick of a needle point in his left buttock and, before he could move, felt pain when something was injected into the muscles.

"That should wake you up in a hurry, lover." It was Lynne's voice and he looked up to see her standing beside the bed, looking down at him with the syringe she had used to make the injection in her hand. "It's a good thing you had Adrenalin in your medical bag," she added as she dropped an empty plastic syringe with needle attached into a wastebasket and began to unbutton her blouse. "Armand taught me to use it on people who get too spaced out from hash or acid. If you hadn't had an ampoule in your bag you'd probably have slept all night."

"Wh-what time is it?" Both vision and consciousness were clearing rapidly from the effects of the powerful central nervous system stimulant, but the figures on the clock were still blurred.

"Only three." She laughed. "The night's still before us."

She hung the blouse over a chair and, reaching behind her, unhooked her brassiere and dropped it on the chair, too. Fumbling at the buckle of the smart beige slacks that set off her lower body so beautifully, her eyes suddenly widened at the indubitable evidence that Mike was definitely coming to life as a result of the injection.

"You *are* quite a man, aren't you, Mike Kerns." She whistled softly in admiration, then as she stepped out of the slacks and one last wispy garment dropped to the floor, added, "Move over, darling. You are about to experience what the French would call *fréquentation à la Tallman*. And believe me, this is going to be a night you'll never forget."

13

The bright morning sun, shining through the south window of the bedroom, woke Mike about ten o'clock. The softness of a woman's breast was against his cheek as she lay on her side, her body still pressed close against his own, as it had been for hours during the night, between repeated bursts of utter rapture.

Moving gently so as not to awaken her, he eased away until he could raise himself on one elbow and look at her, a vision of loveliness as she lay with the sheet pulled up across her loins against the coolness of morning but the upper part of her body as bare as was his own.

He leaned over to kiss the lips that had been so demanding against his during the night, but found them only soft and utterly tender now. Then, as they moved against his own in a sleepy return of his kiss, he saw the pupils suddenly dilate until they were dark pools of loveliness in which, he thought, a man could drown himself gladly. A lovely arm moved up to encircle his neck in a sleepy embrace, then as her breasts touched the bare skin of his chest, she sat up suddenly, looking around with eyes that momentarily did not seem to be aware of where she was.

"Mike!" she cried. "What are we doing here? And like this?"

"You came of your own volition," he told her, afraid yet to believe it was really Janet and not Lynne playing one of the macabre tricks on him that she loved to play. "The evidence is there on the chair and the floor, where you dropped it at three o'clock this morning," he added, pointing to the clothing she had discarded before coming into his arms.

She was sitting up in bed now, the sheet drawn across her breasts in an almost virginal gesture which, he knew, would have set the gamine in Lynne shouting with laughter. "I don't remember anything, Mike, not since I was cooking breakfast in my apartment this morning before going to Randall's laboratory to go over the manuscript of the article."

"That was *yesterday* morning," he told her. "When Father

Julian discovered yesterday afternoon that you had called during the morning and left a message canceling the exorcism—"

"I didn't cancel anything!"

"I'm sure you didn't," he assured her. "When Randall told me you'd skipped the appointment with him yesterday afternoon, I put two and two together and figured Lynne had taken over—"

Janet shivered. "I can't stop her any more, Mike. She can do anything she wants to do, or rather, make my body do it." Her eyes widened suddenly. "Then she—you?"

"*We,*" he said. "Don't you remember anything at all about last night?"

She shook her head. "Nothing—except I remember dreaming we were together somewhere."

"Making love?"

"Yes."

"I'm afraid that wasn't just a dream." He told her how Lynne had given him the drug in elderberry wine, then waked him with an injection of the powerful psychic energizer.

"Did you say she was having some sort of a meeting here?" she asked.

"Yes. A half dozen or more people I've never seen before, or at least I never remember seeing."

"She's planning something terrible, Mike. It doesn't bother her, because even if I'm killed or put in prison, she can just move on to another body. And there's nothing I can do."

"There may be something *I* can do," he said, taking her into his arms.

"Don't tell me, she would only get it out of my mind and stop you." She clung to him. "I'm afraid, Mike, terribly afraid."

"Just leave everything to me."

"She'll destroy you, too, if you get in her way." She seemed unconscious of the fact that the sheet, which had partially separated their nude bodies, had now fallen away, but Mike was disturbingly conscious of the loveliness in his arms.

"You trusted me to make you over, now trust me to make you whole," he told her as his lips sought hers.

"You're my only hope now. Love me, Mike! Don't let her destroy me."

She did not respond immediately to his kiss, so great was her

fear and her anxiety. Then, as his hands moved over her naked
flesh, molding her against him, her mouth opened to his and he
felt her body start to arch in an instinctive response as old as time.
It was a sweet communion, yet a passionate one and, when the
final ecstasy joined them irresistibly for a prolonged instant of
time, Mike rejoiced that it was far more meaningful than had been
his experience during the night with the creature who called herself Lynne.

It was after one when they awakened. "I'm so hungry I could
eat boiled dog, darling," said Janet happily as she headed for the
shower, a nude goddess of incredible loveliness.

"Hurry up or I'll be in there with you," Mike called to her.
"And in case you don't know what that would mean—"

"Don't spell it out, please—and spare me," she said. "After all,
the female reproductive system can only take so much in twelve
hours."

"You're headed for a lifetime of that sort of thing," he told her.
"Right now, how do steak and eggs sound to you? A restaurant at
Indian Head specializes in them on Sundays."

"Sounds great. Throw those slacks and the shirt that hussy was
wearing in the closet to be cleaned. A kiss says I'm ready before
you are."

"I'll take that bet," he said but, when he came into the living
room, after a shower and a quick change to slacks and a polo
shirt, she was waiting in a light summer dress with a scarf tied
around her hair.

"You lose, and don't bother about the kiss," she told him.
"After the way you used my anxiety this morning to take advantage of me, I don't trust you."

"Do me one favor and don't change back to Lynne before I
finish my breakfast. I'm afraid I wouldn't be up to it."

"You'd make out—and I use the term advisedly. What troubles
me is whether I'll be up to being married to the most highly sexed
man in the world."

"You'll never know until you try," he told her as he started the
car, "but I've an idea you'll do just fine—and I do speak from experience."

They drove back to a largely deserted Washington just before
sundown. "Please don't ask to come up, Mike," she told him as he
drew the Porsche to a stop before her apartment house behind her

own car. "I'd only let you stay and right now I need time to think more than I need being made love to—even by you."

"I understand," said Mike. "Be sure and call Father Julian tonight. He has to know you're okay before tomorrow."

"I'll do it as soon as I get into my apartment," she promised. "Believe me, darling, I'm as anxious to get the exorcism over quickly as you are."

"I'll pick you up for dinner here tomorrow night about seven, then," he said. "Sorry I'm tied up Tuesday night with a medical dinner."

"Better make it Wednesday night," she told him. "I'll be busy tomorrow evening and probably Tuesday, too, on the final draft of the *Journal* article I didn't do on Saturday."

As he drove home slowly, Mike reached into the pocket of his polo shirt and took out the slip of crumpled paper that had fallen from the blouse Lynne had been wearing last night, when he'd tossed it into the closet with the slacks that morning to be cleaned. There hadn't been time to examine it closely then but, after driving into the parking garage beneath his apartment house and turning off the motor, he smoothed out the crumpled sheet of note pad on the cowl board.

Even a superficial examination assured him that, in his quick glance at it when he'd picked it up from the floor, he had read the words correctly, though he still couldn't figure out what they meant.

"D day . . . Tues. 10 A.M." was written in the unmistakable handwriting he'd first seen on the surgical permission sheet for the mammaplasties he'd done on Janet, or at least on her body. A date followed, but it had been erased, so he couldn't make out exactly what it had been, then the words: "Fifteen-mile range."

Obviously Lynne had used the crumpled rectangle of paper to jot down some notes that she had stuck in her shirt pocket, probably last night during the conference in the living room Mike had seen so indistinctly in the mirror as he'd crawled back to the bed from the bathroom. He recalled again the man's voice saying the words "fifteen miles," but although the voice had seemed hauntingly familiar, he still couldn't pin it down.

Janet had said, when he'd taken her to Annapolis for dinner the week before, he recalled now, that she was sure Lynne was planning some mischief, and the single sheet with its cryptic notations might very well be a clue to what it was. But beyond the fact that something was probably going to happen on a Tuesday morning at ten o'clock, Mike had no clue as to its nature.

In his apartment, he briefly considered calling Inspector Stafford and asking his advice, but decided against it. Consulting the FBI agent would mean revealing what had happened over the weekend, especially the conference at the cottage of perhaps a half-dozen people he never remembered seeing before. And although he'd told Stafford of Randall McCarthy's double-personality diagnosis in Janet's case, as well as Father Julian's quite different diagnosis of possession, he was certain the inspector had not accepted either theory.

Father Julian called about an hour after Mike reached the apartment.

"I just thought you'd like to know your fiancée is still very anxious to go through with the exorcism, Mike," said the priest. "I gave her all the instructions when she called, so if it's okay with you, we will meet at your cottage early Saturday morning on the weekend after Labor Day."

"That's a week earlier than you'd planned, isn't it?"

"Yes. Another case I had scheduled was injured in a collision and is in the hospital. Miss Burke seemed anxious to get the exorcism behind her, so I scheduled it tentatively for two weeks from yesterday."

"I'll take Janet there myself the night before," Mike promised. "What about Dr. McCarthy?"

"I called him just now and he's free, too. He'll drive down that morning with me and my assistants."

"Thanks, Father," said Mike. "You can't imagine what a load this takes off my mind."

"See you that morning, then. Good night, my son. I shall pray for your fiancée to be healed."

And pray that whatever mischief the other resident of that beloved body has planned isn't scheduled earlier than two weeks from yesterday, Mike added in a silent prayer of his own.

14

When Tuesday morning passed without any sign that it was the day Lynne had scribbled on the sheet of note pad, Mike breathed a sigh of relief. He was busy Tuesday afternoon with the final preparations for the paper he was scheduled to give that evening at a dinner of the Pygmalion Club, a group of Washington-based specialists in plastic and maxillofacial surgery who met every three months.

His presentation was built around the surgery involved in re-making Janet's crushed features and was illustrated with color slides. Afterward the discussion was prolonged, when some of the surgeons present pointed out the danger of malpractice accusations inherent in trying to reshape a patient's features to something that differed in appearance from the original. It was after eleven before Mike returned to his apartment and he considered calling Janet to tell her about the meeting, then decided to tell her the next evening at dinner.

At seven, Wednesday evening, Mike rang the bell of Janet's apartment. When there was no answer, he went downstairs to the one occupied by George Stanfield, but he, too, was out. Thinking she might have become ill, he found the building superintendent, who knew him and opened the apartment with a passkey. Everything was in order, however, except that Janet was not there and her parking space in the garage was empty.

Definitely worried now, Mike drove back to his apartment and went upstairs, hoping she had called in the meantime to tell him what had happened. His answering service reported no calls, so he telephoned the Emergency Room at several hospitals to see whether she could have been involved in an accident and was un-conscious. Drawing a blank at the three of the busiest hospital emergency rooms in the city, he was considering calling the police when the telephone rang. It was Janet.

"Where are you?" he asked the moment she spoke his name. "I've been calling hospital emergency rooms for the past half hour."

"I'm at the Visitor Center: you know, the old Union Station. The police are holding me—"

"For what?"

"The lieutenant they called when I was arrested doesn't quite know yet." He could tell from her voice that she was near to tears. "You see, I don't know how I got here myself."

"Lynne?"

"It must be. I—I had a blackout sometime today and don't remember anything that's happened since breakfast."

"Tell the officers I'm your physician and you're under my care; I'm a police reserve surgeon, so I know most of the top brass in the department. Everything's going to be all right."

"All right. Please hurry."

Fifteen minutes later, Mike parked the Porsche in a restricted area near the massive Union Station, which, with few passenger trains running any more, had recently been made into a Visitor Center. It was a logical move, too, he could see, as he circled the fountain in front of it and went inside, for the station was within walking distance of practically every structure that made up the very heart of the federal government, including both the White House and the Capitol.

He found the police booth without difficulty and, when he came in, Janet threw herself into his arms, sobbing. "Uncle George is in Canada," she told him. "If I hadn't been able to get you, I'd have gone to jail."

A burly officer with the map of Ireland on his face came over to where Mike was holding Janet just inside the booth. "Good evening, Doctor," he said. "Lieutenant Gerald O'Flanagan."

"I remember you, Lieutenant, from one of my classes in emergency procedures when I was a surgical resident. Miss Burke is my patient and also my fiancée."

"And a fine tribute she is both to your skill and your good judgment, Doctor. Now, if you can persuade her to tell us why she was a quarter of a mile away from the station platform inside one of the old tunnels—"

"But I don't know," Janet wailed. "I—I just found myself there with a security guard shining his torch in my face."

"That's the only story she will tell us, Doctor," said O'Flanagan patiently.

"Not *will* tell you, Lieutenant—*can* tell you. Miss Burke suffered a severe concussion at the time of the airplane crash and has been subject to spells of amnesia ever since. They're clearing up slowly, but they're still very upsetting to her when they do occur."

"Is she undergoing psychiatric treatment?"

"Yes, with Dr. Randall McCarthy at the University Clinic. He will vouch—"

"Your word is enough, Dr. Kerns," said Lieutenant O'Flanagan. "I'll take the responsibility of releasing your fiancée in your custody."

"Will she have to appear in court?"

"The worst charge we could make against her is trespassing and that's hardly one we could press, considering that it occurred in a railroad station. She's just lucky that, in her state of amnesia, she didn't choose a tunnel used by Amtrak or one of the few passenger trains of other lines that still come in here from the South."

Mike signed the record and left the huge old station, where the voice of the train callers used to echo back and forth but were rarely heard now. "Do you know where your car is?" he asked Janet. "It's not in your space at the apartment."

"No-no, Mike. The last thing I remember is putting the breakfast dishes in the dishwasher. Randall and I worked until almost midnight and he insisted on following me home from his office, but I don't remember going out at all."

"There's a parking garage close by. Look in your handbag and see if you have a parking ticket for it."

The ticket was there, stamped with the time she'd entered the lot, 6:30 P.M. But when she looked at the note pad in her bag on which she recorded the mileage driven each day, the figure on the pad was almost fifty miles less than the one on the mileage indicator in the car.

"It looks like Lynne has been up to her old tricks again," Mike said as he started the car and drove it down the ramp to pay the bill. "Do you have any dreamlike memories of where you could have been from noon until six-thirty?"

"None at all. The only thing I remember is the sight of a man's back disappearing into a side tunnel a moment after the guard flashed his light on me and shouted for me to stop."

"Did the guard see the man?"

"I don't think so—but I did. It was Roger Coven."

"Are you sure?"

"Absolutely. I got a clear view of his face."

"You know what that means, don't you—about the other black-out when Randall saw you by remote viewing with a man who looked like Coven?"

She nodded slowly. "It had to be him that time, too, which means they've met before, probably in connection with whatever Lynne is planning to do. What are we going to do, Mike? She'll be able to outwit us if we try to stop her."

"*Us,* yes, but maybe not the United States government." He stopped her car beside an outdoor telephone stand across from the station near the area where his car was parked. "Do you feel like driving behind me to the FBI building, if Inspector Stafford happens to be working late? He once told me he often does."

"I'll be all right, as long as I'm with you," she assured him.

"Which is from now on," he told her as he went to the telephone.

At his office Stafford listened in silence while Mike gave an account of the happenings at the cottage over the weekend, omitting of course, his trysts with Lynne and Janet. When Mike spread out on the desk the note pad sheet that had fallen from the blouse Lynne had worn, Janet leaned forward to study it more closely.

"That's Lynne's writing," she said. "Don't you remember, Mike? From the hospital permit sheet I didn't remember signing."

"I recognized it at once and I'm sure Professor Leibowitz will verify the difference, Inspector."

"We often use the professor for handwriting questions and will show the note to him." Stafford handed Janet a note pad with about the same size sheets from his desk. "Please copy what's written there as you would write it, Miss Burke, so we can have the professor make a comparison."

Janet made the copy and Inspector Stafford put it inside a folder that already contained a dozen or more reports.

"We haven't exactly been sitting on our hands, you can see, Doctor," he said. "We have an affidavit from Father Julian O'Meara stating his conviction that Miss Burke is indeed possessed by a demon, probably that of Lynne Tallman." He smiled, a little wryly. "Though I must say that to my knowledge this is the first time such an affidavit has been included in an FBI file."

"Then you accept it as a fact?" Mike asked.

"I accept that Miss Burke is capable of acting as two different people—"

"But not voluntarily."

"The file contains an affidavit from Dr. McCarthy to that effect."

"What does it take to convince you, Inspector?" Janet demanded. "Especially after what just happened at the station."

"Let's say I'm keeping an open mind," said Stafford. "Are you willing to make an affidavit that you saw Roger Coven in the branch tunnel this evening and that he had probably been with you until the security guard spotted you?"

"Not the latter part," said Mike quickly. "She has no memory of how she got there or who she was with, only of seeing Roger Coven disappear into a side tunnel an instant after the security guard saw her."

"We'll settle for that," Stafford agreed.

"That being the case, can't you put Coven under arrest?"

"All things considered, we can hardly arrest him for trackwalking any more than Lieutenant O'Flanagan was able to arrest Miss Burke tonight."

Mike threw up his hands in a gesture of bafflement. "Obviously something's going to happen, probably on a Tuesday morning at ten o'clock, and both Roger Coven and Lynne are involved. Are you just going to stand by and let it happen?"

"We'll certainly place Coven under surveillance, Doctor, but we'd have a hard job finding a judge who would believe Miss Burke is harboring a demon. Even so, how do you control something—someone—that has no material existence, except when it uses Miss Burke's body for its own purposes—and without her knowing what's happening at that?"

A light suddenly burst in Mike's brain, and with it a possible answer to all the riddles. Moreover, the answer had been there ever since Janet had found herself deep inside the maze of tunnels that ran beneath the old Union Station, with no memory of how she'd gotten there.

"Listen to this theory, then tell me why it couldn't be true," he said. "Some important event—probably a terror bombing because, when she was alive, Lynne Tallman and her cult specialized in just that—is almost certainly going to happen."

"But how soon?" Janet asked. "The only time mentioned is a Tuesday morning, and one Tuesday has already passed since it was written."

"It must be going to happen soon, else the meeting at the cottage Saturday night wouldn't have been necessary," said Mike.

"That's logical," Stafford agreed.

"On what Tuesday morning in the near future would Washington be the most crowded and a bombing liable to maim or kill the most people?" Mike asked.

"Tuesday after Labor Day!" Janet cried. "That has to be it!"

"Go on, please, Doctor." Stafford's tone was grave.

"And where else could a bomb be better placed to destroy the very heart of Washington and disrupt the government than somewhere inside the maze of tunnels beneath the old Union Station?"

"I can see two weak points in that conclusion," Stafford objected. "Armand Descaux was the bombing expert in Lynne Tallman's cult group, and, with him dead, I doubt that anyone else in the cult could put together such a bomb. Second, the bomb required would be of such size that it could hardly be moved into the station tunnels without attracting attention."

"Not if they used a small atomic bomb."

"Perhaps, but that would be very difficult to achieve."

"Maybe not as much as it would seem at first glance," Mike argued. "You were able to catch Lynne Tallman originally because of a power struggle within the cult between her and Armand Descaux, weren't you?"

"We think so."

"Descaux used dynamite in the landing gear of the plane because that's the technique he knows best. When the demon from Lynne Tallman's body took up residence in Janet's, however, it couldn't trust Descaux any more so it had to get rid of him—with that call to Chicago and the certainty that Janet would shoot him as an intruder when he came to the cottage. All of which meant that before Lynne could go on with the same sort of destructive campaign against the world she'd been engaged in before, Lynne had to find another bomb expert. And when I took Janet to my cottage, there was one a short distance away: Roger Coven."

When Stafford still looked somewhat doubtful, Mike added, "Coven is capable of making a small atomic bomb, isn't he?"

The FBI agent didn't answer but got to his feet instead. Crossing the room to a large filing cabinet, he pulled out a folder and leafed through the material it contained, then brought it back to his desk.

"This is a clipping from a national Sunday supplement that appeared recently," he said. "A junior at Princeton, majoring in aerospace and mechanical sciences, has written a scientific paper titled 'The Fundamentals of Atomic Bomb Design: An Assessment of the Problems and Possibilities Confronting a Terrorist Group of Non-Nuclear Nations Attempting to Design a Crude PU-239 Fission Bomb.'"

"Are you sure it's for real and not a spoof, like that paper written by a high school kid down in Florida some years ago?" Mike asked.

"It's for real, all right," said Stafford. "The author based his method on pamphlets and other material that anybody can obtain from the U. S. Government Printing Office. And excluding the plutonium, the cost is estimated at about two thousand dollars."

"That's scary," Janet admitted.

"It's worse," Stafford told her. "According to the information I've been able to obtain since this paper was published, the bomb that could be made by following the directions in that paper would be only about two feet in diameter and weigh no more than 125 pounds—an easy burden for a strong man to carry."

"My God!" Mike exclaimed. "Anybody who knew how and felt he had a reason, however screwy, could blow up Washington."

"That's exactly what the Atomic Energy Commission concluded from a study it made recently. Listen to this: 'Amateur bombmakers could probably put together weapons as powerful as one-tenth of a kiloton (equivalent to the explosive force of 100 tons of TNT). Such bombs would be powerful enough to topple the twin towers of Manhattan's 110-story World Trade Center. Or'"—he paused a moment for emphasis—"'the U. S. Capitol Building.'"

"That's their target," said Janet immediately. "If you can find a map of those tunnels under the Union Station, I'll bet some of them run very close to the Capitol."

"You're probably right," Stafford admitted.

"Do you remember Washington or the Capitol ever being mentioned by Lynne Tallman, while you were in Chicago?" Mike asked.

"No. Not once."

"Several other statements in material summarizing from the AEC investigations of just such a possibility are important," said Stafford. "Listen:

" 'With so much plutonium around, terrorists might not find it too difficult to get their hands on it. The AEC is tightening its security measures against theft, but some weapons-grade material is lost during processing and merely written off as MUF (materials unaccounted for). If an employee-conspirator decided to accumulate a critical amount of plutonium by helping himself to a little MUF at a time, the loss might never be detected.' "

"As chief investigator of plutonium loss for the AEC, Coven certainly had access to the stuff," Mike pointed out. "In fact he's been sitting in the driver's seat for years, probably snitching a little of the stuff here and some more there, until he had enough."

"But he's too hardheaded to be a terrorist," Janet objected. "That sort of thing is for crackpots—or demons."

"I think you're right," Stafford agreed. "Coven's a realist and would be far more likely to hold the country up for ransom, with the threat of destroying Washington."

"How would he get away?" Mike asked.

"That would be in the deal. A lot of countries hate us so much that they'd give him refuge afterward, if he succeeded, and even make a hero out of him."

"The Lynne demon wouldn't be interested in ransom," Janet objected. "Her whole purpose would be to create fear and disruption of confidence among the people in the power of the government, even religion, to protect them. Whenever—and however—this event is scheduled, it's a terrorist act, pure and simple, as far as she's concerned. If Roger's in it, he's merely using the bombing as a test of what he could do alone later—for ransom."

"All our experience with the Chicago gang does indicate that Miss Burke is right about *their* motives," Stafford agreed.

"The thing I don't understand is why someone in Roger Coven's position would take such a risk," said Mike, but Janet gave him a possible answer.

"I'm not the only person in the world possessed by a demon, Mike. Father Julian says there are thousands of us—and only a few really want to be free from the power of Satan."

"Is your exorcism still scheduled for the Saturday after Labor Day, Miss Burke?" Stafford asked.

"So Dr. Kerns tells me. He talked to Father Julian Sunday night."

"Then whatever form of terrorism is being plotted will almost certainly take place next Tuesday morning."

"Which doesn't give us much time," said Mike pointedly. "Surely you have enough evidence to justify arresting Roger Coven now, Inspector."

"If he were an ordinary criminal, yes—but Coven has powerful friends in Washington and so far it's all circumstantial. Even if he did have connections with the Tallman gang in Chicago, he's covered his tracks brilliantly; all we could get on him was that brief affair with Lynne Tallman years ago. If I arrest him now, his lawyer could demand an immediate hearing before a District Court judge and the case would be thrown out. Or bail would be granted, leaving him still free to do whatever is being planned. I'd rather have him out under surveillance so, if he does plant this bomb, we can locate and defuse it." He turned to Janet. "Do you think your presence, in physical form, but with the other one in control, is necessary now for Coven's plans, Miss Burke?"

"No."

"Why?"

"Roger Coven abandoned me to the station police, knowing Lynne would probably change me back to myself, as I am now. He may even have counted on my being arrested and held, when I couldn't explain what I was doing in that tunnel. Which can only mean he doesn't need Lynne—or me—any more."

Inspector Stafford closed the folder and put it back in the filing cabinet from which he had taken it. "One thing more," he said as he came back to the desk. "Do you believe Roger Coven realized that you recognized him tonight, Miss Burke?"

"I don't think so. The flashlight the security guard was carrying almost blinded me. If I hadn't turned my head quickly to escape the beam, I wouldn't have seen Roger at all. As it was, I only got a glimpse of him."

"Then how could you be so certain of his identity?" Stafford asked.

"There are lamps set into the walls of the tunnels; I used to watch them flash by when I came from Northwestern to visit Uncle George by way of Philadelphia and the train came through the tunnels into Union Station. The beam of the guard's flashlight was reflected by the thick glass covering the bulb of one of those lamps and, for an instant, Roger Coven was silhouetted in the reflected beam. I could see that he had closed his eyes momentarily because of the bright light, so I'm pretty sure he didn't realize I'd seen him."

"And of course, being under control of Lynne while you were inside the tunnel, you'd have no memory of anything until you suddenly became Janet," said Mike.

"That's exactly what happened."

"Then you're probably in no danger from Coven," Stafford agreed. "Thank both of you for coming by tonight. I'll have Coven watched closely, and if he makes any suspicious move, we'll nab him. We'll also check that garage you told me he was usually working in at the river cottage for radioactivity."

"Do you think the atomic bomb—if that's what he's planning to use—could already be in place inside one of those tunnels?" Mike asked. "After all, we know he's been there twice with the Lynne demon."

"If it is, we'll find it," Stafford assured him grimly. "The first thing tomorrow morning, we'll search every inch of that station and the area beneath it. Meanwhile we'll be watching every move Coven makes."

Outside, Mike put Janet into the Porsche and got in himself on the other side.

"I don't imagine you had any dinner," he said as he started the motor. "Want to go somewhere and eat?"

"I don't want to go anywhere but home." She shivered. "Every time I remember suddenly becoming myself again, with that flashlight boring into my eyes, I get the willies."

"Let's hope that's all over now. Tell you what: why don't we go to the cottage for the Labor Day weekend? It's far enough away to let us find a little peace there."

"How far, Mike?"

"Something over twenty miles. Why?"

"Fifteen miles was what Lynne had jotted down on that sheet of notepaper, so it must be the range of the bomb."

"Which could mean Coven figures he only has to get as far away as Lane Cottage on the river to be safe."

"What about the million people who'll be either back in Washington Tuesday morning from the Labor Day weekend or driving in and less than fifteen miles away?"

"Don't think about it," Mike advised. "Just remember what you've done for all of them by recognizing Coven tonight so Stafford can nab him."

Janet shivered and put her hand on Mike's arm in a pleading gesture. "I don't want to go to the cottage. Why can't you stay with me, darling? I'm afraid of what Lynne may do yet."

"I have no intention of leaving you," he told her as the car drew to a stop before the apartment. "We'll go up to your apartment and pack a bag, then you're going to move in with me until this whole business is over. My place is pretty short of parking spaces, so we might as well leave your car here."

15

Mike had planned to close his office Friday for the long Labor Day weekend, when Washington became, in essence, a dead city, so he was only away Thursday and for hospital rounds Friday morning. At Janet's request, he locked her inside the apartment when he left both mornings and, when he came back Friday before noon, she had already prepared a delicious lunch, with a bottle of rosé from the South of France properly chilled to go with it. Afterward they went to a double feature in a nearly deserted movie house where they could hold hands and neck like a couple of college kids on a date.

Driving back to the apartment, after a long, slow dinner at a small Italian restaurant, Janet lay back against the seat and closed her eyes. After a few minutes, however, she sat up. "Do you know what I'd like to do, Mike?"

"I hope so," he said with a grin. "But tell me anyway."

"I read a book a long time ago—about how to live as a whole person and be only yourself. It described a trick the author recommended highly, as a means of getting away from the humdrum of everyday activity."

"I wouldn't say the past few days have been exactly humdrum."

"Ever since I read the book, I've wanted to try her method of shaking yourself loose from the everyday world. What you do is start driving around a traffic circle."

"There are plenty of them in Washington."

"I know, that's what reminded me of the book. You drive around until something tells you to choose a street leading away from the circle. Then you keep on until you see something that looks different, interesting, or maybe even exciting."

"Why not try it?"

"Would you? Just to humor me?"

"Of course. But we'd better go by the apartment and pick up toothbrushes, a shaving kit and whatever cosmetics you need."

"To say nothing of something to sleep in."

"That I do without—remember?"

"But not me, I still have some modesty. Anyway, let's go."

Fifteen minutes later, with a small handbag and a shaving kit on the back seat, Mike started driving around Dupont Circle while Janet lay back against the headrest, her eyes closed.

"No peeping," he warned.

"And no fudging. I'm waiting for inspiration and I'd better not open my eyes to find you're taking me to some motel where you're sure you won't be recognized."

"Cross my heart," he promised.

He was on his second circuit of the busy circle when she said, "Turn right; this is it."

He turned right obediently and found himself on the broad thoroughfare of U.S. 29 leading west and south into Virginia.

"Where are we?" she asked dreamily a half hour later.

"On U.S. 15-29 in Virginia, headed toward Warrenton."

"How far from it?"

"About ten miles."

"Good." She closed her eyes. "I'll tell you where to turn."

"You've been here before," he accused.

"Just trust me and tell me when we're in Warrenton."

Fifteen minutes later, Mike said, "We're here."

"Turn left at the next stop light."

Mike obeyed and shortly found himself upon an almost deserted state road. "We're on Virginia 616," he said. "I hope you know what you're doing and where we're going."

"Trust me," she said enigmatically.

Some fifteen minutes later they saw the lights of a small town perhaps half a mile ahead; nearer, beside the road, was a sign: "Old Mill Motel." As they approached, Mike saw the lights of a small rustic motel, set back among the trees on the shore of a pond near the looming three-storied structure of a typical antique grist mill.

"This is it," said Janet. "Drive in."

"I hope they've got a vacancy."

"They have," she said complacently. "I phoned ahead while you were in the bathroom of the apartment just before we left Washington. The town is called Bristersburg."

"I still don't see how you knew this place was here—unless you've picked up Randall McCarthy's trick of remote viewing from working with him."

"No such luck," she said. "I drove down to the University of Virginia in Charlottesville a couple of weeks ago to check on some work they've been doing in parapsychology. I do shun-piking whenever I can and stay off the four-laned roads. When I drove by this place it was so lovely, I stopped and had lunch. There's a darling little restaurant inside the old mill."

"So all that business of driving around Dupont Circle was a fake?"

"Not a fake, darling. The minute I saw the place, I thought of how nice it would be to come here with you—when all this double-personality business was over."

"I'm hoping it's over now and that Roger Coven flew the coop when he saw you being arrested."

"It also occurred to me that Roger still might need Lynne for the final working out of whatever they're planning, even though I told Inspector Stafford he wouldn't. If I keep my body here, she can't very well be in Washington, so let's just forget about all that for the next few days."

Mike registered them as Mr. and Mrs. Michael Karnes, an old spelling of his name, and they drove to a small, log-walled building on the bank of the pond. Inside was spotless, with an antique rope bed and tester, a red lampshade of Tiffany glass and the general atmosphere of a high-class New Orleans bordello.

"I didn't look at any of the rooms when I was here before, but this is priceless," Janet cried. "There's even a Boston rocker and a little porch overlooking the pond."

"To say nothing of cane-pole fishing equipment in the chimney corner outside," said Mike. "I'll bet that pond's full of bream and catfish."

"With no TV we can put the world behind us; I'm not even going to read a newspaper while we're here." Neither of them mentioned the most important fact—that the Old Mill Motel was roughly thirty-five miles from Washington.

16

Mike was fishing off the front porch of their small cottage when Janet came out the next morning wearing the white bikini.

"How do you know swimming's allowed in this pond?" he asked.

"There's a diving board at the deep end near the dam and I saw some kids swimming there when I had lunch at the restaurant a few weeks ago. Any luck?"

"These fish are too happy where they are to even look at a hook. Wait till I get my swim shorts on and I'll join you."

They had a delightful swim and a hearty breakfast in the small but equally spotless restaurant that occupied the lower floor of what had been a water-powered grist mill. The pancakes were buckwheat, just like that ground there since before the American Revolution, the waitress told them. The eggs were from the hens they heard cackling in the yard next door, the syrup from Virginia maples, and the bacon from hogs like those grunting in a nearby pen.

It was an idyllic spot and an idyllic time. They ate hugely of delicious Virginia ham and biscuits with honey, or fried chicken and creamed potatoes, made love when they felt like it, and dozed or read old paperback novels they found on a shelf in the closet, trying to shut away the world outside and their own responsibilities to it and succeeding very well—until Sunday morning.

Mike awakened to find Janet in the shower. When she came out, her body wrapped in a nubby towel, he saw a look of purpose in her eyes he'd seen there a few times before. He knew then that her thoughts were the same his had been, when he'd lain awake for an hour after they'd made love last night and she'd gone to sleep in his arms.

"I guess we both knew it couldn't last," he said as he headed for the shower. "Lynne couldn't very well blow up Washington with you thirty-five miles away, but if we go back to Washington now, she might appear and lead Inspector Stafford to Roger and the bomb. I'll check out after breakfast and we can be back in Washington before lunch. Stafford's sure to have stayed in town over the holiday and I can give him a call to see what's happening."

"I hate to even think of what that may be but, no matter what happens, I will have known what real happiness we could have had together."

"Not *have had; will have.*"

"I only hope you're right, darling, but somehow I don't see either Roger or Lynne giving up that easily."

"If they have, you made them."

"And if they haven't?"

"I'm afraid we'll have to play that one by ear."

As they expected, Washington was deserted, with not many cars on the streets besides the usual sightseeing buses and only a few of those visible. With all the government buildings closed for the Labor Day weekend, even the tourists had largely deserted the nation's capital.

"It's hard to believe that less than forty-eight hours from now this place will be the usual madhouse again," Mike observed.

"If it isn't a smoking, radioactive ruin!"

"We can still avoid that by going to the river cottage."

"We can't run away, Mike. If I hadn't been with Lynne on the flight from Chicago that night, the evil spirit that drove her wouldn't have escaped into my body. Which makes me responsible, to a degree, for what she does. Pray God the demon's gone, but we won't be sure until next Saturday, will we?"

"I think we'll know before that," he said as they drove into the parking garage. "If ten o'clock Tuesday morning passes without a mushroom cloud hanging over this very apartment house, we can be sure both Roger Coven and the demon of Lynne Tallman have spooked and gone on to cause trouble somewhere else."

Inside his apartment, Mike rang Inspector Stafford. "Miss Burke and I have been out of town for two days, Inspector," he said. "Do you have any leads on Roger Coven?"

"Nothing. When he disappeared into that side tunnel, leaving Miss Burke to fend for herself, he apparently vanished into thin air."

"What about the station?"

"We searched every inch of it and even opened a toolbox of an antique gandy dancers' handcar we found in an unused tunnel. The stationmaster is giving it to the Smithsonian next week. What about Miss Burke?"

"There's been no sign of the other one, if that's what you mean. We're hoping she's flown the coop, too."

"We did find out why Coven took up with the terrorists, though," Stafford added. "Apparently, even in spite of his rapid promotions, he's resented all along not being given credit publicly for catching the men who were stealing plutonium. On top of that, it now appears that they weren't really guilty, except maybe the first one down at Oak Ridge. Coven was already stashing away a supply for himself even then and throwing suspicion on others."

"What could he hope to accomplish—unless he's a diehard terrorist, too?"

"I got hold of George Stanfield where he was fishing in Canada and discovered that the *Star-News* has had a smart investigative reporter named Jensen checking on Coven. As I told you, the Bureau has been hog-tied because of Coven's high connections, but the reporter teamed up with a friend who works for the Magnes Commission. Between them they're about ready to blow the lid off the whole business—Coven, Magnes and Rita, though she seems to have served only as a mistress for the senator. My guess is that Coven got wind of the investigation and was angry enough to blow the Establishment sky-high."

"Do you think he still plans to do it?"

"That's a possibility, but a remote one, now that he knows we're onto him. The entire Bureau, as well as police all over the country, is looking for him and, when he surfaces, we'll nab him. I also talked to Professor McCarthy and asked him to spend the weekend at the cottage with Rita Coven."

"I'll bet he liked that."

"He didn't seem to mind. He's to call me if Roger tries to get in touch with her."

"Otherwise you're sitting tight?"

"What else?"

"Couldn't you issue some kind of warning?"

"And throw the nation into a panic—probably over nothing? The Chief would spend the rest of his days before congressional committees trying to explain what happened—that is, until the President fired him."

"I guess you're right at that," Mike agreed. "Well, Miss Burke and I will be holed up here at my apartment until it's all over."

"You'd be safer at your cottage, no matter what happens."

"We don't figure that's cricket for either of us."

"I figured you'd see it that way but thought I ought to give you a chance to get out. I've set up a command post here at the office and will keep you informed of any news. You can call me here night or day."

"I don't like it, Mike," said Janet when he gave her a rundown on the conversation with Stafford. "All those people will be coming into the city Tuesday morning, not knowing it may be the last day they'll be alive."

"I feel the same way, but we're all stymied, unless Roger tries to put the bomb into position somewhere and the police or the FBI are able to nab him."

"What are you going to do if Lynne reappears?"

"I've got an emergency plan for coping with her."

She shivered. "The waiting wasn't so bad out at the motel, but now that we can see the city all around us and know what may happen, I almost wish I hadn't persuaded you to come back."

"If you hadn't, I'd have persuaded you. We're playing out the last act of a drama that began when I saw your plane that morning on the way to Dulles Airport. And we've got to stay on stage until the curtain's rung down."

"You'd have been better off if you'd been planning to take another flight."

"Then I wouldn't have been there to save your life or to ever know you existed, except from the newspaper obituary."

She managed to smile. "You could have married that blond nurse like any other young doctor and settled down to getting rich doing face-lifts."

"Compared to what I've got to look forward to now, that sounds like a pretty humdrum existence. Let's watch the football game on TV until it's time to make dinner and I'll prepare my specialty for you."

242

"What's that?"

"Corned beef cheeseburgers; they're out of this world."

The evening was quiet, and so was the night. Most of the "singles" who usually celebrated on weekends in the pool or at impromptu apartment parties appeared to have gone away for the final weekend of the summer social season.

Inspector Stafford was still at his command post in the FBI building when Mike called to check with him, but had nothing to report except that Randall McCarthy had telephoned to say Rita apparently had no idea where Roger was, nor any inkling of his intentions. On the advice of Stafford, however, he was staying on at the cottage until noon Tuesday.

McCarthy had, however, accomplished one thing, according to Stafford. While Rita was getting supplies from the crossroads store, he'd opened the garage Roger Coven used so much as a workshop. The garage was empty, except for some tools. But when McCarthy used the geiger counter Stafford had insisted he take with him to explore it, he'd found evidence of radioactivity, confirming the suspicion that Coven had been using plutonium there, presumably to manufacture a small atomic bomb.

It was shortly after five when the telephone rang and Mike answered. Unexpectedly, the voice at the other end was that of Dr. Elmo Sebastian, Chief of Service at University Hospital and head of the Department of Plastic and Reconstructive Surgery, to which Mike was assigned as an Assistant Clinical Professor.

"Thank God I found you, Mike," said Sebastian. "How soon can you get to University Hospital? There's been a pileup on the Annapolis Road and a girl's pretty badly cut up about the face, a senator's daughter."

"I'm not on call, Elmo. Besides, I—"

"You can't let me down, Mike, no matter who you're with. I'm calling from the Emergency Room with a broken wrist. Fell on my own tennis court an hour ago and have the most beautiful Colles's fracture you ever saw."

"I don't—"

"It's an emergency, Mike; the resident's away and I can't trust an assistant resident to work on the daughter of an important senator."

"One minute, Elmo." Mike put his hand over the receiver and spoke to Janet. "It's Dr. Sebastian, my department head at University. They've got a senator's daughter over there with a badly smashed-up face from an automobile accident and he's just broken his wrist playing tennis."

"Does he want you to come?"

"Yes. I'm the only other person on the staff that's available but—"

"Then you'll have to go," she said at once. "Don't worry about leaving me alone, I'll be all right."

"You're certain?"

"Of course. If you lock me in the apartment, I can't get out and neither could *she*."

"All right, Elmo," he told Sebastian. "I'll be right over."

"Thank you, Mike; there'll be a nice fee in it for you, too. After the job you did on Janet Burke, the senator will probably figure you can do a better job on his daughter than I could—which incidentally happens to be true."

"I shouldn't be gone more than a couple of hours," Mike told Janet. "On the way home I'll stop at a pizzeria around the corner and bring us a nice hot pizza with a bottle of wine."

"Sounds heavenly," she said as she kissed him good-by. "Be sure and lock the door as you go out."

The senator's daughter's face was not as badly crushed as Janet's had been, but she'd been thrown clear of an open car in which she'd been coming back to Washington from Ocean City with her fiancé, unfortunately landing in a gravel pit beside the road. The job took three hours of careful surgery, picking gravel and dirt out of the multiple wounds, trimming skin edges and sewing them together with the tiny sutures plastic surgeons used in facial work.

Dressing hurriedly after the surgery was finished, Mike drove through almost empty streets to the pizzeria and waited impatiently while his order was cooked and boxed. Then, carrying it and a bottle of wine, he went to the apartment, taking the elevator up from the parking garage underneath the building. The door was still locked, so he knocked on it, rather than put down the box to get his keys. When there was no answer, he took them from his pocket, unlocked the door and opened it—to find the apartment empty.

Janet—or rather Lynne, he was sure—was gone.

17

It didn't take Mike long to find the note; she'd left it on the table of the small dinette. One glance at the *e*'s and the *t*'s told him who had written it, even without the large *L* scrawled at the bottom:

Darling Mike,

I hate to do this to the nicest guy I ever met. If I could really become human and love anybody it would be you, but you know how we who serve the Lord of Evil are. Besides I hate fire, and before noon tomorrow, Washington will be a mass of flames.

If you really love your Janet and want to preserve her body as well as yours, come to the river cottage tonight, but don't think you can persuade me or the others to give up the destruction of the nest of perfidy Washington has become. Come with the idea of saving yourself and Janet; when it suits my purpose, I promise to leave her body for another that will be easier to control and not so easily recognizable—thanks to you.

Those are my terms; if you agree to them, I shall expect to see you tonight. If not, you will die and, if I were capable of real feeling, I should mourn the waste of your wonderful talents.

Yours (when I want it that way)

L

P.S. I've been picking locks since I was five, as Lynne Tallman. The double dead bolt on your apartment door took me less than a minute.

It was almost dark outside and Mike wasted no time setting in motion the emergency plan he'd decided might well be necessary, since Janet had called him from the station to reveal that Lynne had deserted her to save herself and Roger Coven from being captured by the station security police. It called for little preparation, except a stop at an all-night drugstore on the road to Indian Head.

Briefly he considered calling Inspector Stafford and decided against it. The FBI agent might, in desperation, try to capture Lynne and that, he was certain, would result only in his seizing

Janet, with all the agony for her that would accompany interrogation and perhaps even a night in jail.

As he drove into the yard at the cottage, he saw that all the lights were on and Janet's car was parked under a tree, revealing the way Lynne had reached the cottage. Once out of Mike's own apartment, all she'd had to do was hail a cab for the short trip to her own apartment house, where her car was in the garage. She came to the door as he cut the engine and switched off the lights, a lovely figure in brief shorts and a halter, for the night was almost sultry.

"Mike, darling!" she called, making no attempt to imitate the voice of Janet. "I hoped you'd decide not to fight me any more."

"How could I stay behind, after the invitation you left me?" He came up the steps and took her in his arms for a long, passionate kiss. "I'm not fool enough to throw my life away, along with a city."

"It's going to make a big boom," she said happily. "We can probably see the mushroom from here but Roger says we'll be safe. The effective range is only fifteen miles and we're more than twenty, aren't we?"

"Something like that."

"I was about to pour my first drink of the evening." As they came into the house he saw how brilliant was the light burning in her eyes, unmistakably this time the hallmark of Lynne. "But since it's your house, you can do the honors."

"Not with that elderberry wine you used to put me out."

"No elderberry wine tonight," she said with a happy laugh. "I don't want to have to give you another shot in the tail to wake you up, even if you did perform so well, once it started taking effect."

"I'm glad you were pleased," he said as he moved toward the kitchen and the small bar, leaving her in the living room. "Bourbon do?"

"It's my favorite. Make mine a double."

"Double it is. Turn on the TV and see whether they've captured Roger yet."

"They haven't, and they won't; he knows those tunnels under the Union Station like he knows the back of his hand."

In the kitchen, Mike quickly snapped the top off an ampoule of the powerful tranquilizer chlorpromazine he'd bought at the drugstore on the way to the cottage and emptied it into her glass. Besides its knockout effect in that dosage, the drug also had the advantage of being practically tasteless.

"How did you happen to select Roger to take Armand Descaux's place?" Mike asked as he came back into the living room with two glasses and handed her the one to which he'd added the chlorpromazine.

"That was *luck,*" she admitted, draining half the glass with one swallow. "Umm! I'm glad you decided not to sacrifice yourself tomorrow morning, darling; you mix wonderful drinks. Oh yes! You were asking about Roger, weren't you?"

"Yes."

"Armand turned me in and tried to kill me with that bomb in the plane, so I had to get rid of him." She looked up and laughed. "Rather cleverly, don't you think?"

"No doubt about that." In the mood she was in, the purpose he had in mind could be best served, he was sure, by going along with her and encouraging her to boast. "But I would have thought Roger Coven would be difficult to control."

"I didn't try to control him. When I approached Roger with a plan for destroying the heart of Washington and the U.S. government with one stroke, he'd just learned he was being investigated by Rita's lover—"

"Senator Magnes?"

"Who else? Anyway, when Roger learned that Magnes was going to sell him down the river to save his own reputation, he was ready to do anything for revenge."

"And you used his anger for your own purposes?"

"Of course. What people like you and Janet can't understand is that we who serve Lucifer will stop at nothing to demonstrate his power over mankind."

"How did your spirit gain control of Lynne Tallman originally?"

"That was easy, like the other bodies I've used. Your preachers rant and rave about immortality, but they forget that we of the Underworld are really the immortals."

"And you cannot be destroyed?"

She gave him a quick, suspicious look. "Got any ideas in that direction?"

He shrugged. "If I destroyed you, I'd only destroy Janet."

"And the body you love to touch." She was in high spirits again and finished her drink, handing him the glass. "Another double, lover—and one for yourself. You can't get me drunk, so there's no use trying, but you'll enjoy the rest of the night more if you're well lubricated."

In the kitchen he quickly mixed two more drinks, making his a single this time. He hesitated only a moment about emptying another ampoule of chlorpromazine into Lynne's glass, then broke the top and quickly shook it in and stirred the mixture.

"Hey! What's keeping you so long?" the slightly hoarse voice called from the living room. "I hardly even feel that first drink yet."

"You will this one," he promised and emptied another jigger of the potent 101-proof Bourbon into her glass. "In fact, I'll bet you'll have trouble staying on your feet."

"The hell I will, I could drink you under the table any day." She laughed. "But I'm not expecting to be on my *feet* very much tonight anyway."

"You can say that again," Mike agreed as he handed her the drink.

"You're a man after my own heart, Mike Kerns. Maybe not really the heart, but, as long as we both know what you *are* after, we'll get along."

"Nothing like being appreciated." Mike lifted his glass. "To us."

"Tell you what," she said as the level of the whiskey in her drink grew steadily lower. "When I've moved along to some other body, like I promised you, I'll call you sometime and tell you where I am. You're really too good a human lover to let go, Mike; that's why I left the note, figuring you'd follow me."

"I couldn't see what I had to lose." He kept his voice steadfastly casual. "If I'd stayed in Washington, that bomb would incinerate me tomorrow and I would be giving up both you and Janet into the bargain."

The antique cuckoo clock on the mantel struck then and Lynne looked at the jeweled wristwatch Mike had given Janet on her birthday early in August. "Just about now, Roger will be setting the timer on that bomb—"

"I still don't figure how you got him to go that far with you."

"He wouldn't have agreed, considering the risk, if Senator Magnes hadn't double-crossed him with that investigation because he wanted to have Rita for himself."

"Isn't she one of you?"

"Rita?" Again the raucous laugh. "She doesn't have brains enough to be worth possession even by a lesser demon. The only place she's any good to anybody is behind a stenotype machine or in bed."

Mike knew at least one thing he needed to know now—Roger Coven had not run away after the incident beneath the station and the bombing of Washington was still on schedule. Nor was there any way to warn Stafford in the city, unless the chlorpromazine he'd dumped into Lynne's drink started acting a lot faster than it had so far.

Lynne put down her glass, which was almost empty again. "I guess you know Inspector Stafford is going to arrest your beloved Janet after I move to another body."

"Can you save her?" he ventured to ask. "A note written now telling of your part in the bombing would establish that it wasn't really Janet who planned all this but you in her body. Besides, the rest of the world would know how powerful you are then."

She frowned and shook her head momentarily, as if to clear it. "That way you can have her too—"

"Just as you promised," he reminded her, only to bring another gale of raucous laughter.

"A demon's promise? What would that be worth?"

"Look at it another way, then. Where would you be, if I had let Janet die there on the floor of the airport?"

"That's easy," she said with a shrug. "In another body; the terminal was full of people."

"But not that of a modern-day goddess. And if I hadn't brought Janet—and you—here, you might not have found Roger Coven. Then you'd never have been able to show the world the power you and your Master, Lucifer, have."

"Don't fret me with that now," she said testily. "I may do it in the morning, if you're good in bed tonight without needing a shot of Adrenalin." She stood up and drained her glass. "Pour me another drink while I'm in the bathroom but lay off any more yourself. You look drunk to me." She got up but staggered a little. "Something's wrong; 's never happened before."

"You drank too fast; when you come back from the bathroom you can lie down for a while."

"'S goo' idea." Her voice was slurred almost beyond recogni-

tion when she slumped against him. Then suddenly her body grew
rigid and she turned to face him, standing alone, without swaying,
the flame in her eyes now one of pure hatred.

"You slick son of a bitch," she shrieked. "You gave me something in that whiskey, didn't you?"

He nodded. "The effects will be gone in a few hours but you're
going to tell me first where Roger placed the bomb."

"Like hell I am." Her knees suddenly buckled from the effect of
the chlorpromazine and, if he hadn't caught her, she would have
fallen. Nevertheless she retained strength enough to lash at him
with her open hand, a blow that sent him crashing against the wall
and left him dazed. But it was her final display of a demon's
strength and, even as he stumbled to his feet, she fell against him,
almost dragging him to the floor with her.

Lifting her limp body in his arms, Mike carried her to the couch
and dragged it to the middle of the room. By now she was completely unconscious and snoring stertorously. He could only hope
the sheer terror of fire, which Father Julian had assured him characterized all demonic spirits, would make her confess where
Coven had placed the bomb in time for him to get them both out
of the flames before they were consumed.

Moving outside quickly to the small building where he kept gasoline for the boat and the power mower, he picked up a five-
gallon can used to fill the boat tank and carried it into the house.
Racing around the room, he opened windows on all sides to let
out the fumes so the whole place wouldn't explode when he
touched off the gasoline. As a final measure of protection, too, he
took down the compressed-carbon-dioxide fire extinguisher from
just inside the kitchen door and put it beside the couch on which
he'd placed Janet's sleeping body and the at least temporarily
sleeping evil spirit of Lynne Tallman.

These preparations made, Mike began to pour gasoline on the
floor and the fiber rug in a circle around the couch, drenching the
rug and the floor until the whole five gallons had been poured out.
Then, tossing the empty can away, he uttered a silent prayer that
he and Janet would come out of this desperate situation alive with
the information he wanted, before scratching a match into flame
and tossing it at the ring of gasoline, whose fumes now filled the
living room.

The flames caught with a whoosh and shot halfway to the ceil-

ing at the first ignition, racing around the ring of gasoline so fast
that he could almost believe they were driven by the devil inside
the sleeping figure of the girl. Even Father Julian's warning about
the power of a demon had not prepared him fully for her reaction,
however. When the heat of the flames struck her body, covered
only by the brief shorts and halter, her eyes opened and she
screamed again and again in terror, rising to stand on the couch as
she shrank from the leaping flames.

Reaching down, Mike picked up the fire extinguisher and held it
where her widely dilated pupils could easily let her see it.

"Where's the bomb, Lynne?" he demanded. "Tell me and I'll
put out the flames."

"You'll never find it," she shrieked in a burst of demonic laughter that changed suddenly to one of terror as a tongue of flame
licked at her body.

He saw her start to move and, realizing that, with the superhu-
man strength of the demon, she might leap across the circle of
flames and defeat him, he dropped the extinguisher and tackled
her before she could jump. The action brought them both crashing
to the floor and, as he rolled close to the circle of flame, Mike felt
a searing pain when the cuff of his slacks caught fire. Meanwhile
Lynne was struggling in his arms with such power that he wondered if he could hold her much longer.

"Where's the bomb?" he demanded. "Tell me and I'll put out
the fire."

"In a too—" The rest of the word that might have revealed the
location of the deadly bomb was drowned out by a cry of horror
from an open window. Looking up momentarily, Mike saw Randall McCarthy burst through the door and tear at the woven
drapery across the top of a window beside it, with the obvious intention of beating out the fire.

"No, Randall! No!" he shouted, but it was too late.

As the psychiatrist beat at a thin spot in the ring of fire, it was
broken momentarily for a space of several feet. Lynne had risen to
her hands and knees when the sight of the other man momentarily
tore Mike's attention away from holding her. Now she lunged for
the open space but, feeling her muscles tense, Mike seized her
even more tightly and they both crashed to the floor again, with
one of her hands touching the drapery that was already smoldering into flame.

For a single instant she writhed in his grasp with a burst of demonic strength that threatened to tear her body from his desperate hold upon her. Then a shriek like a banshee's wail assailed his ears—a sound he remembered hearing, it seemed years ago though it was less than three months, from the radio inside the doomed 727 just at the moment of crashing through the glass walls of Dulles Airport. At the same instant, a blast of cold air partially smothered the flames licking at the now burning drape with which Randall McCarthy had broken the fiery ring.

An invisible force toppled McCarthy to one side as if stiff-armed by a football player carrying the ball, to crash against the open front door of the cottage. At that moment, too, the nauseous stench Mike had detected that day in the rectory with Father Julian once again assailed his nostrils, almost making him vomit.

He realized what had happened immediately for, with the single banshee shriek, Janet's body suddenly became limp in his arms. Driven by fear of the flames and of being consumed, Lynne had dispossessed herself from Janet's body, Mike hoped forever.

18

The flames from the inferno the living room had become were already spreading to the rest of the cottage. They licked at Mike's ankles when he kicked the red tank of the fire extinguisher on the floor beside the couch and sent it rolling toward Randall McCarthy.

"Blast the flames back with the CO_2," he told the psychiatrist as he picked up Janet's limp body in his arms. "We'll go out through the kitchen."

Nodding his understanding, McCarthy seized the extinguisher and, jerking out the pin that secured the controls, closed the handles together, sending a gust of the fire-controlling gas through the short flexible hose connected to it. Blasting the flames before him, he leaped across the momentarily quenched ring of fire to where Mike was standing with Janet in his arms.

Turning then, McCarthy directed the rush of gas at the flames as they backed out through the kitchen door, and the cool breeze from the river struck their faces. The final gasp of the fire extinguisher tank was used to extinguish the cuffs of Mike's pants, which were smoldering where the flames had seared them and the skin of his ankle.

"How did you happen to come by?" he asked McCarthy as they stumbled across the dock and around the side of the house.

"Rita was so damned jittery tonight, we went for a drive. I saw the lights on down here when we were coming back, so we drove down your road."

As they started across the front yard, a dull explosion, followed by another burst of flame, came from inside.

"That was the gasoline can explod—" Mike's words were cut short by the whine of a starter from the front yard and the roar of a motor. "What the hell?"

"Rita must have spooked," said Randall. "I left her out in the car; when she saw the fire, I guess she turned and ran."

"*Spook* isn't exactly the word," said Mike, as they came clear of the corner of the cottage and a blast of heat from the burning living room struck their faces. "Unless I miss my guess, your friend is now possessed by the demon of Lynne Tallman."

"Good God!" said McCarthy. "What were you doing? Staging a makeshift exorcism?"

"I was really trying to make Lynne tell me where Roger Coven put the atomic bomb he's been working on the past month or so. With the help of Lynne and her cult from Chicago, he's going to destroy Washington at ten o'clock tomorrow morning."

While Randall McCarthy was still gaping, the car in which Rita Coven had been waiting for him was suddenly backed in a half circle, gears jammed into forward, and the accelerator floored to send it scratching off in a blast of dirt and gravel before swinging around the rest of the parking circle and into the road leading out to Indian Head Highway. McCarthy shook his head slowly as he watched the red taillight disappear around a curve in the narrow dirt road.

"First you'd better take Janet over there in the grass at the end of the clearing and see if she's okay," he said at last. "Then I want to hear the whole story."

"I had to knock Lynne out with chlorpromazine in Bourbon before I could set the fire and, of course, Janet's knocked out, too.

Demons fear fire more than anything else, so I decided to use the flames to make Lynne tell me where Roger put the bomb."

"You're still talking in circles as far as I'm concerned," said the psychiatrist.

Gently Mike laid Janet in the grass at the edge of the yard a good three hundred feet away from the cottage, where flames were now breaking through the roof to make a fiery beacon in the sky. A brief examination told him she was simply unconscious from the knockout dose of chlorpromazine.

"Looks like Rita and Lynne have flown the coop," said McCarthy.

"It's Lynne-Rita now. When you beat out the ring of flame momentarily with that drapery, the Lynne demon managed to leave Janet's body and take control of Rita's."

"What's going to happen to Rita?"

"Whatever Lynne wants to happen. Your former mistress is now possessed by the worst evil spirit the world has ever known."

"Please, give it to me in smaller doses," said McCarthy. "It's bad enough to have proof of your ignorance smeared all over your face; to lose a good lay in the bargain is a little rough."

"So you don't know any more about where the bomb is than you knew before," said McCarthy when the story was finished.

"All I got out of her was that Roger's probably putting it somewhere in that maze of tunnels under the Union Station right now."

"Do you think Lynne would have told you the rest of it, if I hadn't barged in?"

"I'm not even sure she knew the exact spot herself," said Mike. "But at least I can call Stafford when we get to the highway and have him search the Union Station tunnels again. To be safe if the explosion does come, Coven has to be more than fifteen miles away from the station and Stafford may be able to catch him."

"Which means all of downtown Washington and most of the suburbs will be destroyed if Stafford doesn't find the bomb," said McCarthy soberly. "Well, at least somebody saw your fire," he added as the sound of a siren came from toward Indian Head Road.

"As soon as they arrive, we've got to start back to Washington," said Mike. "Somehow or other, Roger Coven has to be taken and be made to tell where the bomb has been planted."

"You could always put him to the flame test," said McCarthy. "But if he doesn't tell more than your Lynne demon did, nobody's going to be any better off."

"Lynne was a spirit, so she could move to another body. Presumably Roger Coven is a human being, so if we can find him and bring him to Washington, the prospect of being incinerated by his own bomb isn't going to be very attractive to him. He may just cave in sometime before ten tomorrow."

"Roughly a million-to-one shot. I don't mind confessing that I don't like the odds."

"Who does?"

A police car, blue lights flashing and siren whining, pulled into the space under the trees, followed by a red fire truck. Sheriff Knott got out of the cruiser and came across to where they were standing, while the firemen drove the truck closer to the cottage and started carrying a hose to the river to get water.

"Tough luck, Dr. Kerns," he said. "With the weather as dry as it's been lately, I'm afraid not much of your place is going to be left."

"It's all right, Sheriff," said Mike. "I've been thinking of buying a houseboat anyway, one I can berth closer to the city."

"Any idea how it started?"

"I guess it was stupid of me to clean the floors this weekend with gasoline," Mike lied. "I had the can of gas in the house and was going to finish up tomorrow but some rags must have ignited somehow. If Dr. McCarthy hadn't seen the flames from the road and driven down here, Miss Burke and I would be incinerated by now. We were asleep, and when we tried to get out, the fire was everywhere. Fortunately, Dr. McCarthy used a CO_2 fire extinguisher I had in the kitchen and blasted a way for me to carry her out."

"Is she all right?"

"A little too much Bourbon, I'm afraid; I doubt if she'll remember anything that happened." That, he thought, was at least the truth.

"You may have trouble with your insurance company, Dr. Kerns," said the officer. "Having a can of gas and gasoline-soaked rags inside the house could be called criminal negligence."

"I'd be ashamed to make a claim," said Mike. "Fortunately the land alone is worth ten times what my father paid for the whole plot."

"Did you drive here in your car, Dr. McCarthy?" Sheriff Knott asked.

"Yes. Mrs. Coven was with me, but she's deathly afraid of fire. She drove away while I was helping Dr. Kerns and Miss Burke escape."

"That must have been her we met as we were coming in," said Knott. "She was going like all the devils in hell were pursuing her."

You're not far from right at that, Mike thought but did not put it into words.

"Like I said, fire spooks her," said McCarthy. "She'll probably come back to the cottage in a little while, when she calms down."

"If she does, call me," said Knott. "The FBI has just issued an all-points on her husband and I'd like to know whether she has any idea where he is."

"I've been down here all weekend but neither Mrs. Coven nor I have seen any trace of Roger since last Friday night."

"What's he wanted for?" Mike asked.

"I don't know, but Inspector Stafford of the FBI really wants him caught."

From the direction of the cottage came the roar of the pump on the truck as it started pulling water from the river.

"Can the fire department take over now, Sheriff?" Mike asked. "I'd like to get Miss Burke to her apartment in town and I need to get some burns around my ankle dressed on the way in."

"Go ahead," said Knott. "I'll tell the Fire Chief how it all happened and you can make a written report on it tomorrow. Need any help?"

"No thanks. Dr. McCarthy can drive my car while I look after Miss Burke. We'll make it okay."

19

"Think Stafford will catch Roger?" McCarthy asked as they turned from the dirt road leading down to the two riverfront cottages into the paved highway.

"I doubt it. The D.C. police and the FBI have been on the lookout for him since last Wednesday, when he was almost caught with Lynne in a tunnel under the Union Station. He must know the location of all the tunnels and could easily hide there."

"I guess my own performance as a psychiatrist in this case makes me professional chump number one," McCarthy admitted. "But I simply couldn't believe in demons and possession by evil spirits."

"Do you now?"

"I guess so." Janet stirred suddenly in Mike's arms and moaned. "Sure she's all right?"

"She's just out cold from the Mickey I gave her. Her pulse is fine and her breathing's reg—"

He stopped suddenly, for Janet's breathing was no longer regular, nor was she sleeping quietly. With a strength that reminded him of Lynne's when he'd fought tonight to keep her on the couch while the circle of fire crackled around them both, Janet was struggling in his arms.

"The flames!" It was a shriek of pure terror, again reminding him of Lynne. "I can't get out! I can't get out!"

For the next couple of minutes, while McCarthy braked the car to a stop on the roadside, Mike had to use all his strength to hold Janet as she fought against him, obviously in an attempt to get out of the car. Her eyes were open and, when McCarthy opened the car door and came around to help him, he saw much the same terror that had been in Lynne's eyes tonight at the sight of the leaping flames. Then as quickly as it had begun it was all over, and she slumped again in his arms, unconscious.

"What the hell was that all about?" McCarthy asked as he got in under the wheel again.

"I don't know but I've got an idea," said Mike. "What time is it? Janet's back is covering my watch."

"Ten-thirty. Why?"

"I'll tell you later. Stop at the first telephone booth you see. I want to call Stafford."

"Mind if I turn on the radio? I'm worrried about Rita, if that she-devil has seized control of her."

"I'd like to know what happened to her myself. Was she very drunk?"

"Not too drunk to drive and she's a damned good driver. I see a convenience store ahead with an outside phone. Will that do?"

"Any phone is okay," said Mike as McCarthy parked near the store. "I won't be long, but watch Janet for me. If she has another of those fits, yell."

"Okay. Take your time."

Using his telephone credit card, Mike put through a call to Inspector Stafford's office. The FBI agent answered immediately.

"Where the hell are you?" he demanded. "Miss Burke has disappeared."

"She's with me." Mike gave a terse rundown on the events of the evening since he'd left Washington for the cottage in the wake of Lynne's escape and the note she'd left.

"You were taking an awful chance," said Stafford, when he described how he'd set fire to the cottage. "What made you think you'd get anything out of her?"

"Father Julian told me the one thing demons are afraid of, the only thing that can destroy them if they're shut up with it, is fire. I figured if Lynne was terrified enough when I hemmed her inside a ring of fire, she'd tell me where Roger Coven put the bomb, but the demon escaped before I could pin her down."

"Before you both died in the fire, you mean," said Stafford. "Then you didn't learn anything?"

"I doubt now that she really knew exactly where he was going to put the bomb; the last time she saw him was when the station security police arrested Janet in the tunnel. Do you have any idea where he is?"

"We know where he *was*," Stafford sounded angry. "Right under our damned noses."

"Then he did get to place the bomb?"

"I'm sure of it, just as I'm sure he's outwitted us again even though everybody I can muster is busy searching the station."

"Sheriff Knott told me you'd issued an all-points. Why did you wait?"

"The order was issued as soon as we found where Coven has been staying the last few days—and realized I'd need everybody here to hunt for the bomb. Do you suppose there's any chance that Miss Burke may remember anything else?"

"Right now she's out like a light, but I'll remedy that as soon as I can get to the Emergency Room at University Hospital and give her an injection of methylphenidate hydrochloride to wake her up. She won't know anything, though, especially since the demon that's been plaguing her has taken a powder in favor of another body."

"After you get through at the hospital, come on over here and bring Miss Burke and Dr. McCarthy with you. Maybe if we all put our heads together we can still come up with an idea worth using."

"We'll be there in less than an hour," said Mike. "By the way, where was Roger Coven hiding?"

"In an apartment Senator Magnes maintains over in Alexandria for extrasenatorial activities. We got a tip when a woman who lives across the street, and had seen Roger there at other times, spotted the fact that he was disguised when he came out carrying a large package. We missed him by half an hour."

"Time for him to disappear with the bomb into that maze of tunnels under the Union Station where they come out from underground down near the Potomac?"

"Where else? After Miss Burke was picked up by the security police the other night in the station, I got hold of the original blueprints. There are enough cul-de-sacs under that damned building in the neighborhood of the Capitol, plus openings near the Potomac railroad bridge, to keep us hunting that bomb for the next twenty-four hours."

The phone clicked off and Mike went back to the car, where McCarthy was listening to the radio, which was playing a rock-and-roll tune.

"Wouldn't you expect just this in Washington?" he said. "With the whole town about to be blown apart in less than twelve hours, the radio's still playing stupid music like that."

"It's better than the 'Funeral March.'" Mike got into the car.
"Did Janet move while I was on the phone?"

"Not a wiggle. When you administer a Mickey, you do it up
brown, friend." McCarthy was reaching for the gear shift lever in
the floor of the car when the music suddenly ended in a squawk
and the voice of the announcer came on the air:

"We interrupt this program to report the latest spectacular accident in the area during the Labor Day weekend. Vacationists
returning to the city from the south along State Road 225 report
that a car being driven at high speed near La Plata in Charles
County left the road on a curve and dived into a ravine about ten-
thirty tonight. Flames from the burning car kept both spectators
and police from making any attempt to rescue the single occupant,
although she was heard screaming briefly as flames engulfed it.
A fire engine from La Plata is now on the scene attempting to put
out the fire so the driver, who obviously died in the holocaust
following the crash, can be identified."

Randall McCarthy's cheeks were ashen. "What a way for Rita
to die."

"But the only way the demon of Lynne Tallman could be destroyed. What time did he say?"

"Ten-thirty, the same time Janet was struggling to get out. I
guess it was Lynne's final attempt to escape that we were seeing
reflected in Janet's body and mind, even though she was unconscious, but I'm not even going to try and explain how it could
happen."

"Let's get going, this burn on my ankle is beginning to hurt like
hell. Besides, Stafford wants us at the command post he's set up in
his office after we stop at University Hospital Emergency Room."

McCarthy nodded and started the car. Only when they were
back on the road and headed again for the Beltway and the bridge
across the Potomac did he ask, "Any news about Roger?"

"He'd been hiding during the weekend at an apartment Senator
Magnes kept in Alexandria but a woman across the street spotted
him."

"I've been there, it's populated with swingers and that woman
across the street watches the windows with binoculars. If she
hadn't spotted Roger, he could have stayed there a month and

nobody would have questioned him. Are they sure he's already planted the bomb?"

"Stafford is so certain of it, he's got everybody available in the D. C. Police Department and the FBI searching the station tunnels."

"On Labor Day, with everybody off but a housekeeping force, that could take some time. Meanwhile, Roger probably knows southern Maryland like he knows the back of his hand, so he'd stick only to back roads."

"Where could he go?"

"With a fake passport, several beards he could glue on to make him look different every day, and a change of cars whenever he found one with the keys in it, he could make Miami in about three days and a Varig flight to Brazil," said McCarthy. "A man who blew up Washington as a demonstration of his power and got away safely could hold any big city in the world hostage for millions."

"Then you don't think Coven is an out-and-out terrorist?"

"Not the kind that does damn-fool things, just to cause turmoil," McCarthy said without hesitation. "My guess is he decided to use Lynne and her group as pawns to help him make an example of Washington, once he'd discovered government agents were on his trail for accumulating plutonium and Magnes was going to let him be sacrificed to save his own skin from scandal."

"Where would he get the stuff for more such ventures, if he does escape?"

"Roger helped prepare shipments of fissionable elements to every nation in the world that has them," McCarthy explained. "The way India used atomic materials we sent them for generating electric power to set off an atomic explosion means the only thing most nations want the stuff for is to scare the hell out of those surrounding them and maybe make a political deal to their advantage. Roger would have no trouble stealing enough plutonium from any of those to make another small bomb and, with a few million dollars, plus his ability as an atomic expert, Libya would welcome him with open arms while they and at least half a dozen other nations who hate the United States were chortling over the destruction of Washington."

"To say nothing of the fact that the Russians might logically choose tomorrow as D day for an atomic attack, with the whole

federal government in Washington dead and nobody in charge to
press the red button."

"I hadn't thought of that!"

"You can bet Stafford has," McCarthy said as he stopped the
car beside the ambulance unloading platform at University Hospital. "Makes you want to cut and run, doesn't it?"

Mike gave him a probing look. "Maybe you'd better come in
with us while I get this ankle dressed and give Janet an injection
to wake her up. Stafford told me to bring you."

"Why me?" McCarthy asked but he got out of the car on the
other side without objection and went to open the door for Mike
and his sleeping burden.

"You know Coven. Besides, you're an expert on extrasensory
perception and remote viewing, so maybe he wants you to send
Roger a message by ESP that he's ready to make a deal."

"What kind of a deal?"

"In Stafford's place I'd give Roger a free ride out of the country
to the foreign airport of his choice, plus a suitcase full of money,
in exchange for locating that bomb before ten o'clock tomorrow
morning."

"A deal with even a human agent of Lucifer? Who could trust
him?"

"That would have been true, if Lynne were still in existence, but
that Devil's gamble failed, thank God, when she was destroyed
along with Rita in the crash—I hope."

Janet was already waking up when McCarthy started the car
again outside the hospital Emergency Room, where Mike's burn
had been dressed and he'd given her an injection of a powerful
stimulating drug to counteract the effects of the chlorpromazine.

"What happened?" was naturally her first question. "And what
am I doing wearing shorts and a halter?"

"First tell me the last thing you remember," Mike said, as
McCarthy drove them through the nearly deserted streets toward
her apartment house.

"Your getting the call from University Hospital to take care of
the senator's daughter, and locking me in the apartment, so Lynne
couldn't get out while you were gone." She frowned suddenly.
"But she's gone. . . ."

"For good—though I guess *bad* would be the better word for her."

"I can feel that she's no longer inside me, but can I be sure she won't come back?"

"I'm sure you can." Mike went on to explain what had happened since he'd returned to the apartment from the hospital, only to find the door locked and the apartment empty.

"Poor Lynne," said Janet, when he had finished. "Even though she was an evil spirit, I guess she was more interesting, as a person, than I could ever be."

"Provocative, yes, maybe even exciting," Mike admitted. "But you can get the same effect from hash—not that I'll ever want it again."

"It was a strange feeling, being myself and Lynne at the same time," said Janet. "I don't remember much of it, but there were times when I felt she would rather be me, and have you, than be what she was."

"She admitted as much to me," Mike said soberly. "But the power she possessed through being a demon was still a danger to you and to the world, so it's just as well that she's been destroyed."

Janet nodded slowly. "I guess you're right. Do you think she really would have told you where the bomb is located, if she'd remained in control of my mind and my body?"

"We'll never know that, just as we'll probably never know why you cried out and fought to get out of the car at just the moment when the spirit of Lynne was being consumed by the flames of the burning car—"

"It seems like a dream, but I saw that car, just as you say the radio announcer described the wreck." She shivered. "It was engulfed by flame, yet I could see someone struggling to get out."

"We're running into still more impossibles," Mike conceded.

"Not this time," Randall McCarthy said from the driver's seat. "Janet's being able to see that scene, even though it was happening miles away, was a case of remote viewing."

"That could explain it!" Janet cried. "Even though I was partly knocked out from the chlorpromazine, my unconscious mind was awake enough to receive the ELF waves Lynne's spirit was sending me—"

"What the hell are ELF waves?" Mike asked.

"Extremely-low-frequency electromagnetic waves in the 300 to 1000 kilometer region," McCarthy explained. "Some investigators believe they're able to carry messages. Others think a different principle is involved, but no one who took part in the experiments in California and elsewhere will deny that information can be received by almost anyone with a little effort. The work at the Stanford Research Institute seems to indicate some type of electromagnetic waves are involved. And investigators there were even able to describe scenes as far away as Colombia, at the exact moment they were happening."

"That sounds crazy," said Mike.

"Not as crazy as a second set of experiments in which the receiver was asked to describe a place—which hadn't even been selected by those who were going to view it until roughly a half hour *before* it was visited by an observer team and *after they left the laboratory*. In those cases, several experimenters known to have psychic powers—"

"Like you?"

"I'm generally considered to have unusual powers of what those studying parapsychology have now started to call the psi phenomenon."

"Go on."

"As I was saying, some of the receivers in those experiments made better drawings of the places the observers were going to see —*but before they saw them*—than the observers in the first ones made of places while they were being seen. What do you think of that?"

"Another impossible! They're getting easier to believe all the time."

"If you still have trouble believing it tomorrow—provided we're not each a small pile of radioactive ashes—I'll send you a reprint of a definitive article on the research at the Stanford Institute from the *Proceedings of the Institute of Electrical and Electronics Engineers* for March 1976."

It was after eleven when McCarthy parked the Porsche before the majestic-looking headquarters of the FBI. They were expected and a security guard took them immediately to the office of Inspector Stafford. It was the scene of busy activity as couriers came and went, reporting to the haggard-looking agent.

At her apartment Janet had changed from the brief shorts and halter she'd been wearing earlier in the evening, when Lynne had been in control, to slacks and an open-collared shirt. She also carried a notebook and a pen, tools of the reporter's trade.

Stafford introduced the trio to the Attorney General, head of the Department of Justice, and to Andrew Carter, formerly head of a large metropolitan police department and now Chief of the FBI, as well as to a Mr. Horner, identified as an expert from the Atomic Energy Commission standing by to defuse the bomb, if the army of agents and police fanning out beneath the Union Station were able to locate it.

"Any news of Roger Coven?" Mike asked Stafford when introductions were completed.

"Nothing. We've got the Maryland and Virginia police on the alert but my guess is that he got a head start because the woman who recognized him coming out of Senator Magnes' apartment didn't call us immediately. My guess is that he's already far enough away from the city to be beyond the danger range."

"What do you estimate that to be?"

"Roughly fifteen miles," said the AEC man. "A strong wind could cause the cloud to drift in any direction and contaminate a much larger area, but the Weather Bureau says we'll have only a slight breeze tomorrow morning."

"Frankly, Doctor," said the stocky FBI Chief, "there's a lot about this case I don't understand. You say Miss Burke doesn't remember anything her alter ego—if that's what she should be called—either did or said?"

"That's true."

"In some countries there'd be ways to make her remember," the AEC man snapped. "And I wouldn't hesitate to use them."

"You'd get nowhere," said Mike firmly.

"I've put Miss Burke under hypnosis and also given her sodium pentothal—what you call truth serum—trying to determine whether any actions of the other personality could be remembered by her," McCarthy added. "She had no recall whatsoever of what the demon personality did."

"Meanwhile we just sit here twiddling our thumbs and let a whole city, including ourselves and close to a million others at least, be incinerated"—Carter glanced at the clock over the door of Stafford's office—"in ten hours?"

"There may be a way to find Roger Coven and bring him here before then," said Janet and every eye in the room was suddenly focused on her.

"So you *do* remember something?" Chief Carter said sharply.

"No. But Professor McCarthy knows Roger Coven well and he's also recognized in parapsychological circles as a psychic with considerabl psi power."

The FBI head threw up his hands in a gesture of frustration. "This is no science fiction movie we're making about the occult, young lady."

"You *do* want to catch this man, don't you, Mr. Carter?" Mike broke in sharply.

"Of course, but—"

"Then listen to what she has to say."

"Yes, Andy," said the Attorney General. "We won't lose time by listening."

"What did you have in mind, Janet?" Mike asked quietly.

"First I'd like to hear Dr. McCarthy's profile, so to speak, of Roger Coven. After all, he's known him longer than anyone here."

"That's right," said Stafford. "Coven was a student of yours at Duke, wasn't he, Professor?"

"For a year," said McCarthy. "We were trying to analyze the wave patterns by which information travels along psi channels."

"That's the second time I've heard that word in five minutes," said the FBI Chief. "Just what does it mean, Doctor?"

"Telepathy, involving contact between minds; clairvoyance, such as reading a letter you can't see; precognition, which is knowledge of future events before they happen; psychokinesis, the moving of an object without touching it, by will only; psychic healing, which needs no definition—all of these are grouped by parapsychologists working in the field as psi events," McCarthy explained. "Persons possessing these abilities are said to be psychic, but a better definition is that they possess psi power."

"In olden times these qualities were ascribed to possession by demons," the FBI Chief said in a tone heavy with sarcasm. "Are you telling us the devil has you under his thumb, too, the way he has Miss Burke?"

"The demon that possessed Miss Burke over the past few months has been exorcised and destroyed—by fire," Mike said sharply but Carter only shrugged.

"Maybe in another incarnation you were an agent of the Inquisition, Dr. Kerns," he said and turned to McCarthy. "Please continue with your own fairy tale, Professor."

McCarthy flushed angrily at the other man's tone but did not waver. "I have published in scientific journals the results of many experiments that prove my own qualities as a psychic, sir, but psi power isn't necessarily limited to a few people. Those working in the field believe everybody possesses it to a varying degree, and some physicists are certain the phenomena connected with psi power will eventually be traced back to the very foundations of quantum physics."

"That does it!" Carter shot out of his chair and started for an adjoining office. "A whole city is about to be destroyed and we waste time talking to an academic nut."

"I'm sure Miss Burke has in mind something the three of us were discussing on the way here." Mike addressed the Attorney General, as the highest governmental authority in the room. "That being the case, the man Mr. Carter just labeled an academic nut may be the only person who can save Washington from destruction."

"We're all a little uptight here, Doctor," said the cabinet officer, "particularly the members of Mr. Carter's Bureau, who will be blamed if this tragedy should occur. I, for one, want to hear what Miss Burke and Dr. McCarthy have to suggest and I apologize to you both for his rudeness."

"It's all right, sir." McCarthy wiped sweat from his forehead, although the room was air-conditioned and quite cool. "I'm as anxious as anybody else not to be incinerated tomorrow morning."

"If you were Roger Coven," Janet asked McCarthy, "how would you have escaped after planting the bomb?"

"Simple logic," said the psychiatrist. "I wouldn't know for sure whether or not I'd been recognized leaving the apartment, so to be safe I would assume that I had and that whoever it was would notify the police. But having lived in Washington awhile, I could also be sure the message would take some time to go through channels—"

"Too long," said Stafford. "We didn't get it ourselves until an

hour after the woman watching the apartment reported to the
D.C. police that a suspicious-looking man had just left. And before that she had spent twenty minutes finding somebody to tell
her story to—who would listen."

"In the first place, I could be sure that, once the FBI knew I'd
left the apartment where I'd been hiding, an all-points would go
out," McCarthy continued. "It wouldn't bother me much, for in
the days while I'd been hiding I could have used one of those fast
tanning lotions to make me look like an Arab or even darker, plus
a false beard and a few other disguises. I'd know I had to get rid
of the car, though, so I'd look for one with the keys inside."

"I can see you watch the TV crime programs," said Carter, who
had paused in the doorway of an adjoining office.

"On a holiday there wouldn't be too many like that in parking
lots or around stores and, besides, the theft of one of them would
probably be discovered quickly and reported to the police,"
McCarthy continued. "So I'd look for motels and a car belonging
to someone who'd probably come in half drunk and left his keys
in the ignition. Or, failing that, I could jump the ignition with a
piece of wire—Roger had a degree in electrical engineering from
Duke before he took graduate work in the atomic energy field."

"That's pretty good thinking," Carter admitted grudgingly. "Go
on."

"With another car, not one likely to be reported as stolen before
morning, I'd choose a direction the police and FBI wouldn't expect me to take, probably by selecting the Baltimore–Washington
Beltway and head south into Prince Georges and Charles coun-
ties. Roger knows the whole area well and, by sticking to the back
roads, he probably wouldn't be spotted by the police while he
worked his way South."

"Where would he be going?" Mike asked.

"Possibly eventually into Tennessee, maybe near Oak Ridge; he
knows that area well, too. With the TVA lakes all around, he
could rent an isolated cabin after Labor Day and just disappear,
until he could arrange for a fake passport—if he needed it, which
I don't think he would."

"Why not?" the Attorney General asked.

"It's my guess that he already had several; a TV program called
'Sixty Minutes' showed some time ago that all the documents a
person needs to create any identity he wants can be obtained here

in Washington without difficulty. With a fake passport, he wouldn't even have to flee to Tennessee but could go to almost any international airport—Miami, Tampa or New Orleans, for instance—and buy a ticket to any country in the world as easily as he could take a shuttle flight to New York or Boston."

"You're in the wrong business, Doctor," said Carter. "You should have been a crook."

McCarthy grinned. "Thank you, sir."

"Was Coven really a terrorist?" the Attorney General asked.

"He was a radical in student days, if you could call the students at Duke University who rioted because of low salaries paid hospital workers, radicals," said McCarthy. "Whether he renewed ties with the Lynne Tallman group the last time he was in Chicago, I don't know, but he did have a brief affair with her before going to Oak Ridge. And if it's true that he was stockpiling small amounts of plutonium—"

"It's true," said Inspector Stafford. "We were almost ready to move in but wanted to find out who he was going to sell it to."

"Did you inform his friends in Congress of that?"

"Yes."

"Then he already knew he'd been discovered and probably figured he was about to be thrown to the lions, so naturally he decided to set up in business for himself."

"As a terrorist?"

"As a businessman—the business of holding cities for ransom," said McCarthy. "And how better prove your ability to do it than by holding Washington for ransom—or, if that didn't work out, destroy the heart of the American capital?"

"Which he'll probably succeed in doing," said Carter. "We have no idea what he looks like disguised, what kind of a car he's driving now, or where he's going."

"Dr. McCarthy might be able to tell you that," said Janet unexpectedly.

"Don't hold out on us, Doctor," said Carter. "Time's too short for a grandstand play."

"What I meant," Janet explained, "is that in his experiments confirming the Stanford Research Institute reports of precognition, Dr. McCarthy has been able to visualize places where experimenters were going as much as a half hour before they arrive to see it themselves."

"I don't know how trying to find Roger Coven through remote viewing would work out," said McCarthy doubtfully. "Ordinarily it's very difficult to see a moving object."

"He's bound to stop somewhere, so why not try to visualize the next stop," said Mike. "Perhaps we can identify it."

"With that information"—Stafford's voice was suddenly tense with interest—"we could direct the people searching for him where to look."

"What do we do?" Carter demanded. "Sit in a circle and hold hands while we wait for the ghost to start speaking?"

"Shut up, Andy," said the Attorney General. "You're a damn good policeman but right now you're clean out of your depth. Let Dr. McCarthy and Miss Burke tell us what they want to try."

"It would be impossible for Dr. McCarthy to work in an area as hostile as it's bound to be with Mr. Carter around," Janet said to Inspector Stafford. "Could we use the office next door?"

"Of course. What do you need?"

"A tape recorder, a few blank sheets of paper and a pencil for drawing—plus some peace and quiet," she said pointedly. "Okay, Randall?"

McCarthy shrugged. "I'll give it the old college try. We've nothing to lose."

"There's a tape recorder on the desk in the next office," said Stafford. "The blank sheets and a pencil should be in the top drawer. Good luck!"

It took a few moments to move into the other room, shut the door firmly and make McCarthy comfortable at the desk. While Janet took the seat beside it, Mike sat farther away, near the window. McCarthy took the microphone of the tape recorder in his left hand, so he could press the button on the side when he wanted to speak into it. Then, placing a blank sheet on the desk top, he held the pencil in the fingers of his right hand above it.

"It may take a little while to start receiving the ELF waves," he warned. "After a hostile atmosphere like that outside, it's hard to concentrate."

"Carter's trying to be another J. Edgar Hoover," said Mike. "Forget him."

Janet touched her finger to her lips in warning and Mike relaxed in his chair, watching Randall McCarthy. The psychic, too, seemed to be resting and for a long moment did not speak. Then he said softly, "I'm beginning to see something, but the signal-to-noise ratio is pretty high."

"Just relax," said Janet. "In the Stanford experiments, the noise ratio was always high at first. What does the scene look like?"

"It's a road, with an area of sky just above it in the distance, cut by some kind of a trellis."

"A building?" she asked.

"No. It curves upward in a steady rise." Then his voice suddenly grew excited: "I can see a road going up it and the middle is elevated." His right hand had been moving the pencil on the paper as he talked into the tape recorder. "It's a bridge, a high bridge."

"Can you tell where?" Mike forgot to be silent and McCarthy shook his head. "It's fading now."

"Try to focus on the end of the bridge," Janet suggested. "What does it look like?"

"I see something in the middle of the road, like a small house. There's some kind of a framework over it, too, with something on either side." The fingers with the pencil were moving again, shaping the outlines of a second drawing. "Back this side of the archway, beside the road, there's a large sign, I can make out a *T* and an *L,* and above that some number—a 0 and a 1."

"How many numbers in all?" Janet asked.

"Three, I think, but I can only see two of the numerals on the right side of the sign."

"The toll bridge south of Indian Head that carries U.S. 301 across the Potomac!" Mike exclaimed. "It's the only route Roger Coven could take to leave southern Maryland—except by ferry, and they wouldn't be running this late at night—for at least a hundred and twenty miles. You've done it, Randall! Congratulations!" Then his sudden exultation took a nose dive. "Can you tell whether he's crossed it or not?"

The psychiatrist shook his head. "My guess would be that he's near it, but I can't go any further than that. Let's get the others in here."

Inspector Stafford took one look at the toll bridge McCarthy had drawn, with the high-arching roadway and the pattern of girders against the moonlit sky, then at the toll booth and the arching frame above it.

"The Governor Nice Memorial Bridge just west of Allens Fresh," he said softly. "It's unbelievable. Why, that could be a sketch of the bridge done on the spot, Doctor."

"Listen to the description," Janet had been spinning the tape recorder backwards. When she reversed the tape direction, Randall McCarthy's voice began to describe what he was seeing, but Stafford didn't wait to listen.

"The best place to nab Coven will be when he comes off the bridge on the Virginia side of the Potomac. A naval ordnance laboratory is located right there and a group of highway patrol cars can take cover beside the highway."

"Shouldn't you set up a roadblock?" Mike asked.

"Yes, but it should be farther along, probably where the railroad tracks serving the ordnance laboratory cross U.S. 301." He picked up a telephone from the desk and spoke to the operator at the switchboard. "Get me Colonel Thorndyke, head of the Virginia Highway Patrol in Richmond. You may have to ring his home."

It took a few minutes to rouse the head of the Virginia State Police. "Jim," Stafford said, "this is Frank Stafford in Washington. I know it's a hell of a time to be calling, but on that all-points you issued for me earlier tonight, we're pretty sure our man is heading south on 301 and is near the Potomac toll bridge, probably on the Maryland side. Will you order several cars to trap him as he comes off the bridge?"

There was a brief colloquy, then Stafford said, "The Attorney General is here with Chief Carter. We're going to ask the Navy to send a Marine helicopter from Quantico to pick up the prisoner and bring him here. I'll ask them to have the pilot approach from Fredericksburg so as not to spook Coven before you can nab him; it's pretty vital that we have him here as quickly as possible. Good. We won't forget it, Jim."

Stafford turned to the Attorney General. "Will you contact the Navy, sir, and ask them to send a 'copter from Quantico? The pilot can land on the Mall down by the river and we'll have police cars ready to bring him here."

"One minute," said Carter. "Are we going to risk letting the Marines and the Navy know we made fools of ourselves on the basis of a drawing anybody could make by memory of the 301 bridge?" He whirled upon McCarthy, who was still sitting at the desk, with a look of utter exhaustion on his face. "Have you ever crossed that bridge, Professor?"

"Of course."

Carter threw up his hands. "Of all the—"

"It's the only logical way for Coven to escape." The Attorney General was looking at a road map. "Somebody was bound to spot him on I-95, if he'd chosen that as his route of escape. But by driving around southern Maryland for a while on back roads, then coming onto 301 near the bridge, probably by way of Maryland 232 and 234, he could have fooled us completely."

"*Did* fool us, but not any longer." McCarthy had been concentrating, seemingly oblivious of those around him. "I see a car on the road beyond the bridge. It's apparently surrounded by police cars, for I can see lights flashing."

The telephone on Inspector Stafford's desk rang. He picked it up and listened for a moment, then put it down with a pleased look on his face.

"Roger Coven was just captured by the Virginia State Police, when he tried to run a roadblock beyond the Potomac Bridge on U.S. 301," he announced. "The helicopter is on the way from Quantico now."

Chief Carter went over to where Randall McCarthy was sitting and held out a hamlike hand. "I guess I owe you an apology, Professor," he said. "When I was a county sheriff back in Michigan, I used to roust a lot of so-called mind readers. They were mainly pickpockets and con artists, though, and I guess I developed some prejudices, but maybe there's something to this business of seeing things in advance." Then his broad face was creased by a grin. "If you can tell us where banks are going to be robbed before the crooks can get there, you'll save the FBI a lot of trouble."

"I'm afraid parapsychology isn't that advanced, sir," said McCarthy. "But I'm at your disposal any time you need me."

"The next question," said the Attorney General, "is what to do with Coven, now that he's practically in our hands."

"Make him defuse that bomb to save his own skin," said Carter. "What else?"

"But if he's a dedicated terrorist—"

"He isn't," said McCarthy. "Roger's a genius in his field and also a prime opportunist. Right now he's got a grudge against the government for preparing to crack down on what was the beginning of a very lucrative racket. My guess is that when he gets here, he'll have a proposition to make."

"Proposition, hell!" Carter exploded. "We've got him by the——" He shrugged and did not finish.

"What are you saying, Dr. McCarthy?" the Attorney General asked.

"When they bring Roger here, he'll be ready to make a deal," said McCarthy. "Right now I'd say give him whatever he asks for."

"Don't you think he'll crack at the last minute and tell us where the bomb is?"

"Possibly—but can you afford to wait that long?"

There was no answer—until Janet spoke. "If he's going to put the heat on us, why not put the heat on him first by taking him directly to the Union Station and talking to him there? That way he'll know he's sitting on top of the bomb."

"Smart girl," said Chief Carter. "That's about the hottest seat we could put him on, outside of the electric chair."

There was general agreement and Inspector Stafford called the Washington police waiting on the Mall for the Marine helicopter, instructing them to radio the pilot to land on the broad esplanade lying between the Lincoln Memorial overlooking the Potomac on the west and the Capitol itself on the east. After the landing, the prisoner would be brought to the Union Station, lying a few blocks northeast of the Capitol.

20

The moon was shining over a peaceful city as Mike, Janet and McCarthy drove through the deserted streets to the massive marble structure of the Union Station, still one of the most impressive buildings in Washington's central government area.

"It gives you sort of an eerie feeling to know a bomb that could kill all of us is ticking away somewhere inside this place," said Janet as Mike parked the car and they circled the memorial fountain in front of the station.

"If you want to know, it scares the hell out of me," Mike admitted.

"How about you, Randall?" Janet asked the psychiatrist, who seemed to be in what was sometimes called a brown study.

"What?"

"I said it's sort of eerie, knowing a bomb is ticking away inside that building. Or aren't you scared?"

"I'm scared all right," he admitted, "but I'm too busy trying to see that bomb to think of anything else."

"You've already done more than your share by helping capture Coven," Mike assured him. "But please go the second mile, if you can."

The all-night snack shop in the station was open, with a single frowsy-looking waitress on duty inside. Mike and Janet took one end of the counter and ordered hamburgers and coffee for them and for McCarthy, who sat by himself, in a deep study. The government men were at the other end.

By the time they'd finished eating, a uniformed officer entered the lunchroom and nodded to Chief Carter. All filed out and into the office of the terminal superintendent at one end of the great building. Roger Coven was standing there, guarded by two policemen and with his hands manacled behind him. He was looking out a window toward the street outside where some cars were now moving and Mike was startled to see by the clock above the desk that it was almost 3 A.M. Oddly enough, Roger Coven didn't seem perturbed, considering his plight.

"Good evening, gentlemen," he said on a note of sarcasm. "I'm surprised that you would dare to come here but let me assure you that you're perfectly safe"—he glanced at the clock—"for almost another seven hours."

"You're a cool one," said Chief Carter. "It will be a pleasure to see you behind bars."

Coven shrugged. "I've had close shaves before. A station security policeman almost caught me a few days ago, when he surprised Miss Burke and me—"

"Not Miss Burke—Lynne," said Mike.

"I stand corrected, Dr. Kerns. With two people—in spirit at least—inhabiting the same body, it was sometimes difficult to determine when the change from one to the other occurred. As I was saying, when the guard surprised us while we were discussing where best to place the bomb I had made, I was sure the Lynne personality would disappear, leaving the Janet one in charge. I couldn't, however, be sure whether the change of personalities was made before I got out of sight into a side tunnel so Janet wouldn't recognize me. I take it the latter happened."

"I didn't see you clearly, only enough to be sure it looked like you," said Janet. "That's what I reported when Dr. Kerns took me to Inspector Stafford."

"I thought something like that had happened, but the tunnels soon started filling with police and FBI men, so I climbed out where the tracks emerge from beneath the ground and made my way to the apartment in Alexandria."

"Did Senator Magnes know you were there?" the Attorney General demanded.

"The senator is at home in the boondocks, mending political fences, sir. I knew he planned to be away until the middle of the week, so I was safe. Fortunately, the apartment was kept well stocked with food—and liquor—at all times and I lived very comfortably."

"Until a neighbor recognized you early tonight when you left to place the bomb."

"That was unfortunate," Coven conceded coolly.

"Even more unfortunate for you was Dr. McCarthy's trick of seeing the Governor Nice Bridge over the Potomac before you got there. If he hadn't, you could have gotten away scot-free—at least for a while."

"Take my word for it, Chief," Roger Coven said. "I could have escaped easily, once I'd crossed that bridge."

"He's carrying a fake passport, social security and even credit cards, Chief," said one of the policemen who had brought Roger to the station. "He was wearing a false beard and mustache, too, and his skin's dark enough from all that suntan stuff we found in the apartment in Alexandria for him to pass as an Arab."

"Since I may take refuge in an Arab country, the dark skin was a necessity," said Coven.

"The only way you'll ever take refuge anywhere is to be buried there," Carter snapped.

"I may be—eventually," said the prisoner calmly, "but right now I think you gentlemen had better listen to my proposition."

"We'll listen to nothing but where the bomb is—"

"You'll listen to what I have to say." The prisoner's voice was suddenly as sharp as that of the FBI Chief.

"All right, Coven," said the Attorney General. "What *is* your price for locating and defusing the bomb before it explodes tomorrow morning—killing you, I might point out, because you're not going to leave this station before you tell us."   -

"Here are my terms." Roger Coven might have been discussing a small loan with a banker. "I want five million dollars deposited to my numbered account in a Swiss bank. I'll give you the numbers as soon as we come to an agreement and the embassy in Geneva can make the deposit."

"You don't come cheap, do you?" Chief Carter said contemptuously, but Roger Coven ignored the thrust.

"I also want an immediate flight in a U.S. jet to Brazil, landing at an airport near a small city I'll name when the pilot is five hundred miles from the field—plus a diplomatic passport and air passage to Rio later for my wife, Rita—"

"Rita's dead, Roger," said Randall McCarthy. "Mike burned down his cottage exorcising the demon of Lynne Tallman from Janet and Lynne seized possession of Rita's body instead. The car she—they—were driving went off the road not far from La Plata, Maryland, earlier tonight and was consumed. Neither Rita nor the demon possessing her could get out."

Coven was visibly shaken. "You're lying—"

"He's not," said Mike quietly. "Lynne told me you were placing the bomb in the station before I drove her out of Janet's body and we heard on the radio, as we were coming back to Washington, that the car Rita was driving was destroyed."

"She was to meet me in São Paulo," Coven said brokenly, then turned upon Janet. "You're to blame for her death. You and that demon—"

"The demon was destroyed, too; they can't escape fire, when shut up in something like a car," said Mike. "All you did by going along with Lynne and her cult in the plot to destroy Washington was to cause Rita's death, so why don't you give up and tell the authorities where the bomb is located?"

"If you know," Carter sneered.

"Of course I know," Coven snapped. "I placed it there, didn't I? And armed it with the tools I used to build it in the garage at Lane Cottage. You must have found the box when you searched the garage, as I'm sure you did."

"Toolbox!" the word burst in Mike's brain like an exploding firecracker. Lynne's last words at the cottage, he remembered, had been "In a too—" but McCarthy's interruption had kept her from finishing the word. Now the rest of what she had been going to say fell into place with the memory of something Stafford had said, after the first search of the station tunnels, when Janet had been found in one of them by the security guard.

"Inspector," he said urgently. "Do you remember what you told me about the first search you had made of the station?"

Stafford frowned momentarily. "Nothing important." Then his face suddenly cleared. "Yes, I remember telling you we even searched the toolbox on an ancient handcar used by gandy dancers repairing track." He stopped suddenly. "Do you mean . . . ?"

"Before the Lynne demon left Miss Burke's body I asked her where the bomb was and she answered, 'In a too—' She didn't get to finish the word but it must have been 'toolbox.' If the second group of searchers was the same as the first—"

"They were," said the chief of the station security guards.

"Was the toolbox examined again last night when I asked you to search again?" Inspector Stafford's voice was like a whip.

"I'm sure it must have been."

"How sure? Did you see it?"

"No, but—" The guard chief's troubled face cleared. "Alf Porter was in charge of the search detail but he went home—said he felt like he was getting the flu."

"Call him. Ask whether he opened the tool chest a second time or not."

The security chief went to the phone, looked up a number listed on a card taped to the wall with Scotch tape and rang it. "Alf," the listeners heard him say, "do you remember whether you examined the tool chest on that old handcar in Section Thirteen again today?"

The chief listened a moment to the voice on the other end, then covered the mouthpiece with his hand. "He said they couldn't see any reason to open the toolbox, since it had been empty about twenty-four hours before."

"That does it," said Chief Carter to the station security head. "Do you know where that section of track is located?"

"Certainly. It's almost directly under the Capitol Building." Then, as he realized what the words meant: "The bomb; it's under the Capitol."

"Exactly," said Carter. "Come on, Horner. The chief here will show us where the handcar—and the bomb—are located."

"Just a minute!" Roger Coven's voice stopped them as they were leaving. "The detonator on that bomb is very sensitive and had best be handled by me."

"Let's go, then," said Carter. "Time's flying."

"I'll defuse it in exchange for my life." Coven was speaking directly to the Attorney General, who alone could grant him his request. "Is it a deal?"

The cabinet officer wasted no time in indecision. "We could get you for treason, attempting to destroy the life of the President, and a dozen other counts that would carry a death sentence. But giving you life imprisonment in return for saving a million people from possible destruction is a better deal."

"I'll take it," said Coven. "Come on, Horner. You can help me."

When Chief Carter, Horner, the station security chief and Coven had left the room, the cabinet officer wiped his forehead with his handkerchief.

"Whew! That was close, Dr. Kerns," he said. "Your remembering those words of . . ."

"Lynne," Janet prompted him.

"Lynne, then—saved the lives of at least a million people."

"I guess you could say nothing in her life became her like the leaving of it," said Janet. "I'll use that quote when I write the story of what happened here tonight, for the *Star-News.*"

"There isn't going to be any story," said the cabinet officer decisively.

"You mean you really want this whole thing kept under wraps?" Janet asked incredulously. "I can win a Pulitzer Prize with that story."

"Not one word must be printed about it," said the Attorney General on a note of finality. "If the public knew the government had let one man come so close to destroying the very heart of Washington, including the highest officials in the government, there might even be a recall petition to remove the President from office. To say nothing of the fact that, if the explosion had come on schedule, the American government would have been absolutely paralyzed and the Soviets could have considered this the opportune time for a first strike with the nuclear arsenal."

"What are you going to do with Coven, sir?" Mike asked.

"I promised him his life, so I have to give it to him, but an affidavit by two doctors can commit anyone suspected of insanity to a mental hospital. After all, a man has to be insane to attempt what Coven attempted, so you and Dr. McCarthy can have no hesitancy about signing the affidavit."

"What then?"

"Tomorrow morning I will arrange a private hearing before one of the justices of the Supreme Court. By tomorrow afternoon, Roger Coven will be on the way to the Raleigh-Durham Airport in a government plane."

"Why there?" Janet asked.

"Not too many people know it, and we don't want it publicized, but the government has just finished building a maximum-security prison and hospital for very important prisoners in one of the Carolinas. It's way out in the boondocks and, when the gates close there behind Roger Coven, they'll never open again for him."

"Provided we two doctors certify him," said McCarthy. "But what's the diagnosis?"

"Paranoid megalomania," said the cabinet officer. "Do either of you disagree?"

"I guess I can go along with that," said McCarthy. "Planning to blow up the capital of the United States is about as megalo as any maniac could get."

"Ditto," said Mike.

21

The sun's rays were poking their way around the dome of the Capitol to create a lovely pattern of trees and shadows, plus that of the tall spire of the Washington Monument, in the Reflecting Pool adjoining the east side of the Lincoln Memorial, when Janet, Mike and Randall McCarthy came out of the Department of Justice Building and moved toward Mike's Porsche where it was parked at the curb. Janet took a long breath of the fresh fall air, not yet polluted by the exhaust from thousands of cars that would soon be jamming the still partially deserted streets after the long Labor Day weekend.

"It's hard to believe what we've just been through really happened," she said. "Why don't we just treat it as a dream and put it away in our unconscious minds."

"Until it emerges again sometime as a nightmare," Randall McCarthy warned and stepped down from the curb to hail a passing taxi, one of the few out on the streets at this early hour. "I'm for home, two Nembutals and a day's sleep," he added. "What about you?"

"Sambo's Restaurant down the street stays open twenty-four hours a day," said Mike. "I'm taking a hungry fiancée there for steak and eggs before we start covering the waterfront marinas."

"I'm for the steak and eggs," said Janet as the taxi bearing McCarthy drew away from the curb. "But why the waterfront marinas?"

"We're buying a houseboat," he told her. "Didn't I tell you—or was it Lynne?"

Janet shivered. "Don't let me ever hear that word again. But you know something—I think she came as near to loving you as a non-human could get."

Mike didn't comment; as a husband-about-to-be, it was just as well to let an old flame—even if it were a demon—remain extinguished.

AUTHOR'S NOTES

Readers of previous novels written by me know that, where medical and scientific subjects are treated, I make almost a fetish of absolute factual accuracy. In a novel involving both demonology and exorcism, as well as the fascinating realm of the psi phenomena of parapsychology, a great deal of study was required in order to be accurate, as well as believable. Not all of the references used for this story can be listed here but several were of enough importance to be worthy of mention.

For the detailed description of plastic surgical procedures, I am indebted for many reprints to my friend Dr. Kenneth L. Pickrell, Professor of Plastic and Maxillofacial Surgery at the Duke University Medical School. In the field of demonology and exorcism, my most valuable source has been *Hostage to the Devil: The Possession and Exorcism of Five Living Americans,* by Malachi Martin (Reader's Digest Press). In the area of parasensory perception, which figures so largely in the latter chapters of this book, I found much help from *Supersenses: Our Potential for Parasensory Experience,* by Charles Panati (Anchor Press, Doubleday). I am indebted to both authors for permission to quote briefly from their books.

I first learned about the fascinating work in remote viewing being conducted by the Stanford Research Institute from two broadcasts by Jack Perkins, reporter for NBC Evening News. Recognizing its potential for use in this novel, I requested a reprint of the article upon which the broadcast was based and was furnished one from the Institute. It is: "A Perceptual Channel for Information Transfer over Kilometer Distances: Historical Perspective and Recent Research" by Harold F. Puthoff and Russell Targ, *Proceedings of the Institute of Electrical and Electronics Engineers, Inc.,* Vol. 64, No. 3 (March 1976).

The work at the Stanford Institute, as described in the reprint, is absolutely astounding, yet so carefully carried out with every precaution against possible error, that its accuracy and truth can hardly be doubted. It is recommended to anyone interested in the fascinating world of psi phenomena.

An article describing an atomic mini-bomb appeared in *Parade* for May 8, 1977.

FRANK G. SLAUGHTER, M.D.
Jacksonville, Florida